DARK STATE

Empire Games: Book II

CHARLES STROSS

TOR

First published 2018 by Tom Doherty Associates, LLC

This edition published 2018 by Tor
an imprint of Pan Macmillan
20 New Wharf Road, London N1 9RR
Associated companies throughout the world
www.panmacmillan.com

ISBN 978-1-5098-2352-9

1 3 5 7 9 8 6 4 2

A CIP catalogue record for this book is available from the British Library.

Printed and bound by CPI Group (UK) Ltd, Croydon, CR0 4YY

In memory of Anthony Wedgwood Benn MP,
3 April 1925–14 March 2014

TIME LINES

TIME LINE ONE:

History diverged from our own around 200–250 BCE in Time Line One. Judaism, Christianity, and Islam are all absent and the collapse of the Roman Empire into dark ages was complete rather than just partial. Since then, civilization in Europe reemerged and quasi-medieval colony kingdoms sprang up on the eastern seaboard of North America. (The western seaboard was settled by Chinese traders.)

The Gruinmarkt, one such kingdom, was home to the Clan—rich merchant-traders with the ability to cross between time lines. As worldwalkers, they made a good living as the only people who could send a message coast-to-coast in a day in time line one. They could also guarantee a heroin shipment would arrive without fear of interception in time line two. But all good things come to an end, and the vicious civil war that broke out in 2003 (by time line two reckoning) led to the Clan's discovery by the US government. Their escalating cycle of retaliation ended in a nuclear inferno.

TIME LINE TWO:

This is a world almost identical to your time line, as the reader of this book—right up to a key date in 2003. Here world-walkers from the Clan's conservative faction detonated a stolen nuclear weapon in the White

House. They assassinated the president and forced the government to reveal the existence of parallel universes and the technology for reaching them.

Our story starts in time line two.

TIME LINE THREE:

This time line was discovered by Miriam Beckstein. In this alternate world, England was invaded by France in 1760 and the British Crown-in-Exile was established in the New England colonies. There was no American War of Independence and no French or Russian Revolutions. Therefore the Ancien Regime—despotism by absolute monarchy—shaped the world order until the Revolution of 2003. Here, the New British Empire's Radical Party overthrew the government and declared a democratic Commonwealth. The country is now known as the New American Commonwealth.

The French invasion of England stifled the Industrial Revolution in its crib, so industrialization began a century later than in time line two. But economics and science have their own imperatives. And even before Miriam led the survivors of the Clan into exile in the Commonwealth, the pace of technological innovation was beginning to pick up.

TIME LINE FOUR:

Currently uninhabited, this time line is in the grip of an ice age—with an ice sheet covering much of Europe, Canada, and the northern states of the US.

But it hasn't been uninhabited forever. The enigmatic Forerunner ruins pose both a threat and a promise . . .

MAIN CHARACTER PROFILES

ERIC SMITH

Born in 1964 in time line two, Colonel Smith, USAF (retired) has been a government man all his life. He worked for the United States' National Security Agency, then inside a top secret unit within Homeland Security. It was tasked with defending the States against threats from other time lines; these included world-walkers, those who could cross between these alternative worlds and his own time line. Many might consider this easy—after all, most known time lines are uninhabited, or populated by stone age tribes at best. However, the exceptions are the problem. The notorious Clan and their world-walkers came from time line one. And contact with this secretive organization resulted in a national trauma—dwarfing both 9/11 and the war on terror.

Smith knows that there are other inhabited time lines out there. At least one civilization is far ahead of the United States' technology levels, fighting—and losing—a para-time war against parties unknown. And then there's the BLACK RAIN time line, where reconnaissance drones and human spies go missing.

Defending the nation is easier said than done when you can't even be sure what you're defending it from. But you can make a good guess . . .

KURT DOUGLAS

Born in 1941 in time line two, Kurt Douglas grew up in the German Democratic Republic—East Germany—during the cold war. Drafted at eighteen, he ended up in the Border Guards. Then in late 1968 he escaped over the Berlin Wall to the West, and emigrated to the United States. Marrying Greta, another East German defector, he made a new life for himself. Kurt raised a family, and lived quietly with his son, daughter-in-law, and their adopted children—Rita and River.

The East German foreign intelligence service didn't send Kurt to the West to spy on the United States—they had longer-term objectives in mind. However, that was before the end of the cold war and the collapse of East Germany. Old skills don't fade easily, and Kurt has given Rita the best training he could for living in a police state. And she knows, if she ever gets in over her head, that she can count on Grandpa Kurt—and his friends—for help.

MIRIAM BURGESON

Born in 1968 in time line two, Miriam grew up in Boston, Massachusetts. She worked as a tech sector journalist before discovering, in her early thirties, that her mother had been lying to her for most of her life; mother and daughter were fugitives from the Gruinmarkt—a small kingdom in time line one, which had reached medieval levels of technology. They were women of noble birth, whose designated role was to produce more world-walkers and to serve the Clan. Miriam world-walks "home" by accident and is expected to conform. But that had never been Miriam's style. So in short order, she discovered a route to a new inhabited time line and built a business start-up—using it to import high-tech innovations into this new territory. This triggered a crisis within the Clan, reviving a dormant blood feud and causing civil war.

Now seventeen years have passed since the Clan and the Gruinmarkt were both destroyed. Clan reactionaries made a disastrous miscalculation that led to a very brief war with the United States—ending when the US nuked the Gruinmarkt. Miriam saw the writing on the wall and led anti-Clan survivors into exile in the new world she'd discovered. But here she found a revolution in progress—and a new vocation.

Miriam is now older and wiser, and a minister in government. She works for the New American Commonwealth, the ascendant democratic superpower of time line three. She'd taken part in the revolution that overthrew the absolute monarchy of the New British Empire, now defunct. And ever since, she's been warning the new government, "the USA is coming." For seventeen years, she's been working feverishly to ensure that when the US drones arrive overhead, the Commonwealth will be ready to meet them on equal terms. But she wasn't expecting them to be expecting *her*—and to have made plans accordingly.

RITA DOUGLAS

Born in 1995 in time line two, and adopted at birth by Franz and Emily Douglas, Rita was eight when Clan renegades from time line one nuked the White House. Growing up in President Rumsfeld's America she has learned to keep her head down and her nose clean. But there's only so much you can do to avoid attention in a national security state when the government has you under constant surveillance in case the woman who gave you up for adoption (or her relatives) takes a renewed interest in you.

Rita has a history and drama studies degree, a pile of student loans, and no great employment prospects. At twenty-five years of age she doesn't really know where she's going. But that's okay. Because the government has big plans for Rita.

ELIZABETH HANOVER

Born in 2002, just before the revolution that overturned the New British Empire and sent the Crown into exile in St. Petersburg, Elizabeth Hanover is the only child of his Royal Majesty John Frederick the Fourth, Emperor-in-Exile of the New British Empire. Unmarried, she's a pawn in her father's dynastic plans, which will come to fruition on the death of Adam Burroughs, First Man of the Commonwealth. But her father's plans revolve around a royal marriage into the Bourbon dynasty, to a prince twice her own age (who possesses a mistress and, according to rumor, the pox). Elizabeth isn't stupid. She's been watching the Commonwealth's technological progress from afar, and laying plans of her own. Plans which will bring two nuclear-armed superpowers to the brink of war . . .

PRINCIPAL CAST LIST

UNITED STATES OF AMERICA

RITA DOUGLAS, struggling thespian

FRANZ DOUGLAS, Rita's father

EMILY DOUGLAS, Rita's mother

RIVER DOUGLAS, Rita's brother

KURT DOUGLAS, Franz's father, retiree

GRETA DOUGLAS, Kurt's wife (deceased)

SONIA GOMEZ, DHS agent

ANGIE HAGEN, electrical contractor, childhood friend

PAULETTE MILAN, a spy

PATRICK O'NEILL, Rita's supervisor

DR. EILEEN SCRANTON, deputy assistant to Secretary for Homeland Security, Colonel Smith's boss

COLONEL ERIC SMITH, DHS, head of the Unit

DR. JULIE STRAKER, colleague of Rita's

NEW AMERICAN COMMONWEALTH (AND FRENCH EMPIRE)

MARGARET BISHOP, Party Commissioner

MIRIAM BURGESON (previously Miriam Beckstein), Minister for economic development and inter-time-line industrial espionage, Commonwealth Government

ERASMUS BURGESON, Miriam's husband, Minister of Propaganda, Commonwealth Government

SIR ADAM BURROUGHS, First Man (head of state)

THE DAUPHIN, heir to the throne of the French Empire

PRINCESS ELIZABETH HANOVER, heir to John Frederick

JOHN FREDERICK HANOVER, the Pretender, King-in-Exile of the New British Empire

MAJOR HULIUS HJORTH (YUL), Brilliana's brother-in-law, world-walker spy

ELENA HJORTH, Hulius's wife

HUW HJORTH, Explorer-General

BRILLIANA HJORTH, Huw's wife, DPR (espionage agency) director

ADRIAN HOLMES, Party Secretary

ALICE MORGAN, Commonwealth Transport Police officer

OLGA THOROLD, Miriam's director of counter-espionage

PART ONE

PRISONER

America is the place where you cannot kill your Government by killing the men who conduct it. The only way you can kill government in America is by making the men and women of America forget how to govern.

—Woodrow Wilson, 1919

Moscow Rules

Rita Douglas's head was spinning.

It had been scarcely twenty-eight hours since her reconnaissance mission to the time line codenamed BLACK RAIN had gone spectacularly bad, culminating in her capture and interrogation by the National Transport Police in the city of Irongate, near Philadelphia in time line two. The detention of a world-walker from the United States had ignited a firestorm of political maneuvering in the Commonwealth, as different agencies vied to capture her. Then the enigmatic Miss Thorold of the DPR had shown up in Irongate with a warrant and a helicopter to spirit her away to a secret meeting in the capital with a very senior politician—a woman who claimed to be her birth mother—which ended badly.

But now they were letting her go. It seemed almost too good to be true.

In the outer office they gave Rita a leather shoulder bag to hold the diplomatic letters and a DNA sample to prove the identity of her high-ranking contact. Then Inspector Morgan and Miss Thorold—her wheelchair pushed by her bodyguard—escorted Rita back out to the helicopter-like aircraft waiting on the pad behind the ministerial palace. There were no handcuffs or blindfolds this time. None were needed, for she was going home. She ought to have been happy, or at least relieved. Instead of facing further interrogation, she was going home to report to

Colonel Smith. Instead of being buried in a prison cell she'd be able to sleep in her own bed, or her girlfriend Angie's. She should have been happy, but instead her stomach was a pit of curdled despair. *I fucked that up brilliantly, didn't I?* The look on the evil queen's face when she said *I was younger than you are now* was going to haunt her dreams.

The guard helped Miss Thorold into the seat beside Rita. Rita accepted a headset as the aircraft screamed into mechanical life, small jets howling at the tips of each rotor blade. As they lurched into the air, she felt so mortified she half-wished the gyrodyne would crash. The moment passed. Then, a minute later, Miss Thorold poked her sharply in the fleshy part of her upper arm and spoke through her earphones. "Well done, kid. *Very* well done. I hope you're proud of yourself."

"Proud of what?" Rita said defensively. She wrapped her arms around the shoulder bag. "You set me up! You set us both up. And it's true. She put me up for adoption. She abandoned me."

"I see we have some issues to work through here." Olga gave her a critical look. "She was twenty-three. Had it occurred to you that it might not have been a decision she made on her own? I'd tell you to ask her mother, but Iris died fourteen years ago."

"My *grand*—" Rita made a fist of her left hand and jammed it against her lips to hold back the scream of frustrated anger she could feel building inside her.

"Iris was always good at manipulating Miriam," Olga added after a while. "Miriam only really thrived once her mother was gone. This is a horrible thing to say, but Iris was a tyrant. Quite, quite ruthless, although she had her reasons—mainly her *own* mother. But as I understand things, Iris simply didn't want to have a baby around in those days. Especially— in her eyes—a half-caste bastard whelped by a non-world-walker. Iris grew up in the Gruinmarkt before she ran away. It's where I grew up, too. It leaves its mark on you: that's how people there thought. Totally medieval. They were still having honor killings and multi-generational blood feuds when the USAF closed the book on them."

"You're telling me I, I—" Rita choked to a halt.

"Do your job and fuck off back to the United States," Olga said tiredly.

"They'll debrief you, yell at you for getting yourself caught, then send you back here eventually. Because that's easier than expanding their threat perimeter to marshal more world-walking assets. Which is all you are to them, frankly. Meanwhile, my advice to you, which you will probably ignore, is to *think* before you open your mouth again. I know Miriam. If you really don't want to talk to her she'll respect that, but if you want to hit the reset button and start over, I'm pretty sure she'll listen. She likes to think the best of people. Just . . . try to get your facts straight before the next time you gut someone."

Rita nodded, not trusting herself to reply. Then she reached up to the overhead console and unplugged her headphones. She brooded for the remainder of the hour-long flight, her emotional isolation enforced by the muffled thunder of the rotors. *I already have a mother,* she thought confusedly, thinking of her adoptive parents, Emily and Franz: *What does Mrs. Burgeson even mean to me?* But that led to other questions, starting with *What do I mean to* her?—questions that she had no answers for, which left her feeling increasingly queasy.

BOSTON, TIME LINE TWO, AUGUST 2020

Kurt Douglas paid no heed to the early-morning rain shower as he shuffled slowly along a tree-lined path, searching for his wife's headstone in the graveyard.

Greta had died more than twelve years earlier, of emphysema brought on by her lifelong cigarette habit. The echoes of her choking laughter haunted the empty corners of Kurt's life as he rattled around in the clean-as-a-whistle house his son Franz had bought him, next door to Franz's own home in Phoenix. Greta would have helped him fill it—assuming that she hadn't hated it so much she insisted they live elsewhere. *Soulless,* he could hear her ghost tutting in the recesses of his skull.

Kurt shook his head. Droplets of water hazed the surface of the glasses he wore, misting the world around him with damp uncertainty. A normal man might have moved on by now. But Kurt couldn't leave Greta's memory behind as easily as he'd left her body in this Boston graveyard when he followed his son and daughter-in-law to Phoenix. The events of November 1989 had seen to that, shattering their shared life's purpose. Everything since then had seemed like a bitter joke, until now.

Greta was not only his wife but his life-long co-conspirator. They'd come to the United States to perform a mission of vital importance, only for it to be deprived of all meaning by the collapse of East Germany. Now she was here, sleeping beneath the damp green sward of an alien nation she had never really approved of. And *he* was here too, brokenly ticking along like a clockwork man held upright by the rusting armature of a promise he'd made forty years ago. A Lutheran pastor he'd known in his youth had a way with words: *You might not believe in God,* the man had told him waspishly, *but that does not mean God does not believe in you.* Kurt no longer believed in the great work that had brought him to this shore, but it was the cracked and time-worn faith on which he'd built his life. Renunciation would be the final straw: an admission in his twilight years that his entire life had been meaningless.

Greta's resting place resembled an arboretum rather than a cemetery. Tranquil and wooded, the discreet headstones and memorials of those buried here were set back from footpaths, beneath the shade of neatly manicured trees. It could almost pass for a public park, but for the scarcity of surveillance cameras. The dead were no longer under suspicion, sleeping beyond the reach of politics and intrigue. All but one . . .

He found her grave eventually. Greta's remains lay beneath a simple stone, with no religious motif—she had detested all such, denouncing them irritably as superstition—but with a marble flowerpot for decoration. Someone had recently mowed the grass around it, and a handful of lilies, only just beginning to wilt, suggested that the grave had been visited recently.

Kurt lowered himself to his aching knees, leaning one hand on the headstone. It seemed to him sometimes that the better half of his life lay buried here. After so many years his grief was worn as smooth as a pebble on a rocky lee shore. Without her acerbic humor at his side, he felt like a pallid ghost fluttering through a future he was neither trained nor briefed for. A future which had no need for his kind.

Until now.

He paused for long enough to compose himself, then carefully unwrapped the bouquet of red roses he had brought. Fumbling with the flowerpot, he removed the lilies and set them to one side. They lay like the dead, a limp bundle gathered together by a rubber band. He arranged the roses at the foot of the stone, one by one. Then he carefully rolled up the wilted lilies in the sheet of paper he'd carried the roses in. Finally he heaved himself upright and went in search of a trash can.

The finger-sized aluminum cigar tube he'd found among the lilies felt like a lead brick in his pocket, full of dangerous secrets. Greta would have appreciated the irony. But then, she always had been a truer believer and a more dedicated player of the Great Game than he. She'd urged him to maintain the old disciplines, to keep the members of the spy ring they jointly controlled aware that they served a great purpose and had not been forgotten. To maintain the Wolf Orchestra against a time of need.

She would have wheezed herself sick with laughter at the sight of him using her grave as a dead letter drop. And he was certain she would have approved of the use to which he was about to put the Orchestra—even though it was purely by accident that they'd finally penetrated a first-rank target organization, a third of a century after the state they had served was absorbed by its enemies.

His granddaughter Rita was in trouble and he intended to defend her. And when Kurt rose and walked away from his wife's grave, he bore in his pocket a shield and sword: the last legacy of a nation that no longer existed.

CAMBRIDGE, TIME LINE TWO, AUGUST 2020

Kurt's first port of call after the grave of his wife was a car pound in the suburbs of Cambridge, to see a woman about a car. Buses and subway trains and trams were all surveilled these days, so out of a general state of cussedness he walked nearly four miles through the light autumnal rain to get there. The cigar tube rode in his jacket pocket, unseen but always felt, a focus for heightened awareness and curiosity. It was a familiar irritant of a kind he understood well, and he would resist the temptation to examine its contents until he could guarantee total privacy.

He was more curious about the woman he was on his way to meet. He was already aware of her as the granddaughter of an old comrade who had died some years ago, one of the tribe of true believers the Orchestra had been tasked with raising on this foreign shore. His adoptive granddaughter held the woman in some esteem, and Rita's judgment in friendship had never given him cause for concern yet. That Rita was now holding him at arm's reach was worrying, even in light of the identity of her employers. And that her (he hesitated to make assumptions, but the label appeared to fit) *girlfriend* was reaching out to him for help on her behalf, using the old contact protocols, was even more worrying: so Kurt answered the call promptly.

The mission planners of the Hauptverwaltung Aufklärung had carefully studied the followers of secret faiths in order to replicate the feat among the offspring of their agents on foreign soil. Marranos in Spain, vodoun in Haiti, thuggee in India: all groups who lived among their enemies while remaining loyal to a forbidden doctrine, passing their faith down the generations in secret. The HVA's objective had been to raise a crop of East Germans in exile in America, able to pass the most stringent background checks with flying colors while remaining loyal to the cause. The mission had been rendered pointless by the end of the cold war and the absorption of the GDR by West Germany, but the training and the tribal loyalties had lingered. Kurt had taught Franz, and then Rita. His colleague Willy had passed on the hidden knowledge to his granddaughter Angela by way of his son, her father. There were other children and grandchildren. Their parents took care to arrange introductions and many of them became more than friends, marrying within the group: for this was how a persecuted religion persisted in the face of adversity. And so the last true believers of the Socialist Unity Party of

Germany practiced their faith behind closed doors, a secret religious cult embedded within the United States of America.

There was a diner on a street corner in Belmont, sharing the block with a burger joint and a sandwich shop. Kurt arrived around two thirty in the afternoon, during the slack hours between the end of the lunchtime rush and the first trickle of commuters grabbing a bag for the drive or train ride home. He ordered a coffee and a chicken sub, then slid into a booth with a view of the window and pulled out the burner phone he'd bought that morning in a CVS. Making a note of its number, he turned it on, placed a call to a voicemail address, listened briefly, then turned it off again. Content with what he had heard, he slid it back into his pocket and turned his attention to his lunch.

As he was approaching satiety (half the sub remained uneaten: age was slowly killing his appetite) a young woman with green-streaked blue hair opened the door and glanced around. He waved: she came over. "Are you Kurt?" she demanded.

He put the sub down and carefully wiped his fingers. "You must be Angela," he said, standing and offering a hand. She shook, grip firm and emphatic.

"Angie," she corrected, defusing it with a smile.

Kurt couldn't help noticing there was meat on her bones. Black leather jacket, jeans, chunky emerald sweater and chunky silver jewelry: short hair, squared-off unvarnished fingernails, a half-healed scratch on one knuckle. "Angie, then. You are an electrician, I understand?"

"Yeah." She sat down, unslinging a bulging messenger bag. He followed suit. "Rita asked me to get her car out of the pound, and I kind of hoped you might be up to ferry-driving it down to Philly with me tomorrow."

"I can do that," Kurt said. "It's the Acura, yes? Franz's old car?"

"Her dad's? Yep. I've got the paperwork to spring it from the pound where it's been parked up for six months, but I thought I should get it checked over before we bring it to her, and I need someone to drive in convoy with me in case it breaks down. I've got a hitch on the truck but I don't want to tow it three hundred miles if I can avoid it."

"Well"—Kurt gestured at his unfinished meal—"perhaps we can do that after lunch? I have a room in a motel, I'm sure we can park it nearby, and then we can start off early tomorrow." He paused. "I will need to catch a train back to Boston."

"I can give you a ride afterwards," Angie offered. "My truck's got an autopilot mode so I can sleep on the return leg. It'll give us a chance to catch up."

She had a smile like an arc-welder. *Yes, I think I know what she sees in you,* Kurt decided. He was too old and too honest with himself to run after pretty women, but it warmed his heart to see Rita doing well for herself. "I would like that," he said gravely. "You and Rita met in the Girl Scouts, yes?"

"Yeah. Long story. Guess I should save it for the drive back, huh?" She gestured at his meal: "I need to get some food. Be right back."

Kurt worked on his chicken sub while she ordered, silently contemplating her proposed course of action. Yes, it was plausible from an outsider's perspective: a solid cover story. Grandfather helps girlfriend drive granddaughter's car home for her, girlfriend gives Gramps a ride back to his hotel afterward and deadheads home. If anyone asked, *of course* Angie would want to get to know her partner's favorite relative. And with gas under a dollar a gallon, it made sense to drive. A security officer paying attention to Rita's social graph wouldn't even blink. If Kurt wanted to visit Rita and sniff around her contacts, it was a perfect pretext: *your parents asked me to check out your new friend . . .*

He glanced at Angie as she paid for her food. The wolf cub had grown up into a fine specimen. *I wonder how much operational doctrine your parents passed on to you?* If she was a full initiate of the Wolf Orchestra, rescuing Rita would be much easier.

PHILADELPHIA, TIME LINE TWO, AUGUST 2020

The mission to spring Rita's wheels from automobile jail went smoothly enough. The guard at the pound was expecting Angie, the storage fees were all billed to Rita's employers, and the Acura had been stored under a tarp. When Angie checked it over, the tires were low, but the self-inflation system worked, and after running the engine for five minutes they were all showing the correct pressure. "It's probably going to fail its next emissions test," Angie said, listening to the engine, "but I know a shop that'll fix it cheap. Are you up to driving three hundred miles to-morrow, Mr. Douglas?"

"Of course. I need more rest stops than you youngsters, so you should allow five hours for driving and two more on top, but I can do that."

"Great! Well, how about you take her car to your hotel overnight, then phone me when you're ready to set off tomorrow morning?"

They parted company outside the pound. Kurt braved the Boston afternoon traffic with quiet stoicism. When he pulled up behind the hotel he was staying in, he rested his head on the steering wheel for a couple of minutes. Then, as calm returned, he climbed wearily out and went to his room.

Before he showered, Kurt closed the curtains then retrieved the cigar tube from his jacket pocket. Unscrewing it, he looked inside. A tightly-curled sheet of paper met his gaze. It was covered in a grid of hand-written letters, seemingly random. Attached to the bottom with Scotch tape was a neat row of chips: a tiny memory card, and no less than five phone SIMs. Kurt whistled quietly through his teeth, impressed despite himself. The FLASH request he'd sent out, asking the Boston Resident to conduct a roll call, had delivered far more than he'd expected. Ne-glected sleeper rings tended to decay over the years as agents became ill or infirm, died, or went feral. But of the eight families in this part of the United States, five had answered the call. Most of them were undoubt-edly second or third generation descendants: it was possible some of them didn't even know what the Orchestra was, or the purpose it served. But they'd each sent the number of a burner phone and a code word, and the Resident had set up a SIM for each of them. They'd only answer a call from a phone using the correct SIM, and would only respond to the cor-rect code word, but Kurt now held in his hands the key to a ring of sleeper agents, all unknown to one another and (hopefully) the authorities.

Deciding what to do with it—or whether to use it at all—would have to wait until he'd spoken to Angie in private.

Kurt folded the paper and its precious cargo and inserted them in the middle of a paperback he was slowly reading and annotating—Judt on the history of Europe since 1945—then stashed his toothbrush in the cigar tube, placing it in turn in his toilet bag, where it would be just another old man's foible if anyone searched for it. (Decrypting the message was best left until after his return to Philadelphia, indeed for as long as possible. The last thing he needed to be in possession of at an airport checkpoint was an incriminating plaintext message.) Then, for want of anything better to do with his evening, he ordered in a pizza, watched a comedy movie, then went to bed early.

The drive down to Angie's apartment in the suburbs near Philadelphia went smoothly but boringly. Nevertheless, Kurt was light-headed and slightly shaky by the time he pulled into the lot and parked up beside Angie's crimson pickup. He was old and no longer accustomed to driving such distances in a day, and although Rita's Acura had once been comfortable it was now entering its twilight years, with well-pummeled seats, poor shock absorbers, and a collection of arthritic squeaks and rattles to rival his own. Angie materialized from the apartment doorway as he eased himself out of the driver's seat. She looked concerned. "Are you okay?"

"I will be once I stretch these bones." Kurt waved her away tiredly. "And then I must sit down for a few minutes."

"We should go get some dinner. Then I can run you back up to Boston?"

Six hundred and fifty miles in a day. Kurt gritted his teeth: *Don't say you didn't know what you were doing.* "Dinner would be good," he admitted. "Then we can talk."

"I checked my truck when I stopped for gas. Didn't find any new trackers."

"They don't need trackers to follow you unless you go off-grid. The truck itself reports—"

"I know. But mine only tells them what I want it to: I was looking for new passengers."

Kurt sighed. "You won't find them. They are subtle. The hands-free kit and in-cab entertainment system, they are all rooted these days. I could show you pictures from the old days, what passed for bugs in the GDR—they're on the web—it is to weep! I knew technical guys, nerds you would call them, who must be rolling in their graves, green with envy for the shinies of the NSA. But all this is nonsense. We should check Rita's car before we go—*that* is where you will find the extra bugs. There is a reason I had my son give her an old sedan, its systems lack the native intelligence to make a good informer."

Angie frowned. "You really think they'll be monitoring me pro-actively?"

"Yes, because you're a known associate of one of their agents, and servers that can process speech to text are cheap. But you are probably safe, unless they know of the Orchestra, in which case we are both in hot water already." He laid a finger on the truck's passenger door handle. "Shall we eat?"

NEW LONDON, TIME LINE THREE, AUGUST 2020

The Party headquarters within the walled royal capital of New London occupied the former Crown Prince's palace on Central Avenue, which bisected the lower quarter of Manhattan Island. The chaotic maze of offices and departments (many of them organized after the new open plan mode, with fabric-covered partitions dividing up the floors of former ballrooms and state receiving suites like cells in a very busy beehive) provided accommodation to the heads of the apparatus of the Deep State. These were the bureaucratic structures created by the Radical Party during the revolution, to provide a supportive framework within which democracy was to take root and thrive. Naturally there were times when it seemed anything *but* democratic. And that afternoon, Erasmus Burgeson, the Minister of Propaganda and Communications, was running up against it in the person of some of his more obstructive colleagues.

"We have to face facts," Commissioner Jarvis said mildly as he polished his spectacles on one end of his neck-cloth. "Adam is terminally ill, and when he dies the enemy—both without and within—will push as hard as they can to overturn the Party." He referred to Adam Burroughs, the First Man and leader of the revolution seventeen years before that had toppled the monarchy and installed this time line's first democracy, in the former New British Empire.

"Of course the reactionaries will come out of the woodwork!" Erasmus agreed vehemently. "Which is why, from a propaganda viewpoint, the course of action you're proposing is a bad idea: it will play right into their hands. Everyone will expect a, a ham-fisted crackdown on dissent. It won't win friends. In fact, purges are often interpreted as a sign of weakness. Consider the outcome of John Frederick's disastrous crackdown in '86 after his father's assassination . . . All the polling my research department has done points to the inexorable conclusion that one conveys the appearance of strength best by acting as if one is *already* secure, rather than by issuing threats that invite defiance. The First Citizen secured the revolution when he allowed the Emperor to leave peacefully. Doing so was an assertion of power, not an admission of weakness. Similarly, so was his delegation of most of the powers formerly wielded by the Crown to the apparatus of the Party. If we clamp down in the wake of his death, we run the risk of making the Party look as if it has something to fear once the First Man is gone—"

"You are talking about appearances." Commissioner Buccleugh's diction was as sharp as ever, even though Erasmus harbored doubts about his mind—now more than ever, for the man was in his dotage. "But as Albert says we must face facts. Have you seen the foreign intelligence briefings? The Young Pretender is clearly cozying up to the Dauphin, and there has been an upswing in activity at home by the Patriot Societies, the so-called Royalist Party loons who would welcome the return of the jackboot and fetters in an instant—"

An extremely modern woman, one of the new generation of Party bureaucrats, approached their little circle of armchairs. They were off to one side of the cold fireplace in the Commissioners' Dining Room, and so Erasmus was the first to see her approach. "Gentlemen, please?"

"Ah, a message for Commissioner Burgeson?" The staffer extended one gloved hand, bearing a sealed envelope. "Sir, if you need to reply—"

"A moment." Erasmus slit the envelope open with the edge of one fingernail. He scanned quickly, then folded the letter away. "Gentlemen, I'm being called away. Fascinating as this discussion has been, I think we are going to have to agree to disagree—at least until we can put our heads together again for long enough to reach a consensus." He eased himself out of the chair with a moue of pain. "After you, my dear," he told the staffer.

She beat a hasty retreat from the dining room, with its forbidding ambiance of an old man's club: Erasmus followed her as fast as he could. His hips and knees weren't particularly bad for his years, but he was of an age he had never consciously expected to reach, and was finding it full of unpleasant surprises. The constant low-level pain from aching joints and tendons were by no means the worst of it. As they passed through the doorway into the main corridor, he asked, quietly, "Where is she?"

"I left her in your office, sir. She appears to be distressed."

The staffer looked at him with wide eyes. *She can't be more than twenty,* Erasmus realized. Dark suit, blond hair with a permanent wave so tight it might have been lacquered into immobility. Divergent fashions aside, she was of a type he recognized instantly from the imported American political drama shows his wife watched at home when she needed to relax completely after work. (Which was all too seldom, these days.) "How distressed is she?" he asked gently.

"She borrowed my handkerchief, sir . . ."

Now worried, Erasmus sped up as best he could. *Damn this warren,* he thought: the marble floor took a toll on feet and knees. *What can have happened?* His wife was not, in general, given to melodramatic emotional meltdowns—*especially* not in public, wearing her Commissioner's face. *Hardheaded* was an apt way of describing her. She hadn't even cried at her mother's funeral.

He found Miriam in his inner office, wearing a face more suited to news of a friend's passing. "Leave us," he said gently, and shut the door before the staffer could enter. He crossed the carpet to meet her. She leaned into his embrace hard, almost driving the breath from his ribs as she hugged him. She was shaking: "What is it?" he asked.

"The bastards. The bastards."

"Hush." Her shoulders were rigid with tension. They didn't relax as he stroked her back. "Take your time. You've got time, I take it?"

"I'm due in front of the budget select committee in half an hour to discuss next year's requirements, and then I've got a briefing on the teacher in-placement program—" She stopped. "I ought to cancel everything. I can't focus." She slowly relaxed her grip on Erasmus, but kept her chin on the crook of his neck and shoulder. She sniffed, betraying a passing congestion.

"What bastards? What did they do?"

"The US government. I'm convinced"—her bosom pushed against him as she inhaled deeply—"it's deliberate. They knew, or guessed, that I'd survived. That's why they sent her."

"Her? This is the DHS illegal everyone was talking about yesterday?"

"Yes." She let go of him, reluctantly. "Ras, if you learned that Annie—you said she died in childbed, in one of the camps—what if you learned that your child survived? And had been raised by Crown loyalists? What would you do?"

He felt sick to his stomach. "That can't be . . ." He fell silent in the face of her expression.

"You know I had a daughter twenty-six years ago," Miriam said quietly. "Not a world-walker. My mother pushed me into giving her up for adoption. Or maybe I half-wanted to do that anyway: or my first husband, back when we were together . . . it's hard to remember. My little accident. She was *right here*, where you're standing now, just half an hour ago."

"They— How did they find her?" Erasmus stared at her. His wife looked ashen.

"They've got the Clan breeding program records. Hell, *we've* got the records Iris copied from Dr. ven Hjalmar's computer. My people had her on a hands-off watch list for years, keeping an eye on her via social media from a safe remove. A resident agent in Italy, something like that. Anyway, nobody really noticed until the day before yesterday—when the transit cops picked her up, and Olga scrambled to catch up—but her Facebook updates turned oddly anodyne nearly a year ago. It looked like she was posting entries but she wasn't friending or unfriending anyone or joining new apps, there was just a thin layer of Astroturf covering multiple month-long gaps in her time line. She's my girl, Ras, I'm sure of it. We don't have a DNA match yet—the best our people can come up with will take another couple of days to come back from the lab—but she's got her father's looks and she was born on the right day in the right hospital. They made her into a world-walker, Erasmus, they worked out how to switch on the gene or whatever it is in carriers, and she, I think she hates me . . ."

She reached blindly behind herself until she found one of the visitor chairs and sat down heavily. Miriam did not weep easily: nor did she sob loudly. But the tear tracks on her cheeks told Erasmus everything.

"You think they knew you were here, and they deliberately sent her?" he asked, pulling up a chair and sitting next to her. He fumbled for his handkerchief and passed it to her; she took it gratefully and mopped at her face.

"Either that, or they guessed there was a high probability I'd be here. They knew about me back then, after all. They had a profile of the Clan leadership, of their presumed enemies. I can't see what else it could be . . ."

"Miriam. How old are the other carriers your people were tracking? I thought you said they were all teenagers? Your daughter, how old is she, twenty-six? It might simply be that she was the oldest and best-trained."

"Maybe." She sniffed, and looked at him bleakly. "But there are other implications. She's a world-walker. We have witness reports."

"Could they have shrunk the gadget, whatever it is they use . . . ?"

She shook her head. "If they did, the arresting officers couldn't find it on her person. Also, they applied the world-walker containment checklist and report that her reactions were exactly what you'd expect. Finally, she admitted it under questioning. The Department for Homeland Security absorbed the old Family Trade Organization, and that's who she's working for. They're tasked with protecting the United States from threats from parallel universes—sound familiar? She even mentioned an old-timer who sounds like that Air Force colonel Mike Fleming worked for. It's the same people, love, playing the same fucking head games with us. Only this time it's personal."

PHILADELPHIA, TIME LINE TWO, AUGUST 2020

Less than an hour after her inconclusive conversation with Miss Thorold, Rita was in a secure office with Colonel Smith. Smith's boss, Dr. Scranton, had been notified and was on her way. The rubberneckers from head office had been peeled away and sent to a waiting area to cool their heels. And the guards who had nearly machined-gunned her when she jaunted into the middle of the secured transit area had been dismissed. "They're idiots," Colonel Smith fumed. "'Secure the area in case the opposition send us a whoopee cushion,'" he mimicked, fingers waggling in air quotes. "At least now I can tell them to get lost next time they try to stick their noses under the tent flap." He looked as if he hadn't slept for the entire duration of her trip. "How did it go wrong, Rita? Sitrep, please."

"It was a mess," she said faintly. "'Scuse me." She sat down in the visitor chair. Smith looked more concerned than angry. He nodded silently as he waited for her to open up. "They caught me." *There, I said it.* "There's some sort of power struggle going on. The railroad police got me first, and asked lots of questions. They knew exactly what I was: they kept me in cuffs and blindfolded until they got me on the top floor of a high-rise."

Smith swore quietly. "And?"

"They grabbed me almost as soon as I arrived and questioned me pretty much continuously until this morning. No sleep deprivation or violence," she added hastily. "Also—they knew about world-walking, but they didn't seem to know *anything* about the United States. I mean, at one point I got into this crazy loop trying to explain where Seattle is . . . Anyway, then a woman in a wheelchair turned up, acted like"—her eyes narrowed—"Dr. Scranton. Seriously, she had a bodyguard and issued orders and the police tripped over their own feet getting out of her way. She sprang me from police custody, said she was one jump ahead of a rival group from the secret political police. So then she hauled me off to New York in a helicopter—"

"New York?"

"That's where their capital is. There's, uh, there's no D.C. in their time line. Anyway, she took me to see"—Rita swallowed—"my birth mother. Who is something—"

A snapping sound made her look up. The Colonel shook his head. "Continue," he said, carefully placing the broken halves of his fountain pen beside the legal pad he'd been jotting notes on.

"—She's something in their government, extremely high up. She, uh, she gave me a sealed letter for you—"

"*Fuck.*" Smith looked pained. "Excuse my French. Go on."

"—Said she wants, her faction wants, to open diplomatic negotiations. To stop us nuking them, or them nuking us. Colonel, they're in the middle of a cold war! She said, said they've got *nine thousand* H-bombs pointed at, at France? The French Empire? They want to talk. And she gave me a set of times and coordinates that are safe at their end—that is, her people will be waiting if I or, uh, some other world-walker, goes through to deliver a message."

"I see." Smith looked at her, frown lines forming a furrow across his forehead. "What else did you observe? Impressions? Technologies?"

Rita swallowed. The past day was all fading into a jumbled mass of impressions, swirling around the maelstrom of darkness that was her conversation—mere minutes—with the woman in the office. "They've got helicopters, sir. Big military-looking things, like a Black Hawk. Cars, trucks, buildings. They don't go in for skyscrapers like we do, but there's plenty of concrete and elevators and men in uniforms with machine guns. She said they've got nuclear power—"

"We already knew they've got nukes," the Colonel said flatly. "Did the woman who said she was your birth mother have a job? Where was she?"

"They took me to see her in a big, uh, a big neoclassical building.

Instead of downtown Manhattan they've got a bunch of palaces, former royal palaces. She was introduced as the, uh, *Party Commissioner* in charge of the Ministry of Intertime Technological Intelligence. Like it's a big deal . . ."

Rita trailed off, dumbstruck. She'd never thought of the Colonel as a man prone to emotional outbursts or demonstrative behavior. To see him lower his head and rest his face in his hands was profoundly disorienting.

After a moment he looked up. The bruised skin under his eyes lent them the appearance of slowly rotting fruit. "This letter, Rita. Give it to me. And the other papers."

"Uh, I can't, the security detail took—"

"Jesus *wept*." Smith picked up his desk handset and barked angrily: "Gomez, Colonel Smith here. Agent Douglas returned half an hour ago and there appears to have been a mix-up. You will personally locate *all* the clothing and items that were removed by the reception crew, I repeat *all* of them, *everything*, and bring them directly to my office. In particular, there's a, a—"

"—A leather document case—"

"—You are looking for a leather document case. If anyone opened it, have them arrested and bring them here. If it's open and the contents have been removed, find them and bring it. If it's disappeared, notify me at once then put the site on lockdown and arrest everyone who might have handled it. If it's still sealed, keep it that way when you bring it."

He listened for a few seconds, then put the phone down and stared tiredly at Rita. "I'm going to start recording now, Rita. I want you to talk me through everything that happened, and then we're going to go through it again when Dr. Scranton gets here. In minute detail. Take your time, but I want you to get *everything* out. Do you understand?"

"I—I understand. I fucked up," she said hollowly.

"That remains to be seen. We generally apportion blame to the officer who issued the orders, not the hands that carried them out, and in this case Dr. Scranton's orders came from the Oval Office by way of the National Security Council." He picked up the wreckage of his pen, which appeared to be quite an expensive one, and rolled the broken barrel between his palms. "You seem to think we expect perfection. That's not true. We just expect you to do the best you can. We're not omniscient, we're not super-intelligent. Everyone in this business is muddling along in the dark, concocting plans and executing them then revising when the outcomes don't match what they expected.

"And in any case, there are very few rules for conducting the kind of mission we've been sending you on—very few indeed. Moscow Rules, maybe. So." He put down the pen and moved his fatphone into the middle of the desk and tapped at its screen. "Testing . . . good. Colonel Smith, first debriefing of Rita Douglas after return from Phase Three. Rita, in your own words. What happened to you when you arrived in BLACK RAIN?"

CAMBRIDGE, TIME LINE TWO, AUGUST 2020

Boston, at four o'clock in the morning:

A SWAT team was moving in on an enemy of the state.

They'd called in support from the Boston PD and the state troopers, cutting off access to the apartment building where the target lived on her own in a second-floor condo. Drivers trying to take that particular street would find their vehicles under police override, diverted into a nearby parking lot for inspection. Manual cars and trucks—not that there were many at this time of night—would be waved down by the state troopers. Papers would be demanded, DNA samples taken, trunks searched.

Overhead, a pair of silent drones kept infrared cameras trained on the block. Celldar—secondary radar that stitched together an image using the reflections of the pervasive cell phone and wi-fi carrier signals—filled in the blind spots. More recondite backup enforced the blockade. The neighborhood cell stations and wi-fi hot spots were all under government override, calls and Internet connections diverted, the locations of every phone and television and computer pinned down to within inches. Smart gas and electric meters monitored for signs of anomalous power spikes.

Some of the more modern wireless routers, equipped with phased-array antennae capable of beam-shaping their wall-penetrating emissions, scanned buildings and mapped the location of human bodies. Webcams in tablets and laptops in every apartment came to life, activated without a betraying indicator LED: game consoles in dens and living rooms leapt to attention, repurposed as vigilant motion-sensing security guards. A translucent 3-D model of the building assembled itself in the team's war room, every object accurately mapped to within millimeters, right down to the nails and wiring embedded in the walls.

The enemy of the state was asleep in her apartment bedroom. Spyware injected into her phone that night, masquerading as a software update, had boosted the sensitivity of the device's twin mikes. The phone had heard the traitor awaken an hour earlier and shuffle to the toilet for a late night piss. It had listened as she returned to the bedroom, yawned, and burrowed back under her comforter. Breath came uneven at first, then slowed, falling into a tempo indicative of sleep. Analysis software now indicated that she was probably in stage II sleep, moving toward REM sleep within the next five minutes: dreaming deeply, her muscles paralyzed. In a control room on the far side of the city, the officers in the war room put their heads together and came to a consensus. It was time to move.

Five minutes to contact:

The front door to the apartment building obligingly unlocked itself for the SWAT team. Simultaneously, e-locks and fingerprint readers throughout the complex turned quisling. The front doors of all but one of the apartments in the complex sealed themselves shut, securing the residents inside, save only the targeted front door. *That* one silently unlocked.

Four minutes to contact:

The target's phone, sitting in a cradle on the bedside table, had a front-facing camera. The target was lying on her side, facing the device. While the light level was sub-optimal, variations in specular reflection from her closed eyelids suggested rapid eye movements. Meanwhile, breath analysis confirmed ongoing deep sleep. The fire team now assembled on the second-floor landing outside the apartment. Their HUDs updated, showing them an exact map of the interior as they took up their positions.

One minute to contact:

The target was still asleep as a quadrotor drone spiraled down to hover in position thirty feet outside the bedroom window. Curtains hid the occupant from direct view, but the drone's active teraherz radar could penetrate concrete and drywall and glass, confirming the accuracy of the map created by the rooted wi-fi routers. The UAV moved closer, motors whining as it lined its payload up on the window.

Fifteen seconds to contact:

Answering the press of a distant button the suppressed shotgun in the drone's chin turret coughed, propelling a breaching round through the upper half of the window, shattering glass and ripping the curtain away from the opening. The target twitched, began to spasm: then the shotgun fired again, this time aiming at the sleeper. The slug it fired was a fearsomely complex machine, half air bag and half Taser. Exploding to boxing-glove dimensions just before impact, it punched the target down onto the mattress and drove wired barbs through her skin, then unloaded its capacitors through them.

Contact:

The bedroom door burst open and the overhead lights came on. Armed men filled the room, guns pointing, shouting orders. The target moaned in pain, but lay supine as the DHS antiterrorist team zip-tied her wrists, ripped bedding aside to tie her at knees and ankles, then gagged and bagged her in a cocoon-like transporter threaded with biomonitors and a shock belt to enforce compliance. The rendition protocol was designed to minimize risk for the arresting officers, to take by surprise even a hardened assassin, lying sleepless with gun in hand. The target this time was a fifty-two-year-old single white female: unarmed, untrained, and unprepared.

Contact plus two minutes:

The SWAT team carried the pick-up downstairs and out to the waiting prisoner transport. Behind them, the apartment door locked itself, awaiting the arrival of the CSI team when regular office hours rolled around. As the arrest wagon rolled away behind its escort of cruisers with flashing lights, the security perimeter shut down. Cell and Internet services reverted to normal, traffic diversions cleared themselves, state troopers took calls and moved on to the next appointment of the night.

And by dawn, the only remaining sign that Paulette Milan had disappeared into night and mist would be the gaping hole in her bedroom window.

PHILADELPHIA, TIME LINE TWO, AUGUST 2020

Dinner was Philly cheesesteak with fries for Kurt and a big crab salad bowl for Angie. Kurt allowed himself a large glass of wine with his food, and was in an expansive frame of mind when they left the restaurant and climbed back into Angie's crew-cab.

Angie drove cautiously until they hit the interstate. Then she put the truck on autopilot and turned to face him across the center divider, which she had rigged as a mobile office. First she flipped a concealed switch under the dash. Then she opened one of the office cubbies and removed a padded chiller bag. She shook the bag out, then slid her phone inside and gestured for Kurt to follow suit. Once the phones were zipped away behind layers of muffling insulation, her shoulders slumped slightly. "The entertainment system's powered down hard: I'm pretty sure we can't be overheard. Rita hasn't been back for two days," Angie explained. Her voice quavered with worry. "I called her boss—she'd given me a number—but I got the brush-off. Kurt, what do you know about this thing she's been dragged into?"

Kurt finger-flicked a brief acknowledgment. "Firstly, you must be clear on this: my son and daughter-in-law adopted Rita. We learned— much later—that her birth mother, and her mother (who arranged the fostering) were fugitives from the world-walkers. Did Rita tell you any of this?"

"That they tried to kidnap her? Or that the DHS said they did?" Angie's scowl made her suspicions clear. "Yes, she told me about it. I know she's not a, not one of the terrorists. But she didn't tell me what they wanted her to do. Only that they'd worked out how to activate her ability to travel to other parallel Earths."

Outside the windshield, in the darkness, the traffic flowed hypnotically. The truck indicated, then pulled out into the left lane to overtake a tanker.

"They want her for a spy," Kurt said gently. "Quite ironic, is it not?"

Angie looked at him sharply. "Yes! Speaking of which . . . who set the Orchestra up, originally?"

"That's ancient history." Kurt stared at the lane dividers as they strobed past, gradually curving, the truck following the road by itself. "How much do you know about it?"

Angie hesitated. "My parents are part of it. So was Grandpa. I don't remember when I first knew: I think after I came back from the second summer camp I guessed something, but there were games when I was a kid, stuff I barely remember. Papa teaching me a special kind of hide-and-seek in the mall when I was twelve. Socials with friends from the old country, and party games none of the other kids at school knew. A play-set polygraph when I was fifteen, and tricks to defeat it. The special Girl Scouts camps where everyone seemed to have parents who worked for the government and the merit badges were all about cryptography and tradecraft. I didn't realize it was the real thing until I enlisted, during my clearance. They never told me explicitly. But I knew we were different and had to hide it."

She kept using the correct personal pronoun, Kurt noted. He remembered a movie, decades ago: *that word you keep using, it does not mean what you think it means.* "There are two ways of looking at the Orchestra," he said slowly. "Let me give you the children's story first. Once upon a time there was a magic kingdom, which had been conquered by an ogre. And the ogre was unpleasant and bad-tempered and suspicious, and from time to time he ate people. The ogre thought people outside his kingdom were plotting against him, so he took some of his people and sent them abroad as spies. And, you know, there was a little truth in this: the ogre's kingdom wasn't popular, after all it was ruled by an ogre. But then a handsome prince—or maybe she was a princess—slew the ogre and freed the people. The spies were torn: if they went home, the new king, or queen, would not look on them favorably, for supporting the ogre's regime. The people of the lands they now dwelt in would be angry if they admitted what they were! So there was nowhere for them to go but underground, hoping to live out their lives in anonymity."

"Yeah, I got that early. Caused a few raised eyebrows when I came out with it in first grade, you know? But it sounded Grimm enough that the school counselor dropped it after a head-to-head with Mom." Angie took a deep breath. "So I guess you're not big on the workers' paradise and the dictatorship of the proletariat?"

"I grew up there." Kurt reached for his water bottle. "The ogre wasn't *all* bad, but he was still an ogre: nobody sane would want to re-create his kingdom just for the healthcare coverage and the guaranteed employment." A big road sign on a gantry hung overhead, closing fast. Kurt stared at it morosely. "On the other hand, there's plenty wrong with this country, too. Sometimes it seems as if I haven't moved very far at all."

"But you said there's another story—"

"Yes. The other way of looking at things—forget the fable we teach our preschoolers, let me give you the grown-up version—is that Colonel-General Markus Wolf established the last great Communist Bloc spy ring on Western soil during the sunset years of the GDR, in the 1970s through late 1980s. The Orchestra's job wasn't to spy, but to raise a generation of children in situ on American soil, natural-born Americans with perfect cover identities and enculturation, but loyal to the cause. The plan was that some of them would get jobs in government, as spies or agents of influence. But then the wall came down, and the controllers burned their files—starting with the most sensitive, those of the overseas illegals like your grandpa and me. We were cut loose, with nobody for aid but one another. We have no mission but survival, Angie. The nation we served is gone: it disintegrated nearly a third of a century ago. The irony is that my granddaughter, without even *trying*, has achieved an espionage coup—she has inadvertently penetrated a top-secret American

HUMINT operation! The comrade general must be laughing in his grave. If the GDR was still around it would be the intelligence coup of the century."

"But what does it mean?" Angie asked.

"What does *what* mean?" He raised an eyebrow: "It means fuck-all, unless you want to invent a meaning for it! It certainly means I am guilty of conspiracy to act as an agent of a foreign government without notifying the US Attorney General, contrary to the Foreign Agents Registration Act of 1938. The country for which I trained as a spy no longer exists, but that won't help my defense. It means your grandfather and parents are guilty also. But the spying is not so serious: at worst a couple of years in federal prison. More serious is that to talk about helping Rita— you must be very clear on this—makes you a party to a conspiracy to interfere with a federal agent. These people do not mess around, Angie, and I fear that to them Rita is disposable. But I want you to think very hard before you commit to helping her. There could easily be terrorism charges. *Everything* is terrorism these days: downloading, uploading, jaywalking with intent to cause fear. Terrorism has become a meaningless word, our version of anti-Soviet hooliganism, but for all that, accusations of terrorism are not the worst risk we run. What they're using her for, this game of empires . . . if we're caught meddling they might even try and make a treason charge stick. We could be executed."

Angie swallowed. "I got that," she said, and took the water bottle from his fingers.

"It boils down to this: are you to your friends and family loyal first, or to your nation? Or are you loyal to the people who say they are the government of your nation—do this! do that!—are you loyal to those who claim to rule? Because you were born here, and even if you are the child of illegals, this *is* your nation, and in any case the ogre is dead."

She looked at him sidelong. "You know she means the world to me?"

Kurt was silent for a while. "I'm not blind, or bigoted."

"I'd marry her if I could. When they repeal the Defense of Marriage Act."

"Well, good for you," he said, so drily that she stared at him for a few seconds, unsure whether to parse his words as support. "I mean it: you made your choice. Did you know, you could marry her tomorrow if you were in Berlin? Your father can claim German citizenship by descent, and so can you. You were never in the HVA's files: there's no dirt to stick to you, or Rita. You and she could run away from the kingdom of the Ogre's Son—this America—" He shrugged. "It's up to you."

"I'm certain they won't let her go." Her words were heavy with conviction. "I think they attach too much weight to her birth mother. She's a world-walker to them, a tool not a citizen."

"Do you know, back in the GDR 'citizen' was an insult? It meant something like 'subject.' Here, I think they'd say 'civilian.'"

"Stop trying to distract me." She crossed her arms. "What are we going to do?"

"A certain Herr Schurz, a Prussian politician, once said: 'My country, right or wrong; if right, to be kept right; and if wrong, to be set right.' Your choices—if Rita comes back, which I may remind you is not settled—are to look to your own well-being, or stay and fight to set things to rights here. Assuming you consider yourself to be a loyal American." He saw the tension in her shoulders, the wrinkling of her brow: "But you won't have to try and make that choice on your own. If you love her, talk to her. Then tell me what you want to do. Whether to fight or flee. And then I will see what the Orchestra can do to assist my granddaughter and the woman who wants to marry her."

Best Laid Plans

The Explorer-General was entertaining visitors.

A couple of days after his brother departed, a blue-ribbon delegation of VIPs drawn from the War Committee of the Chamber of Peoples' Magistrates—the elected chamber of the Commonwealth's legislature—had buzzed into Maracaibo. They had a long and tiresome list of questions, and seemed to believe they'd get better answers if they asked them in person by spending a huge amount of money on a fact-finding mission. Huw was not officially at the beck and call of the Chamber—the Department of Para-time Research answered to the Commissioner in charge of the Ministry of Intertemporal Technological Intelligence, who in turn as part of the Central Committee answered to the First Man. However, it was sensible to deal politely with the elected representatives of the people. The War Committee had reason to be concerned with the spiraling costs of the JUGGERNAUT program, and the drain of workers and resources it was sucking from both the ICBM program and the embryonic civilian space agency. And as a successful agency, MITI had enough enemies in the Deep State and the legislature to make it a target for empire-builders.

So all Huw could do was swear to himself in private and take a couple of days out from his normal job to glad-hand the lawmakers, conduct the delegation on a dog-and-pony tour of the facilities used for exploring other parallel universes conventionally, and then (having confirmed they had a sufficiently high security clearance) show them the JUGGER-NAUT assembly area itself.

"This is one of the two staging platforms we use for transferring heavy freight across to Fort Bastion in time line twelve, which is our main dispatch and retrieval center for missions," he told his audience of six very important elected representatives and their dozen or so personal assistants. He had to raise his voice to be heard over the hubbub, even though the pilot had shut down the motors of the passenger hovercraft, which had settled on its skirts in the middle of the huge hydraulic lift platform. "Normally we use this platform for heavy freight hovercraft, with up to a hundred twenty-foot containers at a time. But right now the prime mover is unloading an outsize cargo in time line twelve, so we've got the transit platform to ourselves." Not for long: glancing to one side he saw the next freight train slowly rumbling and grinding into the siding, ready for the gigantic container cranes that lined the hangar-like building to unload. "We need this capacity because, as you're going to see shortly, keeping Fort Bastion in business consumes huge quantities of supplies and fuel."

One of the magistrates (a plain-faced middle-aged woman with a pudding bowl haircut, clearly made of stern stuff) raised her hand. "General Hjorth. Is it not possible to produce fuel locally? You have free access to the resources of time line twelve, after all."

Huh: off the script already. Someone's clearly been briefing against us. Huw nodded affably, inwardly irritated. "We considered it, and did the detailed costings," he said. "The problem was that we'd have to build oil extraction sites, bring in tankers to move the crude around, then build a refinery before we could start manufacturing Jet-A or Blaugas. If we planned to run operations on our current model for another two decades, it would be cost-effective, but JUGGERNAUT should make aviation ops obsolete within a couple of years."

He saw heads nodding. They'd seen the JUGGERNAUT line item go through, but it was a black program. And it was what they were really here for. Sticking their collective nose into a state secret that could not be discussed back in the capital, risking mischief when they got back home. Huw had already sent a sharply worded memo up the line, requesting a security review. For now, he'd just have to downplay things as much as possible. (Arresting the magistrates for spying would be indiscreet, and might draw unwelcome attention to the leak: it would be much better to obtain their willing complicity.) "We'll get to JUGGERNAUT after siesta. First I want to show you our current operations in time line twelve. Pilot? If you could set me up, please."

To his left, the pilot nodded and spoke into his headset, then started up the lift fans. Used only for world-walking transits within large buildings, the hovercraft had a paltry battery life—just enough to lift its cargo until it was electrostatically isolated from the ground, and hold it for a minute. The vehicle rose on its air cushion, compressors roaring, and began to drift forward. At a hand-signal from the pilot, Huw reached into a compartment in front of his observer's seat and withdrew a laminated card bearing an oddly reticulated knotwork design. He steadied himself by grasping an unadorned metal grab-rail with his free hand, and focused on the card.

His ears popped, and a spike of pain knifed into his forehead. Behind him, the passengers' gasps were almost audible over the roar of the hovercraft. Huw slid the card back into its binnacle. Beside him, the pilot nudged the craft toward one side of the flat concrete apron, clearing the transit area taped out on the platform. There was no roof in this time line, just open sky above. A huge hangar shaped like a bisected cylinder lying on its side loomed at the other side of the field. A minute later they were parked alongside it, and as the machine settled on its skirts the pilot deployed the stair-ramp. Huw massaged his forehead, then palmed a capsule from the bottle in his hip pocket. *I'm getting too old for this*, he told himself. The blood pressure spike that accompanied world-walking had once been a major cause of mortality for members of the Clan. Even with a well-funded research program and modern medicines the risk of a stroke rose with age and frequency. *Good thing we're due to stay here for lunch and after* . . . The Explorer-General had opened more than his fair share of new time lines. He didn't want to check out due to a cerebrovascular accident incurred while entertaining visiting legislators.

"Please follow me," he told his audience. "As this is an active military installation I'd appreciate it if you could stay with the group, for your own safety." *Just like herding cats*, he thought to himself as he walked toward the reviewing stand.

As he stepped onto the apron the Commonwealth Guard colonel in charge of the hangar crew stepped forward to meet the delegation. Colonel Manning was at the head of a detachment in parade uniforms: he'd brought the regimental brass band, Huw noted, trying not to wince. They were volunteers, not a formal ceremonial unit—a posting here could be prolonged and you needed to make your own entertainment.

"Earplugs, sir," Manning whispered, offering Huw a small cardboard tube.

"Better not: they might have questions for me. But thank you anyway. How's the schedule?"

"Everything's running like clockwork, sir. Maybe a bit too fast—wind's strengthening from the west."

Huw nodded, then straightened his shoulders and stood to attention while the band ran briskly through the Commonwealth anthem then rested their instruments. A faint noise, not unlike feedback from a stringed instrument amp, continued to buzz after the band was muted.

Huw turned to the assembled delegates. "Welcome to Fort Bastion, time line twelve. This is the forward staging area for Expeditionary Task Force Two, from which we conduct preliminary airborne recon flights into newly identified time lines." He glanced surreptitiously at his wrist watch. "One of which is due home just about . . . now . . ."

The buzzing grew louder. Huw looked up, above and beyond the delegates. Behind the bandsmen the radio operator was talking into his microphone. Off to one side, hot sunlight glared from the windows of the field control tower. "Within the next couple of minutes we should be able to see the exploration vehicle—"

The buzzing noise intensified until the airship finally came into view above the hillside overlooking the base. Seen nose-on it resembled an alien moon, silver-gray and faceted. It rose slowly, an illusion caused by its size. The engines, unblocked by terrain, bellowed hoarsely. "This is the AS-4 *Fraternity*, returning from a two week cruise across the South American continent of time line seventy-three. As you can see, at a whisker less than nine hundred feet long she's the largest ship in service in our exploration fleet . . ."

Bigger than the LZ-129 *Hindenberg*—and much safer than the zeppelins of time line two, thanks to the Commonwealth having access to helium as a lifting gas and not using highly inflammable fabric dope—the *Fraternity* took nearly ten minutes to make its final approach to the giant airship hanger at Fort Bastion. In the meantime Huw gave his audience a brisk refresher course in the reasons for using airships as para-time reconnaissance platforms: the need to carry more than one world-walker, to stay airborne for long recovery periods between jaunts, to hover while deploying ground parties, and to cruise for long distances while mapping new territories. Not to mention other, more recondite problems.

"General, what happens to your airship if the time line you send it to has no atmosphere? Or an unbreathable one?" The fellow with the odd-ball question looked to be one of the magistrates' aides: colorless eyes, unobtrusive, diffident manners.

Huw smiled stiffly, not baring his teeth. "We don't send airships through to new time lines without some idea what they're getting into. The first probe mission is always a pair of world-walkers in pressure suits: one to cross over, and a partner to bring them back immediately."

"But if they don't come back—"

"—Then they have had the supreme misfortune to have discovered a time line so hostile that it can kill a pair of armed explorers in space suits in less than a minute." Huw frowned at his audience. "Citizens, this is not a risk-free enterprise. I'd like to remind you that the limitless natural resources we can obtain from these other worlds come at the price of asking a corps of very brave volunteers to play roulette with a revolver. Over the past decade we've lost twelve world-walkers in this manner. In return, they and their colleagues have mapped routes to no less than two hundred and eighty-four time lines, and no less than two hundred and fifty-one where it is safe for human beings to live and work. And we are currently actively working in fourteen."

"If you don't count the United States of America," said the sour-faced woman.

"Yes, that is correct, ma'am."

"What happens if one of your exploration craft finds itself in a time line with another technological civilization?" asked a different rep: a sixty-something man whose olive skin and aristocratic pose bespoke southern aristocratic ancestry. "Like the, ah, *United States . . .*" He pronounced its name with a moue of skepticism, as if he wasn't entirely convinced the fabled high-tech time line existed.

"It hasn't happened yet. We try to avoid such a situation arising; on the first pressure-suited visit our world-walkers deposit a multi-channel data logger and a wireless receiver. Their next mission, a few hours later, is to retrieve the logger—nothing more, it's a quick in-and-out. We only send an aerostat once we're sure there are no radio emissions. Obviously if we run into a civilization so advanced that they have abandoned wireless for crystal balls, we might have a problem—but we would hope to see other warning signs first."

He lost their attention as the *Fraternity* finally came in to dock. The ground crew had wheeled out the mobile mooring mast and ballast tankers, and the *Fraternity's* propulsion fans were swiveling and twitching as its guidance computer held it steady. The weather was good but not completely still. Huw watched with them as the airship nosed up to the mooring mast, then waited for the clang of the docking connector and the rumble of tons of ballast water flooding into the ship's tanks, dragging it gently down onto the wheeled trolley that would carry it into the hangar.

"All right. If you'll follow me this way, into the headquarters building, I can talk you through our operational program. After which the officers' mess has laid on a buffet lunch—and then I can take you to see JUGGERNAUT."

THE MENSHIKOV PALACE, ST. PETERSBURG, TIME LINE THREE, MAY 2020

"Daddy, buy me a palace for my birthday?"

The King-in-Exile winced. "Certainly not, Liz. Birthday presents should be ostentatious, but there are *limits*." He spared her a brief, withering stare, then directed his gaze toward Professor Thompson, her tutor. "Where does she get these ideas?"

A grandiose and excessive claim is best supported by a bombastic back-drop. Knowing this, and being mindful of the proprieties of offering a Brother Emperor sanctuary during the tiresome business of suppressing the protracted rebellion afflicting his realm, His Imperial Majesty Louis XXV had granted His Royal Highness John Frederick the Fourth, Emperor-in-Exile of the New British Empire, a suitable sinecure. In due course he had also extended the same courtesy to his son John Frederick the Fifth, known by his rebellious subjects as the Young Pretender. The Emperor's thinking was that a grand duchy encompassing territories in the Bulgar, Romanian, Ruritanian, and Serbian lands would permit the Pretender to comport himself in a manner befitting an emperor-in-exile, but without sufficient influence to rival the true Imperial house. The British monarch was to be indebted to the House of Bourbon, and provided with a seat from which to campaign for the return of his rightful throne—but not encouraged to pursue any futile and tiresome ambitions he might harbor toward his ancestral lands, these being the islands of Greater Brittany and the duchy of Brunswick-Lüneburg.

So the British Crown-in-Exile occupied the Menshikov Palace on the banks of the Bolshaya Neva, living in straightened circumstances on a purse providing a mere seven million écus per month in taxes.

John Frederick held the palace on a rolling yearly lease, and spent every August praying that the revolution would vanish like a bad dream, freeing him from the need for it. With the passing of the fifteenth anniversary of the lease, his bolder courtiers had begun to whisper behind his back that perhaps it would have been prudent to purchase it instead.

But none were brave enough to bring this suggestion to the royal ear, until his daughter.

"You're *wasting money* on this pile," Elizabeth insisted, with the withering scorn of a late teenager. "I saw the figures. We bleed as much in rent in four years as it would cost to buy the freehold outright! If you were to buy it and deed it to me as my birthright then it would certainly light a bonfire signaling the wealth and power of the House of Hanover—and it would save you money in the long term. Even in the short term! I did the sums when Professor Thompson taught me the laws of usury and compound interest: it's true, I swear! In just four years you would break even. Even if the rebels open their arms and welcome you with flowers, will we abandon court in St. Petersburg so soon? And anyway," she added, "if we move back to New London we can lease it out ourselves, or sell it. Even if we lost a tenth of its value and had to divest after a year, we would be better off than under the terms of the lease Prince Krunichev extracted from Grandpapa."

The skin around John Frederick's eyes tightened: Professor Thompson wilted under his gaze. *There will be an accounting for this accounting,* the Pretender's expression promised. Then he turned back to his daughter. She was eighteen, skinny, and blessed with her mother's brown eyes, black hair, and sharp wits. But she was also barely biddable, prone to back talk, and dangerously close to rebellious: in his opinion she'd spent too much time running wild in the country estates when she should have been learning the social and diplomatic graces required at court.

"We are minded to say no," he said, mildly enough. "You are correct on the accounts. We would break even after a year. But buying the palace would send *another* signal, Liz, one you've overlooked: it would declare us reconciled to our exile in a land that we cannot call our own. If my father had purchased it when we first arrived, it might have passed unremarked. But to buy it now would send a renewed sign of commitment to our continental cousins. Just at the worst possible time."

"Worst?" Elizabeth's brow wrinkled. "Why is this birthday different . . . ?"

"Walk with me, daughter." John Frederick rose and, offering her an arm, gestured with his free hand toward the tall French windows that opened onto the garden at the rear of the drawing room. Liveried footmen, as unremarkable as any other furnishings, leapt to open the doors. "One should like to smell the rosebushes."

Elizabeth rose and took her father's arm. The fashion in St. Petersburg in the twenty-first century was dominated by a baroque revival, with court dress as elaborate as anything from the time of the Sun King. The King-in-Exile led his daughter down the marble steps and along a gravel path between elaborate displays of topiary. A cometary trail of servants followed behind them: footmen bearing wireless telephones and discreet cypher machines, ladies-in-waiting of good breeding in the Princess's service, runners to fetch and carry anything that the royal couple might call for, and a squad of soldiers in dress uniform as overt bodyguards. An autogyro of the Royal Gendarmerie buzzed in lazy circles overhead, watching the approaches to the royal cantonment of Vasileostrovskiy. Doubtless there were other guards concealed in the shrubbery, their uniforms camouflaged and their guns loaded, but they were at pains to be discreet so as not to offend the eyes of their rulers.

"You are nearly eighteen," John Frederick told his daughter. He knew perfectly well that she was ill at ease here, preferring the opportunities for solitary study and outdoor exercise that their dacha in the countryside provided. "And you are feeling the constraints of palace life. The constant scrutiny and public speculation, the lack of friends of your own age . . ."

Elizabeth ducked her head. Some things didn't need saying. "I'm not *that* short of friends, Papa. I have my ladies-in-waiting and my tutors . . . has Donald been reporting to you?"

She was referring to Professor Thompson by his first name: *That will never do*, thought her father. He shook his head. "No, but it's obvious. We all go through it, the isolation of rank. No, Liz. On the one hand, you feel stifled by the intricacies of court. On the other, you are growing into the age of responsibility just as the world stage is changing and the play moves toward its third act. Buying the palace would be a, a bad idea at present. It would send the wrong message not only to my loyal subjects, but to the enemy. And it would send the wrong message to a potential ally, as well. A princess does not need her own palace when she can use any of her husband's."

She let go of his arm and stopped dead in the middle of the path. "What. Husband," she said tonelessly.

John Frederick composed his face. "One is merely speculating about your future," he pointed out. "You are a princess. Not merely *any* princess, either: you are Princess Elizabeth, heir to a certain throne. You'll marry sooner or later, as you wish. We'll not force your hand, nor arrange anything against your wishes. But your rank means you will have suitors by and by, and you lack the polish and political acumen to understand how to make the most important decision of your life. The professor may be able to teach you the arts and natural sciences, but he lacks the necessary insight into politics. So one believes we should broach the topics of new advisors—and of finishing schools."

Elizabeth's shoulders heaved. "Oh Daddy, you had me worried for a minute!" She tentatively reached for his arm and he offered it. "I thought you were getting ready for *that* talk."

John Frederick smiled wryly. "Which one?" They began to walk again, pacing toward the fountain at the center of the garden.

"The one in which you tell me we're to announce my public engagement to that pig Louis," she said blandly. "Wedding to follow on my twentieth birthday, baby by the twenty-first, pox by the twenty-second." John Frederick doubled over, coughing. Footsteps, running: "It's nothing! Nothing, I say! A glass of water for my father, and the physic, that's all!" She pounded on his back, taking a daring liberty. "Stop choking, Daddy, it's *undignified*."

Attention, water, and breathing space brought John Frederick back to himself within a minute. Waving off the servants, he turned to his daughter. "You are a wicked, *wicked* young lady." His finger stopped wagging momentarily. "Where did you hear those slanders?"

"I'm not an idiot, Daddy." She glanced sidelong, checking for overly open ears. "It's the obvious way to rent yourself an army, and it would explain your lack of desire to make any permanent accommodation here . . ."

"Don't be evasive, child, we were talking about the pox."

"I *read*, Daddy. A lot more widely than Louis would approve of, I'm sure. There are pamphlets, you know." Her father's face was a worrying shade of puce. "Don't worry, they don't say anything bad about *you*. But Louis is a pig and a rakehell and has a string of mistresses *and* a worrying habit of retreating to a certain clinic on a regular basis, and no children by *any* of his fancies. I understand the urgency of retaking the family seat in New London, but don't you think you could do better for me?"

Her father tried to collect his dignity. "A two-year engagement would actually be very convenient right now, Liz, if you could bear to announce it with a straight face—no, hear me out! I'm not proposing that you should actually *marry* the fellow. But the chief rebel, Burroughs, is dying. He's going to last less than six months, and when he's gone the wolves will tear into each other. We could be back in the Brunswick Palace within the year, and any marriage could then be postponed indefinitely by the exigencies of reasserting Crown rule over the dominions. Or the engagement ended, after a decent interval. This is purely about short-term expediency, and the need to give him a reason to lend us the troops we'll need—"

"But he's a pig! And if we're engaged and I'm here in St. Petersburg it will be impossible to avoid him. Worse, if I retire to the dacha he'll come and *visit*."

"Yes. Which is another reason I mentioned finishing schools. Madame Houelebecq in Berlin is highly spoken of—"

"—Berlin? It's full of knuckle-dragging racist Prussians and their Huguenot and Jew minions! Why not Vienna or Paris?"

"Louis would insist on offering you the hospitality of his winter court in Versailles, were you to go to Paris. We thought you wanted nothing to do with him?"

"But Vienna—"

"Is stuffy and full of Czechs and Magyars and other undesirables, Liz. One has been there. You would tire of the opera after a couple of months, feel unwelcome and gawped-at at the balls, and as for the rest of it, it's as full of stuck-up Balkan princes as anywhere else. We have discussed this with your mother. You would never be allowed to go to Londres or Dublin or Hanover, or any of our other traditional demesnes. Louis and his father aren't *that* stupid. In Paris or Rome or the other peripheral capitals you would be unable to avoid Louis's hospitality. You could go and hide somewhere like Strelsau, but it's a backwater. Our best option is to dangle you under Louis's nose, encouraging him to dream of a stake in our American properties—then whisk you away to gain allies and learn the necessary graces at a finishing school somewhere inconvenient but unthreatening to a self-deceiving ally."

"You really *have* thought this through, haven't you?" Elizabeth looked up into his eyes—not far, for she was a tall lass, scant inches shorter than her father—and smiled admiringly. Her cheek dimpled pleasingly when she did so, taking two or three years off her apparent age. "If I wasn't your daughter I'd call you a snake!"

"One writhes in the grass and bites ankles so that you shall have a throne, my dear." His cheek twitched. "We can only wish that our father had applied himself to his garden with equal diligence when the sprouts of treason were growing under his nose. Then we wouldn't have to deny you a palace for your coming-of-age present."

He paused for a moment. "Will a crown suffice, instead?"

Later, in the privacy of the Princess's apartment:

"I can't believe it. The slimy squirming *worm* . . ."

"What has he done now, my lady?"

Snort. "He as good as said he'd sold me to the highest bidder! And then he had the gall to say he was doing it for my own good."

"And the highest bidder, would be, oh *no*—"

"Oh yes, *him.*"

"He's not *that* ugly. Or ancient. Is he?"

"If it was merely that he was thirty-two I could close my eyes. But the mistresses and the brothels and the unspeakable habits—he's indiscreet! He would be a laughing-stock, if not for his royal blood. He's thirty-two and nobody has married him and there is a *reason*, Susannah, even if my father refuses to acknowledge it. He's a catch, but there's a catch."

"You can always say no, can't you?"

"That's the worst part: I don't think I can. Father spins a web so fine I can barely see the strands. He wants to send me to a finishing school, Sue. That is, right after announcing the engagement. Two years! In Berlin of all places. Why *Berlin*?"

"Huh, Berlin? It could be worse. Distance is the best chaperone and all that . . . but maybe he wants you out of St. Petersburg for some other reason?"

"Yes, that's what I'm afraid of. He said it was to let me stay away from the unspeakable fiancé, but what if that's just a convenient excuse? What if he suspects me?"

"*Hsst!* Say it's not so?"

"I wish I could, my dear." A pause. "I'm sorry, I've upset you."

"Oh, this is terrible!"

"I'll find a way to take you with me. I won't let them part us."

"But if your father suspects anything he, he, he—"

"He won't. Hear, hug me. Calm down. I'll think of something."

Later, by scrambled telephone: "I broke the subject to her."

"And how did she take it?"

"She understands the diplomatic necessity in principle, and she will even tolerate a public engagement. But you face an uphill battle thereafter: it'll be up to you to woo her. I'm going to send her to finishing school. You'll have two years to work on your public appearance. Take the cure, banish the trollops—or at least make them use the back door—and practice your charm. Liz thinks she's going to school to receive some final polish, make friends, and have her horizons broadened. What's really going to happen is that she'll be a long way from home and desperately lonely. She's going to be surrounded by jealous debutantes who resent her for being betrothed to a prince and who will spite her for the color of her mother's Brazilian skin. Play your cards close to your chest and practice your charm and she'll be ripe to fall into your arms when we bring her home."

"What an excellent plan! I believe I entirely approve. So where are you sending her?"

"Berlin."

"Berlin? But that's—"

"Yes, it's a grim provincial capital full of idiot radicals and smoke-spewing factories. And you must be at pains to stay away for the first year, Louis. Let her stew in her own juice."

"But I don't have any people there!"

"Exactly. By the same token, there's nobody there to spread poisonous rumors against you."

"Oh." A pause. "Not *that* again."

"Yes, *that*. Elizabeth is sharp as a razor. She's not one of those pedigreed Hapsburg cows with the congenital wits of a drunken snail. She takes after her mother. But for all that she's intelligent and cynical beyond her years, she's just a girl approaching marriageable age. She's read the scandal sheets, but as long as you do nothing to inflame jealousy, the noise will die down, and if you are careful to give the impression it's all behind you, you can be her knight in shining armor when you arrive to rescue her from the backwaters of Prussia. Turn her head and put her on a throne beside you before she wakes up. But if you *don't* clean up your act I can't in all honesty commend your hand in marriage to my daughter."

A longer pause. "I understand." Pause. "And thank you for trying."

"I'm not just doing this for myself, Louis. I'm doing it for her future."

"*Her* future? What about your grandson?"

"My grandson doesn't exist yet, Louis. That bit is up to you. What I am minded to consider is the fate of my daughter if I lose at the Restoration game. If this gamble we have embarked on fails. There is no shame in a princess of the House of Hanover becoming Queen-Consort of the Sun Throne, but if I return to New London and the rebels prevail . . . there is a very dangerous precedent in the history of my crown, Louis. The history of the Kings of England and Scotland is still shadowed by the events of 1649. You're gambling your reputation and your father's goodwill, but I'm gambling my *life* on this alliance. If I fail and the rebels keep their heads, they will certainly not suffer me to keep mine. And I would have you remember that."

THE SUMMER PALACE, ST. PETERSBURG, TIME LINE THREE, AUGUST 2020

In due course, the delicate negotiations between the court-in-exile of John Frederick IV and his Imperial Highness, King Louis XXV came to a mutually agreeable and fruitful conclusion. These negotiations coincided with the eighteenth birthday of Her Royal Highness, the Princess Elizabeth. And so a decision was taken to announce her engagement that same evening, at a ball held in her honor in the grounds of the Summer Palace.

For her part, Elizabeth endured the celebrations with dry eyes and grim determination, smiling fixedly through the ceremonials. The birthday gifts were scant compensation: her father bestowed on her a wholly spurious duchy and the titular leadership of an order of chivalry, at the same time as he stripped away her last illusions of freedom. Her new tiara of sapphires and emeralds in a platinum band was so heavy that it threatened to engrave premature lines on her brow: a fitting metaphor for the evening. It would have been graceless to sulk or throw a tantrum on one's birthday, whether or not one was to be engaged to a notoriously dissolute rake nearly twice one's own age. Elizabeth had no desire to be seen as graceless. She had few friends at her father's court, and a mother who, living as a recluse, having abandoned all interest in her daughter's education. So she allowed her newly announced fiancé to lead her through the first waltz, and smiled winningly at the round of applause that followed. For his part he refrained from staring down her bosom too obviously and managed not to tread on her feet, for which she was grateful. (His breath was another matter, enriched with port fumes sufficient to stun an ox.) He was, she supposed, quite a catch. She ought *in principle* to be grateful to have such a husband on the end of her fishing line. But it seemed to her that her tastes ran to dolphins, and he was a vast and ancient whale, white-bellied, barnacle-encrusted, bloated and smelling of rotten seaweed.

The rest of the evening was hardly an improvement. She sailed alone through a sea of the Dauphin's courtiers, their pale faces goggling at her as if she were an alien from the planet Venus. Her head ached, and the news of the day left her feeling not glorious, as a young woman should feel at her engagement party, but grim and full of apprehension. She left as early as possible, and back at her apartments she instructed her servants to pack immediately for her departure on the morrow.

"How long is my lady to be away for?" asked Jessop the butler.

"About two years." She watched his face for signs of disquiet and surprise. Either he had nerves of steel, or someone had leaked her father's arrangements. "I shall be attending a finishing school for the duration. The wedding will be scheduled after my return." Her cheek twitched. "There will be other formalities before then. A trip to Rome, I believe."

Now Jessop twitched in turn. "To see the ruins?" he asked carefully.

"An audience with the Pope." It was a precondition for the engagement, lest the heir to the Sun Throne be born outside the Catholic Church. A compromise her father was willing to accept on her behalf, regardless of her own beliefs.

"Very well, my lady." Jessop backed away carefully, as if she was made of stale explosives and might detonate at the slightest disturbance. Not that the Princess was *devout* by any measure, but when one had been raised to anticipate inheriting the titular leadership of a state Church, being told that one's father had consigned one to marry a Catholic crown was something of a shock. It underscored her father's reckless determination to retake New London so firmly that it left her sick to her stomach when she realized the full implications. Although many of the New British Empire's subjects were Catholic, the Crown had traditionally relied on the support of its Protestant and non-conformist supporters. Her conversion was a necessary precondition to the proposed dynastic marriage, and the marriage was essential to secure the support of the Bourbon

Empire, but it risked a tremendous backlash among the Crown's loyal supporters. The distant memory of Bloody Mary and the less-remote recollection of the Slaveowners' Treasonous Rebellion provided a rallying cry for anyone who was against Papist Plotters. As a strategy it risked setting the North American dominions ablaze, yet her father was seemingly willing to take the risk.

I'm not going to marry, she almost called after Jessop. *Not him, not any man. And I have* no *intention of converting!* But at the last second she remembered to seal her lips. Let word escape! Let rumor fly where it would. Let turbulence result. And let non-conformists all over Europe wonder if the last royal defenders of the faith were about to kneel and kiss the ring, and if the cold sword of imperial conformity would soon be pressed upon their necks. If nothing else, it might make life easier for her eventually, if she had to save herself . . .

"Attend me," she called, looking around for Susannah, her lady of the bedchamber. "I'm ready to disrobe."

"Certainly." Susannah followed her into the dressing room, closing the door behind them. She still wore her own ball gown, having been part of the Princess's party this evening. "So it's going to happen?"

"As planned, I fear." Elizabeth sat down. "Unlace me. I'm not staying in St. Petersburg a minute longer than necessary, Susie. Not with my so-called fiancé on the prowl. The risk—no, the prospect—of embarrassment is mortifying."

"Your shoulders are very tense."

"Yes well, why shouldn't they be? The cat and his tame mice kept *staring*. In front of everybody! I was extremely tempted to make a scene. If Mother had been there they wouldn't have *dared*, but . . . Ah, that's better."

"I didn't see Lady d'Angelou at the ball, though, Liz."

"No, he'd not be *that* shameless, not at my birthday ball. But this marriage . . ." The Princess shuddered. "It's not going to happen. It can't happen. Not only is it unwise, it's a mistake."

"Jolly good," Susannah muttered as she helped the Princess out of her formalwear. "Which dressing gown, my lady?"

"The pale blue yukata, please." Elizabeth frowned minutely. "I intend to depart as soon as possible. Classes at the school do not start until mid-September, but I am sure no harm will come if I travel early and spend a week in Vienna on my way to Berlin. The royal air yacht is available: I told Daddy I wanted to borrow it."

She rose, extending her arms as Lady Susannah helped her into her robe. "You should prepare for bed, Susie. It's going to be a long day tomorrow."

MARACAIBO PARA-TIME STAGING COMPLEX, TIME LINE THREE, AUGUST 2020

Huw Hjorth, as Explorer-General in charge of opening up new time lines for the Commonwealth, spent much of his time apart from his wife, Brilliana—who was herself responsible for the Ministry of Intertemporal Technological Intelligence's espionage operations in other time lines. Being one half of a power couple was not conducive to quiet domesticity. Brilliana spent much of her time visiting MITI's scattered para-time intelligence offices, while he remained in a windowless air-conditioned box adjacent to the Maracaibo staging complex.

But the Explorer-General's younger brother Hulius was happy to admit that when they were home together they set a good table. A formal family dinner party (attended by the two of their four offspring who were not yet of an age to be serving elsewhere) assured Hulius that his brother and sister-in-law were doing well for themselves. Age, experience, and marriage to Brilliana had matured Huw, allowing him to grow into an impressively professorial demeanor. And being married to Huw seemed to agree with her, too, judging by the complicit glances and sentences started by one and completed by the other. Hulius wished he could say as much for himself: the thought brought a mild pang. But at least Ellie and the girls were well cared for, back up north.

"Is it time to talk business?" he asked as the maid removed the last of the dessert bowls from the table. "Or are we still on family catch-up time?"

Brill frowned very slightly, then glanced sideways at Roland, their fourteen-year-old, who was looking distractedly at something in his lap. "Roland, put that *away*."

"Aw, Mum . . ."

She narrowed her eyes. "I saw your homework list. You can play with your Game Boy when it's done." Hulius took note: a game console imported from the other known high-tech time line was quite a prize to be handing out to a bored early teen. "Give it here. You can have it back when you've finished your trigonometry." She held out a hand.

Huw joined in. "Nel, would you mind taking your brother . . . ?"

"Yes, Father." Nel, sixteen and responsible, looked disappointed, but nevertheless rose obediently. "Come along, Rol, they need room for their top-secret management talk. You'd only be bored by it."

"You've got them well-trained," Hulius remarked as Nel closed the door.

"Yes, well." Huw shook his head. "The Game Boy wasn't my idea. Erasmus gave it to him for his birthday. I can guess where *he* got it, and the idea, from—"

"They like to spoil other people's kids," Brill cut in. "Can we change the subject, please?" They were getting close to dangerous ground, Hulius realized. Even though the world-walking Clan didn't exist as a formal organization anymore, old habits died hard. The personal was political, and Miriam had a claim to leadership over the world-walkers by right of birth. She'd also kept them alive in exile through the deadly white-water ride of the revolutionary years. Not to mention by having risen so high in the Radical Party, although her mother Iris's planning and foresight had done much to make that possible. The surviving world-walkers had adopted the dress and mannerisms of the Commonwealth's ruling party elite, and provided service to the state in return for security and privilege. But Miriam's lack of children—she'd been thirty-seven when she'd led them into exile, nearly forty when she finally married Erasmus—struck dissonant notes among those raised in a dynastic tradition. They were led by a Fisher Queen, casting her net through the shoals and waters of parallel universes in hope of bringing back treasure, but with no clear heir to leave it to.

"Well." Hulius paused to dab at his beard with a linen napkin. He was strongly tempted to loosen his embroidered waistcoat. The meal had served to remind him that his stomach was no longer a bottomless pit like one of those black holes that were all the rage on the TV science channels these days. "I assume you didn't invite me all this way from New York just for dinner?"

"No." Brill carefully folded her napkin and laid it beside her plate.

Huw glanced at her. "What is this—" He looked back at Huw. "Excuse me. What?"

"JUGGERNAUT is going to need a pilot." Brill nodded at his blank look. "A classified project you haven't been briefed on that needs a world-walker. I pulled your medical records. For a male in your late thirties you've got low blood pressure. That could be important. You're big-boned, which is a minus, but—"

"You are not pulling my brother into this!" Huw burst out, to Hulius's complete surprise. "For one thing he's not cleared for it, and for another thing, he's, he's—"

"But it's a great cover story though, isn't it?" Brill asked. There was a dangerous light in her eyes. "That's why Olga suggested him. *You* be-lieved me, didn't you?"

"Wait, what?" Hulius looked first at Huw, then at Brilliana, swiveling his head. "What's this 'juggernaut'? What's Olga hatching *now*?" Brill sat still, gloved hands clasped in her lap, looking smug.

Huw shook his head, then pushed his chair back from the table. "Remind me again why I married you," he murmured to his wife. Then, to his brother: "Whisky? I have an excellent Bourbon. And cigars . . ."

"Don't mind if I do."

"Cigars." Brilliana wrinkled her nose. "Not that I mind the smell *at the time*, but you men don't pay the dry cleaning bills. Why can't you smoke something sensible?"

"Well, if you insist . . ."

Huw ferried a decanter and tumblers from the sideboard to the low table between the two chesterfield sofas that dominated the far side of the room, then returned to fetch an ornate multi-stemmed narghile and a silver-chased box which, to Hulius's satisfaction, proved to be overflow-ing with freshly aromatic herb. "Cascadian Gold, from the former Royal Plantations," he told his brother as he primed the water pipe. "My dear, if you'd do the honors?"

Brill nodded grudgingly. She rose and moved to one of the sofas; then, taking lighter in one hand and a flexible-stemmed pipe in the other, she puffed the apparatus into life. She handed the other stems to her hus-band and brother-in-law before sitting down to inhale properly.

After a contemplative moment she leaned back against the sofa and gently exhaled, trying to blow a ring. "I am so very glad that Helge found a new form of arbitrage for us to pursue, all those years ago," she mused. "We would have been in terrible trouble if she hadn't. Even if we were still in business in the United States."

The war on drugs had died with a whimper rather than a bang, but it was dead for all that. And in this time line, the Commonwealth (and the Empire that preceded it) had avoided teetotal crusaders en-tirely—a side effect of the Empire's bloody birth pangs. The sweetly heady smell took the edge off Hulius's urgent sense of inquiry, and a sip of the whisky—an excellent single barrel—settled warmly in his overfull stomach.

"So," Hulius began, "there is something secret called JUGGER-NAUT, and I am sufficiently suited for it that *you*"—he nodded at his brother—"were taken in by your lady wife's proposal that I might pilot it, which *you*"—he met Brill's steady gaze—"thought would make an excel-lent cover story for *something else*. So I am presented with the existence of two secrets, only one of which concerns me. Am I right?"

Brilliana brushed an unseen crumb from her gown, then sat up again, back straight. "You are not wrong." She took a brief sip of smoke, then leaned forward to replace the pipe. "You do not currently need to know about JUGGERNAUT in any detail. All I can tell you is that it's part of our worst case contingency plan for dealing with the US government, or any other technologically-equipped time line, and you will not mention it to anyone outside this room. Think Manhattan Project."

Hulius nodded hesitantly. (The history of the United States' atomic weapons program—and its disastrous fruition—were a matter with which he was regrettably familiar.) "And my involvement is the *cover* story?"

Huw gave his wife a look. "My dear, I think you owe us both an explanation."

"Surely, if you will bear with me. Yul, after we came over here, you spent some time learning to fly, didn't you?"

Hulius blinked rapidly, unsure whether the smoke or the maze of mirrors he found himself within was responsible. "It was Rudi's idea. Rudi thought we needed more world-walkers who were pilots."

"Really?" Huw raised an eyebrow. "You could have told him—"

"Well yes, but that was before we discovered the problems. World-walking while airborne works fine, if you enjoy playing Russian roulette with the weather in parallel universes. Or happen to be on board a multi-engined transport aircraft or a bomber with an experienced flight crew and a few thousand feet of altitude for recovery if there's a storm cell or clear air turbulence in the wrong place when you transition. Rudi and I—" He shook his head. "Private pilot's license, visual flight rules, single engine? I'm not going there, it's a game best played by eighteen-year-olds who are convinced of their own immortality."

Huw looked at his wife. "But he's got a pilot's license. And even Olga thought he was suitable for JUGGERNAUT . . ."

"Yes." She took a slow sip of whisky, looking thoughtful. "It *is* plausible, isn't it."

JUGGERNAUT is some sort of flying machine, Hulius realized. *Paratime capable, almost certainly nuclear armed, and not just a bomber.* Any damn fool general could see that you could put a couple of world-walkers in every cockpit of a bomb wing and have them transition simultaneously while their planes were in the air, three minutes out from an enemy city. Approaching their target's location in another time line, they'd be impossible to detect or intercept, right up until they shifted time lines and began dropping nukes. The Commonwealth couldn't build anything in the same league as a B-2 Spirit or an F-22 Raptor, but it didn't have to. Their existing six-engined subsonic battlewagons, designed to rain instant sunshine on the French Empire in Europe, were in the same class as a

B-52. More than sufficient for a first strike through para-time. So, if JUGGERNAUT wasn't a *first* strike weapon, designed for a swift decapitation strike on the United States, there must be some sort of deep para-time strategy—

His brother elbowed him gently. "Yul, stop thinking. It's not what they pay you for."

"Sorry, I was away with the fair folk." Hulius took a deep breath. "You've got something in mind that needs a world-walker who can fly a plane and warrants an impeccable top-secret cover story. And it has to be someone you trust like your own, uh, brother-in-law." He stared at Brill. "It's deniable. Jeopardy so high that you can't trust an outsider. Something so secret you'd use the Manhattan Project as a cover story. So it's politically embarrassing." He glanced at Huw, who looked as mystified as he felt: "What's going on?"

"It's a deep penetration mission via time line two," said Brill. Hulius felt dawning dismay. In the Clan's old terminology, time line two meant the world of the United States. "The operative we eventually choose—it might not be you, but you're the lead candidate—will travel through time line two and then pop up here in time line three to carry out an, uh, political neutralization." Frown lines deepened on either side of her mouth. "It's a very high level target. Options have been considered, including abduction and assassination, but there's a third alternative that we're pursuing." She met his gaze directly, unblinking. "The target is Princess Elizabeth of Hanover. The only child of the heir to the throne of the former New British Empire. She must not under any circumstances be allowed to marry the Dauphin."

Hulius stared at her, a mild sensation of nausea creeping over him. "You're playing with fire!" *The Pretender is planning on marrying his daughter to the French emperor's son?* Hulius tried not to boggle at the news. The Pretender still claimed to be the legitimate ruler of the British Empire, his Crown-in-Exile a symbol of political opposition to the revolutionary Commonwealth. Then another thought struck him. "She's only eighteen!"

Huw nodded. "She's not much older than Nel."

"Wouldn't it be more expeditious to kill the . . . the French prince?" Hulius speculated.

"Yes." Brill nodded guardedly. "But Olga ruled out assassinating the Dauphin. That would be an overt act of war. It would be equally problematic to act against John Frederick himself. Our priority is to prevent the Dauphin acquiring a legitimate claim to the territories of the, the former British Empire. Sir Adam is dying"—she took in their shocked expressions—"and we will be facing enough pressure for a restoration of the monarchy as it is. So the weak point is the lynchpin of the alliance that our informers tell us is being negotiated."

"Sir Adam is *dying*?" Huw demanded.

"Cancer." She frowned. "The doctors think he may have as little as three months to live. Then the Commonwealth has a constitutional crisis: he's been the First Man"—effectively the President for Life—"ever since the revolution. We know how the succession of powers *should* operate, but the machinery is untested . . ."

Hulius crossed his arms. "I am not going to murder a girl barely three years older than my eldest daughter." A nasty thought crawled out of the darkness, a memory of the way the nobility had done business in the Gruinmarkt: "I'm not going to despoil or rape her either! This Commonwealth is founded on the rule of law, the idea that there are universal standards, basic rights that apply to all. If we stoop to such depths of skullduggery, what claim will we *ever* be able to make for legitimacy?"

Brilliana glanced at her husband. "Told you he'd gone native," she murmured. Hulius twitched: she sounded *approving*.

Huw chuckled. Hulius stared at his brother and sister-in-law, fuming. "Well? What are you holding back?"

"You missed the third possibility," Brilliana said quietly. "Do you think a spirited eighteen-year-old girl can possibly be looking forward to marrying a debauchee who is half her age again, has a mistress, and is also reputed to have the pox?"

Suddenly Hulius had an inkling of where this was going. He leaned forward. "Where did you learn about the impending nuptials?" he asked. "I haven't seen anything about this in the press or on the wire."

"Sources." Brill raised a cautionary finger. "According to the boss herself, we have them." She took another sip of whisky. "Back channels through which deniable negotiations may be conducted. Yul, if you agree to this task, the first cover story is that you are to train as a pilot for JUGGERNAUT. The *second* cover story, for use only if you are captured, is that you are being sent to murder, rape, ruin, or otherwise render Elizabeth, Princess of Hanover, unmarriageable spoiled goods.

"In reality, the mission is somewhat different. The young lady in question—who is currently mewed up in her father's palace, a gilded cage in the middle of the French capital—contacted us herself to tell us she's interested in negotiating the terms of her defection to the Commonwealth. As you might imagine, offering her the moon on a stick is not a problem. The *real* headache is how to get her out of French hands and spirit her halfway around the world, under the nose of the military and intelligence complex of the largest empire on Earth.

"And that's where you come in . . ."

Arrivals

Hulius spent a week with his brother and sister-in-law. He took pains to phone and (later, once he was assigned an account on the base mainframe) to e-mail his wife Elena and their daughters. He was, he assured them, sorry to be called away, but for the next few weeks he was working on a project that he could not discuss. As a world-walker herself, Elena understood the need for regular government service. The quiet conscription of the para-time-capable had been the bedrock of the Clan for centuries, and their forced migration to the New American Commonwealth had merely changed the taskmaster.

In reality, Hulius's week was crammed with preparatory meetings with the DPR's local Latin American and European specialists because Hulius was about to embark on a hazardous clandestine operation.

"Head office set up an identity and a background for you," Brill explained. "Use it well, it's very expensive. Your biometrics will be captured on your way into the Schengen zone, along with your passport details, so you won't be able to operate in the EU under different cover ever again. Or in South-East Asia, for that matter. How's your German?"

Hulius shrugged. "Indifferent to crap. I have a lousy accent, they think I'm Dutch."

"That's actually useful." She slid a passport across the desk toward him: it was drab green, slightly creased, and embossed in faded gilt lettering with PASPOR REPUBLIK INDONESIA. "You are Manfred van Rijnt. You were born in Cape Town but moved to Jakarta when your father took a job in the oil industry when you were eight. Your mother is dead. You have a degree in plant genomics, studied management—you have an MBA—and you work in the rubber plantation industry." She slid a manila document folder across to him. "Read and memorize this backgrounder in case you have to bore random strangers with your anecdotes. Incidentally, you speak Malay—actually Bahasa Indonesia—as well as Dutch, English, and some German."

Hulius cleared his throat. "But I don't speak Malay . . ."

"You won't need to, and there's virtually no risk of you outing yourself unless you spend a lot of time in Amsterdam. The reason we're using Indonesia for your documentation is that they're a weak spot in the global air passenger advance notification system. They don't have a national DNA database or capture biometrics beyond the minimal facial stuff, and it's easy to bribe a passport out of them. Your cover story is that you've been in Brazil and Venezuela negotiating the South American side of a supply deal. Genetically modified latex is going to be a big thing, hypoallergenic and biodegradable. If anyone asks, you're flying to Germany to talk to a medical appliance company. You have a visa valid for entry to the Schengen area, applied for via the Dutch embassy. Your port of entry is Schiphol Airport, and once you're through Dutch immigration you can head for Berlin."

"They'll still capture my biometrics—"

"Yes. But you've never been out of North America before, and the Schengen group of nations follow German standards on data privacy. The Americans don't share domestic biometric captures with foreigners, and the EU only share travelers with the USA if they're flying to North America. So unless at some later date you get on a plane bound for North America, nobody will realize your biometrics match the world-walker the Americans are hunting. You're clean as a whistle, at least for a single mission in Europe."

"Ah!" Hulius beamed. "I see where this is going."

"Yes! We can insert you into the heartlands of the French Empire without anyone knowing—not the United States, nor the French over here. The idea is, we send you through time line two under a clean cover identity. Still in time line two, you establish a safe house, then do the same in time line three. Then when it's time for the pick-up, you can penetrate the Princess's security cordon in time line three and extract her to time line two."

"Yes, but what happens afterwards?" His smile faded. "I don't see how you can fake up a biometric passport for a woman from another time line—"

"We can't. That's not in the plan. But once you've carried her across to time line two, the next step is for you to drive her to an airfield. We budgeted to buy you a Cirrus SR22T. When we've got everything lined up for exfiltration, you'll fly due west—it has a range of nearly fifteen hundred kilometers without ferry tanks—then world-walk and pop the plane's recovery parachute over the Atlantic. It avoids all the air defenses around the French empire and avoids having to fake up ID good enough to get her on an airliner."

Hulius couldn't contain himself. "That's suicidal!" Even without factoring in a possibly unwilling passenger, deliberately ditching a light plane in the middle of the North Atlantic—even one with a built-in parachute recovery system—seemed like a *really* bad idea.

"Not if there's a fleet of spy trawlers waiting right under your flight path with orders to retrieve you. And you won't take off until you get confirmation that they're in position and the weather conditions are favorable." She held up a finger. "Added bonus: it gets Manfred van Rijnt's identity confirmed dead in a general aviation accident. If his biometrics ever filter their way back to the NSA or DHS, they'll be tagged as 'deceased.' Oh, and we get some up-to-date general aviation avionics from the light plane, a bunch of composite materials and one of those neat ballistic recovery systems for the air cadets to pick over. But mostly Princess Elizabeth gets to vanish mysteriously, right under the noses of her chaperones and bodyguards and secret police monitors, avoiding a marriage she doesn't want and an entanglement with the French monarchy that the Commonwealth really doesn't need. And then"—Brill smirked impishly—"the *real* empire games begin!"

VENEZUELA, TIME LINE ONE/CARACAS, TIME LINE TWO, AUGUST 2020

Venezuela, in time line one, was heavily forested and decidedly unsafe for random pale-skinned interlopers—the empire of the Quiriquire took a robust and gruesome approach to intruders on their territory. However, the Department of Para-time Research had constructed a small camp on the steep hillside of the Caracas valley. Electric fences and sharpshooters had taught the neighboring villagers to give it a wide berth. The camp functioned as a forward base and covert insertion site, allowing clandestine agents to cross over into time line two outside the heavily-surveilled police states of North America.

Hulius arrived in the camp as a passenger on the twice-weekly supply hovercraft, along with a couple of tons of trade goods and four other agents. Two were buyers from Technology Acquisition, tasked with obtaining samples of pharmaceuticals and electronics from the more advanced time line. The other couple were research librarians, looting the stored academic heritage of time line two for the benefit of the DPR. They chatted among themselves in rapid-fire Spanish (too fast for Hulius to follow) and seemed to be very excited. Like old-time KGB agents on foreign postings to the decadent fleshpots of the West, they were dizzily intoxicated by the novelty and wealth of Venezuela. The panoply of luxury goods and high technology laid out all around them was fascinating. Despite the Commonwealth's best efforts to catch up (and they'd come a *long* way in the past two decades) visiting time line two still felt like taking a leap fifty years into the future. Hulius, however, faced a more challenging mission than draining academic pre-print Web sites onto storage devices and buying equipment for the MITI teaching labs. He kept his own counsel, reading and rereading his travel briefing.

Finally the duty world-walker arrived, took her seat next to the hover-craft's pilot, and blinked them into a different parallel universe.

The time line two terminal was a windowless warehouse with a thick industrial carpet floor and deafening aircon fans running overhead, the walls lined with foam baffles. As the hovercraft settled on its skirts between the red-and-white barber's pole guides that marked the arrival platform—carefully surveyed and leveled to exactly the same height in both time lines—Hulius grabbed his carry-on and made his way to the gangway. "Manfred van Rijnt. I've got a flight to catch?"

"Certainly, sir. Please follow me." The Resident was a pleasant-faced woman, apparently a local. "There's a taxi waiting for you out front." Behind him the DPR agents were picking up their suitcases and chattering, much like any other group of tourists starting a vacation in the fleshpots of para-time.

The para-time terminal was separated from the front of the operation by a cinderblock wall and a succession of locked doors ending in the inevitable *Staff Only* sign. Up front, it was disguised as a (real) wholesale designer clothing outlet, selling seconds and rejects from big brands. Shoppers chattered and rummaged around the aisles as the Resident led Hulius out to the parking lot. A black SUV was waiting for him, baking beneath the brassy afternoon sun. She leaned close: "This man will take you to the airport. He's prepaid, but you should tip him five dollars."

"Thanks. Take these and return them to Control for destruction." He handed over the last of his background papers—just his travel itinerary, indistinguishable from that of any other business traveler—then climbed in.

"*Maiquetía? ¿Qué terminal?*"

"I'm flying Air France . . ."

"*Si, senor.*" The driver hit the throttle immediately and screeched out into traffic. Signaling was clearly considered giving information to the enemy.

An hour later they arrived at the airport terminal. Hulius relaxed infinitesimally as the driver pulled up, double-parking beside a line of similar black taxis. He passed over a crumpled five dollar bill from the wallet he'd been given, then went inside.

Check-in was routine, security cursory. Huw was traveling on a full-price business class return ticket that guaranteed polite and expeditious treatment. He had a checked bag and a carry-on, a tablet and a burner phone loaded with a promising selection of bootlegged movies and anodyne pornography. If anyone examined it they'd find a carefully curated selection of cloud e-mail and storage accounts with contents designed to lull suspicious border inspectors into complacency. There was nothing overtly felonious on it, but it was risqué enough to explain away any guilty vibes he might exhibit at a border checkpoint.

Over the years the DPR had carefully assessed the best way for a clandestine agent to travel without attracting the attention of the Five Eyes. It was a far cry from the days of James Bond antics. There were no false-bottomed suitcases with silenced guns and knives, no weapons or exotic espionage devices. The only giveaways on his person were the knotwork designs that he needed to focus on in order to world-walk between time lines. They were concealed in a sideloaded app, disguised as pornographic clock faces, and he had a plausible explanation if they came to light: he'd accidentally infected his smartwatch with malware by downloading a movie from the Internet with his phone.

If Brill's back-office people had done their job properly, the Manfred van Rijnt cover was watertight; and if they hadn't, well, he was committed now.

He had some hours to kill after check-in, but with business lounge access and a tablet the hours slid by like cheap liquor until it was time to board the airliner. The wide-body Airbus struck Hulius as wildly, extravagantly luxurious, from the seat that turned into a lie-flat bed once airborne to the in-flight Internet access. He felt a stab of envy as it taxied for takeoff, the engine noise barely rising above a subdued rumble. His last flight had been with Brill aboard a diplomatic courier from New London to Maracaibo. It wasn't any slower than the Airbus, but the wax earplugs hadn't quite blocked the dental-drill screech of the engines, and they'd had to land twice for refueling along the way. The New American Commonwealth was still learning to build passenger jets: the first DC-10-like wide-body wasn't quite ready for passenger service.

Hulius had grown up in the Gruinmarkt—in time line one, where horse-drawn wagons were the height of transport technology. The irony of his discontent with the Commonwealth's early jet airliners was not lost on him. Nothing underscored the technological superiority of time line two like the experience of long-haul air travel—or underlined the importance of MITI and the DPR's work.

Hulius kept his in-flight entertainment screen switched off (to avoid any subliminal in-flight trigger engrams inserted at the request of the US authorities). After a meal served on fine china that stunned his stomach into a food coma, he poked at the button that turned his seat into a bed. The jet rumbled on through the night, trailing frozen water vapor across the stratosphere, as it carried him north and east across the Atlantic. He dozed through the gravel-bumpy flight across the intertropical convergence zone, and as the crescent moon beyond the windows slowly rolled upside down above the equator his sleep was haunted by dreams of black princesses and red queens dueling in the Tuileries of Imperial St. Petersburg.

BERLIN, TIME LINE TWO, AUGUST 2020

Hulius entered Berlin in the back of an airport taxi, eyes closed and mouth ajar, drooling in the grip of jet lag. It was perhaps good for his peace of mind that he slept through the ride from Brandenburg, for his driver took an unholy joy in taking manual control. He pushed the needle insistently past two hundred kilometers per hour as he flung the Mercedes Kombi about the autobahn. He had to slow down soon enough, though, impeded by the growing congestion of the afternoon rush hour traffic.

By the time they arrived at the hotel, Hulius had been in transit for nearly twenty hours. He yawned as he peeled himself out of the taxi, paid the driver, and trudged inside. Five and a half hours of west to east time difference and two flights was enough to scramble anyone's brain: relocating himself safely to the other Berlin, in the heavily policed time line that was his ultimate destination, could wait a little longer.

He napped for an hour and a half on the hotel bed, fully dressed, then woke to his phone's alarm. Still groggy, he showered and changed into clean clothes. He was trying to get his tablet to talk to the hotel Internet when the phone on the desk rang. "Hello?" he asked.

The front desk spoke fluent English: "There is a Herr Reinhardt to see you in reception, Herr van Rijnt."

"Good. Can you send him up here, please?"

"Of course, sir. Have a good day."

A minute later there was a knock on the door. Hulius opened it. "Come in," he said.

"*Danke*, ah, Herr van Rijnt."

His visitor was skinny, with sallow skin and scarred cheeks that supported a pale brown beard that clung bashfully to the line of his jaw. "Mr. Muller, I presume?"

"No, I am Mr. Fox." His English diction was clipped, suggesting that he was a native German speaker.

Hulius stepped backward into the room and gestured at the door. The man who called himself Fox closed it carefully then followed. "Why is Mr. Muller not available?" Hulius asked.

"Because he, he—" Fox momentarily looked irritated and snapped his fingers: "I know, he was, uh, discommoded. That's the password, isn't it?"

"Practicing in front of a mirror generally helps," Hulius suggested. "Sit down. Would you care for a coffee?"

"No thanks." Fox poured himself into the room's single armchair, an expression of hangdog relief on his face. He'd probably been worried that Hulius would murder him if he didn't come up with the correct response to the challenge phrase, unaware that Hulius recognized him from the briefing dossier. Fox wasn't aware who he was working for. He had been led to believe that the DPR was a shady PacRim industrial espionage outfit, contracting for Indonesian and Malaysian multinationals as they played footsie with their Chinese and Thai opposite numbers for lucrative EU contracts. It was a good enough story to account for the sub-rosa posturing and skullduggery. The truth would have panicked him.

Hulius busied himself with the kettle and instant coffee that the hotel supplied. He felt thick-headed and dizzy, as if his head was packed with a fog bank. "What is the current state of arrangements?" he asked, taking the office chair for himself.

"Everything is on course." Fox shrugged. "The SR22T has been paid for and title transferred to the service company I set up for you. A ferry pilot has been commissioned to fly it to Enschede Airport Twente where it will be serviced and provisioned to your specifications. The flight plans you requested have been prepared, but will not be filed until you request them. And the residence you asked for will be available from tomorrow, if all goes to plan."

Hulius gave him a hard stare. "I was not notified of any delays," he said. "What's the holdup with the building?"

Fox shrugged again, nervously. "It took me a while to find premises in the right neighborhood that were for sale or lease, and then to confirm the site survey with your head office. Houses are not so common here in the inner city: most Berliners live in apartment blocks, and obviously there are relatively few ground-floor apartments with direct entry. I had to query HQ twice before we could agree on a suitable target. Then I had to make an offer, and undergo reference and credit checks. This all took time."

"Ah." Hulius relaxed slightly. "But it will be available tomorrow?"

"So I am told. It is an apartment, it is on the ground floor and has its own private street door—also a back door opening onto the common yard. I took it for a one-year lease, with furnishings. Your name is not on the paperwork. If you require it I can have my lawyer prepare a sublease agreement, but then I would have to notify the police of a change of resident and incur all sorts of complications."

"No, that won't be necessary." The kettle came to the boil: Hulius poured his coffee then unplugged it from the wall. "In any event I do not expect to be using it for more than two or three weeks."

"Is there anything else I can help you with?" Fox asked.

"Write your cell number on this pad." Hulius pointed at the desk. "I'll call you to arrange a face-to-face meeting if I need anything else. But nothing of any substance may be spoken of by phone or Internet.

I repeat, phone and Internet are to be used *only* for arranging in-person meetings. Tomorrow, when you receive the keys, you will inspect the house. Then come here and collect me. There is no need to call ahead, I will be expecting you from noon. That is all." Hulius yawned. *Five hours,* he told himself. *Just stay awake for five more hours and you can go to sleep on local time.* "You can go now."

"You won't need any assistance after, afterwards?"

"No," Hulius said tersely. Fox rose, looking uncertain. "I just flew in," he added, "if there's anything more I will tell you tomorrow."

"*Guten tag,*" said Fox. He slithered toward the doorway, gave Hulius a dubious glance, and was gone.

Why do we always end up hiring stringers who act like cheap drug dealers? he asked himself, then yawned again. *Stay awake, fool.* He drank the coffee, his eyeballs fixed to the TV, his mind a million miles away. *Better go for a walk, otherwise I'll be no use to anyone.*

He stood up groggily, and pulled his jacket on, then headed out to hit the streets of this strangely futuristic Berlin.

PANKOW, BERLIN, TIME LINE TWO, AUGUST 2020

Forty-eight hours after he arrived in Berlin, Hulius was ready to visit the Berlin of his adoptive time line: a Berlin of smoke-streaked tenements and sprawling palaces, a Berlin where Friedrichstraße had never been bisected by a wall, or pounded by western heavy bombers and Soviet artillery.

Fox had visited again the morning after his arrival, bearing keys and papers for a *neubau* apartment in Pankow. "Nobody here lives in American-style single-family houses—at least, not unless they're millionaires," Fox explained. "This is a large ground-floor apartment in a modern block. You're lucky I could get one at all, mostly the ground-floor units are occupied by shops or businesses." He presented Hulius with another bunch of keys.

Hulius nodded. Fox was not the DPR's sole asset, and according to his overnight update the lamplighters—advance agents sent in to prepare a safe house for occupation—had already done their business and withdrawn. In time line three, the apartment block was doppelgängered with a furrier's warehouse. The DPR's Berlin Resident had bought the business from its owner for a hefty payout: the employees would be fired on the morrow.

Hulius looked at the keys in his hand, feeling faintly guilty. They'd just stolen the income of several workers, mere weeks ahead of winter. Even though vastly more was at stake than a few starving families, he found it unpleasant to consider. Time line two's Germany had a fine welfare system, but the quiltwork of small states that paid tribute to the Bourbon throne had, at best, forced labor for the indigent. "I understand," he said quietly, unsure whether he addressed Fox or his own conscience.

The *neubau* apartment was modern, airy, and largely lit by artificial lights. Its windows were small and protected by motorized shutters. Fox had rented it on a short-term basis, ready furnished. It featured lots of austere white surfaces, with sensors that activated the indirect lighting and controlled the heating as he moved from room to room. The kitchen, all brushed-steel surfaces and gleaming appliances, was like something from a Commonwealth movie, a futuristic operating theater for daringly experimental culinary surgeons. Hulius hardened his heart against the sense of inadequacy that stole over him whenever he contemplated the technology gap between the Commonwealth and this world. He'd grown up in a stone-and-timber mansion with dirt floors in the servants' quarters, lacking indoor plumbing, never mind glass in most of the windows. Seventeen years in the New American Commonwealth had accustomed him to rapid change: *We'll catch up with these people eventually*, he reminded himself. *Probably before I retire.*

Hulius moved his suitcase into one of the two bedrooms. There was another case waiting for him there, a leather-and-wood steamer trunk with cheap brass buckles. He opened it and inspected the contents. It was like a step backward and sideways in time, a reverse knight's move between worlds. It held two suits, worn but well-mended and not too shabby, such as a working professional man might wear. There was a thick wool coat, a choice of hats, underwear, shirts, boots, and shoes—all in his size, procured locally in the time line he was about to travel to.

A carpetbag at one end of the trunk proved to contain a small attaché case with travel documents, identity papers, and one highly incriminating letter. It would condemn him to the headsman's block if he was taken in possession of it: he treated it with the wary respect due a loaded gun.

Finally, there was one last piece of luggage.

A flat black nylon strongbox nestled in the bottom of the trunk. It was full of anachronisms sourced from this time line. "James Bond shit" as his wife Elena disapprovingly called it. (Not that James Bond was a thing in the Commonwealth, but one of the perks of being a world-walker with connections to the former Clan was easy access to extratemporal media.) There was a set of cardboard cartridges preloaded with imperial coinage, including enough *écus d'or* to buy a house or bribe an official above his own pay grade. There was a handgun with a suppressor and laser sight built into the receiver; a compact set of night vision goggles; and a couple of preloaded self-injecting syringes. He took a deep breath, wishing he could call Elena and the girls, then dismissed the thought. The sooner this was over, the sooner he could see them again.

There was one other device, a peculiar hybrid. Hulius turned it over in his hands, marveling. One face of the milled black-enameled aluminum slab was half-covered in buttons and an e-ink display; the other face (including the power button and antenna jack) was covered by an adhesive label bearing blood-curdling warnings that it was not to be turned on in this time line. It had been assembled and programmed in the DPR's electronics laboratories using smuggled integrated circuits and test equipment. Although laughably crude by the standards of the United States of 2020, it was a generation ahead of any encrypted spread-spectrum radio the scientists of the French Imperium had ever imagined: late 1990s or even early 2000s equivalent tech. "In another decade we'll be building these ourselves," Brill had told him. "But for now we're dependent on components imported from time line two, which is why we're not spreading it around—it's the tech equivalent of heroin. We don't want to get our embryonic semiconductor industry hooked on this stuff when we should be gearing up to build our own."

The French were still trying to make transistors reliable enough to use in simple amplifier circuits. Current Commonwealth intelligence assessments suggested they were still relying on HF/DF to intercept spy transmissions. If Hulius needed to phone home, he could record a voice message on this machine's flash memory—or laboriously key in a telegram—and it would send it out within ninety minutes, as one of the Commonwealth's new military relay satellites flashed overhead. He chuckled grimly. After the evasion protocols he was used to needing on contact missions in the United States, avoiding the Imperial Intelligence Service's signals intelligence people was on a level with taking candy from a baby.

Enough vacillation. Hulius selected an outfit then undressed, showered, applied the temporary tattoo he found in the supplied toilet bag to the inside of his left wrist, and dressed again from the skin out: this time in the costume of a Prussian legal clerk. He double-checked his identity papers, procured by bribery from an issuing official. The photograph staring out at him named him as Herr Julius Gormer, an import/export factor from the Low Countries. "Gormer," he muttered. "*Gormer*." He could feel Herr Gormer settling across his shoulders like an ill-fitting coat. He picked up the shipping trunk—only three-quarters full, now he was wearing some of the contents—and trudged through into the living room with it. Then, on impulse, he checked the second bedroom.

There was a suitcase here, too, waiting beside the made-up bed. Flipping the latches, he opened it. It was full of women's clothing, still in the original store packaging: a trouser suit, a winter coat, a couple of tops and skirts. No underwear or shoes, he noted, but a prepacked toilet bag. He closed the suitcase again, then paused while his own personal flashback passed. *At least I knew what to expect*, he thought. Even the backwoods peers of the Clan had owned portable generators and videocassette players for after-dinner entertainment. They imported soap operas and movies and dramas from America in their personal allowances when they performed the corvée for the Clan postal service. He'd grown up in a rusticated quasi-medieval backwater, but at least he'd known there was another world out there. *Better minimize her exposure*, he resolved. *If she sees too much of this Germany she might have second thoughts about the Commonwealth.* Even if she didn't flip out completely, the culture shock was going to be huge.

Shaking his head, he went back into the living room. The small trunk was a problem: he hefted it, then put it down again and instead moved most of the contents to the carpetbag. Picking up both now-balanced bags, he took a step forward into a section of floor the lamplighter had marked out in red tape. Hulius squinted at the back of his left wrist, and the knotwork design of the tattoo seemed to shimmer and distort before his eyes.

Five minutes later, the apartment's environmental controller dimmed the lights and set back the temperature on the thermostatically controlled radiators. Ten minutes after that, the burglar alarm—having confirmed that the occupant had left the premises—armed itself. And then there was silence, for a considerable length of time.

BERLIN, TIME LINE THREE, AUGUST 2020

Her Royal Highness, Elizabeth, Princess of New England (in exile) and heir to the Throne of New Brunswick, flew in to Köpenick Aerodrome aboard her father's royal air yacht, a three-engined airliner of sturdy construction but not terribly recent vintage. For a Crown Princess she traveled with a remarkably small retinue—just two ladies-in-waiting, two bodyguards, and three servants—and so little luggage that the party required only two automobiles and a small truck to take them from the VIP pavilion at the side of the field. This was not an accident.

Her recent fiancé, Prince Louis, had offered her the use of his royal train, a *much* more sumptuous conveyance. He'd also pressed her with a vastly larger and more overbearing retinue, and an entire battalion of dragoons for security. But neither Elizabeth nor her father wanted to be beholden to the French prince: both had their own reasons. "It will attract the *wrong type* of attention," she insisted. "And besides, I wish to be able to travel at will and see my future domains without dragging a three-ring circus behind me!" Which was true, but not the entire truth.

For the time being her plans would have to wait. She had been sent to Berlin by her father to attend Mme. Corinne Houelebecq's finishing school for ladies of noble birth. Her father's motivation was to protect her from her fiancé's premature attentions (not to mention the miasma of scandalous whispers that followed him around like a plague of bad airs). She fervently approved of this aspect of her father's scheme. Perhaps her father also thought it best to distract her from her usual pastimes of hunting, skiing, and shooting in the northern forests. And perhaps he genuinely thought it necessary for her to polish the social graces of a royal consort. But her own motives were somewhat different. Although she was only eighteen, Elizabeth had her own agenda and plans— plans she did not expect her father or her fiancé to approve of—and the smaller her entourage, the easier her plans would be to execute.

She had set the wheels in motion months ago, back in the palace in St. Petersburg. Regardless of the ultimate outcome it would be a glorious adventure, with minimal—she believed—risk to her person. More to the point, this would be her only opportunity to experience anything approaching a normal life. A solid gold cage studded with diamonds and surmounted by an imperial crown was still a cage. Once she was tied by wedlock to the French imperial crown, she'd be manacled by one wrist to the royal nursery and by the other to the claustrophobic squabbles and intrigue of court life.

As the convoy pulled away from the VIP pavilion, Elizabeth sank back into the leather-padded womb of her car and reached up to tug the privacy curtain forward across the window. "What is it, my lady?" Susannah asked anxiously.

"Face-stealers," she said acidly, turning her head away from the magnesium-flash of the camera lights. "You'd think they'd never seen me before, wouldn't you?"

Susannah leaned sideways and tugged the curtain across the opposite side window. She was just in time, for a moment later there were more flashes. "These ones haven't," she said softly. "You have never set foot in the Holy Roman Empire before."

"Daddy would say I should stop the car, wave and smile for them: but I don't care." Elizabeth crossed her arms stubbornly. "I'm tired, I need a bath, and I know what the headlines will say. And what the cartoons will look like."

Susannah touched her knee delicately. "Anyone who catches the public imagination is fair game for petty cruelty . . ."

The finishing school was located in the former Schloss Britz, near Bezirk Neukölln, some distance from Berlin proper, but the school term had not yet started. Elizabeth had been offered rooms in the Old Wing of the Charlottenburg Palace, but had politely declined. Instead, she'd asked for a suite in one of the grand hotels on Unter den Linden, right in the middle of the excitement and electric lights of the city. It gave her another excuse for declining her fiancé's offer of a cortège fitting a princess. It also gave her the opportunity to slip in and out with only a single chaperone for company, dressed in a mode suitable for an upper-middle-class young lady. She wanted to discreetly sample the public life of the city without attracting a sparkling trail of face-stealing photo-journalists and vitriolic editorial writers keen to expose every public misstep of the "Quarter-Blood Princess" (as the gutter press had labeled her). Not that there were many young ladies in Berlin whose Brazilian mother's blood showed so clearly in their skin, but short of taking a tour of the Ottoman rump or the foot of Sicily, it seemed unlikely she could ever find herself in a part of the empire where she would not stand out.

It had been Princess Elizabeth's misfortune to be born with three burdens: exile, intelligence, and her mother's bloodline. Exile was self-explanatory: she'd been too young to remember the palaces of New York before the revolution that had forced her grandfather and parents to seek uncertain shelter with their long-term rivals, the Bourbon Empire. Her mother's blood was a problem of a different kind. Her father had mildly scandalized New British society twenty years ago by courting her mother, Helena, Princess of Brazil. She was a famous beauty, but like most of the nobility of her province she was descended from the freed African troops who had conquered the southern continent for the Crown in the eighteenth century. Helena had succumbed to neurasthenic depression in exile and had become a recluse, thereby leaving Elizabeth to grow up in isolation in an exiled court, surrounded by an empire where dark skin was a signifier of serfdom rather than southern aristocracy.

But by far the heaviest burden was to be intelligent and active while also being a girl. *If I'd been a boy none of this would be necessary*, she told herself grimly. Princes were expected to set their own goals and trim their sails accordingly, to be players in the dynastic games of monarchy. Princes had agency. But in the ossified political etiquette of the Old World, a princess was merely an incubator for the next crop of rulers. Princes did things; princesses were done to.

If that had been the worst of her fated problems, Elizabeth might have forced a glassy-eyed smile and gone through the motions of cooperating. Even the dynastic betrothal her father had arranged for her to the French emperor's son and heir—though he was nearly twice her age and possessed both a mistress and (it was rumored) the clap—even that, she might have suffered in silence.

But Elizabeth was a quietly voracious, not to say eclectic, reader. It had been a cause for despair and even a nervous breakdown or two among her tutors. Expecting a spoiled and overprivileged brat, they'd been confronted by a whirlpool of ravening intellectual hunger. And, having studied, she could draw her own conclusions. It was apparent to her, if not to her father—or to the other bickering grand dukes and princes of Europe— that the tide of history was turning. While her father had glanced dismissively at the headlines describing the rebel Commonwealth's new artificial moonlet, then snorted, or chosen to make a joke out of the scientific gewgaws coming out of the workshops of the West, Elizabeth had shivered apprehensively. She had begun to make discreet inquiries, paying attention to the more bizarre conspiracy theories coming out of New London, rumors of visitors from other worlds bearing alien technology. She had asked for subscriptions to some additional periodicals (which her tutors approved without demur, for dry academic journals hardly required censorship for the delicate sensibilities of a princess). And she was unsurprised when one day she found an unasked-for and most peculiar history book in her papers. A couple of weeks later, she found a letter hidden among the pages of one of her technical journals. It had been addressed to her, asking if she had read the book, and would like some more. (And it was unsigned, of course.)

She had replied in the affirmative, pulse pounding and palms moist, before replacing the magazine in the drawer of her desk. The following week, there was another letter, which set out a most interesting proposal. At which point she demanded some external evidence, for the suggestion was breathtaking in its audacity—and almost insultingly extreme, as if Herr Polk, her seventy-year-old violin teacher, had calmly asked her to elope with him.

The next letter was terse, and contained six angular parameters and a time, five days hence. She waited expectantly: and when the newssheets announced that the anarchists beyond the ocean had thrown another piece of scrap metal into the heavens, her disinterest was entirely feigned.

That was when she began to make serious plans. For Elizabeth of Hanover had *no* intention of being consigned to the scrap heap of history, like the Dauphin of France described in the book: a bizarre history of eighteenth-century France that ended in a terrifying revolution in 1789—a revolution that was absent from her own world's records.

BERLIN, TIME LINE THREE, AUGUST 2020

There was no engram that could take Hulius directly from the Berlin of time line two to time line three without passing through the chilly, forested wastelands of time line one. Hulius jaunted, sheltered quietly under a tall pine tree until his headache subsided, then jaunted again, careful to stay within the perimeter marked out by stakes in the forest floor.

The warehouse in time line three—Hulius's home time line, that of the Commonwealth and the globe-spanning French Empire—was dark, extremely dusty, and smelled overpoweringly of damp leather. Hulius lowered his bags to the floor then stood in silence for half a minute, trying to ignore the pounding in his skull as his eyes adapted to the gloom. Finally, hearing nothing and feeling marginally nauseous, he relaxed slightly.

The arrival point in the doppelgänger facility was situated in the middle of a sample room. Wooden cubbyholes vanished into the gloom beneath a high ceiling, each stuffed with a fur or a bundle of leather or a brown paper parcel. The lamplighter had drawn a chalk circle on the worn linoleum floor to outline the safe transfer area, within which Hulius could world-walk back to time line one without risking a painful intersection with a tree. *So far, so good.* He moved toward the entrance to the room, then listened for a moment before he pushed the door open.

Wan afternoon sunlight streamed through windows almost completely coated with grime, the soot of a million coal fires that turned sunsets into an apocalyptic symphony of color and choked the lungs. The back of the furrier's warehouse was filled from floor to creaking rafters with bales and bulging sacks. Up front, the cramped business office lay empty, inkwells dry and telephone stilled. Hulius satisfied himself that the premises were empty. Then he went back to collect the carpetbag, let himself out, and locked the office's front door behind him.

The most perilous action for any intelligence agent is a covert insertion into hostile foreign territory. Once in place and oriented, with somewhere to go to ground and local contacts and knowledge, it's possible to hide incriminating equipment and develop a cover story with local alibis. But the moment of arrival is the moment of maximum risk. Most spies are detected within twenty-four hours of insertion, and of those, the majority are caught within the first six hours.

Walking along a gray sidewalk in the afternoon light, Hulius reminded himself to keep his pace slow and his head down, to avoid rubbernecking like a visitor. Maintaining a scan was pointless; if he was already under surveillance his mission was over before it began. Prussia was by no means the most heavily policed province of the Empire. But in the increasingly fearful political climate of a superpower that was falling technologically behind a revolutionary upstart enemy with super-science on its side, it wasn't a good idea to stand out.

Trucks rumbled past, belching diesel fumes. Overhead cables sparked and sizzled against the pick-ups of the trolley buses. Private cars were relatively rare compared to the flock of buzzing sky-blue taxis. An occasional police sedan drove past, big-block engine gurgling, but for the most part the cops hereabouts walked the streets in pairs, or watched from small elevated guard towers at intersections. There were enough pedestrians that he didn't stand out among the foot traffic. Hausfrauen pushed perambulators or trudged under their loaded grocery baskets. Street hawkers and shoe-shine men called their services as self-important clerks hurried around them.

Hulius had memorized the directions left by the lamplighter. He followed them to an intersection of three boulevards a mile from the furrier's warehouse, where a gleam of steel embedded in the cobblestones betrayed a loop of tram tracks curving back toward the center of the city. He didn't have long to wait for a ride. Within minutes a multi-carriage streetcar whined into view around the curve of a residential street and squealed to a halt by the stop. He climbed aboard, and nodded to the guard in his wooden cubby hole. "A single to the Brandenberger exchange, please," he said haltingly.

"Twenty pfennigs." The guard spun his handwheel as Hulius slid the coins across and the tram whined back into life, swaying from side to side. He took the ticket and found a spot on one of the slatted wooden bench seats, studiously ignoring the other passengers. It wasn't hard: as with big city dwellers everywhere, nobody wanted to risk giving the crazy in the next seat a conversational opening.

It was mid-afternoon and the tram was far from full, so Hulius took the opportunity to gaze out the window at the passing scenery.

This Berlin felt curiously backward and dated to a visitor from the Commonwealth, let alone one who had experienced a few days in the Berlin of time line two. In time line two, Berlin was populated by cars that resembled half-melted blobs and often drove themselves, the pedestrians thronging the sidewalks all staring into glowing slab-like fatphones. The Commonwealth wasn't there yet, but signs of hypermodernity were springing up like the first shoots of spring rising from winter ground.

The Commonwealth was installing public computer terminals in former telephone booths; synthetic fabrics had pushed the fast-forward button on fashion trends, and satellites and jet airliners were the hot new things on postage stamps.

In contrast, the Berlin of the Bourbon Empire in time line three seemed to have heard of the modern and decided it wanted none of it. It wasn't that the suburban streets the tram rolled through looked poor or badly maintained. On the contrary: the road surface was sound, the trees and ornamental plants were well-tended, and the painted building frontages clean and free of cracks. But the clouds overhead were tainted with yellow, and streamers of coal-smoke rose from chimneys on every roofline. The few automobiles were oddly archaic, boxes on wheels that bespoke ignorance of aerodynamics and a lack of advancement in chemical processes. His fellow-passengers' clothes were well-made, and far more elaborately decorated than the cars, but their fashions wore the unseen fetters of manufacturing costs. Cleaning and mending was in evidence: working women wore aprons to protect their gowns, while some of the poorer-looking male passengers' outfits showed signs of repair, repeatedly patched at elbow and knee. Fishmongers and butchers displayed their wares on shade-covered unrefrigerated slabs in front of their shops. The streetlights, he noticed with a start, featured rungs for the lamplighters to climb. And drays still clopped along the streets, delivering wooden casks to the bars and reeking horse droppings to the gutters.

Turning another corner, the tram hummed along a street lined with larger shops. A department store window tried to entice Hulius with the prospect of renting the latest radio-gramophone. In the next window along, a preposterously primitive-looking television—black-and-white, its screen a pale green ovoid set in a tall wooden cabinet—occupied pride of place, where in the Commonwealth an equivalent store might offer an early home computer. *You are now entering the Empire: please set your watches back thirty years,* he reflected. But it was, he realized, dangerous to be complacent. Like all unreconstructed monarchies, the Empire was a totalitarian regime, equipped with all the police state tools of repression. It had successfully fought off the virus of revolutionary modernism when the New British Empire had succumbed two decades ago. But it was now confronted by a rival, the revenant Commonwealth which had risen from the ashes of empire, which was clearly pulling ahead. And the Commonwealth seemed bound to leave the French Empire in the dust over the next few years. With no peaceful mechanism for transfer of power when a government was failing, sooner or later there would be a crisis of confidence that would plunge the continent into a desperate cycle of perestroika at best, and civil war at worst.

Another stop, and now the buildings were growing larger and more grandiose. Unter den Linden was only a couple of miles down the track. Hulius stood up and pulled the bell rope, then moved toward the doorway. *Hotel reservation in the name of Gormer,* he reminded himself. He would check in, unpack, eat a late lunch . . . and then it would be time to see about saving this world from an accidental descent into nuclear war.

FORT BASTION, TIME LINE TWELVE, AUGUST 2020

The officers' mess at Fort Bastion had laid on a buffet lunch for the inquisitive legislators. Huw forced himself to mingle with the magistrates and their staffers and make friendly small talk, answering questions that ranged from so technical they verged on an operational security risk to so ill-informed they made him want to groan. Canapés, amuse-bouches, and sushi rolls formed heaps on bone china plates, neglected by their owners in favor of a deafening buzz of conversation. Huw tipped a wink to the headwaiter: his glass received only white grape juice and soda water.

Finally, the trays on the sideboard began to empty and the delegates surrendered their plates one by one. "General." It was Madame Sour-Face—Magistrate Rebeccah Smith, representative for the Riding of North Kansaw. "I'd like to thank you for your hospitality, but I can't help noticing we're running late."

Huw nodded. "Yes, my staff asked for a little extra time to prepare, but they should be ready by now. I take it you'd still like to see JUGGER-NAUT itself, so—" He signaled the headwaiter, then he cleared his throat.

"Excuse me, honorables, if I may have your attention please! We have a lot of ground to cover, so if you'd like to join me at the entrance it's time to start the next leg of our tour of the facility."

Transferring to a passenger bus, they slowly circumnavigated the airship hangars. Huw reeled off facts and figures about the *Fraternity* and its sister-ships. They were impressive but obsolescent, retired from service as long-duration antisubmarine patrol vessels a decade and a half ago, to eke out an afterlife as para-time scouting platforms. They had been extremely cheap to buy, but were becoming expensive to maintain. "They're not fast, but they can cruise for up to ten days without refueling, dropping sample retrieval cages and away teams as they go. On a ten-day mission one of these airships can survey two-thirds of a million square miles, establish four fenced-off landing outposts, drop twelve tons of supplies and twenty ground crew, and traverse up to six double-indirect time lines or twenty-four direct-access ones. Consequently we're opening up an average of one new time line per month."

Huw paused as the bus drew up next to the transit hovercraft. While they'd been touring the hangar, a gigantic freight carrier had come in: the logistics crew were readying it for departure to time line twelve. The driver eased the bus up one of the giant freight ramps and onto the deck of the hovercraft, before a row of stacked forty-foot shipping containers. "To save headaches, I've got us a ride on this freighter for the next sector. Lift-off is due in"—he checked his watch—"six minutes. You might want to fasten your seat belts: it can be a bit dizzying if you're not expecting it."

The gray-eyed representative (a Mr. Cortez, from the state of Patagonia) shook his head. "This is merely another hovercraft, is it not?"

"Yes, but it's a lot bigger. And size has a quality all of its own . . ." Huw gestured at the raised bridge of the craft, where he could see the pilots and the world-walker going through their preflight checklists. The cargo ramps were already rising, and a distant rumble bespoke the hovercraft's starter motor firing up, ready to turn over the huge bank of diesels that drove the lift fans. "We're sitting in this bus along with thirty-six containers, holding roughly one and a half thousand tons of cargo. It takes a lot of power to float that much on an insulating air cushion while the world-walker takes us across—"

The gathering engine roar forced Huw to stop talking. Moments later he reached for his ear defenders as the lift fans howled into life, blasting air into the skirts around the craft. The howl rose to a crescendo and the ground beyond the edge of the freight deck dropped away, as the cushion inflated and the hovercraft lifted them almost twenty feet straight up. Then, from one moment to the next, the sky and the ground outside changed. Huw's ears popped as clouds crowded in overhead, staining the land with the pinkish gray shadow of an incoming storm. In front of the giant freight hovercraft, an overhead crane squatted above a string of flatbed railcars. And to the left—

Huw gestured at the view as the lift fans whined down into silence and the hovercraft's skirts began to deflate. He removed his ear defenders as the magistrates and their assistants turned to gape at an open-sided building that dwarfed the airship hangars they had just toured. "That's the vertical assembly building where we're building JUGGERNAUT. You can't see the launchpad, because it's in time line twelve-B, another transit away—but it's co-located with the VAB." He pointed at a squat building adjacent to the VAB, surrounded by a high fence and watch towers: "That's the fuel package final assembly building. And that"—he pointed at a five-hundred-foot-high pistol cartridge, just visible through the open side of the assembly building—"that's the second JUGGERNAUT prototype itself, sitting on its launchpad, ready for orbit." In front of the bus, the cargo ramp was descending. "Now let's drive over to the VAB, and take a look at the future of para-time exploration—and space travel."

Bred in the Bones

After insertion, the second most dangerous moment for an illegal agent is a first meeting with a source.

Sources generally fall into three categories: people with access to secret information, people who are of interest to the local authorities, and people who are crazy. (These categories may overlap: some sources fall in two, or even all three.) With any of these, making direct contact may expose the illegal agent to the scrutiny of the state counter-espionage apparatus.

Princess Elizabeth was certainly a member of the first two categories, and quite possibly the third—insofar as the sanity of a royal princess holding secret talks with the revolutionary power who exiled her family might be open to question. And sanity notwithstanding, approaching her was a risky process.

In Hulius's opinion (shared by his controllers and superiors in the Department of Para-time Research, not to mention Brilliana's more shadowy operations group), the Crown Princess was about as safe to contact directly as a lump of green kryptonite sitting on top of a critical mass of plutonium in the middle of a fish tank full of rabid piranhas. The DPR focus group that had brainstormed the scenario had issued voluminous and dire warnings, almost as if they were treating it as an exercise in ass-covering. What if it was a false flag op, and the Major was being suckered into a situation where he could be arrested and portrayed as a Commonwealth assassin, sent to murder the Princess on Imperial soil? What if the Princess's request for a meeting was genuine, but she was in the throes of bipolar disorder or an acute psychotic breakdown? What if the Princess's request was genuine and she was sane, but she changed her mind halfway through? What if the Princess was not in fact requesting asylum, but some other member of her retinue was impersonating the Princess for their own purposes? What if the Princess was actually a shape-shifting alien lizard from the fourth planet orbiting Arcturus?

Brill had overruled all these objections, because the upside of the risk/benefit trade-off was an astonishing diplomatic coup that might never be repeated. And, Hulius agreed, it *would* be worth it—if everything worked like well-oiled clockwork. But the level of risk involved made his usual courier missions into the United States look like a walk in the park, and he intended to proceed with extreme caution.

Hulius snorted as he unpacked his bags in the modest room he was renting. It sat above a *bierhall* half a kilometer away from the Princess's far more palatial hotel suite on Unter den Linden. Speculation was pointless: to establish the true picture, someone would have to go and place a pea under the girl's mattress. Or, more prosaically, someone would have to set up a rendezvous and see if she showed up for it—and if the Kaiserlichen Geheimpolizei also showed up. As a world-walker, Hulius ought to be able to dodge the KGP. It would be hairy, but over in time line one this part of northern Europe had been depopulated by the climatological effects of the North American nuclear winter. If he was walking into a stakeout, he could slip through the net, albeit only by the cost of giving the KGP valuable information about world-walker capabilities. *So let's not do that*, he resolved.

That evening, he dined in the *bierkeller* on roast pig's knuckle with sauerkraut and Jerusalem artichokes, with a Berliner weisse to wash it down and a shot of schnapps to ease his stomach. Afterward he went for an evening stroll in a leafy park just off Prenzlauer Allee. The leaves were falling, orange and brown in the glare of the hissing gas lamps. In his jacket pocket, the black aluminum slab was slightly warm to the touch, like an intrusion from the future. He'd coded up a message before he ate. Now, as he walked, he felt a telltale vibration as a download arrived from the satellite overhead. He switched it off by touch then slowly made his way back to the hostelry, deep in thought. An experienced tail might have recognized this for the misdirection that it was: but nobody followed him home. In the absence of ubiquitous computing technology, even the most oppressive police state is always desperately short of the bodies it needs if it is to maintain total information awareness, and his arrival in Berlin had not set any trip wires humming.

In the morning, Hulius dressed and slipped out of his room. He broke his fast with *bretz* and coffee at a street café, then caught the tram back to the furrier's warehouse. There were no signs of visitation outside, and no watchers present when he went indoors. He remained out of sight until, in late afternoon, he emerged and locked the door behind him before taking a tram back toward the city center. And then . . .

BERLIN, TIME LINE THREE, AUGUST 2020

"I should like to go shopping today, Susannah," said the Princess. "*Incognito.*" She glanced slyly in the direction of Bertrand, the head of her bodyguard. Despite his usually imperturbable manner he didn't quite manage to suppress a momentary twitch.

"Your Majesty. Begging your pardon, but I can't see to your safety if you—"

"Lady Susannah will see to my safety. Won't you, Sue?" Elizabeth raised her coffee glass as she watched Bertrand for signs of rebellion. "As I said, I should like to go shopping incognito, as a *bourgeois*. I will take Susannah as a chaperone, and a guard or two, as long as they are discreet and keep an appropriate distance unless they are needed. I won't be wearing my jewels, or standing on protocol, so I am unlikely to attract trouble."

Bertrand shifted from foot to foot. "But Your Majesty, is this really necessary? I beg you to reconsider; there are rumors of Leveler cells and anarchist sympathizers in the city. Without a full escort you will be exposed to any number of petty insults, not to mention being at risk of assailants. There could be demonstrators or worse . . ."

Elizabeth was about to protest when Susannah caught her eye; she shook her head minutely. The Princess nodded, waiting. "Captain," said the lady-in-waiting: "When did Her Majesty last go outside?"

"I—ah." Bertrand nodded in turn. "The day before yesterday, ma'am?"

"And how natural is it for a young lady of any status to stay mewed up in an apartment for so long?"

"Indeed, ma'am." Bertrand looked thoughtful. "But a suitable escort—"

"Will impede Her Majesty's ability to relax, and will actively attract the sort of attention you would prefer to avoid, won't it?"

"Hmm." Bertrand looked at his charge again. "I see." He paused. "You support this plan?"

"I propose that Her Majesty and I will go shopping together. If a pair of gentlemen happen to be walking the same way, not in uniform and at a sufficient distance that they are not *obviously* accompanying us, that would be prudent. They can keep an eye open for pickpockets, if nothing else. And if there is the slightest rumor of trouble we will stay indoors, or return immediately. But I pray you will allow her at least the illusion of autonomy? To be under constant scrutiny is so very wearying."

Elizabeth nodded, not trusting her ability to plead her own case without becoming irritable. It was always better to have an advocate, if so frustrating at times . . .

"How do you propose to avoid attracting attention?" Bertrand asked cautiously. He had the demeanor of a snapping turtle: stubborn, defensive, and seemingly slow—but capable of sudden and decisive bursts of action.

"We will dress below our station," Elizabeth said primly. "People focus on clothes, not faces. I shall wear a headscarf—the weather is poor enough to make that unexceptional—and we shall leave via the staff exit at the rear. If anyone asks, we shall be a pair of governesses on an afternoon excursion. But I assure you, nobody *will* ask so long as we play the part honestly."

"I see." Bertrand was silent for a moment. "It sounds as if you have done this before."

"Yes," said the Princess, thinking, *If only you knew.*

"Not often," Susannah added diffidently.

"I wish you hadn't told me that." Bertrand looked pensive. "Tell me when you are ready to leave and I will send two men to follow you. Please be back by seven o'clock. Any later and your father will have my head."

"Thank you." Elizabeth smiled at him. There would be at least eight men, she was sure, but only two would be visible. "We'll be ready in an hour. I shall go and get changed now." She rose and swept out of the lounge, toward her dressing room.

"Stay." Bertrand fixed Susannah with a chilly look before she could follow her mistress. "Lady Susannah, I hold you personally responsible for Her Majesty's well-being. Do you understand?"

Susannah met his gaze evenly. "I have held that responsibility for longer than you have, Captain. I was with Her Majesty during the bomb attack on the palace three years ago. I was at the winter ball where those horrible anarchists assassinated the Grand Duke of Muscovy. I am very aware of the risks. I would also like to remind you that Her Majesty is a bored and *energetic* young woman, whose energy cannot always be relied upon to flow in risk-free directions. Be glad we're not in the country, I've seen her turn her guardian's hair gray with her riding escapades. Do you have any word of actual threats to her security, or is this caution merely an expression of your desire for a quiet life? Because if it is the latter, I assure you that your life will be a lot quieter if you permit her the occasional taste of adventure—the illusion of freedom, prudently restrained to ensure her safety—than if you lock her in a padded cell until she is driven to break out."

"But it's not ladylike!" Bertrand stopped, as if suddenly remembering who he was speaking to. "I apologize," he said stiffly. "I am sure you have more insight into the mind of a spirited young filly than I shall ever have. There are no current security alerts. But I have been given very specific instructions about not allowing her to be exposed to any risks."

"She won't be. What's going to happen, Captain, is that we shall walk around two or three department stores until she becomes foot-sore. I will urge her to buy a trinket or two along the way, to provide some intercourse with the common folk. Then I will steer her into a patisserie or a coffee shop for half an hour. After that, she will want to visit one last store, and then it will be time to come home and refresh herself then dress for dinner. If Her Majesty is feeling adventurous I will allow her to argue me into riding a tram with her for a couple of stops, then feeding swans in the park—but only in daylight, if the weather is good and there are no signs of trouble." He deflated slowly under her gaze. "All the time, two—or knowing you, four or six or eight—of your men will be following us. Armed, I'm sure, and able to summon help if they become worried."

"And this is necessary? Truly necessary?"

"It is, if you don't want her climbing down the drain pipes after midnight to go carousing in beer halls. At the dacha she used to hare off on skis and hunt reindeer: at least in Berlin you don't have to worry about her playing with guns." Susannah stood. "Now, if you'll excuse me, I should go and change, too. The public might think it odd if they see a young governess being followed around by a lady in a court gown."

BERLIN, TIME LINE THREE, AUGUST 2020

In early afternoon two women—a *jungfrau* of respectable breeding and an older woman, either her governess or chaperone—exited the perfumer on Holzmarktstraße where they had just spent ten minutes. They turned into a side street lined with secondhand bookshops, newsagents, and cozy-looking cafés. "My feet are positively *aching*, Suz," said the young lady. "Can we stop for coffee?" She held her companion's arm lightly, head turning continuously to take in the scene—she wore a black armband and her hat was swathed by a mourning veil that obscured her face.

"I suppose so."

Susannah sounded dubious, but the young lady was not to be dissuaded. "This looks like a decent establishment," she insisted, steering her chaperone toward a coffee house that boasted fresher paint than its neighbors, with window boxes full of ornamental flowers fronting the street. "Shall we try it?"

"If you want," Lady Susannah agreed. As she approached the door, a fellow in a long black overcoat strode up, nodded politely enough, then nipped indoors in front of her. "I *say*," said Elizabeth, feigning mild offense.

"Hist," said Susannah. "At least Bert's men are on the job." She stopped and waited on the threshold. A few seconds later the door opened again. It was the fellow in the black overcoat: he bowed apologetically, then stepped aside to admit the ladies. His colleague loitered on the far side of the street, watching the approaches and discreetly monitoring everyone entering and leaving the café.

The café was furnished in dark brown leather, offsetting the white-washed walls and blackened beams, that fashion so tiresomely dictated for such places. Gaslights fizzed quietly, the better to burn up the blue fumes from the pipes a couple of old veterans smoked in one corner. Susannah and Elizabeth were met by a young waitress, who led them to a corner booth. Susannah removed her hat and coat, giving them to the waitress; after a moment, Elizabeth did likewise, pretending not to notice the widening of the woman's eyes. When they were alone, Liz reached across the table to touch Susannah's hand. "Thank you. My feet are truly sore: my right heel is rubbing."

"You are wearing the new winter boots that were delivered this morning, aren't you?" Her lady-in-waiting glanced around the room. "I'm sure we can send them back to the cobbler for work if they're uncomfortable. But we have walked an awfully long way today, haven't we?"

"Yes. I'll be glad to get the weight off them for at least fifteen minutes." The waitress returned to take their order. She turned to Susannah, not meeting Elizabeth's eye or addressing her. The Princess watched her departing back, her face still.

"Is there a problem, my lady?" Susannah asked quietly.

The Princess's fingers tightened momentarily. "No more than there ever is. I'm never going to be accepted here: maybe I should give up hoping."

She didn't expand on what *here* meant. To her lady-in-waiting it was all too obvious. The social implications of skin color in the old world were very clear, from the slave plantations of the Congo to the caste systems of the Maharashtrian and Bengali dominions. Elizabeth had inherited her hue from her mother, a Brazilian queen—herself the descendant of one of the conquerors of South America, freed from slavery by one Hanoverian monarch and ennobled by another—but in northern Europe she would always be an oddity, whispered about, viewed (if she was lucky) as exotic, or (if less lucky) as a freak. The plantation-owning aristocrats of Virginia and Mississippi had rejected the Imperial Settlement of 1760; their founders were in many cases Stuart loyalist exiles, and the idea of paying taxes and bending the knee to a Yankee Hanoverian monarch had lit the fuse on one of the ugliest periods in North American history. The Slaveowners' Treasonous Rebellion lasted seven years, and ended with the death of nearly nine out of every ten white menfolk in the southern states, and six out of ten women and children besides. Slavery was abolished and government enforced by the law of cannon and gibbet. Mercy was not a commodity that a King with his back to the wall was inclined to dispense freely.

"They can't touch you, Liz. When you become—" Susannah faltered. "After the coronation, they won't dare. It becomes lèse-majesté! Treason, even!"

"And when was the last time you saw some scribbler broken on the wheel before the Menshikov Palace, for writing that the Dauphin picks his nose and eats it?" The Princess raised one chiseled eyebrow. "Prosecuting editors for sedition and slander won't stop the whispering. It only convinces the listeners that there is a fire beneath the cloud of smoke. Suppose you were offered a choice between reigning in Hell, or being a citizen, not even in Heaven, but just somewhere on Earth where you wouldn't be an object of contempt—what would *you* choose?"

"I don't know. I think one should prefer to reign in Heaven, but—" Susannah looked up. The waitress was approaching. "Ah! Our refreshments."

The girl curtsied, then placed cups, saucers, and a milk jug on the table. She filled the cup in front of Susannah from her *cafetière*, then placed the jug on the table and left without a word. Liz stared at her empty cup. After a moment, Susannah fluttered into motion and filled it for her. "My question was not rhetorical," Liz said quietly.

Her lady-in-waiting stared at her. "But where would you go?" she asked thinly. "Where will have you?"

"I should like to go home."

"What? To St. Peters—"

"No; to New London."

Susannah stared at her. "But you can't! Not without your father, and your husband's navy—"

"What if there was a way?"

Susannah shrunk back against the wall of the booth. "Liz dearest, you're frightening me."

Elizabeth glanced down at the thin swirl of cream lightening the top of her coffee. Then she looked up. "Can I rely on you not to betray me?"

"Of course I won't betray you! But. It's not possible. Is it?"

"There is no price on my head," Elizabeth's voice was steady. "There have been no assassination attempts that could be traced to the rebel government, Suz. *None.* They honored their end of the bargain my grandfather made." (The bargain being, essentially, that John Frederick would take his family into exile, and the revolutionaries would let them leave in peace. Nobody wanted a repeat of 1649 or 1688. Or, among the closed inner circle of the revolutionary leadership who had been briefed on other time lines, of 1789, 1917, or 1979.) "The times are changing. The Leveler revolution is nearing its majority. If it was going to collapse imminently, if it was weak, it would already have been swept aside by the tides of history. So . . . I gather that a gentleman has come to Berlin to place a proposal before me."

"Liz, you wouldn't!"

"She did." The speaker was male, of middling years—anywhere between thirty and fifty. He was tall and solidly built, but as nondescript in style and manners as the Princess in her disguise. He had made his approach without Susannah noticing, emerging discreetly from the door to the ladies' room. "May I join you?"

"Oh dear."

"Move along, Suz. Let him sit next to you."

"Oh dear."

The man perched on the end of the bench seat as Susannah slithered sideways, recoiling as if his touch might contaminate her with the virus of sedition. Elizabeth eyed him with interest. "May I ask your name?" she said.

"You may. I might not answer truthfully." He sounded faintly amused. "I take it the guards out front are yours?"

"Captain Bertrand wouldn't let me out of the hotel without them."

"Good." He nodded. "I approve." Lady Susannah's eyes widened. He glanced at her: "I'm not going to kill and eat you," he added. "You're at no greater risk from me than you are from Captain Bertrand's men. In fact, my superiors would be *extremely angry* if I allowed any misfortune to befall you. However, I must insist on you remaining at this table until it's time for me to leave—and I must leave first."

"If you won't tell me your name, what should I call you?" asked Elizabeth.

"Call me Major White: all the other ladies do. At your service, ma'am." He ducked his head at the Princess. *He tries to play the charming rogue,* Liz decided. *But they wouldn't send me an idiot. He's sharper than he looks.*

"I believe you have an offer for me."

The Major looked mildly perturbed, although his expression was nothing compared to Susannah's. "Yes, yes I do." He cleared his throat. "Very well. You understand that the Commonwealth abolished all titles of nobility in perpetuity, and disestablished the monarchy. Yes?"

The Princess nodded.

"An absolute precondition for the offer—an iron-bound one—is that you publicly renounce in perpetuity all claim to sovereignty over the Commonwealth, its citizens, and its territories, both on your own behalf and on behalf of any descendants you may have. You may continue to style yourself a princess, but you renounce all the rights and powers that go with the title. It will be an honorific, not a legal privilege. You will consent to this decree under oath, and it will be publicly broadcast worldwide."

Elizabeth nodded again. "And in return?" She tried to ignore Susannah, whose eyes had grown to the size of dinner plates, almost matching the O of her mouth.

"Let's see . . . we will make arrangements for your travel, of course. We will grant you a full pardon and amnesty for all claims against your person and estates arising from any cause prior to your return to the Commonwealth. There will be a one-time payment to you in exchange for your relinquishment of your rights, followed by an annuity accruing to you and your descendants for the next two hundred years, of ten million pounds initially, and then two million pounds a year respectively. The Commonwealth Guard will provide bodyguards for your personal protection for as long as you require them. And finally, we can arrange the most precious thing of all: citizenship."

"Citizenship with no restriction on my participation in the political life of the nation?" she asked.

The Major nodded. "As a citizen, should you want to stand for election to the assembly, there would be no obstacle save your age. If you wanted to join the Party and become a People's Commissioner, you could in principle do that. You might even rise to the office of the First Man—or First Lady." He seemed to find this idea amusing. "You could not expect to achieve success overnight, but you would not be prevented from trying."

Elizabeth turned and looked at her lady-in-waiting. Susannah seemed almost paralyzed, gaping in bewilderment—whether at the temerity of the offer, or the size of the purse attached (which was considerably larger than Elizabeth had expected, and she had been primed to expect a Princess's ransom). "So, Suz," she said lightly. "Back to my question: is it better to reign in Hell—or should I aspire to be a citizen in the early years of a better nation?"

FORT BASTION, TIME LINE TWELVE, AUGUST 2020

"Welcome to JUGGERNAUT."

Huw had shepherded his delegates into a briefing room in one of the site office prefabs where they wouldn't get underfoot or risk physical injury. The assembly and integration building was factory-like in terms of the hazards it held for the unwary. A row of middle-aged faces looked up at him from the front row of chairs, set in expressions ranging from bafflement to awe.

He couldn't blame them, really. They'd all grown to at least early-adulthood before the revolution, in an age of rapid change—electrification, steam cars, motion pictures, aircraft. Even the superannuated dirigibles operating out of Fort Bastion had been shiny and new relatively recently. But the revolution had been followed by the establishment of MITI and its systematic program of education, industrial espionage, and planned technological disruption. *We're playing the ultimate game of Civ,* Miriam had explained: attempting to duplicate the mystical, barely understood development surge that could take a country like Meiji-era Japan and bootstrap it from medievalism to the cutting edge of technology in a generation. In the United States, they'd gone from biplanes to ballistic missiles in fifty years. In New Britain, they'd gone from piston engines to space launchers in just fifteen—with a bit of help and, more importantly, the full fore-knowledge of *why* they might want to do that, and *how* to get there fastest.

"JUGGERNAUT is our alternative space program. You've all seen the film of the satellite launches, I take it? The rocketry program is, in no small measure, a cover for JUGGERNAUT."

Shocked, white faces all round. Finally Cortez raised his hand and uttered one word: "Why?"

"Because nobody was sure JUGGERNAUT would work." Huw shrugged. "Kerosene-LOX multi-stage rockets like the ones we use for satellites are well-understood. But JUGGERNAUT is based on an untested design. We're the first people to actually build one. A US scientist called Freeman Dyson came up with it's ancestor in the 1950s, but it went out of favor and they never built it. In principle it can lift gigantic payloads very efficiently, and send them anywhere in the solar system. We've resurrected it because we have a key enabler that they didn't have—the ability to build and launch it in an uninhabited time line. And we have a mission for it: to conduct orbital surveys of parallel Earths without risking exposure to surface-level hazards.

"Let me walk you through the history of what they called Project Orion . . ."

It was an old story. Project Orion had been a bomb-powered spaceship, sitting atop a gigantic armored plate with a small hole through which the crew would drop carefully designed nuclear charges. Shock absorbers on the pusher-plate absorbed the brutal impact of the explosions, transferring momentum to the multi-thousand-ton ship suspended above it. A couple of dozen atom bombs would blast the ship from ground level into low Earth orbit; with a full magazine of hundreds of rounds, it could cruise the solar system for years.

The flaw in the design was obvious: takeoff involved nuking the launchpad, distributing a fallout plume downwind that would render the site uninhabitable for years, and fry most electronics within a thousand kilometers. The Comprehensive Test-Ban Treaty killed Project Orion, and by the twenty-first century it was clearly impractical, even for deep space missions. The electromagnetic pulses created by the bombs would fry every satellite in orbit.

"I'm pleased to say that we've solved this problem," Huw continued. "We assemble each JUGGERNAUT unit on top of a large hover-platform, similar to the ones we use for freight transport—then we launch from an uninhabited time line. The crew will include world-walkers. Once in orbit, they'll be able to take the entire vehicle with them when they transition. A JUGGERNAUT vehicle with full crew should be able to survey an entire alternate Earth from polar orbit in twenty-four hours, and carries enough fuel and supplies to operate for six months. In six months—one exploration mission—we should be able to survey as many time lines as the entire exploration program has visited in the past ten years. Finally, JUGGERNAUT returns to orbit in this time line, and the crew and their film payload splash down using a larger version of the capsules that will be flying on one of our chemical rockets next year."

Cortez asked the inevitable question: "Why do we even *need* the rocket program if we've got JUGGERNAUT?"

"Glad you asked. There are several reasons. First, they were an insurance policy in case JUGGERNAUT doesn't work. Secondly, they're propaganda cover for our ICBM program—'rockets for peace.' They're also the real platform for our space program: JUGGERNAUT is merely a highly specialized spin-off. Chemical rockets are more flexible. A single JUGGERNAUT mission consumes a year's plutonium production from the entire Commonwealth, to put a few thousand tons into orbit in one push. It doesn't let us run multiple missions or respond to unforeseen situations, and we had to build up a big enough strategic plutonium reserve for our deterrent program before we started work on it."

"You said consumes, not *will* consume." Magistrate Smith had spotted it. "What exactly do you mean by that?"

Good. "We flew an unmanned prototype JUGGERNAUT stack eight months ago," Huw said blandly. "It was a proof of concept—much smaller than the real thing, with concrete ballast for payload. It had just enough fuel assemblies in its magazine to make orbit. But I'm pleased to say that it went off like clockwork."

He pointed at the projection booth, and gave a hand signal. Moments later the lights dimmed. "Perhaps you'd like to see the launch? We filmed it, after all."

BERLIN, TIME LINE THREE, AUGUST 2020

"Are you *insane*, my lady?"

"I don't think so, Suz. Why do you ask?"

"They, they only need to get you alone and cut your throat, or, or—"

"Don't be silly. If they wanted me dead the good Major would have assassinated me before we even noticed him, wouldn't he?"

"Maybe, but that's not the point!"

"Suz. Think! If they kill me, what happens?"

"They, I, I, I can't think! It's too horrible!"

"Then let me do the thinking for you. Firstly, by doing so they would hand a propaganda coup to my father, and to Louis—nobody would trust them to negotiate in good faith ever again. Diplomats are like Caesar's wife, they have to be seen to be above reproach. Secondly, if they killed me it would *force* Daddy to divorce my mother and remarry, to get an heir. Don't look so shocked! He's been thinking about it for years. The reason he hasn't done it already is that it would make it politically hard for his Most Catholic Majesty to support him. But the next in line after me is his first cousin's idiot son, and the one after that is a wastrel and a gambler. As long as I live he's going to procrastinate and hope I return to my senses."

"You could . . . could you do that? Flee to the Commonwealth, then reverse yourself and avow compulsion?"

"I'm going to pretend you didn't ask that question, Suz. Some questions are best not asked, let alone answered, even in private."

"But. You are *certain* they want you alive?"

"I'd say that was *pretty obvious,* wouldn't you? Not only that, they want me cooperating with their ministry of propaganda. A princess in a dungeon looks bad. But it's hard for outrage to rally to the flag of a princess lounging on a golden fleece in a palace."

"You'd be their puppet . . ."

"And I'm not my father's already? Destined to be Louis's puppet—and his brood-cow—if I don't choose otherwise? A gilded cage is still a cage, Suz. And besides, I palmed a card."

"I'm sure I didn't notice! My lady, were you anyone else I would call your proposed course of conduct treasonable . . ."

"Hush, Susannah. Let me ask you one last question. Who did you think I was negotiating *with?*"

"Why, it was obvious! You're plotting to defect to the Commonwealth, renounce your claim to the throne, and become their—"

"The Commonwealth. Yes?"

"Wait. Oh, my head. You mean the Major wasn't here to represent the jumped-up rebel leadership? There's some *other* faction? Their leadership are split?"

"You could say that, yes."

"Oh, I hate it when you feign ladylike coyness! It's so clearly false! You are a wicked, wicked princess, and a politician to boot! What are you scheming now?"

"As you would know if you had been paying attention to the intelligence packets that come my way so regularly, their First Man, Adam Burroughs, is dying. The Major, who you have now met, is the first emissary to reach me with an offer—as you surmise, it's from the Propaganda Ministry. He will not be the last. There will be an *auction*, Suz, with as many bidders as there are pretenders to Adam Burroughs's throne. Even if our Major is the only bidder, the terms on offer are quite generous. Better than moldering in a freezing palace near Finland, popping out babies for the glory of France while my revolting husband pleasures his pig of a mistress. Stuck in Berlin, or St. Petersburg, I can't *do* anything. But if I'm in New London with you by my side I can influence events. I'm plotting victory, Susannah. Don't blame me: it's bred in my line's bones . . ."

PART TWO

EMISSARY

It is true that liberty is precious; so precious that it must
be rationed.

—Vladimir Lenin

Covert Agendas

Rita's life seemed to be blurring into a barely interrupted series of interrogations held in dingy high-security offices. The costumes and titles changed, but the pedantic, tired, half-hostile questions were the same. Colonel Smith led her through a first round of questioning, breaking off for an hour when Gomez brought him the leather document pouch. Rita was allowed down to the hotel restaurant for a late lunch, eaten in silence under Gomez's suspicious gaze—apparently she was not allowed to speak to anyone until Smith was done with her—then she was escorted back up to the Colonel's office. Where Dr. Scranton was waiting for her.

Dr. Scranton, a middle-aged lady with graying hair and a brusque manner, could have passed for an aging corporate lawyer or a CPA. But she was the deputy assistant to the Secretary of State for Homeland Security (Homeland Security having been put on a par with the State Department in 2003, when it acquired responsibility for parallel time lines). Her down-to-earth, friendly manners were deceptive, concealing a mind like a steel trap. She smiled affably as Rita sloped through the doorway. "Ms. Douglas! How good to see you. Did you have a good lunch? Excellent. The Colonel and I have been discussing what you came back with, and we've got a few more questions for you."

Bend over, here it comes again, Rita thought tiredly. She felt drained, almost completely hollowed out. The past forty-eight hours had left her exhausted. "Sure. What would you like to know?"

Dr. Scranton smiled, in an infinitesimally misjudged gesture of encouragement that allowed slightly too many teeth to come into view. "I'd like you to tell me about the Commissioner, your birth mother. In your own time, please, I'm sure it must be very difficult, dealing with such a personal matter."

"Difficult?" Rita took a deep breath. "*Personal?* Please, can we cut the bullshit now?" She could feel the heat of burning bridges beneath her feet, but there was nothing to do but sprint for the finish line. "You didn't recruit me just because of the world-walking thing, did you? Where there's one there must be others. You recruited me because of *her.* You s-set me up—"

Scranton and the Colonel were both shaking their heads. "No, Rita," said Scranton.

"You've got to understand, we suspected she was out there," added the Colonel. "We hoped you'd flush her out if she was. But this meeting was a stroke of . . ."

"Luck," said the Doctor. She did not, Rita noticed, say it was *good* luck. "I told you a week ago that we would eventually open negotiations with BLACK RAIN. Well, now we know that's where the surviving Clan world-walkers went, and we know they're well bedded in. We weren't expecting your birth mother to be so high up the political ladder, but make no mistake, Rita, we intend to use all the leverage we can get. Which is why I want you to tell me all about meeting her. Including the personal commentary. I want to know how *you* feel about her. And how she responded to you."

"Oh." Rita frowned pensively. "Were you hoping if I met her we'd get on like a house on fire? Like some kind of Hollywood feel-good family reunion movie?" She caught the Colonel's sidelong flickering glance at Scranton before he nodded. "Oops." She raised a hand to cover her mouth. "It didn't happen like that: I, uh, cold-shouldered her when she tried to get all touchy-weepy." She paused. "I've got a lot of unexamined anger, here. Forewarned *would* have been forearmed, and if you had told me this was a possibility I might not have bitten her head off *quite* so hard, you know?"

"So I see." Scranton's tone was mild, but seemed to Rita to be drier than bleached bones whitening atop desert sands. "Did you get the impression that she wanted to meet you?"

"Oh, I don't know. I mean, having her jackbooted minions put me in a military helicopter and fly me to New York for a fifteen minute meeting might *just* have been a hint . . ."

"Enough sarcasm," Smith said sharply. "Rita, this is not a game."

"I didn't think it was." She drew a shuddering breath. "I just spent most of the past two days terrified out of my skull. Colonel, I didn't stand a *chance*. They were hunting for me with a dragnet, and they knew *exactly* how to deal with a world-walker because they run their own. The only reason I'm here talking to you now is because they wanted to send you a message. They're playing nice, for now: they could have sent you my *head*."

Smith opened his mouth, but Dr. Scranton gave him a quelling look: "Eric, chill. Rita, we're very sorry that we sent you into this situation unprepared. We didn't do it deliberately and we'll try not to do it again. But it's vitally important that you lend us your full cooperation. Right now, I've got to prepare a summary for tomorrow's daily presidential intelligence briefing, and you're the lead item. We've got to hammer out a cover story that explains your overdue arrival without mentioning your birth mother, because if we disclose that aspect prematurely it will cause a full-scale crisis. We've got to coach you so that you're ready to deliver this story to the circus of bureaucrats that is going to descend on us tomorrow. And you've got to do it without disclosing anything so sensitive it could blow back. I expect to have a tasking for your next mission tomorrow afternoon. I suspect SecState and SecHomeland are going to reach consensus to send you back to meet your birth mother, or her representatives, again, this time on an official basis. Are you going to be able to do that?"

Rita looked at the Colonel, then back at Dr. Scranton. She opened her mouth, then closed it. She swallowed then cleared her throat. "I will do what I have to," she said quietly. "I can, uh, I can even try and build bridges. If you think it's necessary." She could taste stomach acid at the back of her throat. "It was just a big, unwelcome surprise. I was scared out of my mind when they captured me, off-balance while they were interrogating me—all part of the process—then when they sprang the 'I am your father, Luke' stunt I completely lost my shit."

Scranton nodded. "How do you feel about your birth mother now you've met her?" she asked slowly.

"She's . . . a lot smaller than I expected." Rita paused. "Not physically, I mean: I think she's about my height."

"You can face up to her," said Smith. It was a question phrased as a statement.

"If I know what's coming up." Rita nodded, uncertain of her own resolve. A thought struck her. "Does she have any other children?" *Do I have any long-lost brothers and sisters?* It was an uncomfortable realization, that she might have a phantom family out there—"Miss Thorold said I was her only child."

"We hoovered up her medical records in 2003, when she came to our attention in the context of the FAMILY TRADE operation. She was thirty-four then." The Colonel glanced sidelong at Dr. Scranton. "Your call."

"She was pregnant," Scranton admitted. "Or rather, we have a record of a positive pregnancy test. It was filed about a week before she vanished for the last time. Right before 7/16."

"Oh." Rita fell silent for a few seconds, digesting. "So she aborted or miscarried or . . ."

"We don't know." The Colonel shrugged. "If you find out, it would be useful to us to know. For profiling."

"Yeah, I guess so." Her eyes narrowed. "What happens next?"

Dr. Scranton tapped the leather document folder in front of her. "As I said, after tomorrow's bureaucratic circus dies down we will probably send you back over in a day or two, with a message for Ms. Beckstein. Ah, Mrs. Burgeson, as she now calls herself. Anything you can find out about the presumed *Mr.* Burgeson would also be of interest . . . I am guessing here, you understand, that there will be a reply. As Clan world-walkers need hours or days to recover between jaunts, we would rather you didn't disclose your ability to jaunt rapidly. They might have noticed your multiple rapid arrivals in the railway terminus, or they might not. In any case they probably won't be surprised if you ask to stay there while they prepare their reply. And you can gather more nonspecific intelligence in a couple of days as your birth mother's houseguest than in months of sneaking—"

"Wait, what—" Rita began, but the Colonel beat her to it: "Are you *serious?*"

"I'm completely serious." Dr. Scranton turned her deceptively mild gaze on Rita. "This project will continue to pursue its objectives, which are to deploy HUMINT assets in BLACK RAIN, the New American Commonwealth, and—using this overt objective as internal cover within the DHS and other agencies—to develop a diplomatic back-channel with the Commonwealth government. So, that brings us to the matter of the cover story for general classified briefings. I propose that the best kind of lie is no lie at all: it's just a shortage of truth. Rita, your report—and everything you tell the visitors who are about to descend on us tomorrow—will reflect the reality that you were captured and questioned. It will merely omit certain salient facts: they didn't recognize you as a world-walker, and they didn't take you on a side trip then send you back. Instead, you escaped when they put you back in a ground-floor cell after a second day of questioning. Do you think you can back that up?"

"Yes, uh—" Rita swallowed. Her mouth was uncharacteristically dry. "I can say that. I tell them everything except that the adversaries knew what I was and kept me blocked. Uh. They kept my hands cuffed behind my back, so I couldn't use my key generator until they dumped me in solitary. Right?"

Smith nodded. For the first time, his expression relaxed toward its normal affability. "You got it, Rita. Less is more. Leave the stuff about Olga Thorold and Mrs. Burgeson and the document wallet out, and we can run with the arrest-and-escape story."

"Gomez saw the—"

"Gomez sees what I tell her she sees, and hears what I want her to hear." The twinkle in his eyes was the pale blue of liquid oxygen, chillier than ice despite the crow's-feet wrinkles framing them.

"So we have a story. I leave it to you two to flesh it out." Dr. Scranton stood, picking up the leather document wallet. "I'm going to deliver this to Baltimore in person, eyes-only. I'll be back in a day or two with a sealed reply. We'll discuss what happens next at that point but, Rita, you should expect to spend a few days in BLACK RAIN as a houseguest of the, uh, Ministry of Intertemporal Technological Intelligence." She gave a faint shudder of distaste. "They won't lean on you—not while they're trying to make nice—but they may try to evangelize you. Just be sure you know where you stand and you'll be fine."

BERLIN, TIME LINE THREE, AUGUST 2020

Hulius could world-walk relatively fast by Clan standards, but found it painful to do so—the headaches and blood pressure spikes were a major deterrent. Also, the geography in time line one in the vicinity of Berlin was a chilly pine forest. It made for a lousy rest stop between jaunts. Consequently, he left the rendezvous with the Princess by a more conventional route.

Like many buildings in Berlin, the café entrance opened onto the street, but there was a rear exit into a cobbled courtyard at the center of the block. It was shared by all the other premises and used for deliveries via a gated alleyway. Hulius had entered via the back door and made himself at home in the upstairs storeroom an hour before Elizabeth and her bodyguards arrived. Now, having concluded his business with the target and her chaperone, he took his leave and left via the front door—in full view of her escort.

It was a fraught moment. Thanks to the Princess making clear her desire not to be excessively supervised, the guards had merely glanced inside the café then staked out the front and back access routes, thinking it sufficient. If they'd had even an inkling that her destination was

planned, they would have hurried her back to her apartments while assigning a detachment to search the premises thoroughly. The apparent
spontaneity of her choice of refreshment stop had bamboozled them into
a false complacency. But the instant Hulius emerged, the fellow loiter-
ing by the doorstep brushed past him into the café to check on his charge.
And before he returned, the other nondescript gentleman (watching
from across the street) began to move, tailing Hulius along the street.

He strolled slowly and deliberately away from the café, hands clasped
behind his back, giving no outward sign that the skin on the back of his
neck was crawling. The sense of liminal danger set his heart racing. All
it would take was a stupid slip of the tongue by that sheep-eyed lady-in-
waiting. Or for the Princess, a better poker player by far than any overprivileged eighteen-year-old had a right to be, deciding to throw him to
the wolves in favor of a better offer from some other faction. To betray
unease, even a casual glance over his shoulder, would itself invite suspicion. *Pretend nothing is happening. Because nothing* is *happening.* At any
moment there might come a shout, a command to halt: more likely a
sudden hammering of pistol bullets ripping into his back without warning or quarter. Every breath might be his last, yet he must continue to
take steady, measured steps.

A shop window beside him held newfangled float glass plates sand-
wiched between enameled metal strips. Hulius slowed. He swallowed,
then glanced sideways at the display of cutlery and cookware. There were
rows of kitchen knives, forming a splendidly eye-catching display of stainless steel. He stopped, using them as an excuse to turn his face to the
window. He caught a hint of motion in his peripheral vision, then a
pause. *Retreat.* He turned his head, as if to look at the display of bread
tins. The man in the coat had turned back toward the café and was walking away, his tail abandoned.

Hulius did not relax. The moment of maximum danger was past, but
he was by no means safe yet. He turned back to his direction of travel
and began walking again, lengthening his stride. Thinking, *If I was her*
security officer I would have two teams, a close-in escort and a larger cor-
don farther out. Quite possibly the close-in escort had simply handed him

off to the perimeter team, returning to their primary task of protecting the Princess, while their colleagues tracked everyone she might have come into contact with.

The afternoon was cold and moist with the first chill winds of oncoming winter. The sky overhead was a wall of scudding gray vapor streaked with the yellow of coal smoke, but the humidity was clearing the smog from ground level, dissolving the sulfites, so visibility was inconveniently good. Hulius angled across the street, jaywalking between the back of a receding tram and the front of an oncoming horse-drawn dray. He took the opportunity to scan openly for both traffic threats and signs of followers. The shops and restaurants at this end of the street were more prosperous than at the other, meaning more of them had large, well-cleaned windows. *There. Yes, there.* He spotted the reflection of a man in a long duster-like coat and bicorne hat, following him about a hundred meters behind on the other side of the pavement. Hulius had seen him before, two blocks back. Now Mr. Bicorne was moving purposefully, swinging his head from side to side as he looked for a crossing place. Not a happy jaywalker, then.

Hulius turned into a narrow side street leading to a parallel main road, away from the river, heading in the direction of the park. The rain was beginning to fall, big icy drops spitting in his face. Shuttered windows stared blindly down as he hurried past. He hung an abrupt left at the corner with the parallel road, and turned back on his path.

Two long blocks away lay the park, with trees and footpaths and foliage to restrict lines of sight. Hulius accelerated to a fast walk. He body-swerved around a boy selling roasted nuts from a brazier, sidestepped two middle-aged women burdened by string bags full of kohlrabi, then crossed the road, narrowly missing a diesel-growling bus. Stealing a glance over his shoulder he saw a familiar silhouette bobbing along the other sidewalk. One block still separated him from the hedge-and-fence border of the park. Hulius grabbed his hat and broke into a run. Actual fear knifed into his gut: unhappy anxiety that he might have to ambush and kill a man who was merely doing his job as part of a personal protection detail. Hulius was no stranger to violence. He'd seen more violent death than any man ought to, before he even turned twenty. But committing murder in cold blood was something that he dreaded only slightly less than losing his own life. Such acts came easily only to monsters, and Hulius did not want to bear such a self-diagnosis.

Halfway to the corner he heard a shout, cut off sharply by a squeal of tires and a bang, followed by a discordant braying of horns. He winced but kept going. There was a hedgerow to his right, with a gap coming up ahead. He ducked through the opening, stopped running, and peeped over the hedge from beneath an overhanging tree.

The traffic a block behind him had gridlocked. Isolated horns still sounded, but people were bending over something in the road, a body on the ground in front of a delivery van. There was much shouting and waving of arms as witnesses urged the traffic to back up. He couldn't see whether the man was moving. He feared not.

Hulius took a shuddering breath and gathered his coat tighter across his shoulders as he forced himself to turn back to the footpath. *That,* he told himself grimly, *was altogether too close for comfort.* He hoped the man wasn't dead or badly injured. The automatic pistol holstered at the small of his back weighed on him like a guilty conscience. He hadn't made his pursuer run after him into traffic: nevertheless, *If I'd world-walked instead . . .* He made his way slowly away through the park, zigzagging along the footpaths under the chilly rain, periodically doubling back and changing direction to check for further tails. Only when he was absolutely certain nobody was following him—that the man in the bicorne hat had been his only pursuer—did he set course for his hotel, and the encrypted base station with which he would make his report:

OFFER ACCEPTED PROCEEDING WITH EXTRACTION.

PHILADELPHIA, TIME LINE TWO, AUGUST 2020

The debriefings—now with added misdirection—continued until dinner, then long into the night. Smith (with Gomez's help, to add an adversarial edge to proceedings) coached Rita until she was prepared to recite her lines in her sleep. She needed to be ready for the skeptical and disappointed audience who would descend on the Unit's field office the instant they learned of her return. Then Gomez and a couple of DHS cops escorted the yawning Rita up to a bedroom on the top floor of the hotel. "What is this?" she complained. "Can't I go home?"

"Not tonight." Gomez's gaze flickered to her colleagues and back. "Not until you've delivered your performance. Tomorrow, maybe."

Rita was too tired to fight back. Someone had procured a change of clothes so that she could peel out of the wardrobe department's best guess at Commonwealth women's wear (which she'd been living in for nearly three days now, and which needed washing). But getting out of costume was all she managed before the allure of the hotel bed overwhelmed her.

The next morning she showered and dressed in the clothes she'd found in the hotel room wardrobe, then trudged to the elevator under guard—before breakfast, even before coffee—to face her first grilling. There were three sessions that day. The worst part wasn't lying about the presence of world-walking murderers in the dangerously developed time line next door, but figuring out diplomatic responses to the most inane questions. "But, Ms. Douglas, surely there was *some* sign of the Church of Scientology being present?" Or, "Is the Book of Mormon known to them?" She was a good girl: she did not laugh in anybody's face, or exercise sarcasm or irony. The wardrobe department had supplied her with a dark suit and a cream blouse, an office lady uniform she wouldn't normally be seen dead in—but she got the message: *This is a role I'm acting, serious civil servant woman.* The closer she played it to the point of audience boredom, the sooner she'd be allowed to go home and collapse on Angie's shoulder. So she consciously modeled the delivery of her canned report on the FBI agents she'd trained with, answered questions solemnly and without embellishment, called her interlocutors "sir" and "ma'am," and did her best to convey the impression that she had all the personality of a piece of boardroom furniture.

She must have been doing something right, for after the third run-through Gomez and Patrick rang the curtain down on the last group of rubberneckers. "Good work," Patrick said approvingly after he shooed the last of the visitors out of the bug-swept hotel boardroom that the Unit had requisitioned for the dog and pony show.

"It was very impressive. You almost looked like a real DHS special agent," Gomez added, so drily that Rita couldn't be sure if she was joking (although a joke from Gomez—any joke at all—would be a first).

"The boss says you can take the rest of today off," Patrick continued as if she hadn't said anything. "And as tomorrow is Saturday, you get the weekend off as well. Be back here Monday at nine and, uh, have a nice time."

"Okay." Rita patted her jacket's fake pockets and frowned. "Any idea where my phone and purse got to? I left them with Gladys."

"Come with me." Patrick held the door open for her. Gomez looked as if she was about to say something, but pivoted on one heel and stalked off.

"What's eating her?" Rita asked, once she was out of sight. "She's had the knives out for me ever since . . ."

"Come on." Patrick led her toward a service staircase leading down toward the back of the hotel. "You're not a co-religionist of hers, and you've got something she'll never have. What more reason does she need?"

Rita hurried to keep up. "I suppose . . ."

"Jealousy sucks. Professional jealousy is no different from the personal kind. My advice would be to try and learn to ignore her. Unless she oversteps the line and does something unprofessional, in which case . . ." He shrugged.

"I didn't ask for this shit," Rita said tiredly.

"Nobody ever does. Come on, I think this is where wardrobe is currently holed up."

Ten minutes later Rita found herself sitting in the lobby of the hotel, holding a bag with last Monday morning's leggings and dress, too tired and apathetic to change out of the G-woman suit. Her phone was almost flat, but when Rita called, Angie answered immediately. "Rita! Where've you been hiding? We've been worried shitless—"

"I'm at the, uh, the hotel my employers use. Can you drop by and pick me up? They said I can go home for the weekend."

"Oh baby, you don't have to *ask*."

Half an hour later, Angie bounded in through the revolving lobby doors. "Rita!" She stopped just short of throwing an enthusiastic embrace around her.

Rita smiled weakly. "Hey."

"Hey yourself. You look like you've been interviewing for a new job. Want a ride home?"

"Love one."

"C'mon. I've got a surprise for you. Two surprises, actually, but one's waiting in the parking lot, the other's in the back of my truck."

"Okay." Once they were out of sight of the front desk Rita reached out and took Angie's hand. Angie squeezed back, surprisingly hard.

"I thought I'd lost you," Angie said quietly. "I was so scared."

"So was I." A thought struck Rita. "This outfit—my employers supplied it. I don't know if they stripped all the laundry tags out first."

"The—" Angie nodded, frowning in silent understanding. "Got it. I can put it in the wash when we get home if you want." They were approaching her pickup: "But first, your surprise is in the back."

The passenger door clicked open. Rita began to climb in, then froze. "Grandpa?"

"Rita . . ."

She threw herself into his arms joyfully. "You came!" She gave Angie an odd look: "You invited *him*? Woman, do you have any idea who this is?"

"Yeah, yeah, he's the mad scientist and you're his beautiful grand-daughter, I know." Angie rolled her eyes. "Let's get you home. Then we can talk."

NEW LONDON, TIME LINE THREE, AUGUST 2020

Rank conferred certain privileges under any regime, some small, and some large. Right now, Huw was taking advantage of a small favor, sitting in the jump seat of an airliner's cockpit. He watched, entranced, through the panoramic glazed nose of the jet, as it made its final approach into East Jersey Airport. It was a clear night, and a glittering carpet of lights sprawled out across Manhattan Island beyond the Hudson estuary. The windows of the capitol and the palaces and fortresses of New London burned megawatts of power to hold the darkness at bay.

It had been a wearisome flight—five hours in an extremely loud, barely subsonic courier jet—and it came on top of a long day spent shepherding a second tour group of legislators around the Maracaibo complex, trying to head off their more transparent attempts to dig up dirt. He'd gotten back to his office just in time to receive a FLASH priority message: do not pass go, do not collect £200, fly direct to the capitol and *see me immediately*, signed, the Commissioner. If the Commissioner had not been a distant relative and a long-standing personal friend, Huw might have been angry or apprehensive. Instead, he simply told his secretary to e-mail ahead for someone to organize a toilet kit and a change of clothes. Then he'd requisitioned a seat on the magistrates' flight home.

Rank conferred privileges beyond access to the best passenger seat on the flight. The jet touched down with a squeal of wingtip stabilizers and a roar of thrust reversers, then turned and taxied at high speed toward the VIP reception building rather than the civil aviation terminal. A row of limousines waited below the air steps to whisk the VIPs away. Their baggage, such as it was, would be unloaded later and delivered to their homes by courier.

As Huw set foot on the apron, a sergeant in the uniform of the Commonwealth Guard approached him and saluted. "This way, sir," he said, and led Huw to a limo of different design, parked behind the front row of vehicles. The car had a high roofline, a sliding side door, and windows tinted almost black. "She's waiting for you." Another guard was waiting by the door: he tugged on the latch, sliding it aside to allow Huw to climb in.

"Long time no see," he said, sliding into the rear-facing jump seat as the door slid shut behind him.

"You too. Was it a good flight?"

He fumbled with his seat belt, grimacing, as the driver turned over the engine and moved off. "Lousy, actually. I got the call right after finishing my dinner theater spiel. Grabbed the first available seat, but ended up in the middle of the audience who, as it happened, contained more than my fair share of critics. So I spent the last couple of hours hanging out in the cockpit." He got the belt fastened and took a deep breath. "How are you doing? How is *she*, Olga?"

"Oh, we've both been better." The dome light in the middle of the ceiling shed a sepulchral glow across Olga's face, throwing her eye sockets into shadow. She was in the wheelchair again, Huw noted. It was strapped down in the back of the limo in place of the usual bench seat. "In my case, it's the usual. But I thought I should warn you what to expect before you see Miriam."

"*Scheiss* . . . is it medical?"

"Personal. You're on the briefing list for the American probes." He nodded. "We're keeping a lid on this for as long as we can, but they sent a world-walker. We captured—"

"What?"

"—Let me finish."

"Sorry. Please continue."

"We captured the spy. Or rather, the railway cops did—but they knew what to do and we got her out of their custody one jump ahead of that rat bastard fixer of Adrian's. Whereupon we got a shock. They're inside our decision loop, Huw. The DHS sent us the Commissioner's own daughter."

"They sent *what*? But she doesn't *have* a—"

"*Wrong*. Turns out she does. Miriam got a daughter by a college boyfriend when she was twenty-three. Married the fellow later: it didn't last. Iris forced an adoption because she didn't want a bastard outer family brat muddying the waters of her dynastic strategy. And they both kept it top secret after they surfaced in Niejwein, for obvious reasons. But it looks like the DHS found her, along with the rest of that monster ven Hjalmar's breeding program. Worse, they worked out how to *turn them on*, making lots of little American world-walkers—maybe thousands—who, quite naturally, have no reason to love us."

"Oh Jesus. Fuck. Jesus. Pardon my lack of originality . . ."

"You can say that again." Olga grinned cadaverously. He hadn't seen her for a while: it was frightening how rapidly she had gone downhill over the past few months. "Some of Hjalmar's kids may be as old as twenty-one by now. Rita—Miriam's daughter—is twenty-six. You are *not* going to convince me that they picked *her* rather than some other random sacrificial chick by accident. No, this is a Message, capital *M*."

"Um." Huw clasped his hands together to keep from fidgeting. The limo swayed, taking the roundabout exit for the highway leading to the New London bridge. "Where is all this going?"

"Where do you think it's going? Miriam insisted on seeing the girl. They got along like a house on fire—lots of screaming, swearing, and jumping out of windows. We sent the kid home with a dance card: hopefully she'll be back. The point is, there's clearly a faction within the US government who want to jaw-jaw, not war-war, otherwise they wouldn't have sent her. But . . ." She trailed off.

Huw's gaze sharpened. "You didn't fly me up here to give me the low-down on the Burgeson household soap opera. What gives?"

Olga raised a bony hand to shove back her hair. "Miriam took it badly. Now she's questioning her own judgment, trying to second-guess herself. That's not so surprising: if I discovered I had a long-lost child after more than twenty years and the kid cut me dead on our first meeting, I'd be a bit out of sorts, too. The problem is that it's deliberate: the DHS clearly intend to use Rita as leverage. They'd be mad *not* to. They now know that most of the former Clan ended up here: *hopefully* we got across the idea that we've gone native in the Commonwealth, but things could get very tense. Especially as they just confirmed that Miriam is high up in the administration and there's a succession crisis coming up."

"I already used up this month's ration of 'oh Jesus,' didn't I? Well, *fuck*. What can I do to help?"

Olga tucked a stray wisp of hair behind one ear, then let her hand drop. "We're on our way to Ras and Miriam's place for dinner. Don't worry, they know you've been traveling and they don't normally do formal dining at home anyway. Miriam needs moral support and you've known her nearly as long as I have. She trusts your judgment. The kid . . . we expect to see her again within a couple of days, with a reply. Can you stay up here for a week, Huw? You can use the Ministry office suite for briefings and updates from Maracaibo. I took the liberty of asking Facilities to open up and staff your house: it should be ready for you to sleep in tomorrow, and you can use the time to catch up with what's going on in the 20/21 budget round—it's an easy cover—but we really need your help on this."

"You want me to take a week off-site from JUGGERNAUT just on the off chance Miriam's kid—what's she called, Rita?—shows up?" Huw didn't even try to conceal his incredulity. "Do you have any idea how disruptive that's going to be?"

Olga stared at him. "If it's disruptive to routine operations then it means you screwed up your management responsibilities, cuz."

"Ow." Huw looked away. "Well, maybe I deserved that. No, *routine* ops will carry on regardless. And I don't expect any exceptions that need me on-site to blow up at less than a week's notice. The kids will cope and I might even get some time with Brill, which would be a bonus. But are you sure this is necessary? Isn't it broadcasting a message for everyone with eyes to see? 'Hello, our Commissioner isn't feeling too good, her staff are calling for backup'? Won't that bring the vultures circling?"

"Not if we do it right." The limo began to slow. "But there's another reason I want you here. You did the first real research on world-walking that the Clan ever tried, and you've been pushing the R and D envelope ever since. There's something hinky about Rita, Huw. Don't tell Miriam— she's got too much on her plate already—but tomorrow morning, I want to show you some CCTV footage."

PHILADELPHIA, TIME LINE TWO, AUGUST 2020

Angie drove home manually, excusing herself from the conversation under pretext of paying attention to the evening traffic. Kurt engaged Rita in solemn, slightly stilted conversation, describing his trip to Boston to visit Greta's graveside. Rita apologized for not communicating, citing pressure of too many meetings at work. But all too soon they ran out of things that could safely be said. They shared an understanding that Rita's clothes and phone were probably riddled with snitchware, wireless bugs concealed among RFID tags bearing washing instructions for Internet-enabled laundry appliances. Nor was there any guarantee that Angie and Kurt's phones, or the cab of the truck for that matter, were clean. Rita reached across the backseat and clutched her grandfather's hand. For the time being, it was the only safe communication channel she had.

Back at Angie's flat, Rita grabbed a clean set of clothes from her suitcase and headed for the bathroom to shower and change. She wore last week's outfit, and a hoodie for the weather, which was turning cold. When she emerged she found Angie and Kurt chatting idly about automobiles over the breakfast bar. Angie stood up: "How about we go eat? I've got a surprise for you downstairs, and we can drop your grandfather off at his motel on the way back."

"Motel?" Rita looked at him. "You're staying in a motel in Philly?"

He pushed his empty coffee mug away. "Yes. Angela called me when you failed to come home on Tuesday. I was in Boston. It was no problem, really."

"Really?"

"Let's continue this downstairs? I'm starving," Angie declared. She picked up a battered-looking messenger bag and hefted it, giving Rita a significant look.

Rita stared, then shrugged. "Yes, let's."

Down in the darkness of the parking lot round the back of the condo, Kurt pressed something into the palm of her hand. "Your car."

"Grandpa!"

He smiled in the darkness. "We rescued it from the pound and brought it here. I must say your friend is very good at the mechanical side of things, and it had not in any case been neglected. Would you like to drive?"

"I'm—" Rita swallowed. Drained from the day's debriefs she'd walked right past her own car, but now she could see it plainly, two bays along from Angie's pickup. "I'm tired. And it's manual-only. Best not to."

"I'll drive," Angie suggested. "I know a diner about half a mile away. Give me the keys?"

Huh? Rita handed her the Acura's key fob. "Be my guest." *Why does she want to drive* my *car . . . ?* "It probably needs a good run, right?"

"Something like that."

Sitting in the passenger seat of her sedan while Angie drove felt strangely unsettling. Rita had loved her car, right up until she'd been Tased and shoved in the trunk in a parking garage in Boston. Gomez and the Colonel insisted the kidnappers worked for the Clan, but Miss Thorold flatly denied it. It was a big-ass luxury sedan, completely out of her class except that it was more than a decade old and cheap because the electronics were hopelessly obsolete. Dad had run it for its first six years, then sold it to her for a single dollar. Now the thought that faceless men who'd meant her ill had sat in this very seat made her skin crawl.

"Pass me your phone, Rita?" Kurt interrupted her train of thought. "I want to check your contact details."

"Sure." She pulled it from her purse and passed it back to him, then did a double take as she saw him open Angie's messenger bag and pop it inside. The bag had been lined with some sort of metallic, crinkly fabric and lots of pockets, some of which rustled and babbled quiet gibberish to each other in familiar tones. They were full of cheap Furby knockoffs: electronic toys that spoke a garbled phoneme salad designed to mimic the cadences of indistinct conversation. Procedural voice generation by a chip that could respond to local environmental stimuli was a cheap way of entertaining toddlers. It was also a surprisingly effective way of fooling ordinary acoustic bugs, the kind that simply fed everything they picked up to cloud servers for speech-to-text transcription. And every phone was, by definition, a wireless bugging device. It wouldn't help if you were already under so much suspicion that the listeners had assigned an actual pair of human ears to you, but human ears were expensive, scarce resources. So as long as you didn't do something to attract the direct attention of the Five Eyes, conversation simulators were a useful defensive tactic—although it helped to have a fallback story in case they came checking.

"There are many interesting things about older automobiles," Kurt remarked, "which I shall tell you over dinner."

"Thanks," she murmured. Angie was focused on driving, but Rita caught her eye flicker her way in the mirror. Clearly Kurt bagging her phone did not come as a surprise to Angie. And Rita's car was old enough to lack any kind of built-in Internet connectivity, whether for engine firmware updates or autopilot—instead of satnav she had a cup holder stand for her fatphone. "Where are we going?"

"Surprise." Angie grinned. "My phone's in my bag." In the center console storage. "Can you check it for messages?"

"Sure." Rita rummaged around, found the phone, and wordlessly passed it to Kurt, who stowed it in the chatty messenger bag to join the party. Rita watched in the vanity mirror as her grandfather finally added his own phone to the conversation—its murmuring reminded her eerily of *The Sims*—then sealed the pocketed compartment using some kind of silvery tape. "*Now* where are we going?"

"There's a mall I know with a food court. How does Chinese work for you? I'd sell my soul to the devil for a General Tso's Chicken."

A couple of minutes later Angie parked up against the back of a featureless mall. Rita climbed out and stretched. "Give me that," Angie told Kurt, taking the messenger bag: she slung it over her shoulder then locked the car and handed the keys to Rita. "Now we go somewhere entirely different," she murmured, and set off across the empty parking lot in the direction of the next unit.

"Are we clear yet?" Rita asked, hunching against the increasingly chilly breeze.

"I would say so, yes," said Kurt. "Unless you are carrying a spare phone, or some other devices?"

"They might know where I am anyway." Rita rubbed the inside of her left arm, where the pattern-generating implant ached from time to time. "I have an implant."

"If it's inside your body and there's no external antenna it'd take a lot of power to punch out a signal." Angie took her hand, gave her a worried look: "What does it do again, exactly?"

"I've got this tattoo. Let me demonstrate." Rita stopped and rolled up the left sleeve of her hoodie. "It's got pressure points here"—she wrapped her right hand around her forearm, like a woodwind player fingering their keys—"when I squeeze them I'm entering numbers, like on a keypad. It uses the numbers to generate a geometric knotwork design which it displays using the e-ink tattoo on the back of my wrist, like this." She demonstrated, calling up the trigger engram for the ice age–beset time line in which Camp Singularity's dome and archaeological facilities were located, knowing that she couldn't inadvertently jaunt there. "To world-walk I focus on the knot. I'm not going to do that now." With a double-pinch of thumb and forefinger she dismissed the image, and the black knot tattooed on the back of her wrist faded into invisibility. "Oh, and the e-ink capsules are UV-fluorescent, in case I need to jaunt at night. I just need an ultraviolet headlight."

"Hmm." Kurt looked thoughtful; Angie's eyes were wide. "E-ink, as in e-book readers? That is a very low-power technology, is it not?"

"Yeah. They said it's powered by some kind of fuel cell that scavenges my blood sugar."

"Come on." Angie took her by the right hand. "Let's go eat." She glanced at Rita sidelong, her expression unreadable.

"Where, exactly?"

"Up here, through this gap in the fence . . . over there." Angie led them across into the next car park over, then up to the side entrance of another windowless building. "And we're not eating Chinese. I just wanted to ensure that if they're *actively* watching us they'll go to the wrong place first. They'll catch up with us eventually via video and cell-dar, but it'll take them a while to work out where we've gone, and if we pick a food court with lots of background noise and talk while we're chewing to fuzz the lip-reading software, while the phones chat among themselves in Sim Jail . . ."

"You think they're tracking and bugging us continuously." Rita shivered, and not from the cold.

"They set you to work exploring a time line, world-walking?" Kurt snorted. "I know what I'd do if I was your boss. I'm surprised they let you out at all, even though you came home."

"You're her grandfather."

"And you're my FB partner." Rita smiled and gave Angie's hand a squeeze. "Didn't you have a top secret clearance, anyway? When you were in the Army?"

"Yes, but it expired—"

"But they had you on file. So letting me go home with you guys wasn't a big no-no. It's not like I'm hanging out with illegals from a hostile power or something, is it?"

Angie rolled her eyes, but Kurt tensed up. "Don't joke about it."

"Joking is the only thing keeping me from losing my shit right now!" Rita shivered. "Can we go inside? I'm going to catch my death if we stay out here much longer."

An hour before closing, the mall was almost deserted. Angie led them through a Macy's, then into a central atrium that smelled of floor polish and sweat, decorated with winter-wilted potted trees that needed natural light to thrive. The food court was still open for business, albeit quiet. Kurt staked out a table in the middle, while Angie and Rita fetched the food: a burger for Angie, pizza for Rita and Kurt. "I think we're alone now," Angie said quietly. A solitary restaurant worker was clearing up in the wake of the after-work rush, and Rita had to watch Angie's lips to hear her over the noise of a floor cleaning machine. "What the fuck happened?"

"They sent me back to the same time line. The one they call BLACK RAIN. It went completely off the rails and I was captured." Rita took a bite of pizza, chewed methodically and swallowed, all the while relishing Kurt's concern and Angie's wide-eyed attention. *Look at me, it's my best performance ever! Well, not so much with the* best. "It started Monday morning." She launched into an account of her trip, but stopped short of describing her meeting with her birth mother. "Grandpa, before I go on I need you to tell me everything you know about my birth mother's mom. Because she, uh, died a few years ago, but I met her daughter." *Deep breath.* "Was Iris Beckstein part of the Orchestra? Or just a fellow traveler?"

"Neither: I was certain from the start that she was a ringer." Kurt's cheek twitched. "*Morris* Beckstein was another matter. A lovely man. Hopelessly naive, but idealistic: a useful idiot. He would not have stood a chance back home in Dresden. Iris met him when she was young and alone with the baby—she turned up one day, with a stab wound and a dead companion: we know why, now—and he fell for her. She, she loved him in her own way, I think. But she was a skilled manipulator. I am not sure any of us ever saw her true face. If she was a man I would have said she was FBI, a COINTELPRO provocateur, but the FBI did not employ young women in those days, especially young women with babies. At least, this is my recollection of how Iris met Morris. I myself was not inserted until a few years later."

"So she was manipulative?" Angie asked, giving Rita a speculative glance.

"Oh yes. Iris had no papers, you see? She got Morris to pull some strings, ask friends of friends—people with drug connections. The baby, this Miriam, they made to look like an adoption for some reason or other, perhaps a secondary cover in case the people who had tried to kill Iris came looking. Iris and Morris never had another child—he told me once that he had mumps as a boy. Most convenient for her, but very disorienting for the child. To grow up being told you were adopted, to be made to give up your own child, then to learn that—"

Kurt stopped. He was talking to an empty seat. Rita was walking, stiff-backed, in the direction of the restrooms.

"Please tell me that's a bad joke?" Angie glared at Kurt.

He looked at her sadly. "No joke. Iris raised Rita's birth mother telling her she was adopted because Iris had problems she wanted to spare her daughter. But I made Franz and Emily promise never to lie to Rita about that, you know? I told them to bring her up as their adopted daughter and never to lie because that kind of lie always ends in betrayal."

"Kurt. I like you, you're a mensch, but sometimes you're really slow on the uptake. Probably because you're a man." She stood up. "Wait right here. Don't go away: I may be some time . . ."

NEW LONDON, TIME LINE THREE, AUGUST 2020

A dinner at home with old friends should not have felt like an ordeal, but the strain was having a visible impact on all present. Huw, already tired, felt as if he was navigating a minefield blindfolded whenever he opened his mouth. Erasmus, clearly worried, was twitching and alternating between jovial bonhomie and extreme solicitude. Miriam, as Olga had intimated, was withdrawn and pensive. It wasn't like her. She didn't raise the subject of the DHS world-walker program and Huw didn't dare dig. Rather than behaving like a woman who'd just rediscovered her long-lost child, she seemed distant and shocky, as if she had received a terminal diagnosis. Huw tried to imagine what she was going through, but found himself at a loss. Maybe if Brill suddenly served him with divorce papers, taking Nel and Roland . . .

The opportunity to discuss it passed with the meal. "I have to go now," Olga announced, in a matter-of-fact way that suggested she was too exhausted for elaborate rituals of withdrawal. "I'll send a car for you tomorrow," she told Huw. "Please take care of him," she added for the benefit of the Burgesons, as her current bodyguard pulled her wheelchair back from the table.

"Good night." Miriam waved tentatively. Then she, too, stood. "I'm retiring early," she announced, and followed Olga out of the room.

"But it's only—" Erasmus gave up. He caught Huw's eye. "Olga told you the news, I suppose." Huw nodded. "The personal was always political, in the land your people come from, wasn't it?"

"I suppose discovering your long-lost only child is on the other side in a potential war must be very hard." Huw deliberately kept his tone neutral. "Will she be able to do her job?"

Erasmus frowned. "Do you really need to ask that question?"

Huw raised his half-empty wineglass. "Normally I wouldn't. But she's been under a lot of stress lately, there is the succession issue to consider, and now this. It's obvious the adversary had some inkling she might be here, and they picked their tool *extremely* well."

"Indeed." Erasmus picked up the wine bottle and aimed it across the table like a pistol. Huw extended his glass, to intercept it halfway. "I think it's going to get worse before it gets better. Olga wants to see you tomorrow. Listen to her, not me; I'm an outsider to your people's ways." He topped up his own glass. "I wish I didn't feel so helpless around her."

Jenny, the housekeeper, saw Huw to a guest room on the third floor of the row house—a former grace-and-favor residence for the King's household attendants, on a gated crescent inside the palace security cordon.

Huw fell asleep almost as soon as his head hit the pillow, awakening only as the cloud-diffused dawn light strengthened across the wall above the bed. While he slept, someone laid out a fresh suit of clothes and removed his travel outfit for cleaning: a sealed toilet bag waited in the bathroom next door.

An hour later a ministerial car delivered him to the front steps of the MITI headquarters building. The front desk had a badge and an escort waiting for him. Ten minutes later he was ushered into a blandly anonymous corner office on the fourth floor.

"Cuz." (It was an acknowledgment of shared origins rather than a close blood relationship.) Olga gestured vaguely at the more comfortable-looking of the visitors' seats: "Make yourself at home. Did you get anything out of her after I left?"

"No." Huw planted himself opposite her. She looked somewhat better this morning. Which was not saying much: the evening before, her illness had left her looking half-dead. "Miriam went to bed immediately after you left. Ras didn't open up much: he's clearly very concerned. If I didn't know better I'd say she was suffering from work-related burnout."

"There's an element of that, yes. But now I want to show you the cause of our family crisis. The long-lost prodigal daughter comes with some worrying complications that I don't think Miriam has noticed yet, and I want a second opinion before I bring them to her attention."

"Complications?" Huw leaned forward.

"Move your chair round here so you can see the screen without straining your neck."

"Hey, that's an imported monitor!"

"Top marks for observation. We get to play with *all* the best toys in my department. As long as the air gap is measured in parallel universes it can't snitch on us to the NSA."

Huw shuffled his chair round to see the screen. The exploration arm he worked in—or ran, if he abandoned false modesty—didn't have clearance to use imported equipment. They were required to eat their own dog food, using only domestically-produced electronics to avoid becoming critically dependent on a stream of imported super-science gadgets which could dry up at any moment. Yet here Olga had a monitor a quarter of an inch thick on her desk, displaying millions of pixels in glorious color, rather than one of the clunky vacuum tube displays Huw had to use.

"We don't have the CCD fab lines to roll out cheap closed-circuit cameras everywhere—not yet, not for another three or four years—and we don't have the videotape manufacturing volume to record everything our existing cameras can see. But rail and air terminals are a special case when it comes to monitoring. When we learned we could expect a visitor from the DHS to show up I ordered saturation coverage and 24/7 recording in the Irongate South switchyard that serves the Quakertown Tank Factory, and in Irongate Station itself." Irongate was the industrial city that had grown up near the location of the United States' Bethlehem Works. "Here's a reel my staff put together. First, here's a streetcar platform at the west end of Irongate Station, about ten minutes before dawn last Monday. Watch this. The action starts twenty seconds or so in."

She blew the grainy, monochrome image up to fill the screen, until the raster lines expanded like horizontal prison bars. Huw, squinting, managed to make out the shape of the platform and the track bed beside it. For long seconds nothing happened. Then, from one frame to the next, a woman appeared between the tracks. She stood still for a couple of seconds, then stepped toward the brick wall separating the tracks from the street beyond. Something moved near the edge of the frame, expanding rapidly to become visible as the front of a tram: the figure vanished abruptly.

"Time from world-walk one to world-walk two was less than twenty seconds, Huw. Now let's cut to the camera that was monitoring the south wall of the station from the outside, at the same time."

The reel switched to displaying a view of a block-long brick wall. Seconds passed: then a figure appeared, halfway along it. They walked rapidly away.

"The camera feeds were synchronized. Elapsed time from world-walk two to world-walk three: about ten seconds."

Huw swore. "How is she *doing* that?" A Clan world-walker who crossed between worlds so rapidly would be curled up on the sidewalk, vomiting— if they were lucky. Even with the drug cocktails the DPR's tame medics had developed over the past decade, the migraine-like side effects from jumps minutes apart were crippling. The blood pressure spike could well be fatal.

"Next clip." Olga tapped her trackpad. "This is the interview room at the police station." This time the CCTV footage was in color, and of higher quality. A door opened: two cops frog-marched a smaller figure in. There was a bag over her head, and her arms were cuffed behind her back. "So far so good: they've been trained in the care and handling of world-walkers. Now they're going to sit her down and unhood her, and their inspector is going to tell them to uncuff her. She's not going to try world-walking, she knows she's on the eighth floor. Watch her arms."

They placed a wooden chair behind the prisoner, and made her sit. The hood came off. One of them stepped behind her. A few seconds later she shrugged, brought her arms out from behind her back and began to massage her wrists. The camera operator—*They must have a one-way window*, Huw realized—zoomed in.

"No wristwatch. No tattoo either," Huw murmured.

"Right. Jack and I tag-teamed her. Inspector Morgan had already gone through all her personal effects. She had a couple of gadgets with displays—an inertial mapper and a fancy light-field camera—but no lockets, no wristwatch, no hidden knotwork designs. Nothing stitched into the lining of her clothes."

Huw swore again. "Does this get any better?"

"Uh-huh." Olga gave him the ghost of a smile. "Final piece of the puzzle: I had to go to Miriam to confirm this. Rita's father was a man called Ben Mittal. He was her college boyfriend and first husband. They divorced about a year after they married, and that was a year after the baby. He's a medic these days. And of course he isn't a world-walker: not even outer family. Rita told us under questioning that the DHS sent her to a clinic where they activated her world-walking ability. That was a few months ago. I have to presume she was telling the truth."

"Oh hell." Huw leaned back and crossed his arms. "You're saying they can turn outer family members, recessive carriers, into world-walkers. That they don't suffer side-effects when they world-walk—in fact, they can do it repeatedly, seconds apart. And they can do it *without* a knot-focus?"

Olga was shaking her head at the last. "Not necessarily. We didn't find a bug-out knot, but she might have something fancy—an ultraviolet-fluorescent get-me-home tattoo, something like that."

"But they probably got ven Hjalmar's breeding program list. So in addition to their black boxes for aircraft and insulated ground vehicles, we could be facing . . . what? A battalion of special forces soldiers who can world-walk at will without hangovers? A legion of super-spies?"

"Don't know. Insufficient data." Olga looked as if she'd bitten a lemon. "I think they've only just begun to ramp up this capability: Rita is a prototype. And the others won't be as effective, in some ways. Only about a third of the breeding program kids are likely to be medically fit for military service—that's the running average—and even fewer are going to be willing to serve, much less willing and able to kill. They're young, too. So we're not facing a battalion: maybe a platoon, or at worst a company. That's still bad enough, of course. I've asked our assets to schedule an out-of-season web-stalk for all known breeding program kids who are in the military or of age, and to look for signs of them going zombie on Facebook—that'd be a red flag—but I think even if they're building a unit of world-walkers they'll use them as spies, not soldiers." Olga hunkered down in her chair. "What I desperately want, Huw, is to know *how* they activated Rita. Because if—"

"Our oldest are only fifteen, Olga."

"Yes, but *if* we can figure out how it's done, we'll have our own force multiplier by and by."

"But they're *kids*." Huw frowned. "It was a stupid idea, anyway: look, why don't we use artificial insemination to breed up a fuckload of spares to replace the bodies we lost, two generations down the line, because that worked out so well last time!"

"The context was completely different, though—"

"Easy for you to say. You weren't required—*ordered*—to donate."

"They might not have used your sample, cuz."

"No, really? I think they very probably used *everybody's*. To minimize the risk of in-breeding down the line. *Not* one of the Clan's finest moments, cuz. Not one of the First Man's finest moments when he signed the decree, either."

"No? I remember things differently: it was a requirement for our confinement in that vile camp being ended—that we were to sow in the Commonwealth seeds that would grow into a mighty forest, bound by loyalty not to the Clan but to the revolution. And I don't remember you protesting very loudly at the time—"

"No? Brill was pregnant! And the epidemics running wild on the other side of the fence—"

"Bygones, Huw." Olga shook her head slowly. "Water under the bridge. The point . . . we've opened a channel. Rita will be back, sooner rather than later, with a message. Rita is—rightfully—suspicious of me, but if you happen to be around, you can at least try to befriend her. Brill too, when she's in town. If we can get Rita to reconcile with Miriam, then there's another angle we can play, but it's much riskier. Let me talk to her when she's slept, and see if she thinks it's worthwhile. But meanwhile, if Rita visits for a few days, even if she won't talk to Miriam, I want you to befriend her. Give her the dog and pony show. Requisition a courier plane and fly her down to Maracaibo, show her the beach, take her for an airship ride or something. Show her how we open up new time lines. Nothing secret—just keep her entertained, and see what you can learn from her. Oh, and make sure she sees enough that her bosses will figure out why a decapitation strike won't work."

Huw thought for a minute. "I'll need guidelines. What you want her to learn about us, and what you want to withhold. Besides the obvious classified stuff. I mean, she's an agent for a foreign power: obviously she needs to be sandboxed, right?"

"Right. But she's also Miriam's daughter. They sent her to us on a fact-finding mission with a side order of head-fuckery. We shall therefore send her back with a head un-fucked and full of facts. We will just have to be very careful to ensure she is only exposed to the facts we want her—and her controllers—to learn."

"And if she's willing to kiss and make up with Miriam?"

"Then"—Olga's face was studiously expressionless—"things will get *interesting*."

Exchange Visit

Angie caught up with Rita in the bathroom, bent over a sink with the tap running. The sour smell of vomit from one of the stalls told its own story. She didn't speak, but went to the paper towel dispensers, discovered (to her disgust) that they were empty, then grabbed a double handful of toilet paper and brought it to Rita.

Rita splashed water on her face, then took the tissues with shame-faced thanks.

"Don't apologize, girl." Angie leaned against the countertop. "You weren't to know."

"Oh God, I had *no* idea."

"Do you think your—employers—knew?"

"That's—" Rita wadded up the sodden tissues into a ball and threw them, underarm, through the open doorway of a stall, then she turned to Angie. "You think they knew about her? About the adoption thing?"

Angie nodded. Then she took Rita in her arms and hugged her. She was shivering. "Triggery issue, huh?" The point of Rita's jaw dug into her collarbone. "Well, it was a really fucking weird coincidence—if it *was* a coincidence, hmm? And the kidnapping. A cynic might wonder if they set you up. To set *her* up. She's something important in the, the BLACK RAIN time line's government, isn't she?"

Rita hugged her back, painfully hard, then let go abruptly. "Let's t-talk to Kurt," she said, wiping her eyes. She wasn't wearing mascara or eye-liner, Angie noted: she hadn't been when she'd picked her up, hadn't put any on for this outing. Almost like she'd unconsciously been expecting to lose her shit.

"Can you face him?"

"Not his fault." Rita hugged herself. "That woman. What I did to her, without understanding—"

"You were set up to push her buttons. Weren't you?"

Rita's expression hardened. "I wonder how much they know about her? And why they didn't tell me? Yes, it *smells* like a setup. And Grandpa taught me never to assume coincidence when enemy action is possible."

"Now you're thinking like a Wolf . . ."

Back in the food court, they found Kurt poking at the wreckage of his pizza with a plastic fork. He turned a world-weary face toward his grand-daughter. "I am sorry: I do not think about things from that angle."

"It's not just you." Rita took his right hand and squeezed his knuckles. "I sometimes lash out. When I see her again I'll find it hard to look her in the eye." Angie made eye contact with Kurt. He nodded, slowly. "What?" asked Rita.

"Your employers recruited you straight into a sandbox," said Kurt. "They faked an abduction. They fed you lies about the woman who is your birth mother. That is not how you handle a friendly, Rita. It stinks. They are playing a deep game, and you are the pawn who is sacrificed to keep the other side's queen locked down."

"But I— What can I do?" She looked at her grandfather, then back at Angie. "What am I going to *do*?"

"Nothing yet. You must orient, observe, and decide before you act." Kurt nodded to himself, then reached a decision. "But it is time to start a new game of Spies, just like when you were little. Only this won't be a learning game. Rita, you will be the Double. Your mission is to learn everything you can about these people—"

"Which people?"

"Both your DHS controllers and the New American Common-wealth. Everyone who is not us, who is not a Wolf. Our first loyalty is to our own: you are ours, and we are yours, and everyone else may be a threat. Angie will play the part of your Resident: you will brief her on everything that happens. Angie: I am your Control and you will keep me informed. We will discuss protocol later. I will handle threat assessment and provide analysis. For now, we can expect no significant developments until your next jaunt to see your, your birth mother. I don't expect the Colonel to expend you as a weapon against her until your utility as a source is exhausted, which gives us at least one, more likely three or four, visits to BLACK RAIN. Thereafter, though . . . thereafter I may have to ask you to give me a piggyback ride across to this Commonwealth. I think your birth mother and I will have much to discuss."

IRONGATE, TIME LINE THREE, AUGUST 2020

"Sir?" The Transport Police sergeant on the front desk in Irongate looked worried as he covered the mike of his telephone handset with one palm: "I've got a call from the front desk—a Mr. Pierrepoint is askin' to see you."

"Tell him I'm busy—" Commander Jackson stopped in mid-speech, then mouthed two monosyllables. "Wait. Pierrepoint? Is he official?"

The sergeant on reception nodded vigorously. "Says 'e's from the Special Counter-Espionage Police." He raised the handset and spoke into it, briefly. "With an escort of doorbreakers from the Revolutionary Defense Force. Living it large in our lobby!" He looked indignant, as well he might. The RDF were far from popular with the official police forces of the Commonwealth.

"Shit." Jackson took a deep breath. "Tell the front desk to send Mr. Pierrepoint up to see me. Alone—he leaves his heavies downstairs or he doesn't get his toe in the door. I'll be in my office." Jackson stood and looked round the suite. "You've had your show. Get back to work," he said curtly. The heads that had been paused in motion, listening in on his instructions, bent back to their desks. Once again, the clatter of teletype keyboards filled the room.

Richard Jackson closed his office door behind him and leaned against it for a moment, eyes closed, composing himself. He hadn't risen to Commander in the Transport Police by virtue of being easily rattled or having a thin skin. He got there through being good at managing the daily legwork of lifting fare-dodgers and deterring wreckers and royalists from messing up the permanent way. But to attract the attention of two competing factions within the Party inner circle was disturbing. Pierrepoint's remit included internal affairs and counter-espionage, and his minions included the SCEP men. Bad enough that Olga Thorold had showed up *in person* to whisk the hapless chit of a world-walker girl off to some dungeon in the capital, without Adrian Holmes's personal fixer ringing the doorbell a couple of hours later with a squad of black-uniformed political thugs for backup.

By the time the expected knock on the door came, Jackson had found his center again. "Come in," he called. Sitting behind his desk, using his uniform as a shield, he focused on the job in hand: convincing this bastard to piss off back to New London as rapidly as possible.

"Sir." One of the front-desk sergeants opened the door, then stood to attention and saluted.

Well, isn't that wonderful, Jackson thought as he stood and bowed minutely. "Mr. Pierrepoint, do come in. I apologize for the wait: we've been quite busy today."

Pierrepoint entered the room. A thirtyish man, skinny and with a diffident air, he walked like a pigeon: stiff-legged and with swiveling eyes, as if he was on the lookout for enemies of the revolution who might leap out from behind police station filing cabinets, twirling their suspiciously French mustachios while brandishing poisoned daggers sheathed in Royalist propaganda tracts. He looked harmless enough at first sight: a misleading impression, of course. "Ah, you must be Commander Jackson." Pierrepoint unfolded a rumpled smile from the pockets of his cheeks. It didn't extend to his eyes. "Shall we skip the preliminaries?"

"I'm sure you're a very busy man," said Jackson. "Why don't you have a seat and tell me what you want?"

"The world-walker. Why did you hand her over?" Pierrepoint remained standing.

"Well, sir, as you doubtless already know, all world-walkers are the responsibility of the Ministry of Intertemporal Technological Intelligence. They're subject to the Elite Conscription Act of 2003, and as such any adult world-walkers who are not already assigned to duties by the Ministry may be construed to be draft-dodgers. When a duly accredited director of said Ministry arrived here *with a warrant for the world-walker's arrest*, I had no choice but to hand the prisoner over." Jackson frowned. "Despite having brought prior charges against her, I had no alternative, sir. Trespassing on the permanent way and riding without a ticket are minor offenses covered under the bylaws, while evading the ECA—if that is indeed what she was doing, as was alleged—would be a serious felony." He crossed his arms.

"Ah. And it never occurred to you that a world-walker from a hostile para-time power might fall within the remit of the Special Counter-Espionage Police?" Pierrepoint looked amiably quizzical, in much the same way that the gape of a venomous snake might resemble a grin.

"I saw no evidence of espionage," Jackson said, minding his words carefully. "She's not French, and the, ah, United States of America is not listed in the schedule to the Espionage Act that identifies designated hostile powers."

"That's an oversight! She's a damn foreigner—"

"And the Act was drafted rather tightly, was it not, lest it be used as a convenient bludgeon by the overenthusiastic?" Jackson mirrored Pierrepoint's unfriendly smile. Both of them had been young head-breakers during the street fighting that followed the revolution. Only the First Man Adam's turn away from revenge and toward cautious reconciliation had prevented a widespread bloodbath. God alone knew what had motivated his change of heart, but in Jackson's view the Commonwealth had dodged a bullet—a bullet to the head, self-inflicted. Some, like Pierrepoint's master, hadn't forgiven the Royalists for the atrocities they'd committed back in the day. They still bided their time, holding a torch for the witch hunt they hoped might someday erupt again. "Mr. Pierrepoint, it is my job to enforce the law. I can't simply bend it on a whim. So on the basis of legal advice, I handed the suspect over to the agency responsible for dealing with her kind."

He half-expected Pierrepoint to swear petulantly, but the man had more self-control than he expected. Pierrepoint merely nodded. "Your point is taken, Commander, as, I trust, is mine. I understand your inability to keep her from falling into the tentacles of MITI, but I submit that MITI marches to a different drum, as it were, to a different beat from the other organs of this *fine* Commonwealth that we both serve. It might have been the *lawful* thing to deliver her into their grip, but it wasn't terribly clever. So I have two requests to make of you—mind, these are merely polite requests: I have no right to order you around. Firstly, should the woman—or any others of her kind—come into your custody again, would you please notify my office immediately? It would save an inordinate deal of annoyance later. And secondly, for the record, would you mind giving me a copy of the charge sheet laid against her, relating to the transport offenses you mentioned?"

BERLIN, TIME LINE TWO/THREE, AUGUST 2020

For an illegal agent in a foreign country, the third most risky activity one can undertake is to go about in public. To visit a land where one is a stranger, with speech and mannerisms that set one apart as an alien, is to constantly invite scrutiny. And in an empire which requires its subjects to carry internal passports; where informers hang out in every café or beer hall; where everyone inhabits a pervasive media fog of warnings about the need for vigilance against spies and revolutionaries: in such an empire, to invite scrutiny is to risk arrest, purely as a precautionary measure.

But if there's an equal risk to being seen in public, it's *avoiding* being seen in public. Normal people don't huddle in hotel rooms from one week to the next. Normal people don't shy away from contact. There is a fine line to be walked between courting the risk of scrutiny and drawing attention to oneself by furtive behavior.

Hulius followed a protocol designed to deflect the wrong kind of attention by providing a semblance of public interaction, while not giving much away. Early each morning he rose and ate breakfast in the coach house's barroom. Then he walked and caught the tram to the furrier's warehouse, within which he locked himself away for most of a working day. He only surfaced to return to his room in mid-evening. At lunchtime he sometimes visited one of the neighboring beer halls or restaurants: if asked, he freely discussed his business. He'd been hired, he told anybody with ears to listen, to do a thorough stock-take and audit of the warehouse. The absentee purchaser was a cheapskate who was only paying for one auditor, and the work was going slowly: the place had been allowed to fall into disarray and chaos, the former owner a compulsive hoarder who allowed bales of waste scraps and low-value rabbit pelts to pile atop valuable arctic fox or ermine. Hulius's crib-notes were copious and detailed. They were also a fiction, generated by a team of back-office busybodies, and updated regularly via e-mail to a tablet which he kept in the doppelgängered premises in time line two. His listeners' eyes tended to glaze over rapidly once he got his head of steam up, and after he ignored their halfhearted attempts to engage him in political debate or illegal gambling, instead turning the subject to an enthusiastic tutorial on the various grades of commercial cowhide, the local police informers filed him under "annoying but harmless" and learned to ignore him.

This suited Hulius just fine, because most days he went home with a splitting headache.

World-walking too frequently was a recipe for disaster, but he had established a pattern of working long hours and had built himself a doppelgängered hide in the forest in time line one. He now had the luxury of an hour to rest up and recover between jaunts. If anyone had broken into the warehouse during the long afternoons they might have wondered at finding it deserted, but Hulius considered it a low risk. Every morning he returned to the warehouse, locked the door, then world-walked first to the forest hide and then to the apartment in the Berlin of skyscrapers and Internet access. And he only returned to the capital of the imperial province ten hours later, grimacing and dry-swallowing a cocktail of painkillers and antihypertensives.

In between, he worked on mission prep and took flying lessons.

Hulius was not a professional pilot, but years ago, back in the early days of the Clan survivor's exile, Rudi had drafted him into a scheme to train world-walkers as aviators. World-walking while flying turned out to be a bad idea—nearly as bad as playing drinking games behind the steering wheel. Air pressure, humidity, wind direction, and weather all varied semi-randomly between time lines. Even if the pilot wasn't trying to cope with a blinding near-migraine experience, simultaneously losing thirty millibars of pressure, most of your visibility, and thirty knots of headwind made for a flying experience which could euphemistically be described as exciting. It went a lot better with the aid of an autopilot, an up-to-date weather report from the target time line, and either several thousand feet of extra altitude or an aircraft that had multiple engines or was lighter than air. Such as the Continental Bombardment Force's high-altitude strategic bombers, or the DPR's airship fleet. Single-engined light planes need not apply.

But despite the conventional wisdom, the DPR planners had dreamed up a scheme that relied on it. Somebody probably thought it was a Really Neat Idea: somebody who wasn't expecting to fly the maneuver themselves but secretly wanted to be Jason Bourne when they grew up. Hulius, when he first heard about it, used a variety of choice expletives.

The Cirrus SR22T was a modern, single-engined light aircraft. A four-seater made out of carbon-fiber composites and equipped with a glass cockpit, its principal claim to fame was the Cirrus Airframe Parachute System: a ballistic rescue parachute able to soft-land the plane vertically if all else failed. (The airframe would probably be totaled, but the passengers should walk away from the crash uninjured.) Hulius was to exfiltrate the Princess from time line three into time line two, the Germany of ICE trains and lasers, by way of a short world-walk into time line one and out again. (There was no direct route between time line three and time line two.) He would then drive her to an airfield, take off, and fly due west across the Atlantic. Once over the designated recovery area, he would world-walk to time line one, make sure his transponder was squawking, pop the chute, and world-walk *again* to time line three—all in under a minute. The Commonwealth Navy would then do the rest, including rescuing the ditched plane and holding the bucket for him to throw up into.

Advantages: the Princess would simply vanish from the French Empire's territory and reappear in the Commonwealth, as if by magic. There would be no need to procure a valid passport for her in time line two, or to coach her past airport security in an unfamiliar world. By flying her out via time line two the pilot would have access to positioning satellites, air traffic control, METARs, and the full panoply of support for general aviation that was absent from the howling wilderness of time line one. Nor would he run the gauntlet of the French Empire's air defense network and Atlantic Fleet in time line three. He would be able to guarantee his arrival to within a mile or two of the designated pick-up point. And if he had to abort the mission partway, well, there were contingency plans.

In practice . . . Hulius had learned to fly in the Commonwealth, where glass cockpits and ballistic recovery parachutes were the stuff of magazine articles about the white heat of technology rather than part of the curriculum of flight schools. Nor was he entirely sanguine about world-walking twice in mid-air, then parachuting into the North Atlantic in autumn with a frightened princess as a passenger. The phrase "crazy-ass James Bond stunt" had been uttered more than once when the plan was explained to him. Certain points had been criticized scathingly, and the plan amended accordingly. Not dropped: merely changed. For one thing, there was now a boat with a weather station in mid-ocean in time line one, with a courier standing by to give a meteorological update by short-wave radio before he attempted to world-walk. And for another thing, Hulius was currently driving out to the nearest general aviation field three or four times a week, for a couple of hours of touch-and-go landings and cross-country hops under visual flight rules as he cross-trained on the Cirrus. Not to mention hours spent cramming meteorology and navigation refresher courses, and renewing his instrument rating.

Not even the most starry-eyed of the DPR's mission planners were so impractical as to ignore the agent in place's impassioned demand for a training work-up before he attempted to put into practice a story line stolen from *Mission: Impossible*.

The identity the DPR had supplied for Hulius—an Indonesian passport showing him to be of Dutch extraction—was getting a real workout this month. Luckily Germany had managed to cling to its constitutional aversion to surveillance (which was itself a hangover from the downfall of a far nastier police state than the one currently waging the Global War On Para-time). While his identity would be disclosed to the police and security agencies every time he filed a flight plan, it wouldn't—shouldn't—be exported to the USA unless he filed a plan with North America as his destination, or did something else to attract the direct attention of the Bundespolizei. Consequently, Hulius was punctilious in his behavior. Using taxis and public transport, refraining from alcohol, tobacco, or narcotics, paying bills and filing all the necessary paperwork correctly. He was even at pains to maintain his cover with the flight school, chatting with the instructors and letting it be known that the Cirrus was his personal obsession, one he'd been saving for over a five year period. After completing his current job he was going to fly it home to Bandung in one of those epic international vacation-adventures any plane owner daydreamed about: across the Atlantic via the Azores and the Caribbean, across Central America, island-hopping all the way home across the Pacific and Australasia. It was great cover for the preparations for his upcoming real mission.

Hulius wouldn't be ready to fly without a work-up that would take nearly four weeks. Nor would it be prudent to make face-to-face contact with Elizabeth again and risk the renewed attention of her guards until it was almost time to go. So he went about his routine, refreshing his aviator's training, getting used to the Cirrus, and familiarizing himself with the streets and people of the other Berlin, in readiness for the day of extraction.

NEW LONDON, TIME LINE THREE, AUGUST 2020

Meanwhile, in New London, the business of the Party was ongoing.

"Good morning, Mrs. Bishop. And how are you today?"

Margaret Bishop inclined her head stiffly. "As well as can be expected, at my age: still happy to be alive. And yourself, Mr. Holmes?"

Adrian Holmes, Chairman of the Party Secretariat beamed. "I'm fine, fine. Won't you take a seat? I'm so glad you could make time for me in your busy schedule." He stepped around his desk and pulled the heavy visitor's armchair out, making room. Mrs. Bishop shuffled forward and leaned on his arm as she lowered herself into it. The years had not been easy on her, and she had already been over fifty in the year of the revolution. Arthritis was taking its toll on the former coordinator of the New England Underground, who had chaired the Commonwealth Resilience Committee during the crazy years following the overthrow of the Crown and the near–civil war that had followed. In contrast, Holmes was young enough to be her son. He was the sort of son any mother ought to want, for he was both handsome and personable, energetic and intelligent. Indeed, he was the very model of a highflyer in the ranks of the Radical Party, the animating armature at the heart of the Commonwealth. However, their relationship was barely cordial, and anything but familial.

"You wanted to talk to me," Mrs. Bishop cut through the niceties. "I'll not withhold my portfolio's full cooperation on matters of state, but I hope this isn't to be a canvassing session. You're wasting your time."

Holmes returned to his seat. "I think we both know where we stand," he said, pleasantly enough. "So no, I do not expect you to reverse yourself on the matter of the succession. Frankly, I would be worried if you did: the Party needs men and women of integrity, not courtiers. But yes, this *is* about the succession—indirectly."

Margaret cocked her head to one side and regarded him warily. "If you didn't invite me here to canvass my support, then what possible reason is there to discuss it?"

"Well, now. You know I intend to put my name forward as a candidate when the Council of Guardians meets? It's possible that I will be the next First Man; or perhaps some other candidate will make the cut. Regardless, whoever the new First Man is, you will have to work with him—or her. And so will I: after all, we are both loyal servants of the revolution. The reason I wanted to talk to you is that very soon after the succession is announced—if not before—we are going to face two very serious threats, and I think it is important to have some idea of how we are going to respond to them while our leadership is paralyzed or absent."

"Threats." Margaret Bishop fixed him with a gimlet stare. "I'm aware of two threats. Are they, perchance, the same as yours?"

"I don't know. What are *you* afraid of?"

"A threat from overseas, and a threat from over*time.* Overseas: the Pretender would be an imbecile not to realize that this is going to be his last opportunity to attack the Commonwealth for at least a decade, if not ever. He or his daughter will make a play to return to American soil, either in the name of reconciliation or with a French grand fleet at their back. Probably the former: I am told that a face-off between their ships of the line and our Navy's new supercarriers can only end in the adversary's defeat. The other threat is rather more complex, but if I am to believe the daily briefings, we have intercepted unmanned drones sent by the United States of America—do you know anything about that? And the attack alert the other month was part of one such interception. So we may have to deter two different types of enemy simultaneously: a Monarchist pretender with delusions of popular support, and what our analysts call a pseudo-democracy or inverted totalitarian state intruding from a parallel world where history took a different path from our own." She paused. "Your nightmares now, Adrian?"

"They're not totally dissimilar, actually," Holmes admitted. "But I think I have some fresh light to shed on both threats. Unfortunately, it's not very encouraging. Which is why I think it best to build bridges and seek consensus now, before the headsman sharpens his axe for us."

"New light? What kind of new light?"

Holmes shook his head, as if troubled by a fly, but there were none about, it being fall, and the office well provisioned with insecticide strips. "You know as well as I do that we are riven by factionalism. It's the besetting vice of our revolutionary constitution, by design: if you can't trust one pillar of the state, set up another to keep it honest. A tripod is more stable than a bipod, as Adam puts it. My office—part of my office's remit—is to keep watch over the structures we depend on, and to provide early warning to the Council of Guardians if it appears that a faction is preparing to slip the leash. It's not as if we haven't seen what can happen when an agency, or group of agencies, decide that their mission supervenes all the other requirements of good governance." He fixed Bishop with a mild-eyed gaze. "The United States, for example. The situation reports from the Department of Para-historical Research make for frightening reading. That nation's obsession with security in the wake of the admittedly heinous attack on their capital led them to pour resources into a monstrous precautionary bureaucracy. They're nominally a democratic republic, but they could give the Bourbon Crown lessons in how to run its secret police. And then there's the DPR itself, and MITI."

Margaret's spine stiffened against the back of her chair. "What do your informers tell you about MITI, Adrian?" Her tone was deceptively gentle.

"'Trust but verify.' That's what Adam told the first council of guardians he had dealing with Mrs. Beckstein—Burgeson, now. The First Man accepted her Clan's offer of service in return for refuge during the revolutionary crisis, but kept them under lock and key for nearly two years, until satisfied that their intentions were aligned with those of the Commonwealth. Yes, I went back and reread the original minutes, Margaret. And yes, I think it was well worth it to give them their head back then. Mrs. Burgeson is an able and energetic commissioner, and her ministry has brought incalculable benefits to the Commonwealth. MITI is a huge success, anybody can see that. And so we've placed an awful lot of responsibility on her shoulders. But it seems to me that we have been slack in our attention to verification of late, so six months ago I took steps to enhance my understanding of MITI and the DPR's current activities."

He sounded weary beyond his years. Margaret sat in silence for almost a minute, processing. Finally she responded, in a low monotone. "What did your agents provocateurs dig up?"

"Firstly, they aren't agents provocateurs." A faintly aggrieved tone rose in Holmes's voice. "I wanted *information*, Margaret, not a pretext. Only a maniac would want to slaughter a goose that lays a continuous stream of golden eggs. Our GDP has grown by eleven percent per year, on average, for seventeen consecutive years. Growth is actually trending *upwards* at present, and we have a series of new technologies arriving in the next decade that are like something out of a philosophical romance: atom-powered spaceships to the planets, pocket computers with wireless data networks connecting them to the sum total of human knowledge, artificial organs, cures for cancer. We can't even cast doubt on these claims, because they're here *right now* in the DPR's laboratories, borrowed from the world next door. I've *seen* them.

"But Margaret, technologies are not value-free. If you choose a technology, you are implicitly accepting the political imperatives that provide the context the technology operates within. If you want railroads, you must accept coal and steel industries, compulsory seizure of land for rights-of-way, standard railway time, and central stations. If you want magical pocket computers with glowing sapphire screens that give you access to a vast communications network, then you accept the politics of communications surveillance, the interests of cable laying combines that carry the backhaul signal, the ownership of the airwaves.

"So I set two types of agent to work on MITI and the DPR. The regular informers are mundane enough, and what they told me was worrying but not unexpected. There are signs of mission creep, of the DPR undertaking adventures both in the United States and across the water, in the Empire, on its own cognizance." He leaned toward her: "They have at least two operations in train right now that have the potential to blow up into huge scandals, Margaret. And one of these borders on outright treason, which is why I wanted to bring it to your attention: I would be very grateful if you could investigate these and tell me whether I am over-reacting."

He picked up a slim document folder and held it out toward her. She accepted it warily.

"What's in here?" she asked.

"The DPR's attempt to meddle directly in succession politics. Frankly, I think their scheme is harebrained and dangerous, but unlikely to succeed . . . still, someone—someone who they do not consider to be an enemy or a dangerous rival—should take Mrs. Burgeson in hand and suggest to her that trying to organize defections exceeds the remit of her commission, and might well be misinterpreted by some of our more excitable colleagues. The scope for blowback is enormous and would tarnish not just her own reputation, but that of the Party as a whole." He gave a small, self-deprecating smile. "But there is worse. I have included a report by a couple of magistrates from the assembly on a tour of a secret DPR research site that has been soaking up quite amazing amounts of money for some time. You might want to take her aside and ask her just how she thinks our rivals across the water will respond to this, this JUGGERNAUT, should they learn of it? Because, while I am sure she thinks it nothing but an excellent contraption for exploring new time lines, His Imperial Highness won't see it that way *at all*. And of course there's a third matter, but my agents are still investigating for the time being, because if true it's a deadly threat to the revolution. I'll be sure to share my notes with you as and when there is something concrete to report, but until then I would prefer not to alarm you unduly."

Margaret Bishop tucked the file under one arm. She'd always had a good poker face, but to Holmes's eye her expression was somewhat more glassy-eyed than normal: somewhere between stunned and pole-axed. He gave her another gentle smile, then continued.

"This stuff is, well, it's all about individual projects. They should be investigated and either endorsed by the council, or quietly terminated. I leave these matters in your competent hands—hands which, unlike mine, the Burgesons will not shy from reflexively. But the projects my informers have unearthed are all individual operations, and as such they are trivial. I'm far more worried about what my analysts are telling me.

"I asked them for a report on the cultural and social impact of the MITI Ten Year Plan for the period 2020 to 2030, based on the technologies they intend to introduce—the ones that they told us they are in the process of introducing via the National Incubator Program and start-up grants. The report was to address three key questions. Firstly, in broad strokes: what is their likely impact on the general economy and well-being of the Commonwealth. Then, a step back: what are the political issues that will be raised by the introduction of these new tools? The equivalent of eminent domain for railroads, only for heart transplants and hypertext and moon rockets, so to speak. *These* are quite alarming. And a final step back, to reopen the trust-but-verify question: *if* the world-walkers of MITI and the DPR are planning to benefit from these technologies at the expense of the Commonwealth, how might they go about doing so?

"Margaret, their report makes for very scary reading indeed." Adrian slid another folio toward her. His smile disappeared. "I think we've been too trusting. The Clan was, as well we know, a political power in its own realm before their final disastrous encounter with the government of the United States. For fifteen years they have been building a power base within the Commonwealth. This report"—he tapped the cover— "is speculative: it analyzes the capabilities implicit in the technologies they benevolently shower upon us." He took a deep breath. "It doesn't look good."

"Tell me." She took the folio.

"Ever since their nuclear war, the United States of America has been spiraling down the slope of increasing internal repression. But unlike our neighbors in the old world, their police state is based on the ubiquitous deployment of surveillance technologies, rather than armies of informers and agents. My analysts tell me that the latest MITI plan proposes the introduction of too many of the enabling technologies for such surveillance for my peace of mind. I have a very bad feeling that Mrs. Beckstein is, with the enthusiastic support of her ministry—which is one of the most important players in our industrial and educational sphere— laying the groundwork for an internal coup, and the creation of a counter-revolutionary police state. And the worst part is, I'm not even sure that she's *consciously aware* of what she's doing, or whether she's being manipulated by a faction among the world-walkers whose first loyalty is still, and always has been, to their aristocratic Clan relatives rather than to our revolution . . ."

AN UNDISCLOSED LOCATION, UNDISCLOSED
TIME LINE, AUGUST 2020

For the first six hours of her detention, Paulie's life narrowed to a concrete-walled tunnel of pain, humiliation, and fear. Then it broadened out into a windowless cell: pain and humiliation swapped shifts with boredom and despair, while fear did a quick costume change and reappeared on stage as the black dog of depression.

For the past eighteen years she had been expecting a day like this to come. It seemed to her that ordinary people got to angst quietly about ordinary horrors: assailed in the privacy of their own skulls by the nighttime specters of heart attacks, cancer, car crashes, debt, despair, suicide—their own or their loved ones. Almost everybody had morbid thoughts and depressive ideation from time to time, even if they denied it—just like masturbation. But Paulette Milan had drunk from an extra-special fount of gloom, and she had drunk so deeply that it had warped her entire adult life.

Twenty-two years ago she'd landed a job as a researcher and junior sub on a local tech magazine called *The Industry Weatherman*. It was back in the days when advertisers paid for glossy print on paper and investigative journalism was still a thing. She'd worked with a highflyer, predestined to rise to her own syndicated column if she kept going long enough: a woman called Miriam Beckstein. But Miriam had gotten them both shitcanned for sticking her nose in the wrong money-laundering operation, and then her distant relatives had come crawling out of the woodwork to drag her down to an alien time line without modern conveniences like flush toilets and electricity—

And somehow one thing had led to another, and then another and another, until Paulette, dragged along in Miriam's charismatic undertow, came to the full apprehension of her destiny only as she was frog-marched in shackles down a stained concrete-walled corridor in a slaughterhouse for human animals. Her head pounded from whatever knock-out fix they'd hit her with, and her stomach felt as if she'd been gut-punched. She couldn't see where she was going—they'd hooded her—but as the clouds cleared, replaced by a throbbing hangover layered atop the usual aches and pains of middle age, she realized that her personal doom had arrived.

Hi. I'm Paulette Milan, and for the past seventeen years I've been spying on the United States of America for a hostile superpower. They told me that the antibiotic formulae that I stole from Big Pharma saved eighteen million babies from dying of diarrhea. Do I get a medal?

They removed the shackles and hood then left her alone in a windowless coffin-shaped cell. No questions were asked: they knew who she was, and at least some of what she'd done. The only furniture was a thin foam pad on top of a metal platform bolted to the floor, and a stainless steel toilet/washbasin combo behind a low modesty wall. The lights were recessed into the ceiling, flat LED panels behind wired glass. They'd taken her clothes and put her in something like hospital scrubs. A loose V-necked top and pants, cotton so thin it would tear before she could twist it into a noose. The sink and toilet were designed to prevent drowning. She looked up and counted at least six pinhead-sized cameras watching her from the ceiling, like a malignant constellation of black holes: holes that sucked light in, seeing all, returning nothing.

The boredom and dread were bad—the dread less so: she knew her life was effectively over, that from now on her hours were to be spent in spaces like this cement oubliette—but gradually the light began to bug her. It was constant. *Utterly* constant, invariant over time, never dimming, never changing. Once in a while a slot at the bottom of the door would open and a cardboard tray would slide through, loaded with something that United or Delta would have been ashamed to serve the self-loading freight in coach class. It was just barely edible. She had to eat it off the tray, and the first time she'd taken it a stentorian synthesized voice had warned her there'd be no more food unless she returned the tray within fifteen minutes. Whatever a minute was in this timeless, shadowless void. But there had been several meals since then, and a couple of sleeps (despite the undimming lights). Food, she suspected, came at fixed intervals. She'd tried to keep count, but lost it after five or six—what if a meal came while she was asleep, retracting silently on the quarter hour mark?

She'd had some idea what to expect, of course. Life in solitary in a supermax prison. No human contact, and probably no trial—her case would be heard by a court, but it would be a FISA court sitting *in camera*, her case pled before the bench (of judges, no jury) by a defense lawyer with a security clearance assigned by the very same agency that had arrested and prosecuted her. Her defense would be classified, so that she might never even learn the name of her faceless attorney. Nor might she be given the details of the prosecution brief. Even the charges and the verdict could be classified secret, if disclosing the fact that one Paulette Milan had been tried and found guilty under the Espionage Act might be construed as giving valuable information to the enemy. Whoever the enemy was.

It was even possible that, despite her guilt—guilt that Paulette embraced wholeheartedly, for she was beyond self-deception and entirely clear on the fact that she was, in fact, an enemy spy, for this was not the United States she had grown up in and recited the pledge of allegiance to at school—it was even possible that she had been arrested *by mistake*. After one particularly grim crying jag she laughed herself to unquiet sleep over the possible irony that they might have mistaken her for a North Korean spy, or even—much funnier—an agent of the Clan.

After fourteen or fifteen meal times and a few sleeps her apathy was interrupted by an abrupt recorded announcement: "Stand with your back to the door, your legs apart, and your hands behind your back."

"What—" Paulie began, before the recording repeated itself.

She didn't seriously consider ignoring it. There was no telling what they might do. They could flood the cell with CS gas, or Tase her, or simply leave her alone to starve. And besides, the light was bugging her almost as much as the boredom. She stood, as directed: hands using unseen slots fastened chains around her wrists and ankles, then the door opened. They didn't hood her this time, but the guards (male, built like football quarterbacks) wore masks, and in any case there was nothing to see but endless painted concrete. They marched her along a corridor then through a door and along another corridor, always beneath the vigilant gaze of a galaxy of cameras.

There was a door at the end of her journey, and on the other side of it a white-painted room with a white-topped table and a hard chair. It was bolted to the floor, of course. This time there *was* a window—a mirrored one, spanning the width of the wall opposite the chair. "Sit down," said a recorded voice. She sat, and the guards padlocked her leg manacles to a ring in the floor. Then they ran a chain from it to her wrists, behind the back of the chair, tested the restraints, and left her alone in the room with the one-way mirror.

Am I supposed to stew in my own juice? she wondered after a couple of minutes. She shifted in the chair, finding the limits of movement. Her shoulders were going to hurt if she had to sit here for more than a couple of hours. And her back was already sore from the shitty thin mattress. She peered at her dark reflection in the window. Cheeks thinner, hair a flyaway mess tangled beyond easy repair—someone would have to give her a bob cut to restore order. Age sank in. *What a mess I look*, she thought listlessly. Another morsel of human food, gulped into the belly of a Hobbesian beast, driven mad in its torment by powers from another world—

"Paulette Milan," said a voice.

"Yes?" She looked round.

The voice was obviously filtered: they were using Auto-Tune to disguise the speaker and adding a bit of specious bass that gave it an unrealistic resonance, like something from one of the goth and industrial records her elder sister had liked in the late eighties. The door was still shut: she was exposed beneath the panopticon gaze of the one-way mirror.

"You are under arrest subject to Section Four of the Defending the USA against Extradimensional Terrorism Act, 2003." The DUET Act had suspended habeas corpus, driven a stake through the rotting heart of the Fourth Amendment, and seriously undermined the First and Fifth: passed in the wake of 7/16 and rubber-stamped after a pre-arranged appeal by the rump supreme court appointed by President Rumsfeld, it had taken the ball from the USA Patriot Act and run all the way to a successful touchdown at the end of the Bill of Rights. "The Miranda rights do not apply in your situation. The Fifth Amendment safe harbor from self-incrimination does not apply in your situation. You will now be questioned under penalty of perjury. Failure to truthfully answer all questions put to you may result in additional charges being laid against you." *Pause.* A subtly more human, less distorted voice continued: "If you cooperate willingly the prosecutors have signaled their willingness to waive requesting the death penalty."

DUET had established in law that assisting world-walkers from another time line was treason within the meaning of Article Three of the US Constitution. It carried the death penalty. Paulette thought of her cell, and of her former life, before she opened her mouth. Her tongue felt like timber as she spoke, her voice wavering only a little. "Go fuck yourselves."

It was oddly liberating and pants-wettingly terrifying at the same time, like letting go of her life. But she'd had a long time to think it through: not just a double handful of supermax meal periods, but many years of leaden dread. All the lonely nights spent lying awake in fear of exposure. And she *had* figured it out. She was past any fear of being dead, of the judgment of Heaven or Hell. But the prospect of being buried alive in a concrete coffin ten feet by four for years or decades to come . . . *that* scared her.

"You're making a mistake," said the voice behind the mirror. It, or he, sounded very sure of himself.

"Oh, I don't think so." She squinted into the dark glass. "You're never going to let me go, so why not cut straight to the chase? I'll take the needle, thanks. It's better than being buried alive."

"There are worse fates than a secret trial and execution." Pause. "Unmarked bizjets fly around the world every week. Some of them go to countries you've never heard of. We can broaden your horizons with foreign travel. Of course, then you'll wish you'd told us everything: but once in Turkmenistan or Algeria it will be too late for regrets."

Another voice, of lighter pitch—possibly female, behind the Auto-Tune tricks—chipped in. "After they've extracted everything you know they'll sell you on to a prison hospital in Hangzhou. They don't execute donors these days, they harvest one organ at a time. It can be months until they find a buyer who's a good match for your heart or liver. But the corneas usually go first. Also, they usually harvest one kidney and the bladder—lots of cancer patients in China need new bladders and you can piss in a bag for a few weeks. There's a designer drug, MPTP, they use to pacify the donors, to stop them kicking up a fuss . . ."

"We can fast-track you for execution, if you want," the first speaker interrupted. "But if you're really good, we can swing a deal: get the prosecutors to ask for life without parole, but served in the general prison population. It's not like you're violent. So what's it going to be, Ms. Milan? Are you going to cooperate within the rule of law, or are you going to force us to outsource you to the Far East for recycling?"

Paulette closed her eyes. This was inevitable, of course. To extract cooperation from those facing execution, it made sense for there to be a fate worse than death waiting in the wings. "Well *fuck*."

"I'll take that as conditional consent to our proposal that you cooperate with the prosecution in pursuit of a plea bargain, shall I?" said the second speaker.

"We really do have your best interests at heart," said the other. "It kinda sticks in the throat to send US citizens to the PacRim donor theaters, doesn't it? Even if you forfeited your citizenship by spying for a hostile power."

"Ms. Milan? Ms. Milan, are you listening?"

Fifteen minutes in manacles in a white room and they'd cracked her resistance without laying a finger on her. *I'm useless*, she thought drearily. "Ask whatever you want. I'm listening."

"Very well, Ms. Milan. Let's take it from the top of the list then, shall we? The sooner we get through this, the sooner you can go back to your cell and we can tell the prosecutors you've been a good girl. So, let's just clear up some easy questions first."

"Yes . . ."

"Ms. Milan. In your own words: when did you start spying for the Deutsche Demokratische Republik . . . ?"

PHILADELPHIA, TIME LINE TWO, AUGUST 2020

FEDERAL EMPLOYEE 004930391 CLASSIFIED VOICE TRANSCRIPT

COL. SMITH: So how did POTUS take the report?

DR. SCRANTON: She wasn't happy about the unplanned contact, but she's going to play ball. That's the TL:DR version, anyway. The longer version . . . We've got a lifeline and a diplomatic channel. State are already in the loop, and SecState is working with POTUS and SecHomeland on how we approach negotiations with the Commonwealth—targets, strategies, desired outcomes, that sort of thing. It's a major embarrassment that the adversary ID'd our HUMINT asset first, but the fact that they're eager to talk is a decent counter-weight. We are 100 percent responsible for execution and they agreed to keep this fast and light, so the firewall remains in place, this time with official backing from the very top. If something goes horribly wrong they'll hang us out to dry—but that's not going to happen on my watch.

AGENT O'NEILL: Well, that's a relief, ma'am.

DR. SCRANTON: You'd better believe it. Meanwhile, going forward, Sec-State will provide us with a sealed communique for delivery to the adversary's leadership at the next available pre-arranged safe mail drop. And we're to take it from there.

COL. SMITH: How are we going to utilize Rita in this context? What about DRAGON'S TEETH?

DR. SCRANTON: Good questions. For now, Rita has been burned as an illegal in the Commonwealth. We've got to assume that even if they don't have a national DNA and biometrics database as good as ours, they're aware that such things exist, will have taken samples from her, and will be working to develop such a capability. She's still got utility outside the Commonwealth, and she's still clean for use in other time lines, so she remains in your inventory. But for now we'll use her as an overt asset, a courier. She is *not* cleared to know about DRAGON'S TEETH, and from now on she's outside the firewall. Anything she knows, they could learn. The flip side is also true. While she's over there she can soak up all the local color they give her access to. We know they've been spying on us, so as long as she can't give them any-thing useful we could end up ahead on points . . . on the other hand, it would be a good idea to preload her key generator with a termination jaunt. Just in case she's tempted—or coerced—into showing them how it works and where it can take a world-walker.

AGENT O'NEILL: A termination jaunt?

COL. SMITH: I would prefer not to deploy that unless it's absolutely, utterly necessary.

DR. SCRANTON: So would I, and that's why I'm trusting you to make suitable arrangements and define the activation protocol if we have to, have to cut her loose. The criteria for termination are high likelihood of imminent, or actual, defection. Alternatively: if she's been captured, is unable to escape, and they're pulling her apart to see how she works . . . but the primary criterion is loyalty, which makes it a value call, which in turn means it needs to be determined by the officer with greatest insight into her state of mind. I personally don't believe we'll need to use it—she doesn't exactly seem to have hit it off with her mother—but we need to cover all the bases. If possible, you should come to me for confirmation before going through that gate. But as of now you've got authority to terminate her if these circumstances arise.

COL. SMITH: (sarcasm) Thank you ever so much.

AGENT O'NEILL: Let's hope it doesn't come to that.

COL. SMITH: It's not going to be easy to issue that kind of order.

DR. SCRANTON: I think we can all agree on that. I picked you for this task, Colonel, precisely because you won't do it lightly. We owe her that much. Now, moving on: when will Rita be ready to deploy again?

COL. SMITH: We could go tomorrow if you give us the call. Deployment to a pre-arranged rendezvous with a welcoming party is a totally dif-ferent ball game from what we've been doing so far. There's no need for a wardrobe session or special equipment if the other side are ex-pecting her as a guest. We should sanitize her—no phone—but there's no harm in giving her a camera, a notepad, and a pen, and telling her to declare them. Worst case, they're confiscated. Best case, she brings back a diary and vacation snapshots.

DR. SCRANTON: And this is useful because . . . ?

COL. SMITH: Per original mission goals, we're moving into an utterly un-documented, closed society—like China or the USSR in the 1950s. Our predecessors knew *nothing* back then, and it made it really hard to oper-ate. Just what she's learned already is going to keep a room full of ana-lysts busy for months. She may not need to know about DRAGON'S TEETH, but don't you think DRAGON'S TEETH will stand a better chance of success if they go in with a good quality pre-brief?

DR. SCRANTON: This isn't about DRAGON'S TEETH, but your point is taken. Do it.

AGENT O'NEILL: Do we have any other actions around Rita, other than BLACK RAIN Phase Two prep?

COL. SMITH: I'm a little worried by this business with her grandfather. And the girlfriend.

DR. SCRANTON: What are you worried about, exactly? She's got strings. I thought you wanted her to have strings.

COL. SMITH: Yes, but the strings are in danger of getting tangled.

DR. SCRANTON: Explain, please.

COL. SMITH: I asked Sonia to keep a close watch on Grandpa Kurt. Then Rita swan-dived into Angela's bed, so I told her to add Angela to the MKCrossbow Tracklist—

DR. SCRANTON: MKCrossbow?

COL. SMITH: Enhanced number plate recognition, phone cell tracking, government override with voice monitoring enabled on the phone's mikes, proximity-activated CCTV and celldar, domestic appliance monitoring. The panopticon treatment, in other words. It generates *way* too much data for a manual trawl, but it comes with some Bayes-ian behavior analysis tools—basically a deep learning software bot that models her behavior and flags up anomalies, generates a timeline around suspicious incidents. Gomez is tasked with reviewing the ex-ceptions and generating daily reports for my eyes only.

DR. SCRANTON: So what did your crystal ball see, Ms. Gomez?

AGENT GOMEZ: A couple of events over the past two weeks have us really worried, ma'am. On one occasion Ms. Hagen went over to Boston and enlisted the grandfather's help in collecting Rita's car from the pound. Mr. Douglas was in town to put flowers on his wife's grave and go drinking with some old friends—he does it at least once a year. They drove back in convoy, then Angela gave Kurt a lift to his motel and went home on auto-drive. Oddly, they were conversing for much of the drive but the speech recognition software degraded significantly. In fact, when we pulled the raw recording later it sounded like Furbyspeak—the speech synthesizer equivalent of *lorem ipsum*.

Something similar happened again when Ms. Hagen collected Douglas after the most recent clusterfuck. They went back to Ms. Hagen's apartment, then departed again in Rita's car. The vehicle in question is too old to have a cellular uplink to the manufacturer's service agency for firmware monitoring—all it has are tire inflation transponders, our standard Remora tracker, and a couple of pinhead mikes powered by induction from the in-car electronics loom. The pinheads are terrible, and the audio capture from their phones turned to junk. They were heading for a diner in one mall, and per the feed they reached it and parked up, but then they crossed the edge of the parking lot and ended up in a different mall. The lack of forward intentionality indicators meant that we had no in-place monitoring, so all we got was the standard mall CCTV and gibberish from their phones. They sat with their backs to the nearest cameras, so no lip-reading.

DR. SCRANTON: Shit. Pardon my French.

AGENT GOMEZ: Request permission to offer an opinion, sir, ma'am.

COL. SMITH: Go ahead, Sonia.

AGENT GOMEZ: I believe the little cow has blabbed to her grandfather, and possibly to her girlfriend. Her grandfather was a Communist border guard back in the eighties, and the border guards were part of the East German secret police, not regular soldiers. The drop-outs stink of tradecraft and point to his situational awareness exceeding that of a normal civilian. The girlfriend stinks of it, too. Ms. Hagen went to a Girl Scouts camp a few years running in Maryland. I did some checking, and it turns out the place was famous: it's where a lot of NSA, CIA, NRO, and other INTELCOM folks sent their daughters. Sir, nearly *two thirds* of the girls in that camp had parents with security clearances! It was such an open secret that the girls called it Camp Spooky. I mean, they had day trips to the National Cryptologic Museum and merit badges for dead letter drops. Sir, ma'am, I am *very* disturbed . . .

DR. SCRANTON: You're telling me we've been penetrated by the Girl Scouts?

AGENT GOMEZ: It's not funny!

COL. SMITH: Or maybe the ghosts of the Iron Curtain are rattling their chains?

AGENT GOMEZ: Sir, *all* the indicators—

COL. SMITH: Noted, Sonia. Pause for a moment, though, and consider: the girlfriend went to Girl Scout summer camp near the city she lived in. We in the trade have a technical term for this: we call it a *coincidence*. Just like it's a coincidence that a few years later Angie enlisted in the Army and did a term as an intelligence specialist. You don't need to invoke Communist spies to explain them showing rudimentary signs of tradecraft-awareness some years later when they try to evade surveillance over pizza and chicken pot pie—especially when the Communist nation in question ceased to exist three decades ago. I agree, spoofing their phones is suspicious. I agree that it looks circumstantially as if Ms. Douglas has loose lips in the direction of her lover and her most intimate family member. But they're by no means the only folks who do that from time to time, and it could just be that they assume monitoring is still carried out by human ears, and they wanted to discuss something embarrassing: Rita and Angie coming out to Kurt, for example. Or asking for advice about how to handle Emily and Franz Douglas. From an ideological standpoint they're about as damaging as, as, your co-religionists, for example: there's no need to go hunting reds under the bed—

AGENT GOMEZ: Reds *in* the bed, more like—

COL. SMITH: When it might just be a false positive. Sonia, I know what you're going to say and my answer is that we can't afford to haul Kurt and Angie into a secure debriefing suite and give them an opportunity to clear themselves of negative engrams on the basis of a suspicion. If we do that, then we'll turn Rita against us, and we're going to need every edge we can get if we're playing footsie with that bitch Miriam Beckstein.

AGENT GOMEZ: What are you going to do?

DR. SCRANTON: May I make a suggestion?

COL. SMITH: Please go ahead, ma'am.

DR. SCRANTON: Sonia, you should continue monitoring the subject and her associates. Pull in any additional resources you need. The instant you get any positive signals—not just drop-outs and signal degradation, but actual *positive* evidence of malfeasance—bring it to us. We will then determine whether to file it under leverage and leave Rita running, or to haul in Kurt and Angie for adversarial debriefing, or take more drastic measures. Eric, if you think Rita has been turned and is acting for a hostile agency then you already have termination authority. Or you can take the gloves off and run Rita adversarially, using Ms. Hagen and Mr. Douglas as leverage to keep her on track. It's your call. But our priority for now—I shouldn't need to remind you—is to keep the channel open while SecState and POTUS dicker with the other side. Which means Rita stays in a sandbox and doesn't know we're on to her—if indeed she's up to anything at all. When we don't need the channel anymore, or move to a more conventional system . . . then I wash my hands of her: she's all yours, and if she's been fucking around behind our back I expect you to bury her in a supermax cell for the rest of her life.

DR. SCRANTON: But until then, I suggest you watch, but don't touch.

END TRANSCRIPT

Diplomats

After dropping Kurt off back at his motel, Angie drove Rita home. Rita was so drained that she fell asleep as soon as her head hit the pillow. She awakened in mid-morning, to find Angie cooking breakfast in the small apartment's food preparation area: the smell of eggs, breakfast sausages, biscuits, and gravy finally sufficed to raise her from her bed. "You smell wonderful. I mean, you're making wonderful smells," she explained sleepily as Angie embraced her enthusiastically. "Don't set fire to the kitchen!"

It was a Saturday, and Angie had the weekend off. "I work emergency cover twice a month, but not this time," she explained as Rita ate. "Wow, they've been starving you."

"Not the job," Rita tried to explain around a mouthful of omelet. "I mean, *work* haven't been starving me. It's the hotel restaurant. There's no local competition so they serve overpriced junk food. And room service was all I got for two days."

"Two days . . ."

"There were a *lot* of meetings and interviews. 'Scuse me. You didn't hear that," she acknowledged for the sake of the (hopefully merely hypothetical) microphones. "They grilled me for days, but I got the weekend off. I'm back on the job on Monday: I may be traveling for a while, no idea when I'm going to be home. I mean, it could be three hours, it could be three weeks."

"Then we'd better make the best of what time we've got, huh?"

After breakfast Angie dragged Rita out to Target, Walgreens, and a local supermarket for food. That chewed up most of the morning, but it was unavoidable—Rita had been living out of suitcases and hotel rooms for so long that she was short on everything from toothpaste to pillowcases. In the afternoon they hit Macy's and a couple of other clothes stores to fill the gaps in Rita's wardrobe. Then they changed and headed out for dinner and an evening at Angie's favorite women-only club. Angie seemed to take inordinate joy in introducing Rita to all her friends, and Rita was more than willing to play along with it, despite the sour note of insecurity it hinted at, the faint suspicion of bitch-talk happening behind her back. The comfort of public affirmation, of having a lover whose hand she could openly hold (at least in safe spaces like this), of having someone she could get sweaty on the dance floor with and who would take her home afterward, had gone to her head. Nothing could undermine her happiness.

But in the small hours of the night Rita awakened and, finding Angie also awake, wept quiet tears on her shoulder. "What am I going to say to her?" she whispered in Angie's ear.

Angie rolled over and held her. "Ssh. It's going to be all right. Don't overthink it."

"But I didn't know!"

"So? Just tell her that. *I'm sorry, I didn't know. Can we start over?* She'll say yes."

"She must hate me—"

"I'm sure she doesn't."

Rita sniffed. "Now you're just trying to be reassuring."

"Guess I am. Wanna wipe your nose?"

"Oh God, I'm a mess." Rita sniffed, then sat up. "Back in a minute."

The flat glare of the bathroom LEDs, tweaked to a moonlight spectrum with added blacklight to aid makeup removal, turned Rita's mirror image into a skeletally shadowed death's head. She blew her nose and dabbed at her eyes, then sat down until the sniffles passed. She cradled her left arm in her right hand, playing chords on her pattern generator.

Luminous knots swirled and formed on the back of her left wrist, glowing under the UV overspill from the bathroom spots. She took care to stay in the calmly unfocused state of mind where jaunting simply didn't happen. If she slipped between the worlds in a third-floor bathroom it could be disastrous. *I can end it any time I want to,* she realized with a frisson of dread. *I'm such a fuck-up.* They must be certain she wasn't a suicide risk, otherwise they wouldn't have given her the device, she thought edgily. Then another insight struck her and she began to scroll back through the stack of saved engrams.

There was a note-taking facility, so she could add eight character long names to identify where she'd been and where the sequence of knots would take her. **Commonwe. CampSing. Station~.** *Hang on.* She squinted at the name. *That's the, the black hole, one jaunt past Camp Singularity, isn't it?* A blue-glowing halo around a blind spot, barely visible without a telescope through the thick glass cupola of the recycled space station module. She backed and then ran forward through her stack. The **Station~** engram showed up twice, for some reason, along with a bunch identified by random hexadecimal numbers rather than descriptive names. *Did they preload me with a bunch of known time lines?* she wondered. *Hey, I could go exploring on my own, if I had the stones . . .*

"You coming back to bed, sleepyhead?"

"Yeah." Rita rose and flushed. She walked slowly back to the bedroom and lay down beside Angie, who welcomed her into her open arms. "Feeling better now," she murmured.

Angie nibbled the curve of her neck amiably. "Show me," she said, and so Rita did.

AN UNDISCLOSED LOCATION, UNDISCLOSED TIME LINE, AUGUST 2020

Already numb and teetering on the edge of despair, Paulette was unable to parse her interrogator's question. Her ears couldn't make sense of the words: they were so strange, so unexpected, that she couldn't extract any kind of coherent meaning from them.

"What?"

The first interrogator: "How long have you been spying for the GDR? For East Germany? The, uh, so-called German Democratic Republic?"

She opened her eyes. The looking-glass wall reflected the chaos in her head. "What are you asking? I don't understand."

The second interrogator spoke tensely, rapidly spraying words Paulie instinctively recognized were not meant for her ears: "This is useless, I told you she doesn't—"

The voices shut off abruptly, as if a microphone had been switched off. A few seconds later the background of white noise resumed. It was the first interrogator. "Ms. Milan. How long have you been a Communist spy?"

She couldn't help herself. She could feel a deep howl welling up inside her. It was laughter born not of mirth but of despair. If she gave in, part of her knew, they'd find a way to punish her. But she began to giggle despite herself, frightened and appalled, but completely lost in the holy madness of humor. It started as a giggle, then she throttled it back to a titter—then it broke out again, in full-throated hysterical sobs of mirth and loss.

"Ms. Milan! Focus! (We're losing her. I told you—) We know who you're working for!"

"Maybe she doesn't—"

"(Trust the functional teraherz monitor.) Bullshit. Ms. Milan, Paulette, listen to me. The woman you knew as Iris Beckstein was involved with some very dubious people during the late 1980s and 1990s. You may not have known who they were, but—will you stop laughing? This is *serious*. Your future depends on it."

Paulette hiccuped. She swallowed, trying to suppress the giggles. She was shaking, she realized distantly. Behind the numbing curtain of apprehension, the sum of all fears approached: she was in the hands of maniacs, lunatics with the power of life and death. Of life and a fate worse than death. She hiccuped again, mirth morphing into gut-watering terror. "What."

"We know you have been collecting items to order and supplying them to your controller. You may think you are doing so on behalf of the narco-terrorist Gruinmarkt Clan, and you would not necessarily be wrong. However, there is more to the Clan than you are aware of. Their methods betray their motives. Have you ever asked *why* they attacked the United States, Ms. Milan? Did Miriam Beckstein ever discuss her mother's politics with you? Or her mother's fellow travelers from East Germany?"

Paulette cleared her throat. "I *know* why they attacked the United States," she said. It was as good as a confession of guilt, but in her present situation it didn't seem likely to make matters worse. The espionage charges had ripped away her right to counsel and her harbor from self-incrimination, as far as the courts since Chief Justice Scalia were concerned. "It was an internal power play by the faction with the stolen nukes. I don't even know where you're getting this crazy Germany shit from! Anyway, it's just garbage. They executed the perpetrators afterwards, by the way."

"That might be what they want you to believe," said the first interrogator, "but it's not true. Did Mrs. Beckstein—Iris Beckstein—discuss politics with you at any point? Specifically, German pre-reunification politics?"

Oh Jesus. Paulette tried very hard indeed not to roll her eyes. "Mrs. Beckstein, as you call her, was her false identity, in exile in the United States. In the Gruinmarkt she was known as Her Grace the Duchess Patricia Thorold Hjorth, younger sister of one of the most powerful lords in that nation. *She was a feudal aristocrat.* Communist revolution was *not* on her bucket list."

"And you believe that?" The first interrogator's voice rose, then the sound cut out again.

Paulette closed her eyes. *They're not just lunatics: they're amateurs,* she realized despairingly. Not that she, herself, was a trained interrogator, but she'd worked with enough journalists, back before the Internet gutted the profession, to know how you ran an interview. And she'd met enough spooks to know that once you began wandering through the funhouse mirror halls of counter-espionage, coincidences stacked up until even the most bizarre conspiracy theories came to seem credible. A high proportion of working counter-spy officers ended up receiving a medical discharge for acute paranoid psychosis. Feeding the subject your own theories was just plain *wrong*: it violated the first rule of intelligence, that information goes in, not out. And it told her that the crazies on the other side of the one-way mirror had fallen for some filter-bubble groupthink theory that the Clan was a secret cold war Communist front organization. *What happens next, do they start grilling me about the Illuminati?*

She didn't have long to wait. After about a minute the white noise returned, and with it, the voice of the second interrogator. His voice was clipped and businesslike. "Ms. Milan. It is in your best interests to ignore everything my colleague said. Not all of us are uncleared suppressives. My colleague will not trouble you again. You will now answer my questions truthfully, or not, as you wish: just remember that if you try to mess around I will fuck you up so badly you'll remember it for all your future incarnations. Do you understand?"

Paulette licked her suddenly dry lips. *Oh God, this one's* differently *crazy.* "Yes."

"All right then. First question. In 2002, from April onwards, you were in receipt of funds totaling approximately $89,560 from an unaudited source. The line of funding increased to $160,422 in fiscal year 2003. You spent the money on, among other things, rental on commercial property in Cambridge, office equipment, and vehicle lease-purchase. Who gave you the money, and what was your understanding of what you were doing with it?"

At last: a question I can answer! "Uh. That was Miriam Beckstein, you know? We'd both been laid off by *The Industry Weatherman* in early 2002, and then she discovered her long-lost relatives—it came as a big surprise to her. I didn't know what was going on until a few months later, when she dragged me out for a coffee and made me a business proposition . . ."

PHILADELPHIA, TIME LINE TWO, AUGUST 2020

Monday morning dawned cold and damp. The leaves of fall, orange and russet and brown, were piling up atop Rita's car when she said goodbye to Angie and drove to the Unit's temporary headquarters in an industrial unit in Allentown.

She parked up beside the trailer the Colonel was currently using as a site office and went inside. Smith was already at his desk and looking grumpy. *Monday morning,* she guessed. "Reporting for duty, sir," she said, hoping the formality would help defuse the tension evident in his posture.

"Sit down." He pointed: she sat. He glanced at the door as it swung closed, then slumped inside his suit coat as he looked back at her, visibly deflating. "Okay, Rita, here's the score. This is where we start to play things by ear."

"By ear," she echoed.

"Yes." He picked up another of the archaic printed-paper dossiers the operation seemed to run on and pushed it toward her. "Your Phase One jaunts were overplanned and overscrutinized because we had a very specific wish list generated by a whole bunch of stakeholders. We're now into Phase Two. Phase Two is strictly between you, me, Dr. Scranton, and our security detail. As far as the rubberneckers with clearances are concerned, Phase One is still ongoing. This file—you need to memorize it—is a narrative of your ongoing Phase One explorations. You will repeat it to anyone who asks you what you are doing who has clearance for Phase One but who is not part of Phase Two."

Rita blinked. "Just so I'm completely clear on this—you're ordering me to lie, if necessary, to superiors? To anyone who isn't in on Phase Two?"

"Yes." Colonel Smith blinked at her. His eyes were reddened and the skin under them was baggy, as if he hadn't slept for days. "And yes, I'm putting a note to that effect in writing in your HR file. Loosely enough worded to cover your ass if it blows up in our face, but not naming the specific project."

"Got it." Rita picked up the file. "What else should I be aware of?"

"Well." Smith leaned back in his chair and made a steeple of his fingertips. "In an hour or so I am expecting Dr. Scranton to show up. She'll have a sealed attaché case for you. You will deliver the case and its contents to your contacts, Ms. Thorold or Mrs. Burgeson, and to nobody else. If someone else tries to gain access the mission's a bust and you're to come straight back. Assuming it's a success, what happens afterwards—" He shrugged. "It's up to you. If they send you back, fine. But if they ask you to stay around, that would serve our purposes very well indeed. The Clan's world-walkers can't jaunt as rapidly as you can. An inherited malfunction in the way their Q-machines are activated causes a norepinephrine cascade which triggers a hypertensive crisis. They get really bad headaches: if they jaunt too often they can stroke out. So it's totally plausible for you to ask to hang around until there's a return message, and in the meantime do some sightseeing. And if you do that, they'd be idiots not to use you as a channel to feed us whatever crap they want us to know about them. So I expect them to give you a dog and pony show. And we'd be idiots not to let them, always bearing in mind that they know that we know—" The Colonel cracked a pained smile. "This rabbit hole is lined with funhouse mirrors all the way down."

"Do they know I don't have that problem?"

"Insufficient data." Smith paused. "The treatment Dr. Lane gave you fixed it at source, by the way. But you don't need to tell them that, or anything about the process. Leave them guessing. You should base your threat assessments on the assumption that they know you can jaunt rapidly, but behave in their presence as if you're sure they don't know that. Don't give it away needlessly, in other words, but don't make plans that assume the adversary is ignorant."

"So I just"—Rita glanced around—"go as I am?" She'd dressed that morning in the office attire they'd given her when she got back from her last trip: a pin-striped trouser suit and blouse, very definitely not the height of Commonwealth fashion from what little she'd seen of it.

"Yes. You are to leave all your personal effects behind, your wallet and phone and anything else you're carrying. You can take the camera and mapper—they've already seen them and you may get some use out of the kit. Dressed like that you'll stand out, but it sends the message that you're an official visitor, not a covert one."

"Okay . . ."

"There's some other stuff," Smith added impatiently. "Their rendez-vous list included printed trigger engrams for, uh, for the Gruinmarkt and for getting you to the BLACK RAIN time line. You should use those papers for your jaunts rather than your key generator. I've also got a list of keys you should load into your gizmo's memory. They're bug-out options that will take you to other time lines we've got covered, in case you get into a situation where you're actively pursued by a world-walker."

"Pursued? But if they can't jaunt repeatedly—"

"We don't *think* they can jaunt rapidly, but we *do* know they have a history of using antihypertensive medication. They'd be fools not to have thrown every research asset they've got at the problem, and if we could fix it, they might have a work-around too. So"—Smith slid another sheet of paper across the desk—"I want you to enter these knot parameters into your key generator."

"What, right now?"

"Yes. Because your next act will be to witness and sign off on me destroying this sheet of paper, which is the only extant record of the escape vectors I'm giving you."

"In case of—hmm." Rita moved the page closer and began to read. "Are you afraid they might have a spy inside DHS?" she asked quietly.

"They've been spying on us for decades. We have no idea how well-developed their HUMINT capability is, so we always assume the worst, even though we hope for the best. The crown jewels are stored on paper only, put there using a manual typewriter. We burn the ribbon afterwards. Get keying, Rita: I've got a meeting in half an hour."

"Okay." She unbuttoned her cuff and pushed her left sleeve back, then began to squeeze the trigger points. Numbers appeared in boxes on her skin, black and white tattoos depicting dot-matrix digits; they faded within a second each time she pushed the memory store button.

Smith waited patiently while she did the data entry job. Then he pulled open a drawer and removed an ancient-looking glass ashtray and a Zippo lighter. "Are you done?"

"Yes." *I hope I got them all in right*, she thought. They *should* be right: each set of coordinates came with a check digit, and the trigger generator would throw an error if she tried to enter an invalid destination. But *should* was not the same as *is*. "What now?"

"This." Smith picked up the sheet of paper and folded it twice while Rita buttoned up her sleeve. He balanced it on the ashtray, and flicked the lighter. The paper must have been specially treated: one too-bright flare of light and it crumbled into ash. "Okay, that's done. Sign here." He slid a tablet over to Rita. It displayed a form with space for signatures witnessing the destruction of whatever it was that had been burned. Evidently a log of document destruction was less of a security risk than the paper-only document itself: the difference between primary data and metadata. Rita signed, and Smith closed the file. "Good." His cheek stretched into a forced approximation of a smile. It made him look uncharacteristically insincere. "So far everything's going to plan today, which is more than could be said yesterday . . . you have another paper file to read. Eyes only. It stays in this room, and so do you, until I get back. I'll be about an hour, then we'll burn it. And then it's showtime."

BERLIN, TIME LINE THREE, AUGUST 2020

"This weather," said Elizabeth, pensively staring at the rain streaming down the outside of the tall sash windows, "is truly *vile*." It had been raining for two days, rendering excursions into town unappealing. She'd been mewed up in her suite at the grand hotel for nearly three days, unable to take any healthy outdoor exercise, and her patience was wearing thin.

"Not to worry, Your Highness!" Susannah said cheerfully, approaching her chaise from the doorway: "I have here a letter for you from Mme. Houelebecq! I'm sure it concerns the arrangements for your arrival, for term is due to start the week after next."

"Oh really." Elizabeth sighed irritably. She was, she admitted, bored. The hoped-for round of social engagements had simply not materialized. Either Berlin lacked both polite society and a bohemian alternative for it to sneer at, or the two cultures were simultaneously snubbing her. Her capacity for distracting herself with needlepoint, reading, music, and other indoor pastimes deemed suitable for a young lady of refined breeding was running low. She would be vastly happier skiing, riding, or shooting. Nor was she the prayerful kind. While Elizabeth dutifully attended the Church services that were expected of her as future head of the worldwide Anglican communion, she found them boring and fusty rather than a source of comfort. "At this rate it can't come soon enough. Open it, Suz. What does it say?"

"Ah, let's see—Your Highness, we are deeply honored by your father's request that you attend our school this year. As term commences on the seventh, we would be grateful if you could arrange for your personal effects to be transferred to our premises no later than the fourth of September. We have furnished for you a room of your own, adjacent to the headmistress's chambers. We politely request"—Susannah slowed— "because of the nature of this establishment, the presence of personal servants is discouraged? Chaperonage is provided by the mistresses of the establishment, as are the usual household functions. We recognize that Your Highness is of an unusually elevated rank to grace our humble establishment, but we would be grateful if for the duration of your residence you could consent to set aside the style of Her Majesty and instead be the Miss Elizabeth Hanover . . . well, I never saw such a thing! It's scandalous, Liz—Your Highness! The effrontery!"

"Give me that." Elizabeth took the letter from her lady-in-waiting's nerveless fingertips. She read quickly. "Hmm. Yes, I see." A faint smile emerged, like weak sunlight filtering through storm clouds. "You are overzealous, Susannah. This is not a slight. Quite the contrary: they're offering me as much anonymity as I might ask for." Her smile warmed. "I assume that Captain Bertrand has already made arrangements for discreetly securing the schloss? After all, it would be inappropriate to station soldiers inside a ladies' finishing school."

Susannah nodded weakly. "Do you want me to summon him, my lady?"

"Yes, I believe so. It will be necessary to discuss the disposition of my household, yourself included, while I attend the school. I will retain the use of these rooms for the holidays"—which she had no intention of still being in Berlin for—"and in any case I shall only be able to take a small part of my wardrobe. Yes, fetch the good captain, if you please: and also Anders"—the chauffeur, responsible for the car Elizabeth's father had provided for her use—"and Mr. Leverhulme," the butler, first among her servants. "It is time we discussed arrangements directly."

Susannah raised an eyebrow. "But—the other thing?"

"You will keep it to yourself," Elizabeth said sharply. She continued in an undertone: "Never fear, I will remember your loyalty and discretion and send for you once it is safe to do so. But for now, I have no way of knowing which of my other servants are informers on behalf of my father's chief of security."

"I understand." Susannah dipped a brief curtsey. "By your leave?"

"Go. Begone! With my thanks."

Elizabeth walked toward the rain-spattered windows as her lady-in-waiting disappeared about her business. She fanned her face with the letter as she stared across the broad avenue at the imposing town house opposite, the urban seat of some lickspittle baron or jumped-up count who had not seen fit to invite her across his threshold despite her proximity for several weeks. *Snub me, will you?* She challenged the city: *We'll see about that.* Berlin, she had decided, would go down in infamy in the annals of the royal family, not to mention her secret diary. If Berlin's bohemian artistic and philosophical salons couldn't be bothered to invite an imperial princess to dinner—if her elevated persons of privilege had a fit of the vapors at the mere idea of inviting a quadroon to a ball—then, she thought with the brutal self-confidence of late-teenage royalty—Berlin could go hang itself, and she'd happily pay for the rope.

As for the school, well: their offer of an *incognito* identity might come in very useful indeed, if the Major's arrangements failed to come to fruition before the start of term. And if he was late, or—being prudent—if circumstances changed in such a way as to force her to review her planned defection, then at least it would make for a less stultifyingly claustrophobic year than would otherwise be her fate.

PHILADELPHIA, TIME LINE TWO/NEW LONDON, TIME LINE 3, AUGUST 2020

It was three o'clock in the afternoon when Dr. Scranton finally arrived with the promised attaché case. Rita, nesting in a corner of the Colonel's office, had managed to memorize most of his semi-indigestible dossier of lies. Despite not feeling at all hungry she'd forced down a tasteless ham sandwich for lunch. It was probably for the best: Scranton was impatient to get things moving. "Come on," she said briskly, "let's get you on your way."

"Okay." Rita stood. Her legs felt leaden. The idea of seeing Mrs. Burgeson again filled her stomach with dreadful embarrassment. *Mortifying.* She picked up her handbag. "Uh, Colonel, can I leave this here?"

"Stick it under my desk." Smith was carrying a leather satchel. He now opened it for her to see. "This contains the same camera and mapper you carried on your last trip. If you can use them, fine, but don't shed any tears if the opposition confiscate them." There was a side pocket sized for an old laptop computer. Scranton handed him the attaché case and he slid it inside. "All yours," he said.

"Witnessed," said Scranton, as Rita accepted the bag gingerly. "Let's go, people. I have a plane to catch."

Miss Thorold's list of secure transfer locations and times ran to several pages, listing times and GPS coordinates where a world-walker—Rita, by implication—would be met by a reception committee. The locations had given the Colonel (and everybody else with an interest in operational security) a bad case of heartburn because of what it implied about the Commonwealth's ability to spy on US territory. (GPS coordinates were not, after all, a natural measuring system.) But it made it considerably easier for them to find the rendezvous, Rita had to admit.

Gomez was waiting in the parking lot in an official sedan. Rita, Dr. Scranton, and Smith climbed in, and Gomez took off, heading for the interstate on autopilot.

The transfer location was in a big green space in Union, off the Garden State Parkway. Gomez parked the car in the lot next door to a McDonald's, and they crossed the road into Kawameeh Park together. The trees alongside the avenue cut them off from traffic and the incurious gaze of restaurant customers alike. "This looks to be the place," Gomez murmured, checking their location on her phone.

"Close enough for government work," Dr. Scranton murmured with a small, ironic smile. "Colonel, please proceed."

"Rita." Smith squinted at her, half-worried: "It's three forty-six. You've got a two-hour window, starting at three, ending at five. We'll be waiting over the road in McD's until five, if you need to come straight back. Otherwise, Gomez or Jack will be waiting at each three 'til five transfer window until you show, for the next week."

"And, uh, if I come back prematurely and not via a scheduled window or rendezvous—"

"Don't worry, we'll know," Smith said with total self-assurance. "It may take up to an hour for us to have somebody pick you up, though."

"It *could* take that long," Gomez agreed, sparing Rita an amiably menacing glower.

"Right." Rita rubbed the inside of her left elbow, near the persistent phantom itch caused by the map generator implant. *You don't even care that I know you chipped me like a cat, do you?* She forced a smile, shifted the shoulder-strap of the bag so that it hung more comfortably against her hip, then raised the printed card. She clicked her heels: "I'm gone."

Staring at the knot on the card felt subtly different from focusing on an e-ink tattoo, but it had the same effect. Rita jaunted. The grass in the Gruinmarkt's shattered time line was damp: a light rain fell. She flipped the card, then jaunted again, blinked, and swallowed to clear her ears as they popped with the pressure change.

The ground beneath her feet had changed from grass to cement. Where there had been trees there was now a wall with shuttered double doors: rails ran under it. The far side of the compound was stacked with the discarded Lego brick shapes of multimodal freight containers. They were indistinguishable from the ones so widely used back home because they were copied from them, of course. *It's another stockyard*, Rita realized, turning on her heel. Then she saw a pair of bodies in double-breasted greatcoats and peaked hats walking toward her. One of them waved. "Ah, Miss Douglas. We meet again."

"Um, yes. Yes, we do." Rita swallowed. It was Inspector Morgan of the Commonwealth Transport Police, accompanied by a tall man with a mustache luxuriant enough that if nailed to a pole it could serve as a broom. The Inspector's expression was deadpan. "You're my reception committee?" asked Rita.

"The Commissioner requested my services. And had your arrest warrant quashed." The Inspector sniffed, looking her up and down with a raised eyebrow. "I have a car waiting. Miss Thorold is expecting you."

Someone had been briefed, or chosen for her discretion, Rita realized. At any rate, the Inspector passed no comment on her outfit.

This time there were no handcuffs or blindfolds. The car was something of a shock to Rita. It seemed bulky and crude, but was bulbous and smooth, like a sixties muscle machine that had been subjected to a wind tunnel and streamlining then stripped of all the chrome brightwork. There were no electronics to speak of, but a two-way radio (with dials, yet) bolted under the dash. "In the back, please," said Inspector Morgan. "The seat belt is mandatory."

At least it *had* seat belts, even if you had to tighten them with a lever. Rita strapped herself in as Mr. Mustache made the starter motor shriek. It seemed to go on for a long time before the engine caught, and he kept gunning the throttle for some reason. The whole car shook as it crept toward a side entrance that Rita hadn't seen for the shipping containers. "Is the engine all right?" she asked, worried by the odd sounds and the vibration.

"Why wouldn't it be?" Inspector Morgan craned her head round. "It's only a year old."

"Oh." Rita shrugged. So they had cars, with seat belts and head restraints and a big-block engine—a V-8 by the sound—that gurgled and snarled as it drank gasoline. But it felt curiously crude and unfinished, lacking the dozens of computers and electric motors that made even Rita's ancient Acura feel like a real car. *This must be what they were* all *like in the old days*, she realized.

"Floor it, Greg," Morgan told her driver, then reached up for the grab-handle. Rita braced herself as Greg mashed the gas pedal and the car surged forward. There was a road outside the stockyard, but it was quite unlike the interstate she'd arrived by with the Colonel and Dr. Scranton. This one was three lanes wide in each direction, but the inner two lanes were occupied by streetcar rails, and the outermost lane was rendered inaccessible by a raised curb. Seconds later Rita realized why, as they rushed past a clot of motor-assisted bicycles.

Rita settled back for the ride, peering at the urban landscape flashing past to either side. She occupied herself by taking mental notes. Houses here looked very different. There seemed to be lots of three- and four-story apartment blocks, with streetcar stops outside their shared entrances. Dense urban farms or community gardens plugged block-sized gaps. The sidewalks were lined with tiny shops at street level, apartments piled above them. In the distance, smoke-spouting factory towers loomed. Businesses—warehouses, even small factories—were scattered throughout the residential suburbs as if zoning laws didn't exist. Bicycles were everywhere, as were delivery vans, trucks, buses, and streetcars. There were surprisingly few private automobiles.

Eventually they turned onto a recognizable cloverleaf, and then an ascending overpass that joined a bicycle-free highway in the sky. Greg accelerated to a precarious-feeling sixty miles per hour as they shot toward Staten Island and beyond, the lights of the imperial city glowing against the darkening sky in the east.

Rita's stomach clenched at the prospect of the meeting to come. If she was lucky Olga would take the pouch and send her straight back to Dr. Scranton. If she was lucky Mrs. Burgeson wouldn't be in town. No uneasy confrontation, no brittle silences, and no fraught conversational minefields lay in her future—if her luck held out. *Who am I kidding?* she wondered dismally as the road deck flew through a painted cage of red bridge trusses, carrying her toward an alien future.

The demands of empire imposed a certain kind of architectural similarity on capital cities and administrative centers. The common need for large ministerial buildings within easy walking distance of mass transit made for similar layouts. An outer loop road, with modern office blocks sprawling to either side of it, formed a defensible perimeter around inner avenues that were closed to most vehicle traffic. Police or soldiers in discreet checkpoints controlled access to the palaces, courts, and legislative chambers in the middle. That was how it was in Baltimore now, and how it had been in D.C. before the attack. In the case of New London there was a wall around the entire complex—a fortification dating to the late eighteenth century. The bones of the fortress city were still visible through the flab of modern construction, with sloping ramparts recessed into ditches to resist direct cannon fire, polygonal bastions poised to rain fire down on the heads of any force trying to storm the royal residences. These days, the ditches had been turned into sunken gardens and the bastions held only ceremonial guns. Nevertheless, as her ministerial limo approached a ramp leading into an underpass beneath the bastions, Rita's breath caught in her throat. The wall enclosed the entire southern quarter of Manhattan Island, as if a gigantic pre-industrial Death Star had fallen to earth. It must have soaked up the sweated labor of hundreds of thousands of slaves or captured enemies, back in the early years of the Hanoverian ascendancy over the Americas. "Where are we going?" she asked.

"I'm to take you directly to Miss Thorold's office," said the Inspector. "She will be able to tell you more."

"Wh-where exactly is that?" *What does Miss Thorold do when she isn't commandeering police officers and military transport helicopters?* Rita wanted to ask. *She said she used to run the Clan's security organization, whatever that was . . .*

"In the Department of Para-historical Research offices." Lights strobed by overhead as Greg took the underpass.

"And the Department of Para-historical Research is what, exactly . . . ?"

She caught the Inspector watching her in the vanity mirror of her sun visor. "What the name says: they explore parallel time lines and deal with security issues. Much like your Homeland Security organization, I believe?"

"I, um—" Rita was still trying to work out what to ask next as the car slowed and turned into a side route that led to the surface. They turned again onto a quiet side street that ran between anonymous marble-clad neoclassical office buildings—an architectural style that this time line seemed to have inherited from the same Roman lineage as her own. Greg braked, then drove through a pair of wrought iron gates and stopped at a barrier. He lowered his side window to converse quietly with a uniformed guard. Rita couldn't help noticing the other soldiers who stood well back behind the barrier, holding submachine guns. Whatever Greg told the guard worked: seconds later the barrier rose and the man stepped back from the car, saluting as it crept forward. "What is Miss Thorold's position in the Department? I mean, who is she?"

"Didn't she tell you?" Inspector Morgan sounded surprised. The car slid to a halt in a courtyard beside a broad flight of marble steps leading up to a portico-fronted entrance. Greg got out from behind the steering wheel and opened the passenger door for Rita. "She's the Director of Covert Operations, Ms. Douglas. Congratulations: you have come to the attention of very important people . . ."

NEW LONDON, TIME LINE THREE, AUGUST 2020

The steps were not particularly steep. Nevertheless, Rita's heart was pounding by the time she reached the reception desk in the echoing, imposing atrium. Inspector Morgan got there first. "Signing in a visitor," she said, presenting her badge. "Rita Douglas, VIP code. She's expected."

The men behind the desk wore comic-opera uniforms but had the universal hallmark of security: a gimlet gaze Rita associated with cops, suspicious of everyone. "Yes, ma'am," said the guard Morgan had addressed. His colleague turned to a Rolodex-like file. "Rita Douglas, for . . . ?"

"For Olga Thorold."

A slight stiffening told Rita that this was both the correct answer, and a significant one. Guard number two pulled forth a printed card badge and a lanyard. "Wear this at all times," he told Rita. "Stay with your guide. Good day, Inspector."

"Good day," said Morgan, as Rita slid the lanyard over her head. "Come on." She strode toward a bank of elevators in the shadow of a wide, formal staircase. Rita hurried to keep up. Greg, the driver, followed behind. *Stay with your guide*, she repeated silently.

Despite the neoclassical exterior, this was clearly a more modern office, functional in design and lacking the intricate cornicework and classical paintings of the other building. There were fire doors and she caught glimpses of cubicle-partitioned office pools beneath old-style fluorescent tube lighting. There was background noise: telephones ringing (their tonal cadence and pitch unfamiliar) and people talking. Once, they passed a widening in the corridor that was occupied by photocopiers, giant hulking things operated by uniformed men and women who serviced the copy requests of the office workers. Their uniforms were weirdly retro—bicorn hats and blue wool tunics with gold frogging—but formal uniforms always lagged public fashions. What caught Rita's attention was the way they were worn, with everyday touches seldom seen in theatrical costumes. Here a patched elbow, there a belt with a worn leather pouch, pencils and a ruler protruding. Some things, however, seemed to be universal—like the signs saying NO SMOKING.

They came to a closed door fronted by a desk and another security guard. "Passes, please." Rita held up her badge. "Proceed." The door hissed open in response to an invisible switch. Beyond it lay another corridor, this time decorated with thicker carpet, wooden paneled walls, and the paintings that had been missing from the outer offices.

They came to a door that was ajar: Morgan knocked. "Come in," called a male voice. "Hello, Alice. I see you've brought us Ms. Douglas?"

Rita stared at the speaker. He was skinny, a little over six feet tall, and somewhere in the indeterminate thirties. He wore an expression of intense curiosity behind his pince-nez. His suit was a fusty black and looked decidedly lived-in: the only spot of color was a peacock-bright cravat, worn inside the black stand-up collar of his shirt. "That's me," she admitted. "Who are you?"

Morgan cleared her throat. "This is—" she began, just as the fellow said, "Your second cousin once removed, I believe. Huw Hjorth, at your service."

"The Explorer-General," Morgan added, after a stuttering, uncomfortable pause. "Sir." She ducked her head in his direction.

"Olga asked me to meet you here," Huw added. "She'll be ready in a minute. In the meantime, please come in and take a seat . . ."

It was clearly a public office, with a big—and empty—desk, and two doors at the back of the room, presumably leading to an inner sanctum. Huw, Rita noted, didn't take the chair behind the desk. Was he just another guest? "What kind of Exploration do you . . ." Rita stopped, suddenly acutely aware that while curiosity was her job, too much curiosity was reputedly felicidal: and that she had a police officer for an escort, even though Morgan appeared to be doing her best to fade into the wallpaper.

Huw Hjorth looked amused. "Let's not mess around, you probably already figured we're in the business of opening up new time lines, don't you? So that's my job—supervising that."

"And you're my, uh—"

"All world-walkers are relatives, if you trace it back far enough." He shrugged. "It's the family trade." A familiar noise emanated from behind one of the doors: "Ah, she'll be with us in a minute or two."

"Oh." Rita moved her messenger bag around to her front and wrapped her arms around it. The flushing toilet reminded her that she'd been on the move for nearly three hours now. "Does that mean you're related to, uh, Mrs. Burgeson?"

"Distantly." Huw's smile slipped. "Inspector, I thank you for bringing Ms. Douglas to us, but I think we can handle things from here, and we have matters to discuss that you don't have need to know."

"I think I'll just wait here until Miss Thorold emerges and then I'll take my leave, if you don't mind." Morgan's tone sharpened. "Orders."

"Have it your way." The leftmost door swung outward, revealing its occupant. "Miss Thorold? Miss Douglas, as requested."

"Good." Olga raised a handkerchief to her face. "Thank you very much, Inspector: please leave us now."

"Certainly." Morgan gave Huw an unreadable look, then turned and marched away, her back straight.

Huw stood and closed the door behind her, then turned to Olga. "Do you need anything?" he asked, clearly sounding concerned.

Olga waved him off. "I'll be all right," she said. Then, to Rita: "I'm glad you could come. Do you have anything for me?"

Rita reached inside her bag and touched the attaché case. "I have a message for Mrs. Burgeson. Or you."

"Well, then."

Rita pulled out the case and made as if to hand it over. "Ah, no," said Olga. "If you'd put it over there on the side table, please? Over—"

"Wait," said Huw. "Let me open it. I'm disposable."

He reached for the case but Rita pulled it back: "What?" she demanded shrilly.

"Stop it, both of you!" Miss Thorold barely raised her voice, but Rita and Huw both froze. "Huw, you're not thinking. Rita, please accept my apologies. Now put the bag on the side table and step over here." She gestured to the opposite side of her desk.

Rita complied. The side table in question was oddly undecorated, and featured a bulky metal body, trailing what looked to be a power cable. "What's that?" she asked.

Olga picked up the bulky telephone handset and punched in a number. "Security Office? Miss Thorold speaking. Please send the duty screening officer up to my office. Yes, now." She put the phone down. "Rita, the last time your employers sent Miri—Mrs. Burgeson—a personal message, it exploded. Obviously I don't expect them to do anything so stupid this time around, but I *have* been known to err on the side of optimism. Huw, you are not even *remotely* disposable. Neither is Rita: in fact, none of us are. So let's refrain from opening the package until the specialists have pronounced it safe, shall we?"

"You think they'd give me a *bomb*?" Rita demanded.

"Not if they're negotiating in good faith." Olga wheeled up to her desk. For the first time Rita noticed that it sported a recognizable computer—not one of the strange Commonwealth boards and vacuum tube displays, but familiar QWERTY and a flat-panel monitor. The side of the desk opposite its occupant was solid, as if it was designed to provide protection. "But last time we dealt with the US government directly they played dirty, and it's not my job to take risks." There was a knock at the door. "Answer it," she told Huw. As he did so she glanced at Rita and half-smiled. "Younger cousins: answering doors and running sub-departments is all they're good for."

A uniformed woman entered. "Where's the package?" she asked.

"There. I want a non-destructive check on it. I had a fluoroscope sent up—"

"Got it." The screening officer picked up the attaché case then opened the lid of the table—no, the fluoroscope—and placed the case on a shelf inside. "If you'd stand back, please?"

"What for—" began Rita.

"Metal zipper, paper clips. Am I expecting anything else?"

"No, that's all," Miss Thorold said. "As long as there are no unpleasant surprises you can switch it off now."

Huw turned to Rita. "It's a portable X-ray machine," he explained. "Nineteenth-century technology, actually." He walked over to the fluoroscope and accepted the package from the screening officer, then presented it to Miss Thorold. "All yours."

"Good." Olga waited until the screening officer was finished and had left, then unzipped the case. She reached inside and removed a slim white envelope. "How civilized."

"Watch out for white powder," warned Huw.

"Now *that* would be amateurish. And Colonel Smith is not an amateur." Olga slit the envelope open, then read rapidly. There were several pages. "All right, this is going to take some time to respond to." She put the letter down. "I'm going to have to take it to Miriam, and then we're going to have to formulate a suitable response." She looked at Rita. "Have you thought about what I said last time we met?"

Rita swallowed as she nodded. "Yes."

"Well then." Olga tapped a finger on the letter. "If you want to, you can go back right away. The Inspector will take you to a surveyed transfer point. I don't know how long this is going to take, but we won't have anything for you before the day after tomorrow at the earliest—my guess is this will take three or four days of meetings to thrash out a response. So you can go home and check in every day for our reply, *or* you can stay here until we've got a take-home for you." Her cheek twitched. "I'm sure your boss gave you a nudge along those lines."

"How did you know?"

Olga ignored the question. "Huw, seeing you're in town for a few days, would you like to play host? I'm sure you can give Rita a useful and informative tour of our department's public activities, and—" Huw cleared his throat. "What?"

"In case you'd forgotten, my wife's *also* in town this week." Rita glanced back and forth between Olga and Huw. Their body language was coded, opaque: it suggested the presence of a long-running subtext that she was not privy to. Almost as if they were actual, not figurative, family members. "We planned to throw a small dinner party tonight." His gaze slid sideways to take in Rita. "You'd be very welcome, but I gather your last meeting with Miriam didn't go too well and she'll be there. What do you say?"

"I, uh—" Rita froze like a deer in the headlights of an onrushing truck. "But I didn't bring any spare clothes, I don't have anywhere to stay, and, um—"

"That can all be seen to," Huw said briskly. "Brill and I are rattling around in a nearly empty town house, and I'm sure she can find you something to wear. Also—"

"If I'm serious about pushing the reset button this is my chance," Rita said slowly, making eye contact with Miss Thorold. "That's what this is about, isn't it? Am I allowed to say no?"

Olga spoke gravely. "Yes, Rita, you are allowed to say no." She hesitated momentarily, then added: "But I think you'll regret it afterwards if you do."

"Well then." Rita bit her lip. Sometimes knowing you *could* say no made it easier to say *yes*. "All right." She looked at Huw. "Thank you for your invitation. If you're sure it'll be all right? You know we, um, had a bad misunderstanding?"

"I think everyone does by now," he said drily. Rita tried not to cringe. "All right." He stood. "Let me take you home and introduce you to Brill. I think you'll like her. Then tomorrow we can give you a tour of the capital, just to keep your boss happy . . ."

Learning Exercises

Okay, this is a setup, Rita told herself as Huw led her to a rear exit opening onto a long driveway. *It's all about family. Because that's how these people roll.* "You're related to Miss Thorold, aren't you?" she asked.

"Yes. We're first cousins, actually," Huw added, waving in the direction of a black limousine. It slowly rolled toward them, gravel crunching under tires. "The world-walking ability is a recessive trait, so the Clan practiced first cousin marriages. A *lot* of first cousin marriages." The car arrived beside him, and he opened the rear door: "After you, my lady." He said *my lady* as if he meant it, totally unironically. Rita boggled slightly as she slid across an acre of high-grade leather, unsure whether to feel insulted or flattered. Huw leaned close to the sliding window that separated them from the human chauffeur. "To the residence, please."

The limousine slowly made its way down the drive. "So, um. You're the Explorer-General?" she asked, succumbing to the anxious impulse to fill an uncomfortable silence. After all, she was alone in the back of a limo with a strange man: and while Huw was anything but threatening, she had no idea what she should do. "What does that mean?"

"It means I mostly front a bureaucracy and set policy these days." He busied himself with a seat belt. Either VIPs weren't above traffic stops here, or it was a habit he'd picked up somewhere else. "It used to consist of three people and a dog, but over time it sort of grew. Now . . . we've got research institutes, remote exploration bases in other time lines, university departments studying everything we find, cooperatives and companies supplying us with specialized equipment. Thousands of people, really: tens of thousands, even. Managing it is a committee process, but it helps to have a front man." He sat back. "It's much the same job that the DHS's Para-time Transportation Safety Agency does, facilitating industrial and scientific access to other worlds."

"You know about the PTSA."

He caught her eye and nodded. "Yes. You're wondering if we're spying on the United States, aren't you?" It was Rita's turn to nod. "Well, we'd be idiots not to, wouldn't we? After what the USA did to the Gruinmarkt."

Although inarguably true, his reply killed the conversation for a while. Luckily the ride was short. The limo left the driveway and cruised through a curving maze of row houses—all of them remarkably well-maintained—until, less than a mile later, it halted outside a white-painted three-story dwelling fronted by cast iron railings. Behind the railings a flight of steps arched across an open-topped cellar with basement windows, ending at a front door trimmed with polished brasswork. "Welcome to my town house," said Huw. "It's where Brill and the kids and I live when we're here—in the city—on business. We don't own it, it's an official residence."

"When you're not in the city"—she was already on the front steps—"where do you live?"

He smiled. "Wherever they send me," he said as he opened the door and called, "Hi honey, I'm home!"

Someone, Rita told herself, *is laying it on too thick.*

"Halloo!" The answering war cry came from a parlor adjacent to the front hallway of the house. It was clearly a woman's voice: seconds later she bounced through the doorway and grabbed Huw in a bear hug, then detached from him and took Rita's hand. "I'm Brill. You must be Rita? I've heard so much about you!" Brill pumped Rita's arm as if it were the crank handle of an ancient car, staring into her eyes as she did so. Brill overflowed with a dangerous energy, but seemed genuinely delighted to see her. In her mid-thirties, a brunette verging on redhead, she wore the tunic-over-trousers combination that Rita was beginning to peg as the equivalent of a trouser-suit in the Commonwealth. "Come in, come on in. Are you going to be staying with us? Not just for dinner, I mean, we have a spare bedroom. Clothes, if you need them—you're about Nel's size, and I'm sure she won't mind until we can get you some made?"

"I, uh, that is—" Rita spent a couple of seconds untangling her tongue. "Yes, I guess so." *You all just want to meet the long-lost cousin, don't you?* On the other hand: *points for not flipping out over my skin color.* If Colonel Smith wanted her to spend time between courier jaunts getting a handle on the local culture, this was a golden opportunity—just as long as she could stomach it. *Act the part,* she thought. *These people never abandoned you. They didn't even know you existed.* The idea of suddenly discovering a small army of long-lost blood relatives made her feel curiously unbalanced, as if she'd opened a wardrobe door to discover a pathway lined with streetlights leading through a twilit snowed-in forest. She just wished she knew what the Wicked Witch was planning for her. "If it's not impolite, can I ask about your family connection?"

"It's not impolite." Brill led her into the parlor, which was furnished to excess with floral-fabric flounced drapes, flocked wallpaper, and club chairs: "I was Helge's lady-in-waiting at Court in Niejwein. Uh, that's the Duchess Helge, as she was called there. You probably know her as Miriam Beckstein. Your mother."

Rita boggled. "A lady-in-waiting? What did you do?"

"Oh, the usual: manage her household, escort her to formal functions, look good in a ball gown, shoot assassins. I was assigned by the head of Clan Security, initially as an informer and personal protection detail, but I swore personal fealty when she became queen and organized her bodyguard—"

Suddenly there was an over-stuffed chair under Rita's backside. She was extremely grateful for its presence. "Became *what?*" she squeaked.

"Queen of the Gruinmarkt, in the middle of a really nasty civil war. Huw, would you be a dear and sort out coffee for us? She needed bodyguards badly back then, there were a number of assassination attempts between the coup and the miscarriage—"

The room spun around Rita's head. "Miscarriage?"

"You were supposed to have a younger brother," Brill said, peering at her from the opposite chair, head tilted to one side. "You can blame medieval dynastic politics and a very unscrupulous doctor. I'm sorry to dump this on you so fast, but I'm assuming nobody gave you a briefing—I can cut through the bullshit because I'm your mother's right hand and she expects me to deal with this stuff. Internal Clan politics is nothing like as important as it used to be, but they'll all have been walking on eggshells around you, and you need to understand the family politics in case you accidentally say something inappropriate. Your mother—back before the Gruinmarkt holocaust—grew up in the USA in ignorance of all this, much like yourself, but she was shoved into a position of power while the Clan was in the middle of a civil war. Initially she was set up as a puppet figurehead by her mother, who was running a coup against *her* mother, but Miriam learned just enough political judo to turn it into this, this exile. The Clan doesn't officially exist anymore and the Commonwealth has other plans for producing new world-walkers. But she's still the leader of the modernist faction. And here in the Commonwealth, she and her husband of fifteen years are now very important People's Commissioners."

Rita shook her head numbly. *My mother was a* queen? *What the fuck does that even* mean, *am I a princess or something? What* is *a princess, anyway?* Disney images of carefree young women in enormous pink frocks vied with a more cynical definition. *A princess is the larval reproductive host in the life cycle of a parasitic hereditary dictatorship,* as Kurt had told her after one Disney-induced, sugar-fueled, pre-teen meltdown too many. The bit about a missing younger brother she would shelve until later: *I've already got a younger brother, he's called River, and he's a pest.* "What's a Commissioner?"

"We've got a politburo that's elected by the Party membership and approved by the Council of Guardians. The politburo in turn elects a number of Commissioners to run important ministries. The politburo sets policy and the Commissioners keep the, the civil service—Miriam calls it the Deep State—on track to execute those policies. Meanwhile, the Chamber of People's Magistrates are elected directly by the public, they're lawmakers, but the Deep State holds everything together at a constitutional level. Your mother runs the Ministry of Intertemporal Technological Intelligence, which is tasked with accelerating the industrial and scientific development of the Commonwealth. Erasmus—her husband—is the Minister of Propaganda. Or the Minister of Happy Fun Distraction, as he calls it. He's in charge of television, radio, newspapers, and the movie industry. Oh, and computer games once we start building consoles: the first eight bit games platforms are due for rollout next year. He's basically the chief censor."

"*Censor?*" Rita squeaked.

"Yeah, he's a regular Joseph Goebbels." Brilliana's cheek twitched in something that might have been a wink. "Wears a swastika armband and personally blue-pencils the headlines every morning. Um, no: it doesn't work that way. The Commonwealth is a democracy and we are *supposed* to have freedom of speech, so the tools of political propaganda and censorship have to be a lot more subtle than in a monarchy or a dictatorship. Ras is a big fan of Noam Chomsky; calling it the Propaganda Ministry keeps things honest, he says. Like having a Ministry of War rather than a Department of Defense, or Counting Other People's Murdered Children instead of talking about Collateral Damage." *Now* her cheek twitched. "We try to learn from other folks' mistakes. Especially when lives are at stake."

Overload. Rita shoved her hair back from her forehead as Huw entered the room. A woman in what was probably this culture's version of a maid's uniform followed him, pushing a trolley bearing a French press and a set of china coffee cups. "I think my head's going to explode," she said.

"I know, dear. That's why I wanted to drop it on you *right now*, before you're doorstepped by face-stealers. Paparazzi, I mean." Brill turned to the coffee trolley. "How do you take it? Milk, sugar? I'm sorry, we don't have artificial sweeteners."

Rita mentally translated *latte* into old-school filter coffee: "Milk, no sugar, thanks." *Paparazzi?*

"She may be under the impression she's still a covert asset," Huw remarked, watching Brilliana like a hawk. "Olga hasn't scheduled her first press conference yet."

Brill flinched as she poured, almost spilling the coffee. "Impossible!" she protested.

Rita tensed. "Imposs—"

"If we keep her under wraps"—Brill offered the coffee cup to Rita—"I'm sorry, but if we keep *you* under wraps, you're vulnerable. You've got to understand: the existence of the Clan, and of the United States, has been common knowledge within the Radical Party for seventeen years. It's been public knowledge for the past fifteen. Miriam has run her election campaigns within the politburo on the slogan *The United States is coming* for the past decade and a half, and you are the living proof of that proposition.

"If we don't show you in public, SCEP will find a pretext to arrest you at the first opportunity. You'll be a pawn in an internal power struggle. But if we make a public announcement and show you in public, then anyone who tries to touch you has just publicly declared open season on two government ministers and a diplomatic courier from another superpower, and I'm pretty sure Miriam and Erasmus can lean on the Foreign Office to give you limited diplomatic immunity."

"But I—" Rita floundered, then raised her coffee cup for a sip. It rattled noisily when she lowered it back to the saucer. "I don't want this! I had no idea!"

"Tough." Brill looked at her husband, who nodded then picked up the thread.

"Rita, you're here as a go-between, admittedly at a low level, in the process of arranging direct talks between two governments. Even if they're just talks about how and when to start having *real* talks, and even if the news is under lockdown and embargo in the United States, it's not a secret *here*. We can't cover up the Air Force shooting down drones with nuclear-tipped missiles off the New England coastline, as happened a few months ago. Or the Continental Bombardment Force going to war alert. Everyone wants to know what's going down. Oh, and there's going to be a snap election some time in the next few months"—Rita saw Huw and

Brilliana exchange a sharp look of worry—"which Miriam will be involved in, and which will influence the direction of those negotiations."

"But I don't even know if I can talk to her!" There, she'd said it. She planted the half-empty cup on a side table with a loud rattle: coffee slopped over the edge and pooled in the saucer.

"Try," Huw said bluntly. "If not for yourself, then for everybody else." His eyebrows furrowed. "For your own people, whoever they are."

"My own people are—" Rita's tongue stuck to the roof of her mouth. A wolf pack with no leader, roaming a forest in the grip of an eternal winter, starving for lack of purpose. *Who are my people, really?* She shook her head. "I'll try."

"And you'll stay for dinner?" Brilliana smiled.

"Of course."

"Good. Then I'll show you the spare room and bath, and we can find something for you to wear . . ."

BERLIN, TIME LINE THREE, AUGUST 2020

Boredom is the midwife of mischief. And Elizabeth was nothing if not bored. Winnowing her wardrobe for a season at school hardly occupied her mind, the weather was too vile for sports, and Captain Bertrand was uneasy about her desire to explore the city. Perhaps her security detail had spotted the Major when he made contact. Nothing had been said to her, but the sudden solicitude of her guard gripped her like too-tight stays, suffocating in the name of propriety.

After a week of waiting, with only a couple of days to go to her departure for the schloss, Elizabeth cracked. There was a protocol. *We should meet and talk about arrangements*, she wrote. *I cannot leave. Can you meet me here?*

An unwelcome answer arrived the next day. *No. Security perimeter too tight: will contact you at Schloss Britz next Tuesday.—H.*

Elizabeth frowned, reread the note twice, then tore it into tiny scraps and fed it to the drafty fire that rumbled flatulently beneath the stone chimney breast in her sitting room. *Idiot*, she thought petulantly. Whether she meant herself or her correspondent was immaterial. But she'd done what she could, so she dismissed the matter and instead summoned Susannah to give her a list of items she required for the opening term.

Mme. Corinne Houelebecq was fifty-five, pretty in a somewhat retiring kind of way—not remotely in keeping with Elizabeth's image of the headmistress of an exclusive finishing school—and still wore half-mourning for her husband, even though the Baron had died more than four years previously. "Good day, Miss Hanover," she started, then smiled tremulously, like a flower opening. "Welcome to my establishment. Please follow me? First I shall show you your rooms, then I thought we might take tea together." She turned and glided toward the central hall, without waiting to see if Elizabeth would follow.

"Suz, I'll be in touch." Elizabeth gripped her lady-in-waiting's hand.

"Really?" Susannah seemed adrift, almost frightened. Behind her, the porters were already leaving, having deposited a neat row of trunks alongside the door to the servants' quarters. Outside, Captain Bertrand's guards had finished checking the grounds and would henceforth maintain their watch from a discreet distance. "You'll write every day?"

"Of course." At least, at first. Liz squeezed her hand again, then glanced at Mme. Houelebecq, who showed no sign of noticing. "Remember, I'll make arrangements to summon you to me. Hold tight!" She leaned forward and kissed Susannah impulsively, then pulled back before the woman could respond. "*Au revoir*."

"A close friend, your maid," Mme. Houelebecq commented tonelessly as she mounted the stairs.

"Lady-in-waiting, actually," Elizabeth said. Then, momentarily, corrected herself: "Maidservant, if you like. That would be best here, wouldn't it?"

"Yes." Mme. Houelebecq reached the landing halfway to the second floor and paused. Elizabeth looked down on black-and-white marble tiles framed by carved oak rails, then glanced up at the marvelous crystal chandelier, studded with unlit electrical bulbs. The wallpaper was silk, perhaps in tribute to the eighteenth-century owner who had introduced silk farming to Prussia. "The other girls are of noble birth, but I believe we have only one other royal this year, and no other heirs. Jealousy is very unbecoming and it would be best not to give it any opportunity to take hold. Don't you agree?"

"Yes, I think." Elizabeth chose her next words carefully. "They will work out who I am easily enough, but as long as I do not wave it in their faces there will be no friction."

"Not true, alas." Mme. Houelebecq sighed. "There is *always* friction. But you do not need to pour flammable spirits on them, if you follow my meaning. Your father's instructions to me were very specific on the matter."

"Ah." They came to the head of the staircase: a long corridor that connected the second-floor function rooms, the gallery overlooking the main ballroom, and the wings of the house where the apartments lay. "I think so."

Elizabeth's rooms were not spacious, but they were sufficient for a single lady of noble birth, traveling without the circus-sized retinue that would be expected of a crown princess. She had a bedroom adjoining a small study with a desk and a high-set window. A door in the study led to a small room that had originally been a privy (now equipped with a flushing toilet, thank God) and an enameled iron bathtub. The bedroom held two narrow beds. "The other girls share: you will not be expected to do so," Mme. Houelebecq told her.

Elizabeth looked up at the study windows. "Are these safe?" she asked.

"I am sure the gendarmes have found them so. Come now."

Mme. Houelebecq led her back along the corridor, back stiff and gaze directed ahead. The schloss felt curiously empty and hollow, like a jaw without a tongue, expectantly awaiting the animating spirit of gossip. Elizabeth had been invited to move in a few days ahead of term, so that she could be settled before the other girls arrived—and perhaps to ensure that she was dutifully playing her new role as a biddable young lady rather than an imperial power. Elizabeth followed the headmistress, keeping her reservations to herself. It was a game, that was all: a new and mildly interesting distraction, but not a role she should take seriously. It was not as if she intended to live within its constraints for long.

Mme. Houelebecq lived in a small suite on the third floor, directly above Elizabeth's rooms—the east wing had been extended upward at some time in the nineteenth century—with a parlor in which to receive visitors. Once Elizabeth was settled in a chair and the maids had served tea and withdrawn, Madame unwound very slightly. Expression returned to her face as she inspected Elizabeth over the rim of her teacup. "I imagine you are wondering why you are here so early," she said. "Are you?"

"Yes, madame." Elizabeth nodded. She could do *biddable* when it served her needs.

"I thought it best to take a look at you in isolation, as it were." Mme. Houelebecq's expression was cool, and for a moment Elizabeth had an alarming premonition that the headmistress had seen right through her. "This is an unusual occurrence, you understand. I would be astonished if you were not already adequately educated in etiquette and court protocol, not to mention the other arts and graces that we attempt to instill in our girls. It would be sheer dereliction of duty on the part of your tutors had they not done so. But you have probably not spent much time among the social stratum immediately below your own. You know princes and kings, of course, and you know servants: your equals and those too far beneath your notice to worry about. But between these levels there is another one, of people who you can inadvertently crush by accident. The wives and daughters of baronets and knights, or even commoners of means—magnates and merchants. Your father wrote to me in confidence"—Mme. Houelebecq sniffed—"to give me a specific task. It has been said that a true lady never *unintentionally* gives offense. But you, Your Majesty, are not destined for life as a mere lady. Your father wishes for you to learn how to manage jealousy and other unpleasantness, in a setting you can leave behind when the time is right for you to join your husband's court. After all, even a crushed wasp can sting. And I am very much afraid that from next week, you are going to be the center of a hornet's nest of vicious gossip."

BERLIN, TIME LINE THREE, AUGUST 2020

Later, settling into her rooms at the schloss, Elizabeth found a letter on her study table.

At first she overlooked the plain white envelope, for she was still digesting Mme. Houelebecq's explanation of the reasoning behind her presence at the school. Between shedding her coat and hat—then swearing to herself and, after a brief search for her maid, recalling that she was supposed to attend to such chores herself, thereby necessitating a search for the hat rack and closet—she was mildly disgruntled by the time she got her boots off. So she decided to kill time by examining her spartan rooms, and that was when she found it.

The letter came in an anonymous white envelope, addressed to her as **E. Hanover**. When she finally noticed it sitting atop the table it rattled her considerably. For a panicky moment she wondered if someone had slipped into her study while she was in the bedroom next door. While she knew that the school was in principle protected by Captain Bertrand's people, and that the servants had been carefully scrutinized before her arrival, more than one ancestor of hers had been taken by surprise under similar circumstances. The servants had placed her portable writing-slope atop the table. She flipped it open, reached into one of the storage slots, and withdrew her letter opener—a slim, ornamental knife which was of water-patterned steel, honed as sharp as a razor. She carefully checked the hallway, ensured her front door was locked and bolted, made a quick pass through her rooms, then retrieved the letter.

> Elizabeth: arrangements are now in place for your extraction, as per our conversation last month. If you wish to proceed, reply by letter (a simple "yes" will do) and leave the sealed envelope, addressed to "H," where you found this one.
>
> The staff here stored your steamer trunks on the shelf in the front hallway above the coat hooks and hat rack.
>
> If you confirm your intention to proceed, a disguise will be

placed in the smallest trunk the following day. You will also find a letter with a date and time. Half an hour before the designated time you should retreat to your rooms, lock and bolt the door, and change into the clothes provided.

(The garments will be unfamiliar to you but will render you inconspicuous en route.)

If you are unable to be extracted at the designated time, you should remove the small ornamental potted plant from the side table in the corridor outside your rooms. Its absence will serve as a signal that you cannot proceed, and we will reschedule subsequently. If it is present, it will signal that we are to proceed.

You should then wait for me in your study.

—H.

With hands that trembled only slightly, Elizabeth put pen to paper and wrote a reply:

Yes.

    —E.

She folded it and sealed it in an envelope, then left it on her escritoire. Going through to her bedroom she noted that the servants had laid the fireplace. She crumpled the Major's letter and shoved it down among the kindling; tucking her skirts out of the way, she struck a match and watched pale flames caress the edge of the communiqué. Once the fire was properly lit she moved the fireguard back into place. Then she returned to her study and prepared a pot of tea (by herself, unaided). That night she slept with the letter opener under her pillow.

The next morning the envelope had already vanished. It was clear that her unseen correspondent meant her no immediate harm: stone walls and security guards seemed to mean nothing to him. With this confirmation that the offer of extraction was genuine, some of her nastier fears disappeared. Despite her outer confidence Elizabeth had entertained lingering doubts until now.

But now all she had to do was settle down to wait, and trust the Major from the Commonwealth to do his job.

PHILADELPHIA, TIME LINE TWO, AUGUST 2020

Angie hadn't played the Game of Spies since she was in fifth grade, but the rules were so deeply ingrained that it was a physical reflex, like riding a bicycle or swimming. It was one of those skills that were hard to learn the first time round, when you were trying not to fall over or drown. But once it clicked you could no more forget how to do it than you could forget how to breathe.

The Game of Spies was a meta-game, like the Game. In the Game, you could only lose: you lost by thinking consciously about playing the Game, and then you had to announce your loss. In the Game of Spies, the first rule was that you lost by disclosing that you were playing the Game of Spies to anyone who was not part of your team—in other words, your controller or your Resident. It need not be a verbal admission: *yes, I'm playing the Game of Spies and Kurt is my controller.* Any public sign was an admission. And that meant any sign that might be noticed by a hypothetical adversary who could be watching you at any time, for the Game of Spies was played inside the panopticon of a police state.

In the old days, before Moore's Law and computers in hotel door handles and CCTV cameras on every block corner . . . in the old days before everyone carried a fatphone with multiple video cameras and GPS and orientation sensors, before the DEFEND Act required the NSA to log all electronic communications, before high-quality face-recognition and lip-reading software existed . . . in the old days, it was still possible to talk to the agents under your control in public spaces. It was in private places that you had to worry about bugging devices and eavesdroppers. But sometime in the past decade technology had turned all the old certainties upside down.

Last year's tinfoil hat was this year's sartorial good taste. The act of popping the battery from your phone might activate the tiny microphone and GSM phone stage built into the battery itself, prompting it to phone home to the NSA and relay your private conversation if you were a person of interest. There were chips in credit and debit cards for securing your accounts. Rumor had it that Visa and Mastercard also carried embedded microphones, powered by capacitors energized every time you used an ATM, recording everything and transmitting it back to the government via the banking network. Metal door keys were going out of fashion (a distant camera snapshot and a 3-D printer made it disturbingly easy to fake up a blank). But how could you be sure that the shiny new proximity lock on your front door wasn't recording your movements and listening in on your conversations?

Any car manufactured after 2015 was an informer by default unless you took it to an ICE shop and had it lobotomized, invalidating your after-sale warranty and simultaneously guaranteeing that the government took a keen interest in your motivation for damaging your vehicle. The pressure transponders in your tires were radio-frequency snitches, identifying your car even if you swapped out the plates. Any clothing above the level of a $1 T-shirt had smart RFID washing tags to stop your shiny new washer/dryer from wrecking it by running a damaging program. But RFID tags were *also* low-power chips, and how could you be sure that your bra wasn't also recording your speech and skin conductivity and pulse—not only a snitch, but a snitch with a built-in polygraph?

Cosplay and auto firmware hacking were popular hobbies among paranoiacs and dissidents this decade. Angie preferred to rely on Goodwill instead, and relied on other means to keep secrets from her pickup truck and her clothes.

Her washing machine and tumble dryer were ancient castoffs with bizarrely complex mechanical controls. Half the clothing she bought took a brief trip through the microwave oven: the other half was hung, unworn, in the side of the closet reserved for secret police informers. Her laptop and tablet were bugged, of course, but everybody knew and expected that. Where possible she bought her tools secondhand through eBay, or tormented them with alternating current.

Her truck was a problem of a different type. She hadn't taken it to an

ICE shop, but she'd lobotomized the tire wiring and painstakingly gone over the body with a hand-made antenna connected to a signal processing board she'd soldered together herself. She was pretty sure that she'd found and suborned all the microphones and brainwashed the in-car Bluetooth. The story they told now was a synthetic-voiced farrago of lies generated on-the-fly by a matchbox-sized computer she'd wired into the glove box. And she'd subverted the truck's CANbus components with black market firmware.

The bug detector, lie-bot, and hacked vehicle firmware all ran software she'd found on hacker darknets frequented by everyone from unlicensed Mexican plastic surgeons to fly-by-night family planning clinics working up and down the no-choice state lines. She'd found her way in via pointers from an online community where paranoid schizophrenics gathered. They used it to compare notes on the best way to fool the Illuminati and avoid the orbital mind control lasers operated by the gangster computer god on the dark side of the Moon. She used it because it was a good source of more practical survival tips for the professionally discreet.

This was a terrible century to be a paranoid schizophrenic. The real world had become a target-rich environment for conspiracy theorists. Meanwhile everyone suffered the consequences of designed-in insecurity. Paradoxically, the very measures that made it easier for the State to monitor the People—the mandatory backdoors that riddled the Internet of things—made it easier for paranoids and cybercriminals to evade surveillance and hack their marks: casual identity theft and credit card fraud were rampant. There was a gigantic herd of graynet subcultures flying under the radar, people of no actual interest to the national security state who feverishly armored themselves against the cybernetic equivalent of the Black Helicopters. And so the real dissidents lurked amidst the vendors of word salad, hiding in plain sight. Angie had learned how to tell them from the unmedicated casualties of the war on consensus reality by examining their punctuation. Real people pretending to be madmen might throw in the odd cut 'n' paste rant, but in general they wrote in paragraphs and didn't use ellipses as duct tape between their disconnected ramblings.

Only the insane could truly appreciate the Kafkaesque nature of the twenty-first century—the insane, and those who stood consciously outside of society, like lone wolves and spies. It was an ironic truth that the last illegals of the East German Stasi could only feel truly at home among crazies and dissidents.

The families of the Wolf Orchestra, living on as illegals in America, had drilled their children in the Game of Spies as a matter of survival. Like conversos, Jews practicing in secret after those of their faith had been forcibly converted or expelled by post-Reconquista Spain, they lived under permanent threat of exposure by the Inquisition. At first the Game of Spies had simply been part of the process of training their children with the survival reflexes they'd need if they were to avoid betraying their parents by accident. They had never intended or expected to need to pass on their other skills, let alone their contact protocols and cell neighbors. They hadn't realized until after the nuclear attack on 7/16 and the horrifying response that their own upbringing and training, as trusted inmates in the open prison of Actually Existing Socialism, was the best possible way to equip their children for life in Ubiquitously Surveilled America.

The morning after Rita said farewell and headed back to the other America, Angie set to work with a heavy heart. She plugged away until early evening. Then, leaving the breaker board she was in the process of wiring up to a new-build condo, she headed back to her truck. The evening stretched ahead, empty and surprisingly dull. She pulled out her phone and tapped the thumbprint reader to tell it to switch from its work personality to her home identity. It vibrated, twice. There were messages from Kurt: Angie read swiftly. (1) ANY WORD FROM RITA? And (2) DINNER?

Angie smiled faintly as she interpreted his coded signal. DINNER SOUNDS GREAT, she texted back. WANT ME TO PICK YOU UP?

The reply took seconds to arrive: YES. The game was afoot.

NEW LONDON, TIME LINE THREE, AUGUST 2020

Dinner parties with political movers and shakers were well outside Rita's comfort zone. In fact, dinner parties in general struck her as a middle-aged thing. They were an implicit confession that the local restaurant scene was expensive or dismally bad, if not both. And formalwear was a stage costume as far as she was concerned. Prom was far in her past, and most of her friends were too beset by student debt and spiraling rents to afford a wedding, or gay and living in back-to-the-closet states. But Brilliana was hard to say no to. She led Rita to a spare bedroom, showed her the bathroom (with recognizable but somewhat odd fixtures and fittings: everything from power outlets to toilet paper rolls was subtly different in size and shape), then insisted on going through a huge wardrobe in search of an outfit for her. "You need something to wear, for tonight and for any other occasions that might require it. We can get you measured tomorrow, but in the meantime—"

Formalwear fashion in the Commonwealth was currently loose and enveloping rather than figure-hugging and tailored, which was extremely convenient. Rita was a lot less happy about the jewelry Brill insisted she borrow—big enough to be outrageous paste gems in costume settings, heavy enough to feel disturbingly authentic—but she was still punch-drunk from the discovery of her rapidly inflating social identity. Unsure whether to be more scared of meeting Mrs. Burgeson again, or the political implications of failing to make a good impression on everyone else, she was easy meat for a former lady-in-waiting to royalty who had her shit together.

Two hours later she was clutching a glass of sparkling wine in the front parlor with her hair up, wearing a small fortune in gemstones and a kaftan so fancy it made her feel like an imposter. "Relax," Brilliana advised her as she made a final pass through the room, "they'll be here soon."

Rita tensed self-consciously. "Who are you"—a doorbell rang— "expecting? Apart from the Burgesons?" But Brill was no longer beside her: she was meeting the new arrivals instead.

"Hello, my dear." A man's voice, slightly hoarse. "So pleased to meet you—"

"Olga sends her apologies, she's running late." A woman's voice, semi-familiar. Rita tensed up even tighter, as overwound as an abused carriage clock. "God, I've had a crap day—"

It was all piling up too fast: Rita had no time to react as everyone came through the door in a rush, Brilliana leading a man with thinning gray hair and a gaunt face who wore a fancy cut-away jacket with tails over trousers and a frilled shirt, and then a woman whose face dried up the words in her throat.

"Rita?" said Mrs. Burgeson, stopping dead in the doorway.

"Um, yeah." Rita stared right back, frozen in the headlights. *You're not my mom. That's Emily.* She forced a tense smile. "Hello?" She hoped it didn't look like she was smirking.

"That's a gorgeous outfit. Where did you find it?" asked Mrs. Burgeson.

"It's borrowed." Rita managed not to flinch. "Brill insisted." In the sudden silence she took in her birth mother's appearance. "Nice earrings."

Mrs. Burgeson smiled. "You think so?" Motion resumed around them.

Rita shrugged uncomfortably. She was agnostic about pearl earrings—they weren't her style—but suddenly she had a tenuous feeling that if she could keep the conversation on neutral ground it might not end in tears before bedtime.

"Drinks, everybody?" It was Huw, gawking in through a small side door (*servant's passage*, Rita realized). He made a beeline for the sideboard.

"I'll have whatever she's having," said Mrs. Burgeson, nodding at Rita. "This is my husband, Erasmus. Say hi, Ras. She won't bite you."

"I . . . won't . . ." Rita extended a hand, expecting to shake: it was better than stammering.

The Minister of Propaganda smiled at her. "Charmed, I'm sure," he murmured, and actually *bowed* to kiss the back of her wrist. "I've heard a lot about you."

Rita failed her saving throw against cringing. "Shit—I'm sorry!" She took a deep breath. "I've been wanting a chance to apologize," she told

Mrs. Burgeson. Breathlessly, her composure leaving her: "There's a lot I didn't know."

The Minister for Intertemporal Technological Intelligence—*the Minister for Spying on America* Rita translated silently—accepted a tall glass of wine from Huw, then shrugged gracefully. "Thank you, and I accept your apology. You must have been half out of your mind with fear at the time—"

"No, it's not that: my grandfather told me about your, your mother." Everyone was staring at her, Rita realized. "I'm really sorry. I didn't know . . ."

But Mrs. Burgeson wasn't interested in further apologetics. She stepped closer, pupils dilating. "Your grandfather *knew* my mother?" She sounded like a thirsty woman in a desert who had just sighted an oasis.

"I, uh, yes—"

Someone chose that moment to hit a small gong with a drumstick. "Dinner is served," announced a bland-faced man in the knee breeches and white stockings that passed for a butler's outfit here.

"After dinner"—Mrs. Burgeson flashed her a smile that was almost feral in its intensity—"I want you to tell me *all about* your grandfather."

Rita took a risk. "If you tell me about your mother?"

Mrs. Burgeson met her gaze evenly. "Yes, let's do that. If it's easier for you, you can call me Miriam," she said. "To keep things straight in your head, I mean."

"Thanks. Miriam." Rita tried the name. She was right: *Mrs. Burgeson* was too formal but *mother* felt like a mistake.

"I hope you enjoy the food," Miriam added. "Brill is serious about her entertainment. But I should warn you, her taste runs to the fiery."

AN UNDISCLOSED LOCATION, UNDISCLOSED TIME LINE, AUGUST 2020

They took Paulette back to her cell only when she was reeling with exhaustion and hoarse from talking. Some time during the interview her interrogators had swapped over—more than once, she suspected afterward. Thereafter she tried to keep count, because shift changes would give her a handle on how long she'd been there. She half-wondered why they didn't just dose her up with modafinil to keep her running, but concluded that most likely they wanted her sleep-deprived as part of the process. (One of her DPR contacts had told her sleep deprivation was the most effective tool of torture in the interrogator's arsenal, insidious and almost irresistible if applied correctly, and far less likely to induce panicky lies than water-boarding or physical pain: it just took patience and teamwork.)

They left her in her cell and she lay down and switched off at once, even though the overhead light was as bright as ever. She slept like a log, undisturbed by sounds from elsewhere in the prison. It was almost as if she was the only inmate. Far too soon, a harsh buzzer brought her back to consciousness. A meal came sliding through the door, and then it was time to go back to the interview room, groggy and stumbling in her leg irons, to be shackled to a chair and asked the same goddamn questions all over again.

Paulette lost count of the number of interviews some time after the fourth session. It was impossible to tell how long it had been going on for. She suspected no more than a couple of weeks had passed since her arrest, but it felt like months. A thirty-year sentence of white-walled boredom stretched her sense of time to fit. She was too tired to feel any emotion beyond numb despair. Hell, it seemed, was not a fiery pit full of demons but a room with a mirror behind which bored officials repeated inanely misguided questions endlessly. Her only ray of hope was that the lunatics from the first shift didn't make a reappearance. None of her subsequent interrogators expected her to confess to being a Communist or touched on Scientology beliefs. In the rare free moments she had between waking and interrogation she considered suicide, but her captors had gone out of their way to make it difficult: and in the depths of depression she found it hard to muster up the energy for self-harm.

They came to take her to the interrogation room once more. Paulie complied wearily, not balking as the guards shackled her to the ring in the floor. It had become routine by now, and she waited patiently for them to unhood her and start the cycle of boredom anew. But this time, when the hood came off she found herself facing a table—and on the other side of the table there was an empty chair.

A *chair* implied a string of disturbing consequential concepts, starting with a *person who is seated*, who might be *an interrogator*, or possibly *a prosecutor*, here to offer her a plea bargain. (A *visiting friend or relative* seemed hopelessly optimistic.) A cold sweat broke out in the small of her back, then she began to shiver, flushing hot and sweaty all over. She felt weak, as if gut-punched. *Here it comes*, she thought. The light at the end of the tunnel could only be an onrushing freight train. And she was shackled to the floor in front of it, unable to escape.

The door behind her opened with a click. Then a man in a dark gray suit walked around the table, drew back the chair, and sat down opposite her.

"Good morning, Ms. Milan," he said, politely enough. He studied her over his gold-rimmed half-moon spectacles. He was balding, the remains of his hair a peppery gray; crow's-feet wrinkles framed his eyes. He was about her age, give or take a few years—somewhere in the uneasy gap between early middle age and declining sixties—and he wore a badge on a lanyard over his plain blue necktie.

Paulette focused on the badge. Something about it, she knew, made it very important. Possibly all-important. She tried to read the words on it, but they blurred. Her eyes were watering. He was the first human face she'd actually seen aside from her own reflection in the one-way mirror in weeks. The guards she had glimpsed only sidelong in the moments when she'd been unhooded, their backs turned to the interrogators' window. It was remarkably upsetting.

"Who—" She cleared her throat. "Who are you?"

"You can call me Eric, Ms. Milan. And I'll call you—hmm. Do you prefer Paulette, or Paul, or Paulie? You don't strike me as being a Paul, but one can never be sure."

"Paulie will do." Her voice nearly cracked at the tiny kindness. "Why?"

"Well." He shrugged, flexing the padded shoulders of his jacket. "I've got some good news for you. I've read the transcripts of your questioning, and everything checks out—you're not lying to us about anything I can put my finger on. And your story is consistent with Mike Fleming's."

She stared at him in shock. "You knew Mike?"

"I was his manager until he disappeared."

"He disappeared—" Paulie's voice froze up. In the wake of 7/16, Mike had wanted to leak the existence of the disastrous chain of mistakes that had led to stolen atomic demolition munitions falling into the hands of the Clan. He'd tried to rope Paulette in with his scheme. She'd demurred. That was the last time she'd seen him: the truth never made it into the news media, so presumably he'd failed. "Did you people get to him?"

Eric shook his head very slightly. "You don't ask the questions in here, Paulie. You should know it doesn't work like that."

"Oh. Well."

She thought about saying something more, but decided against it. They sat in silence for a minute or so, until Eric finally spoke. "You were told that you could face treason charges, or that you could be rendered to another jurisdiction for destructive debriefing and recycling. But there's another alternative open to you, depending on how cooperative you're feeling."

What's my price? Paulette shivered. "Eighteen million children's lives," she said haltingly.

"Eighteen what?" Eric looked perplexed.

"Antibiotics." She cleared her throat again. "That was the latest figure. Children's lives saved, because of what I did." *By the* valuable intellectual property *I obtained for the Commonwealth.* Medicines from the 1960s and 1970s, cephalosporins and beta-lactamase inhibitors, long out of patent control, rendered useless in this time line due to the antibiotic resistance that had emerged following their reckless misuse by the cattle feed industry. "What do you do for a living, Eric? Does it have anything to do with saving children's lives?"

"Not directly." His eyes narrowed. "But I don't have to lie awake at night thinking up justifications for why I'm betraying my nation, either."

He's breaking his own rules. She smiled, her cheeks hurting. "I haven't deserted my nation: the nation has deserted its own citizens. This isn't the country it was before 7/16; what are *you* doing to make things better?"

She wasn't sure what to expect. A back-handed blow across her face; a cold dismissal back to her empty cell; a curt rejoinder. But Eric merely stared at her with barely-concealed contempt. "I'm working as hard as I can to *prevent a nuclear war*, Ms. Milan. Is that good enough for you?"

Well now. "That's a start," she conceded.

"A *good* start, in my opinion, or I wouldn't be sitting here taking shit from a traitor." He took a deep breath. "Okay, Paulie. Here's the proposition. I'm going to ask you to do some things for my organization. If you do them well, if we succeed, there won't be a war. Instead there will be negotiations, and summit meetings, probably some kind of treaty process, and other trust-building exercises. Somewhere along the way the other side will ask about you. *If you cooperate fully*, at that point I'll see you charged under the original terms of the Espionage Act, sentenced to time served, stripped of your citizenship, and expelled into their custody. That's how the game used to be played with the Soviets, and that's how we're going to play it this time round." He said it as calmly as a weatherman describing tomorrow's cold front passing overhead with a belt of rain leading the drop in temperature.

"What do you want me to do?" she asked, more out of boredom than curiosity. Whatever it was, she'd do it: it was inevitable, even though she strongly doubted he'd deliver on the deal. It was simply bait to keep her pliant and cooperative. But it was preferable to returning to her solitary cell with a life sentence ringing in her ears. As long as she cooperated she could continue to pretend that her life wasn't over.

"You can start by telling me everything you know about this man." Eric pulled a fatphone from his suit coat pocket and tapped the display. A CCTV Magritte showed Paulette a video of the back of her own head, a half-eaten burrito sitting on the table in front of her. She sat opposite a man who went by the code name Jefferson these days, although she'd known him for nearly two decades, long before he'd been assigned any aliases. "We know he's a world-walker. We know he's Clan, or ex-Clan, whatever they call themselves these days."

"Oh." Paulie fell silent for a moment. *I don't suppose it matters,* she realized. *They're not idiots. They'll know I've been turned.* She'd never caught them at it but she was certain the DPR had protocols in place to ensure that they only made contact when she was confirmed clean. "His name is Hulius Hjorth. Major Hjorth. Cover name Jefferson. He works for the Commonwealth Department of Para-time Research."

"Good." Eric tapped the screen again. It showed a new photograph of the Major, in different clothing.

"Huh." Paulette squinted. "Where was this taken?"

"In Germany. The day before yesterday." Eric picked up his phone and slid it away again. "And what is your rank in the DPR, Ms. Milan?"

"My what?" She met his gaze. Smith's eyes were very blue, as cold as liquid oxygen. "They told me I'm a Colonel." She shrugged. "Presumably there's a pension attached. Not that I expect to claim it."

"Well, Colonel." He smiled, as if amused by something: "As I said, this is your lucky day. You can go back to your cell now, but don't get too settled. I'm going to arrange for you to be released into the custody of my unit. And then we're going on a little trip. To Berlin . . ."

PART THREE

DEFECTORS

Rudolf Rassendyll: "I was hoping that our skeleton was
safe at home in our family cupboard."
Fritz von Tarlenheim: "Some skeletons are prodigious
travelers."

—Anthony Hope, *The Prisoner of Zenda*

Dining with the Devil

Dinner with Huw and Brilliana was a regular fixture for Miriam. The extra guest was another matter. Like a close encounter with an extra-solar body, distorting the regular orbits of the planets as it barreled through the solar system, the kid's presence warped the conversation around her presence. *The kid*, Miriam reminded herself, *is older than I was when I gave birth to her.*

Rita remained silent while she drank her soup, as if unaware of the effect of her presence. Brill suddenly playing society hostess again, a role she'd grown rusty at in recent years. Huw unusually reticent, Rita's presence clearly inhibiting his normal tendency to talk shop at the table. (Admittedly, any outsider would have had the same effect, given the nature of his work.) Of them all, only Erasmus was his usual self—mainly because a dinner party with his wife's inner circle was one of his few opportunities to switch off and enjoy life. They were all highflyers, and these monthly dinners usually oscillated between serving as an unofficial kitchen cabinet meeting of the DPR's most senior directors and nostalgic reunions for Miriam's all-but-abandoned coterie of Clan modernizers.

On the other hand it gave Miriam an opportunity to observe her daughter, for which she was cautiously grateful. Their traumatic first meeting had dredged up unwelcome memories of Miriam's breakup with Ben, nearly two and a half decades ago. Maybe that was why she'd taken it so hard, she speculated. Getting pregnant in pre-med had been bad enough, and Iris's push to organize adoption had seemed like a welcome intervention at the time. But afterward, after graduation, she'd married Ben—perhaps trying to salvage a dying relationship, or maybe propelled in part by unadmitted regrets. It hadn't worked out and they'd separated acrimoniously. The adoption had been one of the wedges that opened the gap between them until it was unbridgeable. She'd thought that period of her life was a closed book—or even a bad joke. But now the punch line was sitting across the table from her, avoiding eye contact in a borrowed evening dress that didn't quite work for her.

She couldn't escape feeling that Rita's silence was prickly and sensitive, a thin layer of ice concealing a hot spring of anger beneath. But it hadn't seemed like that in the parlor when Rita had offered up something that might have been an olive branch: *my grandfather told me about your mother.* Yes, but what did he say? And how much did he know?

Iris Beckstein—alternatively, the Duchess Patricia Thorold-Hjorth—had died more than a decade ago. The medication for her multiple sclerosis wasn't easy to obtain by stealth in the aftermath of 7/16, and she'd become increasingly debilitated. In the end the flu epidemic of 2005 did for her. Olga appeared to have inherited the MS via a different route. The Clan's careful sequestration of the recessive trait they depended on for their family trade—the world-walking ability—had come at a heavy price. *I'm as old as Iris was when she organized the adoption*, Miriam realized. *How well did I know her?*

Iris/Patricia had held her cards close to her chest as she played a vicious game with her own mother. The dowager Duchess Hildegarde had led the Clan's conservative faction—the reactionary fools who had thought you negotiated with a democracy the same way you dealt with a hostile monarchy. That had been the last generation to keep to the old ways. Before Iris, the Clan had kept their youngsters close, training them in the ways of Gruinmarkt nobility. By Miriam's generation, they had mostly been shipped to the United States for education to college level and even postgraduate degree courses. (Not to mention the odd enlistment in the

US military, which was a useful finishing school for aspirants to a war-rior nobility.) Iris had been the freak exception, born on the cusp of mas-sive change. Ostensibly a runaway and a deserter, she'd fled an abusive marriage arranged by Hildegarde, escaping with the connivance of Iris's brother, the Duke Angbard.

The genetic determinism imposed by the desperate need to con-serve a valued recessive trait, combined with the frankly dismal status of women in a roughly medieval society, had turned the Clan's politics into a double-layered game. Male aristocrats danced to the puppet strings of the grandmothers who arranged the braided marriages that kept the breeding program running. Angbard had provoked—or revived—a civil war within the clan by secretly approving a plan to use a fertility clinic in the United States to generate a host of carriers (and then, in the second generation, world-walkers) who would be loyal to the organization rather than the dowagers. His goal had been to put an end to the blood feuds that had almost destroyed the world-walkers during the twentieth century. But the backlash had been disastrous.

And now, as the maids cleared the soup bowls and prepared the table for the entrées, Miriam found herself sitting across the table from a young woman with skin the color of latte and an unexpected claim on her heart—and as the emotional squall of meeting Rita began to subside, Miriam found herself pondering disturbing questions.

"Do you know why Olga is late?" Brill asked Miriam. "I know she was working this evening, but . . ."

Miriam looked up from her place setting. "It's something to do with Hulius, I think." She glanced around the table. Huw nodded slightly. (Of course, he knew.) Erasmus was asking Rita something about stagecraft and the girl was talking to him, quietly but intensely. "Does everyone here know what she's engaged in?" Miriam asked pointedly, glancing askance at their visitor.

Brilliana shrugged. "We can talk around it. Or not, if you think it prudent."

Miriam blinked, then reached for her glass. "We need to discuss it later." She'd barely touched her wine. "For now, naming no names—I'm very worried that this scheme could backfire. The potential for embarrassment is enormous. High risk, high payoff. I gather Olga said Yul got the go-ahead, so she's lining up all the billiard balls ready for him to break. And that takes time. But—"

The doorbell rang. Brilliana rose gracefully: "Guess who?" she asked with a smile. "I'll handle it."

Miriam realized Rita was watching her. "You're avoiding talking business around me, aren't you?" Rita said.

"Guilty." Miriam put her wineglass down. "We try to dine together at least once a month, but we're all workaholics and the business conversation can get a bit technical." She smiled to defuse her next words: "Also, we haven't forgotten who you work for."

"But I—" Rita stopped. "I don't have any choice in my employers," she said defensively.

"I didn't have much choice either, when the Clan discovered I existed." Miriam put her glass down. Rita's was empty. "Refill?"

"Yes please . . ." Miriam got to the bottle before Erasmus or Soames, the butler, could intervene, and managed to top up Rita's glass at arm's length without spilling it on the tablecloth. It felt important that she should be the one to do it. "Thank you," Rita said as Miriam filled her own flute. "They tried to pretend I had a choice, but I didn't, really." She stared moodily. "I'm a conscript. I don't know what would have happened if I'd said no to the job offer, but I got the impression it wouldn't have been good. I suppose it's a job, and someone has to do it, and I guess as long as I'm not harming anybody . . . Anyway, they know I've got to go home."

"Go home because they've got something on you, or go home because you want to go home?"

"A bit of both." Her pensive expression deepened. "It's just, um, what was the quote? No man is an island."

"Family?" Miriam raised an eyebrow. "Boyfriend?"

"Partner," she corrected automatically. Miriam blinked. *What does that mean, exactly?* She made a guess then filed it away for future discreet inquiry. Yet another sign of how things were changing back in her former home time line. Rita continued. "I have family, too. When you came here, did you leave anyone behind?"

"Not intentionally—"

They were spared further intimacy by Brilliana's return, pushing Olga's chair. Olga was arguing. "You don't need to do this, I'm fine—" She held a pair of crutches over the arm of her wheelchair, narrowly missing the door frame on the way in.

"I don't want you tiring yourself out," Brill told her.

"Let me be the judge of that. Stop right here." Olga pulled the brake handle and Brilliana surrendered to the inevitable as the other woman planted her crutches and laboriously stood. "I'm better than I was yesterday, and I need to know I can walk . . . that's better."

Huw hastily rose and moved a chair into position as Olga approached the table. She'd come straight from the office and was still dressed for work. "Thank you," she said gratefully as she lowered herself onto the dining chair beside Rita, who, after a momentary startled look, took the crutches and leaned them against the wall. "What a day!"

"Any problems?" Huw asked as he returned to his own seat.

"Your brother . . ." Olga pulled a face. Then she cleared her throat and nodded at Rita. "With all due respect, we should have this conversation some other time."

"Problems?" Erasmus looked up.

"Nothing yet. Just the meteorology reports." Olga's frown deepened. "The forecast has to be just right, twice over—" She glanced sidelong at Rita. "I'll have whatever she's drinking, please. It's been a long day."

Miriam looked round the table. Soames was bringing the next course. Olga's arrival had brought the level of classified projects in the conversation to some sort of critical mass. *I need to put a stop to it*, she thought. Taking a risk: "Rita, you mentioned a grandfather. Would you like to tell us about your family?"

"My family?" Rita looked startled: "But I thought you knew . . ."

"Please. Pretend I don't?" Miriam managed to smile. "My mother handled the ad—everything. I don't think I ever met your parents." She managed not to stumble over the word. "Let alone your grandfather. Do you have any brothers or sisters?"

"Oh, sure." Rita composed herself. Her eyes unfocused slightly as she realized she was being diverted away from a patch of conversational black ice, where she might lose her balance and fall painfully. "Okay, my parents are Franz and Emily Douglas. I've got a younger brother, River— also adopted—and one grandfather, Kurt, Franz's father. Emily couldn't have children of her own. I grew up in Boston and went to college there but while I was in college Dad's company opened a plant in Phoenix. Mom telecommutes, so they moved—Phoenix was depressed enough that they could afford to buy two houses, one for us and one next door for Gramps, and property's rising there again. So." She shrugged. "I prefer the coastal cities, so I stayed in Boston for college."

"The climate in Phoenix doesn't agree with you?" asked Miriam.

"You could say that. Uh. You know how old I am. You know about the no-choice states? Arizona's one of them, it's a *really* bad place to be young, single, and female. I mean, if anything went wrong, if I got raped or something."

Miriam did a double-take. "I thought that was a fringe thing, isn't it? Dominionists? Or is it mainstream these days?" She'd been rooted firmly in the Commonwealth for so long that she'd stopped paying much attention to US domestic politics.

"No-choicers run about half the states," Rita said defensively. "Places they're in charge aren't good places for people like me to live. Single women, gays, Muslims, immigrants. But I stay in touch with my parents: they're only there for the job and the, the real estate opportunity, as Dad puts it. Gramps is visiting in Philly right now. We stay in touch. We're close. But I can't—people like me can't—live in one of those states. It's not safe."

Erasmus had gone totally still and silent, fork frozen in mid-air. As Rita finished speaking he completed the movement, taking a mouthful of duck a l'orange and chewing slowly. Miriam recognized the signs: another two o'clock conversation was coming, in which she tried to translate her increasingly irrelevant and rusty memory of American culture and politics into Commonwealth terms, predigesting it for the next week's editorial policy meetings.

Huw whistled quietly. "Sounds like things have gotten a lot worse since I was last there," he said, attracting a pointed stare from Rita.

"Things have gotten *better* over the past few years—" Rita stopped and seemingly remembered there was a plate in front of her. "This is good," she mumbled. "Don't want it to get cold."

Olga spoke up. "Let's not mince words. 7/16 broke lots of things, and not just in Washington, D.C., and the Gruinmarkt: it broke the collective sanity of a huge number of folks in red state America. If 9/11 was bad, 7/16 tipped them over the edge. Yes?"

"Well, you people would know about it." Rita put her fork down carefully. "Wouldn't you?"

Oh, we were bound to have this conversation, weren't we? Miriam took a mouthful of wine to cover her immediate expression. "No," she said, very firmly.

"No?" Rita looked startled.

"The people responsible for 7/16 are dead," Miriam said firmly, trying to keep a wobble of rage out of her voice. "We hunted them down and killed them. Except for a couple of idiots in the US government who we couldn't touch."

"But the US government didn't—"

"We warned them," Huw said grimly. "They didn't listen. They tried to kill Miriam when she tipped them off. Using an exploding phone."

"An *exploding phone*?" If Rita's eyes got any wider they'd be the size of dinner plates.

Miriam took a deep breath. "Yes. We were in the middle of negotiations, handled via a, a cutout. Trying to warn them about the stolen nukes. They sent us a mobile phone, it came from a Colonel in the agency they'd just set up for dealing with world-walkers. It turned out to be a cell phone with a bomb in it. When we called the Colonel's boss to warn him about the stolen bombs he sent the detonation signal. He obviously didn't think we had any electronics chops. But he didn't need our warning: he already knew about the bombs."

"But the Clan planted the bombs—"

"Rita, the Clan consists—*consisted*—of a couple of thousand people with wildly diverging agendas of their own, to the point where it went through two bloody civil wars in the past century. As I said, we warned Colonel Smith's boss"—Rita flinched violently at the name—"and we did our best to stop it happening. But 7/16 wasn't just bad for D.C. The bastards who blew up the president and tried to nuke the Pentagon also murdered a bunch of my friends that day. They tried to kill me. The bombings in D.C. were part of a coup attempt within the Clan. The plotters failed, but in the process they fucked *everyone* over, not just the White House and the Capitol and the Washington Monument. So I will thank you for not blaming me personally for 7/16, all right?"

Rita looked as if her head was about to explode. "Colonel *who*?" she demanded. "What was this agency?"

"We got the details afterwards from"—Miriam caught Olga's warning glance but plowed on all the same—"intelligence sources. Our contact was working for a Colonel Eric Smith, who was part of an agency that was then called the Family Trade Organization. FTO. It's part of DHS these days, they renamed it a few times . . . what is it?"

Rita wasn't calming down: if anything her distress was growing. "My boss is called Colonel Smith," she said shakily. "He's not a Colonel anymore, he retired from the Air Force—but he's DHS. And he was there from the start. Oh my God. Oh my God." She jammed her fist against her mouth. Miriam stared at her. So did everyone else.

Miriam cleared her throat. "Hey, we're not going to hold it against you," she said softly. "Rita. Please listen?"

Rita looked at her with horror in her eyes, then nodded rapidly.

"It was your Colonel's boss who did it, and he's long since moved on. A neocon political hack from the, the last administration but two. I'm pretty sure that *nobody* wants another nuclear war, least of all your boss. But these are the stakes we're playing for. And I think we've all got a duty to do whatever we can to avoid it happening again, haven't we?" Rita nodded. *Good: I'm getting through to her,* Miriam thought. "You're among friends here, at least at this table. Let's finish dinner and maybe talk some more. Then we can figure out how to stop anything bad from happening."

NEW LONDON, TIME LINE THREE, AUGUST 2020

Later, Miriam found Erasmus in his dressing room, nursing a glass of port in his dressing gown.

"Mind if I join you?" she asked.

"Go ahead." His grin was lopsided. "I see you came prepared."

She sat down beside him on the chaise, holding her whisky tumbler away from her robe. It was empty. "I needed it. That's usually a bad sign, isn't it."

His smile slipped away. "You just met your daughter for the first time, love." He raised his glass. "Panic-induced histrionics don't count. Office ultimata don't count. If you were insisting it was business as usual I'd be worried for your sanity. As it is"—he sipped his port—"I think it went quite well."

"What do *you* think of her?"

"Prickly. Bright and sharp as a nail. Still a bit naive, but she'll grow out of that. She has inherited your brains, I think. I confess I didn't realize you dallied with aristocracy in your youth, my dear—"

"Aristocracy?" Miriam spluttered. "Oh, you think—" She snorted. "It doesn't work that way in the United States, I assure you. I hear her father's a consultant physician these days. His family weren't poor, but nobility? Hardly. They came from Pakistan—sorry, from the country where the French Punjab Dominions are in this world. Not exactly the elevated descendants of imperial conquerors—at least not in the past couple of hundred years."

"Hmm." Erasmus nodded to himself. "Well, then. Then the resemblance is probably coincidental."

"Resemblance? What resemblance?"

"You haven't been following the news from St. Petersburg about the Dauphin's new fiancée, have you? It's really quite funny: if Rita wants to pursue a career on the stage she could make a fortune impersonating the Princess."

"Oh, come *on*." Miriam sipped her drink, covering her confusion. If it had been anyone else, or on any other occasion, she would have found it amusing. But everything relating to Rita was still raw, like a new scar from which a protective dressing had been removed for the first time. And Erasmus zeroing in on the matter she'd been trying to discuss with Brill earlier in the evening was just uncanny.

"Humor an old man's whimsy?"

"Never." She punched Erasmus lightly on the upper arm. "But still, she held up quite well, I think."

"Did she now? I'm astonished she didn't flee screaming into the night, the way you laid into her."

"You don't say. Brill went a couple of rounds with her first, I gather. Laying out the facts of life. I thought"—Miriam focused on some inward vista—"honesty was the best policy."

"She's just discovered she has a second family and they're a nest of scheming vipers?"

"That's about it," Miriam admitted. She reached for the bottle of port: Erasmus got there first and tipped a generous measure into her tumbler. "Ras, I don't like this. Colonel Smith—most likely, his superiors—are playing head games with us again. If they can activate the ability in outer family members, in carriers, then they've got access to potentially thousands of world-walkers. Some of them only a few years younger than Rita. And they could have sent a helicopter instead, couldn't they? Or a bomb wing with nukes, like they did to Niejwein and the Gruinmarkt, although two can play at that game nowadays . . . But instead they sent Rita. There's no way I can read that as anything other than a personal threat aimed directly at me. Using blood as a weapon."

"Psychological warfare has always held a peculiar fascination for spies," Erasmus observed. He took a mouthful of his fortified wine. "Maybe they're trying to put a thumb on the balance, to tip it against you by convincing the likes of Adrian Holmes that you're conspiring with the United States against the Commonwealth."

"But I'd never . . . !"

"Of course not. But will Adrian believe that?"

NEW LONDON, TIME LINE THREE, AUGUST 2020

Rita awakened slowly, in an unfamiliar bedroom. The mattress felt wrong, weirdly lumpy and bouncy at the same time. *Springs,* she realized fuzzily. *Didn't they use metal springs in the old days?* She rolled over and opened her eyes on a view skewed at sixty degrees to reality. There was wallpaper, but the patterns were unfamiliar. There was furniture, but the wooden chair and the handles on the chest of drawers looked wrong. They were the products of nearly three centuries of divergent design decisions, embedding subtly different traditions in popular culture. *I'm in the Commonwealth,* she remembered, and the previous evening came crashing back in a mortifying rush: *kill me now!*

Either the Colonel had lied to her, or these people—strangers who happened to be her blood relatives—were lying to her. Maybe both, but she was fairly sure that in the course of her questioning she hadn't mentioned Colonel Smith by name. Inspector Morgan's questions had focused on protocol and tradecraft, on the precise methods and techniques of her reconnaissance, rather than on personalities. Then Mrs. Burgeson—Miriam—had dropped her bombshell, and it all fitted together horribly plausibly, the exploding phone and the double-cross story. Either Miriam was trying to psych her out, or everything she thought she knew about the people she was working for was wrong . . . or was it?

It wasn't as if she could go home and start asking questions about what really happened on 7/16. Everyone knew what happened that day in D.C. Asking questions would make you look like a tinfoil hat case at best, or one of the weirdos who still insisted that the twin towers had been mined with demolition charges on 9/11. And that assumed that her birth mother was trying to gaslight her, that her inside job theory was false. If it really *was* an inside job and the Colonel had been involved, asking questions sounded like a suicidally bad idea.

Rita rolled over and buried her face in the pillow. Her tradecraft self tried out a different narrative to see if it held water. Suppose Olga had sucked her in and surrounded her with her own allies and friends, establishing an intoxicating party atmosphere with freely flowing wine and everyone primed with the same story to—*no, that doesn't work either.* There was no rational reason why they'd need to turn Rita to their way of thinking, was there? *I'm just a courier,* she thought. *A go-between whose birth mother just happens to be* . . . fuck.

It all revolved around the fact of her existence. The Unit, the DHS, the earlier Family Trade Organization: whatever name it went by, the agency had a history with Mrs. Burgeson. With Miriam. And even when she slipped through their fingers, they'd kept a vigilant eye on her remaining connections. They'd been tracking Rita since she was eight. The Colonel had said as much to her face. The abduction attempt at the car park—*fake,* she realized dismally. It had been as fake as a three dollar bill. These people had helicopters and armed police and all the panoply of big government, just like the USA. They wouldn't send a pair of two-bit thugs to carjack their target. If they wanted her they'd have sent a SEAL team. What other experiences that she took for granted had been rigged, a theatrical trailer designed to hook an audience of one? Had they deliberately assigned her to Philadelphia just to trail her past Angie and see if they could make her—*no, that's not possible.* Rita shook her head dazedly as she sat up. But she kept circling back to the idea. Facebook was owned by the government agencies, everybody knew that. So were the other social networks. What if they'd drilled down deep enough to work out how she felt, then purposefully recruited Angie the way they'd reeled in Rita—*no, Angie's not part of the Unit, not a ringer like Julie. The only role the Colonel has for her is a hostage for my good behavior.* She felt unaccountably grubby even for thinking it, although she'd showered before dinner and slept between clean sheets.

The Colonel was a manipulative shit, but he wasn't omniscient. He couldn't have predicted that Rita would fall straight into Angie's arms after eight years separation, could he? She frowned again. On the other hand, when you had enough data about someone's behavioral profile you could use deep learning techniques to infer things about them that they weren't even aware of. Like supermarkets showing young women ads for maternity products before they even realized they were pregnant. Or political campaigns that could micro-target propaganda to pander to your prejudices and nudge you to vote their way, based on which FB posts you'd liked. Maybe there was a social graph heat map somewhere inside DHS, labeled RITA CONTACTS. And maybe they'd picked the site of this test operation in accordance with the gnomic advice of some incomprehensible deep learning neural network, some software oracle that looked at the phase of the Moon and the state of her Facebook feed and gave a higher probability of her proving loyal if they ran her in Philly instead of Boston . . .

Her office garb was folded neatly on top of the dressing table. She dressed quickly in the pale light filtering through the thin muslin curtains. The top floor bathroom was next door to the guest bedroom, and it was unoccupied. Morning ablutions and brushing out her hair bought her more minutes for uneasy introspection before she had to go downstairs and face Huw and Brilliana.

I'll have to go back, she realized. *They've got their hooks in me.* "They" being Colonel Smith and Dr. Scranton. They knew how she felt about her parents and her grandfather. They *for sure* knew *all* about her and Angie and their illegal-in-Arizona relationship. They knew about everything except—she hoped—the Wolf Orchestra. They'd sent her on this mission (*call it Operation Headfuck,* she thought bitterly: although whether the head in question was hers or Miriam's was unclear) only after they had made sure she had something to go home *for.* Whether or not they'd aimed Angie at her was irrelevant at this point.

That was something the Stasi's Hauptverwaltung Aufklärung—the Main Reconnaissance Administration—had known. Unless you're *absolutely* certain of an asset's loyalty, never send them abroad without sufficient ties to bring them home again. Hold hostages. If necessary, *manufacture* hostages, lest they defect. The home leave and the weekends off had to be seen in this context. Colonel Smith had sent her into the Commonwealth knowing there was a risk she'd begin to empathize with her newfound cousins. Or to bond with the woman who'd had her arm twisted into giving her up for adoption all those years ago. He wouldn't have done that without a hook firmly embedded in her lip, so he could reel her back in when the time was ripe. Or hooks. Hooks called Kurt and Angie and Mom and Pop . . .

James Bond didn't have any hooks, she mused as she tied her hair back. But then, *Bond was a sociopath, wasn't he?* With a heavy heart, she went downstairs.

The Explorer-General and his wife occupied a government-owned row house within the walls of the fortified palace-city of New London, granted by grace and favor (formerly imperial grace, now the favor of the ruling party, whatever that meant) when they came to town. It didn't have much of a yard and it looked small from outside, but looks were deceptive. Rita had to descend three flights of stairs to get to the first floor, where the dining room, parlor, and kitchen facilities were located. She'd slept late. The clock on the landing said it was well past eight when she paused in the dining room doorway.

"C'mon in," called Huw. He was sitting at the table, munching on a bread roll while reading an odd-sized newspaper page. He seemed to be alone. "Cook'll sort you out anything you want for breakfast. Coffee?"

"Yes, please," Rita said gratefully. Huw reached for an ornately detailed silver coffee pot and poured a stream of thin brown liquid into a cup. "Is Brill still here?" She'd indicated she had plans for Rita's day the evening before, but Rita's memory for trivia had blurred under the impact of one significant revelation too many.

"She's around," Huw said noncommittally. "I think she wants to talk to you before she heads to the office."

Ten minutes later Rita was working on a bowl of something not unlike muesli when Brilliana paused in the doorway. "Oh, there you are," she said. She wore a coat over her tunic-suit. "Did you sleep well, Rita?"

"Well enough, thank you." Rita felt her hackles going up defensively. Brill was probably just trying to be friendly, but the words "bossy" and "intrusive" also sprang to mind.

"Good. I've got to be in the office today, but Alice Morgan will be dropping round in an hour to take you shopping, then—"

"Shopping?"

"Yes." Brilliana looked slightly impatient; Huw leaning back, stayed out of the firing line. "If you're going to visit for any length of time you need clothes you can be seen in without every street urchin you pass calling the Polis to report a foreign spy. You also need a personal protection detail, at least until Ras introduces you in public as his wife's daughter, and therefore somebody it would be unwise to arrest on charges of, oh, trespassing on the Permanent Way, for example? Inspector Morgan is in the know, so we might as well use her. And she'll be a good deal better at steering you around department stores and preventing you from committing fashion crimes than his lordship here." Brill reached over and tousled Huw's thinning hair affectionately. He managed to keep a straight face, but Rita recognized the dynamic at work with a twinge. "So: you're to go shopping this morning, then after lunch you have a session with Erasmus's people, and then Huw can show you around the DPR survey offices in town. I'm sure Colonel Smith will be fascinated by your report!"

"Um." Rita paused a moment. "Can I ask a favor?"

"Sure." Brill's response was so studiously noncommittal that Rita almost chickened out. "You can ask, whatever you like." A quick flash of a smile: "I can't guarantee to give you the answer you want."

"Is it possible to send a message?" Rita licked her suddenly dry lips. "I mean, if I write a letter, would there be some way to see it gets into a USPS mailbox with a stamp on it?"

"A letter"—Brilliana focused on Rita with the intensity of a laser beam—"to whom, and why?"

Huw cleared his throat. "Sending an anonymous letter to someone in the United States is *extremely* dangerous for whoever has to do the job," he said. "We're not exactly welcome there. What you're asking for would—hypothetically, I mean, assuming we have any such people—expose a covert asset to an elevated risk of arrest. And while we could in principle arrange to have a letter or postcard mailed from somewhere outside the

Continental United States, it'd be scanned as soon as it crossed the border and it'd take up to a week to get there *and* it's still not a trivial job. Essentially you're asking for an international courier package, a scheduled para-time transit drop, and someone to actually go and execute the task and then confirm the letter was mailed as specified. This is a government bureaucracy: mailing a letter in another time line normally requires committee approval and costs the equivalent of six or seven thousands of dollars."

"But you could just send an e-mail," Brilliana suggested.

"An e-mail—" Rita nearly choked on a mouthful of coffee. "How is that even possible?"

"Oh, we have our methods." Brill's face relaxed into a smugly bland mask.

"Stop playing with her." Huw sounded amused. "Rita, we have people— agents—overseas, outside the United States, in places where they don't have to worry about the DHS breaking down their door or the CIA dropping a Hellfire missile on them. There are some countries the USA doesn't mess with: China, Brazil, Indonesia. Every few hours we ship a memory stick over, and every few hours stuff comes back. It's called store-and-forward, it's slow—it's *no* way to surf the Web—but it suffices. So if you can remember an e-mail address, we can get a message to it, and fetch you a reply. But—this is a big 'but'—we'll be reading your correspondence before we send it. And the NSA will be reading it on its way to your recipient. And we'll be reading your reply."

Rita took a deep breath. "I don't want to be any trouble," she said, "but . . ."

Brilliana looked at her. "You're thinking about your family, aren't you?"

"Yes." She took another deep breath. "If Colonel Smith's been keeping me in a sandbox, he thinks I'm disposable." There was no point denying it. "If he tries to dispose of me, that's one thing. But what about my . . ." She trailed off.

Huw and Brilliana exchanged a look. "It hasn't happened yet," Brill said calmly. "And it probably won't." *She's trying to be reassuring,* Rita thought queasily. *She's trying to spare me.* "And—this is hard—when that sort of thing happens, it's up to them, up to your relatives, your partner, to decide what they want to do next. If you ask for asylum we can help you. And if they want refuge, we can do something about that. But you can't make their minds up for them—"

"What she forgot to say," Huw interrupted, "is that yes, we'll help you warn your relatives if it becomes necessary—but it probably won't do any good. You can tell them the sky is about to fall, but they'll probably smile and ignore you and go about their business as usual. And if they're your relatives, Smith's people are certainly monitoring their e-mail, so your message will be spotted."

"Been there, done that," Brilliana said, and fell broodingly silent for a few seconds. "So. Is that all . . . ?"

"I guess." Rita pushed her bowl away. She didn't feel hungry anymore.

NEW LONDON, TIME LINE THREE, AUGUST 2020

The Chamber of People's Magistrates occupied the premises of the disgraced and disbanded House of Lords. It had been built in the 1960s by the last king's grandfather, in an attempt to abolish adversarial party factionalism by requiring their Lordships to mingle with no clear dividing lines, and the debating chamber consequently featured a horseshoe-shaped arc of seating. But after the revolution, the elected magistrates—elected only if their views met with the approval of the Radical Party's Commission for Democracy, which basically meant being opposed to the restoration of the monarchy—had gradually partitioned into a rainbow of beliefs. Those who trod dangerously close to monarchical restorationism tended to sit at one edge of the aisle, to the left of the Speaker's seat. Their foes, the Egalitarians and Ranters, spread to the right.

Both wings had their own preferred dining rooms and drinking dens in the complex scattered around the Chamber building. And it was in one that leaned to the right that Adrian Holmes took his lunch with Commissioner Sánchez of the War Ministry.

"I'm worried about the Burgesons," Holmes said bluntly. He'd already laid his groundwork. Sánchez, a heavyset man of late middle age, with lugubrious features and a bulbous red nose, nodded tacit agreement as he bent over his seafood platter. "I don't know how much you've heard about what they're doing right now, but I thought I should keep you inside the charmed circle."

Sánchez laid his fork down and swallowed. "Do, please, by all means," he said. His voice was surprisingly mellow and high-pitched for such a large fellow. It was not the most surprising thing about him. The grandson of an Amazonian logger who had migrated to the coastal islands of the Incan dominions and made a fortune importing guano, Sánchez had gone on to spend his inheritance on a low-level guerilla war against the brutal Samurai tax-farmers brought in by the last king's own father—losing everything, then gaining a new respectability in the wake of the revolution. Now he was a member of the commission charged with defending the Commonwealth from royalist and imperial conspiracies abroad, the sword and the shield of the Party. He was not a particularly subtle man, but his loyalty to the principles of Democracy and Revolution was unimpeachable.

"You are privy to the background briefing on the Department of Parahistorical Research," Holmes began. "You know we are dependent on these world-walkers for access—a small clique of families who have a highly unusual talent that runs in the direct bloodline. What you might not have paid much notice to is the fact that it appears the primary power in time line two, the alternate the Burgesons are always warning us about—the United States of America—has for some time had access to *machines* that can transport payloads across para-time. They're ahead of us in some ways—"

"I've seen their gizmos." Sánchez snorted. "And the other stuff." The War Ministry had access to samples supplied by MITI, dangled tantalizingly in front of them as proof that the super-technology MITI promised to deliver in future was actually possible. Wonders like 3-D printers able to extrude turbine blades, sniper rifles with supercomputer-assisted gunsights. Nothing the Commonwealth could manufacture for itself *yet*—not for another decade, anyway—but nothing they wouldn't be able to match eventually. "Where did they get para-time machines from, though?"

"There are rumors about chopped-up brains in boxes." Holmes's expression of distaste was genuine. "When they stumbled across the world-walkers they were desperate. On a war footing. In confidence: we know there's something odd in world-walkers' brains. The Ministry of Health has been conducting some discreet research, and our electron microscopes are apparently good enough to see—well, a handful of world-walkers die every year, and they're all Persons of Interest, and MiniHealth are in charge of the autopsia program, so of course some slides were prepared. We're *not* going to be building any world-walking machines—it's all the proverbial ten years away, like fusion reactors and landing on the Moon—but I believe some of our colleagues are working on it." He pointedly didn't say whether or not such a research program was being conduced under the auspices of MITI. That way, Sánchez could maintain deniability.

"Well then." Sánchez picked up his fork and resumed eating, stolidly focusing on his meal. Holmes wasn't fooled: he had the Commissioner's full and undivided attention.

"I am pretty certain that Mrs. Burgeson and her relatives must have guessed this is going on. They'd be fools not to. They'd also be fools not to realize that they have had a tidy little monopoly for nearly twenty years, and sooner or later it will evaporate. So some or all of them will be making plans for the future, for a time when they are merely citizens with a curious and useful talent rather than the gatekeepers of unimaginable riches. And, of course, they must be considering their probable future after the First Man takes his final curtain call and leaves the stage. As are we all."

Sánchez merely nodded.

"I *think* Mrs. Burgeson herself is fundamentally loyal to the Party," Holmes continued. "She supported our cells in Boston before the revolution, that much is a matter of record. And Erasmus is Erasmus: he's as twisty as a left-handed corkscrew, but his dedication to the cause is above question. What worries me is what their protégés might be planning. I've received some disturbing reports of activities conducted by the DPR in *our* time line. Activities which *might* represent a melted stovepipe between Propaganda and what is admittedly a highly competent intelligence agency, but which might equally well be a rogue operation, or even preparations for an act of treason on an unprecedented scale."

Sánchez dropped his fork. "Treason?" he echoed.

"That is a worst-case interpretation," Adrian averred, dabbing delicately at his lips with a handkerchief. He picked up his glass and took a sip. "I sincerely hope I'm wrong. But consider the nature of the world-walking ability. It's an inherited trait, one that those of us not born within the charmed circle can never hope to emulate. As such, I submit that all world-walkers are unconsciously predisposed to elitist deviationism. Not through malice, as might be the case among the rent-farming aristocracy"—he noted the subtle tell as Sánchez's face stiffened—"but simply because of what they *are*. So a couple of years ago I directed SCEP's Office of Internal Affairs to keep an eye on the senior management of the DPR, in case they were running wild. And about two months ago a report crossed my desk concerning the sudden redeployment of a Major Hjorth, who happens to be both a world-walker and the younger brother of the Explorer-General. Which means he's related by marriage to the very top of his own reporting chain, to one Brilliana Hjorth, who directs para-time intelligence operations in the United States."

"Major in which agency?" asked Sánchez, his tone ominously mild.

"Commissioned in the Army, on permanent secondment to the DPR's Acquisition of Technology Program. Late thirties, special forces training, pilot's license, fluent in at least three languages. He is one of the few officers considered sufficiently acculturated and reliable to operate in the other New York as an illegal from time to time—you are aware that they are a full-blown police state, yes? Miniature television cameras trained on everyone all the time? Invisible flying killer robots to assassinate their enemies at home and abroad? Well, Major Hjorth is a heavy hitter. One may speculate that the only reason he topped off at Major is that he is a hands-on kind of fellow, disinclined to administration. Anyway, he's gone under deep cover, and SCEP is getting some very suggestive reports."

Sánchez pushed his plate aside. "Do you want me to reel him in and squeeze him?"

"Not yet. You probably couldn't find him, anyway. Our reports suggest he's in Germany, of all places. In Berlin."

Sánchez frowned. "What's in Berlin?"

"Have you been reading the weekly digests about the Pretender's household activities?"

Sánchez's frown deepened. "Wait, now I recall—oh no, you *cannot* be serious—"

"I hope I'm wrong, Commissioner."

"Surely you can't believe the world-walkers are going after the Crown Princess?"

"*I don't know.* Short of arresting Mrs. Hjorth or confronting Mrs. Burgeson directly there's no easy way of resolving the question. But I find it highly suspicious that elements within the DPR are engaging with the Pretender's court at the very highest level, behind our backs, just as we ready ourselves for the greatest leadership crisis the Commonwealth has faced since the revolution. My fear is that as instinctive elitists, their minds turn more easily towards an elitist solution to the question of succession than to the preservation of democracy . . ."

"You fear they may be preparing a coup on behalf of Elizabeth Hanover. That would be your treason right there, would it not?"

Holmes smiled tightly. "You read my mind."

"Your mind is an open book, sir—when you leave the bookmark in view." Sánchez's normally affable expression darkened. "And if you're right I believe we are going to have a fight on our hands."

PHILADELPHIA, TIME LINE TWO, AUGUST 2020

FEDERAL EMPLOYEE 004930391 CLASSIFIED VOICE TRANSCRIPT

DR. SCRANTON: Sitrep, please.

COL. SMITH: Rita first: she's over there. Transit confirmed. Gus . . . ?

LIAISON, AIR FORCE: The Dragonfly micro-UAV dump confirmed

successful contact. They had a car waiting for her. Dragonfly only has a fifteen minute loiter time when it's carrying a transit pack, so all we really know is that she got into the limo without obvious signs of duress. By the time the second Dragonfly sortied, the transponder in her navkit was out of range, so at a guess they were heading for one of the turnpikes we mapped. Range is about ten klicks, so an undirected search was obviously not going to work, but I took a gamble on Manhattan and requested another Dragonfly sortie, and it hit pay dirt. Her transponder is in a row house near the downtown administrative complex, in what would be Little Italy in our New York. The transponder data dump says they drove her up the highway, stopped at another government building, then she went to a different row house, then to this one which is about a quarter of a mile away. And she's been there ever since.

DR. SCRANTON: So we can assume she's in the administrative capital. What they call New London. Is that right?

LIAISON, AIR FORCE: Yes.

DR. SCRANTON: Okay, Colonel, please continue.

COL. SMITH: We've had no direct inputs from Rita: there isn't enough bandwidth in those micro-UAVs to upload the entire audio recording from the bugs in her camera and navkit without risking interception, especially in a high-security zone like their capital. So unless you *really* want it, I'd prefer to wait until she brings them home. She's only been there 18 hours—

DR. SCRANTON: Understood. Proceed as planned for now. The others?

AGENT GOMEZ: Nothing significant to report on Kurt except that he went online to American Airlines yesterday to book a flight back to Phoenix, departing next Friday. It's likely he's planning on sticking around Philadelphia until Rita returns. He phoned Angela this afternoon but it was all trivia, apart from a brief reference—by Angela—to Rita being, quote, away on business, unquote. As for Angela, she drove Rita to the office then went to work as usual. No new audio drop-outs, no signs of evasion. Whatever they were talking about the other evening seems to be over for now.

DR. SCRANTON: Okay, that's looking good. Now, in the short term I'd be astonished if Rita returns in less than 48 hours elapsed—more likely 3–5 days. So I'd like to work up a plan to drain the audio capture, if any, with minimal risk of exposure if it turns out she's on a protracted jaunt. Can you figure out a safe way to send a transponder over that isn't going to attract attention? Assuming she's in a safe house.

LIAISON, AIR FORCE: I think we can do that, if they aren't observing COMSEC around the items. I wouldn't like to bet on these people being unaware of our capabilities . . . I'll need authorization for another two Dragonfly sorties to get an exact fix on the house, maybe peep through some upper story windows as well. Then we can send a small return-capable robot through at night, *inside* the building. If possible we will identify a handy piece of furniture for cover—a bed or a chest of drawers or something it can hide under, within radio range of the bugs. I'd call this a medium-risk strategy, but we can minimize the hazard by sending the probe packages on ten second jaunts at dead of night during the mapping stage. Once we've mapped out the interior of the house and identified target spaces, we can do all sorts of things: download the voice dump from the bugs, send insects and micro-UAVs through, turn the whole DARPA/CIA toy chest loose on them if we turn up anything interesting.

COL. SMITH: There won't be, unless they're idiots. But if they *are* idiots . . .

DR. SCRANTON: I really hope they're not. They have lots of nuclear weapons, remember?

END TRANSCRIPT

NEW LONDON, TIME LINE 3, AUGUST 2020

Going shopping for clothes with a girlfriend was one thing. It was entirely another thing to be taken shopping by a middle-ranking cop with orders to buy a wardrobe for a leading politician's daughter to wear during an election campaign. Doing it in a foreign country with unfamiliar fashions was just the icing on the stress cake.

Inspector Morgan turned up shortly after breakfast time, with a car, a driver, and a businesslike attitude. "Right," she said, "there's a department store uptown, Messrs. Cook and White's, which should get you started. I have a list and we can bill it to the Minister's account. Let's see how fast we can burn through it, shall we?" Rita interpolated the rest of the sentence—*so I can get back to my real job instead of babysitting you*—and shrugged.

"Okay—yes," she said, and surrendered to a very unfun experience.

From the moment Alice Morgan marched her through a side door and handed her over to a matronly store clerk with a tape measure, along with a shopping list and a stern admonition to let those who knew best sort her out, Rita lost all volition. The store wasn't laid out like anything she'd encountered before. There were no bar-coded tags here, no racks of cheap manufactured items from sweatshops in Bangladesh and the Congo. They took her to a fitting room, stripped her down to underwear, and took more measurements than she'd imagined possible. They punched holes out of a credit-card-sized piece of cardboard to record her sizes. Then Morgan and her personal shop-jailer escorted her through a variety of claustrophobically small rooms stacked floor to ceiling with drawers full of items, some of them mundane, others unfamiliar. Pants and skirts and blouses were familiar enough, if prone to fastening weirdly, but the shalwar suits and kimonos and some of the undergarments for the formal outfits left her wishing for a user's manual. More numbers were taken, added to another odd-shaped card. Then they moved her on again to a cobbler's department, where it seemed she wasn't expected to try on shoes, but to have her feet measured for bespoke footwear.

"That's it," Alice said half-approvingly just as Rita was getting ready to drop. "I think we're done. Mrs. Murphy, it's all to be billed to the Ministry of Propaganda. I have a letter of authorization. When can you deliver it by?"

Mrs. Murphy—the store clerk who was now more familiar with Rita's body than anyone but Angie—bobbed something not unlike a curtsey.

"Everything but the shoes can be with you this evening, ma'am, if the tabulator says we have them in stock. The shoes will take two days, even if we rush them. You'll be wanting us to retain the lasts, I'm sure?"

"Do that," said Morgan. "All right, let's talk to the accounts department."

Accounts—indeed, all payments—were handled by a hollow-faced fellow sitting in a wooden booth fronted by a transom. While Morgan was waiting for the man to duplicate her invoice (using a photocopier hidden in a back office, via pneumatic tube), Rita tugged her sleeve nervously. "Do we take anything away at all?" she asked. "Or is it always delivered . . . ?"

"It's all delivered to order." Morgan looked at her oddly. "After the alterations. Or do you do your fittings at home, where you come from?"

Rita shook her head. It took a moment to work it out: *So that's what the measurements were for.* "It's very different. Most stuff is off-the-shelf, ready to wear. No alterations." Something about this, she realized, was important: something about the way they managed supply chains here that the Colonel would want to know. But it stubbornly refused to come into focus in her mind.

"I imagine it must seem strange." The Inspector turned back to the payments clerk, accepting a form to sign in triplicate. "Well, we've just spent half a year's universal basic income on your wardrobe: I hope you get some use from it. Come on, I believe you have an appointment with Mr. Burgeson's people in under an hour."

Rita managed to conceal her disbelief. How had they spent a couple of months' money? Was clothing really that expensive here? On the other hand: everything was altered to fit. The measurements had been very detailed. If they'd never developed a culture of cheap overseas production and disposable garments, then everything must be made like expensive business suits or couture items back home. And they'd run at least five outfits past her, three suits and two formal gowns. She followed obediently as Morgan led her back to the side entrance and out onto the street, where a car was waiting for them. *They're serious about parading me in public,* she realized with a sinking sensation. The idea of being a pawn in a recondite political game didn't appeal. But unless she was willing to run back home with her tail between her legs, thereby annoying the Colonel (and risking whatever measures he might consider necessary to motivate her to greater effort), there didn't seem to be any alternative.

The next stop, back inside the walled complex at the foot of the island, was another bland ministerial building. This one had no windows less than twenty feet up, and appeared to have been designed to be defensible in event of a siege. An overbearingly large statue of Hermes dominated the entrance plaza, bearing a message scroll and a somewhat anachronistic bullhorn. As Inspector Morgan led her past its plinth, Rita couldn't help noticing a scattering of droppings. It seemed the messenger of the gods got scant respect from the odd red-breasted pigeons that swarmed hereabouts.

Alice Morgan led her past reception (staffed, like Mrs. Burgeson's ministerial offices, by men and women in unfamiliarly styled quasi-military uniforms), into an elevator, and up to a level consisting of a warren of open-plan offices. Every desk seemed to have a bulky glass-tubed computer terminal atop it, their screens swimming with fuzzy blue-gray text; dotted around the edge of the hallways were recording studios with sound-deadening double-glazing, bulky open-reel tape recorders, and mixing desks adorned with a fearsome array of sliders and thumbwheels. Rita found it odd how imposing the obsolete technology looked. Back home in the United States this could all be done with a cheap tablet and a couple of microphones, but here it took a wall of flashing lights, needle-twitching dials, and minions to change the spinning tapes. "Let's see," Alice muttered. "Room 3041, Donald Truax. That's 3029, here's 3033, ah . . ."

She opened a thick glass door and gently shoved Rita through it. "Mr. Truax, this is Rita Douglas, as requested. I'll wait outside."

"Call me Don." The man in front of the microphone, his middle-aged and thinning hair crushed by a bulky headset, managed a brief hand-wave in her direction. A younger guy hunched over the mixing desk with ferocious concentration, unable to spare even the briefest eye contact. "Come in, Rita."

"Um, do you know why I'm here?" Rita shuffled closer to the table then perched one hip on the wooden interviewee's chair.

"Let's see." Don picked up a letter: "Special request from the Director-General, at the advice of the Minister. Please record a human-interest segment with Rita Douglas, diplomatic courier from the government of the *United States of America* in the next universe over, ready for broadcast on next Saturday's show. Prior clearance and censorship applies, priority A-star." He shrugged. "That's pretty unequivocal, huh?" He smiled at her, only slightly pityingly. "So I guess that costume isn't a prop from some drama shoot?"

"I, oh hell, I had *no* idea!" Flustered, Rita almost stood up: then she had second thoughts and sat down again. "I'm, uh, not supposed to be public. I mean, I was told these were low-key talks about talks, not like . . ." She trailed off. *Anchorman,* she realized with dawning horror. *Broadcast news and commentary. Holy shit!* It was every spy's nightmare writ large.

"These talks might be low-key wherever you come from." Truax looked past her. "If I had to hazard a guess, they might still be. But this came with clearance and censorship confirmation which means the Minister himself is behind this. So he wants a segment in the can, ready to roll, but I wouldn't go mouthing off about it in the meantime, huh, Brad?"

Brad glanced up from his mixer. "What?"

"Forget it. Miss Douglas, if you'd be so good as to take a headset, let's start with a sound check? Then Brad will start recording . . ."

Action This Day

There was a valley in a forest on a cold continent on the edge of forever, and in the valley there was a dome that had already been ancient when the pyramids in Egypt were built.

Men had most recently rediscovered this place a dozen years ago, and around the skirts of the dome they had built a base. It sheltered behind tall steel razor-wire fences, surveilled by cameras and the muzzles of robot guns. The guns pointed inward. Nobody lived on this continent, for human life had never evolved in this time line, and the builders of the dome had been wiped out millennia earlier. Nevertheless, the personnel of Camp Singularity felt safest knowing that the dome was well-guarded.

People worked inside the dome. Their ranks included soldiers from the Army Corps of Engineers, archaeologists from Homeland Security, and spooks from the Colonel's Unit, which focused on emergent high-technology threats from other time lines. Latterly, a team of technicians from the National Reconnaissance Office had arrived, escorting a low-leader. This bore a payload shrouded in a white-walled container, antiseptic in its clean-room wrapping. The NRO folks played tourist within the limits of their sky-high security clearances, discreetly gaping at the ruins of the ancient alien para-time fortress when they weren't attending to their assignments. As employees of the federal agency tasked with launching and operating spy satellites and other military spacecraft, they didn't get to visit other time lines very often—much less ones hiding technological secrets on a par with anything they dealt with at work. They were here to prep the payload in the big white box for delivery to the other side of the gate inside the dome.

The gate was an enigma wrapped inside a mystery. Nobody knew for sure who'd built the dome in the first place, although they had been dubbed the Forerunners—a long lost human civilization that had spread through a myriad of parallel universes, of which the agencies of the US government had so far explored less than two hundred. The para-time transport technology controlled by the DHS had been developed from the nanoscale artificial life machinery harvested from the brains of captured Merchant Prince clan couriers. In vitro cultured neurons could be stimulated to in turn activate the self-replicating intracellular Q-machines that caused whatever they were in electrostatic equilibrium with to tunnel into a parallel universe. But the gate was something different: a permanent portal, an open wormhole leading into another realm—one where the Earth itself no longer existed.

The far end of the gate hung a little less than three and a half thousand nautical miles above a black hole the size of a walnut—a hole with a mass disturbingly similar to that of the Earth itself. The Unit had constructed a pressurized bridge through the gate, and the observatory at the end of the bridge had spotted debris in close orbit, whirling fast around the hole. But the observatory couldn't deliver a conclusive reading on whether the debris were artificial or merely captured near-Earth asteroidal debris, for they were small and fast-moving and thousands of miles away. After much bureaucratic wrangling, a decision had been taken to request the NRO's assistance in investigating the suspected Forerunner wreckage. And the payload in the launch shroud was the NRO's initial response.

By NRO standards, the satellite on the low-loader was small beer. It weighed less than a ton, cost less than a jet airliner, had taken only two years to design and assemble (largely from spare parts left over from other programs), and lacked most of the bells and whistles of the spysat agency's normal toys. After all, a *real* spy satellite was the size of a school bus—far too big to pass through the gate—and cost as much as a Navy cruiser. This payload was simply a proof of concept and an experiment, nothing more. On the other hand, to the Unit it was an *exciting* experiment. It had the potential to disrupt an entire industry. Various manufacturers of medium-payload boosters, from United Launch Alliance to Raytheon, might be *very* unhappy if it worked. If they could combine the availability of the gate, a black hole, and para-time transfer machines to launch payloads using gravitational slingshot maneuvers rather than rockets, it stood to disrupt more than an industry. There were diplomatic and arms control implications to be understood, a whole new balance of power angle that the National Security Council would have to grapple with—

Julie Straker was sitting in on the Bridge Control Room with Jose Mendoza, the watch officer, when the phone from the guard house up at Camp Singularity buzzed.

"Straker here." The phone knew who she was, recognizing the pattern of veins in her hand as she answered it, but the speaker at the other end might not: "How can I help?"

"Gateway? Captain told me to warn you, you've got a VIP inbound. She'll be with you in about twenty minutes. Meant to be an unscheduled inspection, so you didn't hear from us, m'kay?"

"Got you." Julie nodded. Here in Nova America 11, lots of stuff that would have been committed to logfiles if it happened back home never got recorded. Landline calls between remote security offices being one of them. She grinned. "Tell the Captain thanks from everybody down here." There were few enough people permanently stationed at the bases in Nova America 11 that they took a less rigorous approach to security than some people back home might expect. After all, leaks were impossible—aside from the steady trickle of air past the seals around the bridge, whistling thinly into the big emptiness around the hole in space, of course. She glanced over at Jose. "We've got company," she said.

"Right." He put down his tablet then glanced back at the row of CCTV screens showing the clean room and the Bridge Approach Room. The

BAR was a white corridor, windowless, rectangular in cross-section and as sterile and functional as the space station module it was derived from. The bridge was supported from one end—the Nova America 11 end—and terminated in hard vacuum, sixty feet beyond the far end of the gate between time lines. From the other end it dangled an airlock and a remote manipulator arm above thousands of miles of radiation-drenched vacuum. The far end of the bridge wasn't in orbit around the hole: it kept station with the point where the Earth's surface should have been, if the Earth had still been a feature of the other time line. Consequently it drifted around the hole once every twenty-four hours, instead of orbiting it once every ninety-odd minutes. Right now two of their colleagues and four payload specialists from the NRO were carefully sliding a handcart along the floor of the corridor. The white box strapped on top of it was perhaps five feet long and three feet wide and high. Orientation markings and red badges warned of dire peril should the device be tilted beyond a safe angle, or struck with a sharp implement in the vicinity of its shrouded fuel tanks.

"Huh. That sucker's not doing the floor loading any favors." Jose squinted at a false-color display of the stresses playing across the structure of the bridge module. He reached for the mike in front of his desk: "Control to team. Please check lateral drift on payload, keep to within twenty centimeters of the painted centerline on the deck." A ton of payload and nearly half a ton of suited-up personnel put a considerable strain on the floor of the one-ended bridge, shortening its life. The indoor astronauts paused to inspect their cart and nudge it back toward the middle of the tunnel, just as Julie's phone blatted for attention.

"Straker here—" She sat up unconsciously. "Yes, ma'am. If you come straight to the control room, I'll log you in. Yes, we're still"—she glanced at the big clock up front—"fifty minutes until launch."

She put the phone down and turned to Jose. "Our visitor—it's Dr. Scranton."

"Doctor—" Jose paused. *"Her?"*

"Yup, the grand-boss." Dr. Eileen Scranton gave the Unit's chief executive, Colonel Smith, his marching orders. "Looks like she wants to watch this herself." Scranton was about as high up the chain of command as it was possible to get without being a purely political functionary who couldn't sneeze without a retinue of assistants and facilitators running to pass the tissues and take notes. But she tried to kid herself that she was keeping her hand in by directly supervising a project or two. If she wanted the excuse to sneak away from the interminable committee meetings for a few hours every week, who was Julie to criticize?

Jose frowned, pensive. "She's going to want to talk to you." Julie was technically part of the Colonel's small inner team, rather than one of the bridge controllers, although she was certificated to work here. "Who's on standby?"

"Max. I'll page him." She pulled up the shared staffing calendar and sent a priority message to his phone. "Wish the doctor'd given us some warning."

Half an hour later the technicians on the main screen had maneuvered the payload capsule up against the pressure door at the end of the bridge tunnel. They were locking down the connectors and checking the seals behind the outer door, ready to let the satellite out, when Dr. Scranton stepped inside. Max was logged in, sitting at the workstation beside Jose. "As you were," she said as Julie began to stand. "I'm just here to watch the launch. Nothing more."

Julie smiled at her grand-boss. "Glad you could make it. Unfortunately there won't be much to see from here . . ."

"I am aware of that." Dr. Scranton's answering expression was wry. Julie had come to her attention on an external assignment, which marked her as one of the Colonel's highflying youngsters. "Why don't you talk me through the mission profile?"

"Uh, okay . . ." Nonplussed, Julie took a few seconds to realize what was different about Dr. Scranton today. She was in her late-fifties, unobtrusive and handsome in the mode of so many older female Washington insiders. What was new was a pair of thick-rimmed spectacles. Tiny compound eyes glinted at the corners of bridge and arm—easily mistaken for decorative crystals if you weren't expecting the sensors of a federal lifelogger. "This is on the record, isn't it?"

"Pay no attention to the cameras." Scranton shook her head minutely.

Ah, Julie realized sickly. "Uh, yes, ma'am." So this was an official visit: today's launch was important enough to rate someone who reported directly to the National Security Council as an observer. Even though the dome crew was barely into double-digits. (The dome counted as a hazardous posting: all the supporting personnel were stationed well away from the gate.)

"All right. ERGO-1"—she pointed to the crate visible in the middle screen, sitting up against the airlock door—"is the first in a series of Ergosphere Reconnaissance Gravity Orbiter probes. Uh, ergosphere . . . black holes spin, right? It's got all the mass, and angular momentum, and the magnetic field, of the planet that used to be here, squished down inside a golf ball? So it's spinning *really fast*. The ergosphere is a zone just around the black hole where relativistic frame-dragging means we can extract info—" She stopped, seeing Dr. Scranton's polite expression freeze. "I can get you references for later, if you want? Uh-huh. Anyway, ERGO-1 is designed to get in really close and probe the region right around the hole. It's powered up and undergoing systems self-test and thermal equilibration, controlled remotely from base camp, while it comes up to ambient temperature and pressure—" Dr. Scranton nodded seriously, as if she hadn't sat in on the budget committee meetings that signed off on the specifications.

Julie took a deep breath and continued. *For the record, right.* "It's basically a satellite, minus the regular launch platform—the big rocket we'd normally need to throw it into orbit. Here, we can just wheel it up to the door and throw it out. At which point, it begins to fall towards the gravitational singularity, because we're not in orbit around it. We're circling around the hole's polar axis once per day, like the planet the other end of the bridge is anchored to. Because of the lateral velocity component, and the fact that we're some way north of the equator, ERGO-1 won't drop directly into the black hole. Instead, it'll spiral towards it then end up in an elliptical orbit, oscillating above and below the accretion disk with an apogee—maximum altitude above the hole—somewhere below our current ground level."

She paused and checked the main screen. The bridge crew were with-drawing: the box containing ERGO-1 was now latched to the inner air-lock door. In a few minutes, once the crew were clear, they'd depressurize the bridge completely and open the doors. "Of course we're not going to leave it there."

ERGO-1 had a rocket motor. Not a very powerful one—although like all rockets it contained enough highly explosive fuel to kill or injure the bridge crew if anything went wrong while they were preparing it for launch. It was just sufficient to give ERGO-1 a kick as it made its closest pass to the planetary mass singularity, barely fifty kilometers away from the ergosphere. A kick that, thanks to something called a relativistic Oberth maneuver, would slingshot the satellite back up toward the level of the bridge station with vastly higher momentum than it had descended with. Once it rose above mean Earth surface level, the satellite would jaunt back to the skies above Camp Singularity, and squawk its teleme-try log at the ground station there before disintegrating as it slammed into the atmosphere at well above escape velocity. *How to burn through one hundred million dollars in less than three hours.*

Dr. Scranton was still nodding as Jose spoke up: "Bridge crew are clear of the number three pressure door. I counted them out and I've counted them in. We're clear up to the thousand second hold." Like all space launch processes, there was a countdown sequence with built-in hold-points where the ground crew could review the telemetry from the payload and verify everything was all right before proceeding. Rattling was audible from the other side of the control room wall, which ad-joined the clean room disrobing area. The NRO folks would be un-locking their helmets and high-fiving one another when the probe itself powered up.

"Well then, you may proceed." Scranton pulled up one of the office chairs and folded herself down to watch the show.

In Julie's opinion it was the world's dullest space launch. There were no exciting rocket flames and noises to reward them for plowing through the checklists. They'd already pushed out three cubesats this week—

fist-sized titanium cubes, ten centimeters on an edge—via the number two lock. This was simply the same, on a bigger scale. It held all the excitement of taking the trash out to the Dumpster.

Join the DHS, tour the multiverse, train as an agent, and spend your life clicking through computer checklists with an obsolete mouse. Sometimes Julie couldn't figure out what she was doing here. The job varied a lot—the Colonel had deliberately kept the active core of the Unit small, so that everybody had to do a bit of everything—but some of the variations were tiresome and repetitive, so boring that only self-discipline saw her through her shifts. Jose and Max were part of the regular bridge crew: all Julie could do was watch screens when they pointed her at something, check off items in a list—

"One hundred seconds," said the synthesized voice of the launch clock.

"Nearly ready," Max remarked to nobody in particular. "Close out on oxidizer tank, pressure nominal—" Just like the stages in a real satellite launch, without the big-ass rocket sitting underneath.

"Switching to onboard battery power now—" The voice echoed down the link from base camp, where a rather larger team were monitoring their progress from a safe distance.

"Fuel filler line disconnect. Oxidizer filler line disconnect. All tanks pressurized—"

"Thirty seconds." The clock's time check was accentless, dispassionate.

Julie was aware of Dr. Scranton sitting up tensely, watching the big status display at the front of the room over her shoulder—

"External door coming open now." Jose bent over the airlock control panel. "Internal door in ten seconds—"

"Confirm launch window open—"

An obstructed view appeared on the main screen: it showed something blocky and indistinct surrounded by a thin rind of darkness, as if the camera had macular degeneration. The darkness around the edge gradually brightened.

"Ten seconds. Nine. Eight . . . three, two, one . . ."

The indistinct circle of darkness began to shrink and sharpen, details filling in. Now she could see the back side of a spacecraft, the bell nozzle of the main engine surrounded by a rat's nest of pipework and the ducting of gas generators and attitude control thrusters. It slid smoothly out of the box, shrinking as it receded from the camera it had obscured. ERGO-1 began the long, silent fall through thousands of miles of vacuum toward the knotted pinprick of space-time that had once been a planet, before someone had murdered it.

"We have complete separation," said Max. He sounded smug. "High-gain transmitter is up and running, ERGO-1 says hello world."

"Range one kilometer and opening, fifteen seconds, mark." This, from Jose.

Julie turned to Dr. Scranton. "That's it for now," she said. "Perigee is about fifteen minutes away: ERGO-1 is running through its final test cycle. Main engine ignition is due in eight hundred and thirty seconds from the . . . mark. Between now and then it's going to be about as much fun to watch as paint drying. Can I interest you in a coffee?"

Scranton nodded. "Regular, half and half, no sweetener," she said, her eyes intently tracking the main status display as the numbers attached to the blocky diagram of the probe's schematics spiraled rapidly up. "Officer Mendoza. The wide-angle array is tracking the inner debris belts, correct?"

Julie didn't hear Jose's reply: the door to the control cabin closed behind her as she turned toward the break room coffee station. *Debris belts* . . . she paused. What *had* dragged Scranton out here to the politics-free backwater of Camp Singularity? The probe launch on its own didn't justify her presence: she had far bigger fish to fry. *Unless* . . .

She shuddered as a thought struck her. She opened the door to the break room and crossed to the coffee robot, punched in Scranton's order, and her own, and Max and Jose's regulars. *No,* she thought, *they* wouldn't *be that crazy.* Could they?

A probe with a rocket motor on the base and a conical front end looked more like the maneuvering bus that carried a nuclear missile's reentry vehicles than a regular research satellite. It had an ARMBAND unit for jaunting between time lines, and a conveniently compact black hole to provide a hefty change in velocity—enough to fling it on a ballistic trajectory that could come down anywhere on any other Earth in para-time, streaking in from the zenith without warning. *But it's not supposed to survive reentry*, she reminded herself. *Or is it?*

She shook her head, dismissing the thought. *Don't be silly, nobody's planning a nuclear first strike on another time line so they can't be testing a para-time ballistic missile*, she told herself. *That's a crazy thought.* She stacked the coffee mugs on a tray and walked them back to the bridge control room. *Nobody in the administration today is stupid enough to try and play* that *card again. Are they?*

BERLIN, TIME LINE THREE, AUGUST 2020

The game's afoot.

Hulius was not the only world-walker the DPR had assigned to the extraction mission. There were clearly at least two others, a lamplighter to scout out and secure the safe houses, and a courier to collect and deliver messages. But he was the only agent who would make direct contact with the target, and to preserve operational security he worked in isolation, never seeing his colleagues. Quite likely they never saw him either, so that if one was taken they could not lead their captors to the others.

So Hulius was profoundly relieved to receive Elizabeth's response via a dead letter drop in a bar near his hostel, operated by a maidservant who had been bribed or blackmailed by the unseen courier. He'd finished his conversion training on the Cirrus, and was cautiously confident of his ability to make it do what it was supposed to, weather in two time lines permitting. And he'd been getting bored lately, which was an ever-present danger during a covert operation. Covert ops overwhelmingly consisted of "hurry up and wait," but bored agents cut corners and allowed themselves to get sloppy, which was how they graduated to being blown agents, or even dead agents. Neither of these outcomes was desirable, in Hulius's opinion. But now that the Princess had signaled her intention to proceed, he could set the wheels in motion.

The next morning Hulius headed for the tram stop as usual. He didn't tell his landlord that he didn't expect to return. The morning's mission might yet abort, and anyway, what the hostel owner didn't know the hostel owner couldn't blab to a nosy secret police agent. He rode out to the furrier's warehouse in silence, mentally reviewing his plans. In the office, he lifted the loose floorboard beneath which he'd concealed his satellite transceiver. He keyed in a brief coded message: EXTRACTION IMMINENT EXECUTE TOMORROW CONDITIONAL. Then he made the headache-inducing double-jump to time line two, to continue his preparations.

The rented apartment in the other Berlin was aseptically sterile. He took his standard medication dose, massaged his aching forehead, then changed into local drag and made a brief sortie to check on the car parked outside. The BMW's engine started perfectly: he checked the indicated fuel, oil, and coolant levels, allowed it to adjust its tire pressure, let the engine run for a couple of minutes, and shut it down again. Back indoors, he phoned the hangar at the airfield. "Yes, I'll be flying out tomorrow," he told the secretary of the service company he'd contracted to maintain the Cirrus. "I'll arrive around eleven hundred. The flight plan's already on file: two pax, full tanks. Bill it to my account and I'll settle in full before departure."

He hung up, satisfied for the time being. There was a backup plan, of course, one that didn't involve a James Bond–style world-walking stunt in a light plane—but it was actually riskier. If the Cirrus went tech or the weather was bad, he'd have to drive a very long way with a freaked-out young lady who might by then be having second and third thoughts. He'd have to go to ground while Control obtained a false passport for her, then coach her through the process of boarding a civil airliner to South America, or a boat ride out into the Bay of Biscay with a two-person hot air balloon on board . . . the risks exploded exponentially the further down the decision tree he got. Unlike Hulius, the Princess had no idea how to handle herself in the Germany of time line two. The world-walking light plane plan was technically risky, but minimized her exposure to an alien culture.

But the hard bit was always going to be the extraction of Elizabeth Hanover from Schloss Britz, Berlin, the Holy Roman Empire, time line three. It had to be done under the noses of her guards, who were motivated and highly professional, and without scaring the lass into a state of panicky intransigence. Everything depended on her willing cooperation.

But Hulius had one huge advantage over her bodyguards. He could penetrate their outer security cordon invisibly, while they were officially forbidden from operating inside the grounds of the ladies' finishing school.

Entering the apartment's spare room, Hulius collected the bag that the lamplighters had prepared. They'd used a shopping list supplied by head office. Quite how they'd gotten hold of Elizabeth's dress size and other measurements he had no idea: perhaps they'd suborned one of the servants at the school. Hulius would have found it quite disturbing if they'd done it to his own daughter, but . . . *that's the price of fame*, he told himself. There was a certain comfort to be taken from being invisible, obscure, ordinary.

Delivery of the extraction package had to be carried out by the officer conducting the operation. The courier and lamplighter in time line three couldn't come into contact with the package, for if they were taken with knowledge of its contents, the target's security detail would then be able to set a trap. And delivery of the package would constitute a dry run for the extraction officer.

One risk factor in the extraction was that the Princess would probably find mainstream fashions in time line two scandalous. So Control had ordered up a Muslim outfit: nobody in Berlin would look twice at another dark-skinned Turkish girl in long dress and headscarf. The disguise only had to hold up until Hulius could get her to the airfield. He repacked the outfit in the otherworld carpet bag he'd bought for just this purpose, wrote down a concise set of instructions, wrapped it in a brown paper shopping bag he'd brought over from time line three, then returned to the car and drove off.

In time line two Schloss Britz lay in the suburb of Berlin-Neukölln, rather than outside the city itself. It was open to the public as a museum, along with the beautifully preserved manorial park that spread out around it. And unlike Mme. Houelebecq's finishing school, the Kulturstiftung Schloss Britz wasn't swarming with imperial guards.

Hulius parked up in the visitor's lot, then walked to the public entrance. He paid cash for admission then headed directly to the house itself. He ignored the dubious temptations of the ornamental garden— with fall setting in, it was unsurprisingly deserted. He walked through the vestibule, then entered the terrace room, with its grand piano and rococo antique chairs, then the painted magnificence of the hunting room. Off to one side there was a discreet entrance labeled STAFF ONLY. He paused for a brief inspection, then eased the door open and stepped inside. The former servants corridor led through narrow passages past rooms refitted as offices and now all but deserted. He stopped at a janitor's closet, stepped inside, then, taking a deep breath, pulled out a small locket on a chain around his neck.

The room went away, replaced by forest. He stood atop a mound of compacted dirt, held in place with planks and carefully flattened to provide a platform at the same level as in the time lines where the schloss existed on this site. Despite the throbbing in his head, Hulius turned around slowly, checking for signs of disturbance. Then he sat for ten minutes while his headache eased. Finally he flipped the locket around and focused on the design on the opposite side of it.

He looked around at a dust-sheeted furniture storeroom, occupying the same floor space as the closet in the time line two version of the schloss. He checked his watch. He had plenty of time for it was nearly eleven, the ladies would be attending their classes, and his headache had intensified: he needed to rest up. So he crossed to the door and inserted a pair of wedges to hold it shut. Then he removed his chinos and hoodie, revealing the knee breeches and lace fronted shirt of a servant. He shoved the discarded clothes under a chest of drawers. Then he took two pills, dry-swallowed them, and sat down on a covered chaise to wait for the pounding in his skull to subside.

When he was ready to open the door, Huw walked straight to the staircase and ascended, performing the part of a man who was exactly where he knew he was supposed to be. He'd walked this route before, of course: reconnaissance was essential. But every such exploration brought with it a risk of exposure, and there was no margin of error on this mission.

Emerging into the main second-floor corridor, he headed toward the bend where, in that other Berlin, the house had been extended and the mistress's residence added to the new wing. It was a short walk to the Princess's rooms, but this was the most hazardous part of the job: he was in possession of items that could not be explained away if he was challenged. Hulius walked calmly along the corridor, exuding confidence. He held a key: as soon as he recognized the vestibule leading to Elizabeth's rooms he extended it to the lock.

"Excuse me, sir." A woman's voice, challenging. "What are you doing?"

Hulius turned slowly, and gave a half-bow, keeping a tight grip on his expression. The woman was about thirty years old, her morning gown as impeccable as her cut-glass accent. Evidently one of the tutors. She looked curious rather than outraged. Hulius made a snap decision: "There is a special delivery for Lady Hanover," he said apologetically, raising the carpetbag. "Her lady-in-waiting requested it to be delivered. I am to place it inside while she is attending her lessons."

"Good man." She took in his key ring. "Well, go on, then." But she showed no sign of leaving him unattended.

Hulius unlocked the door. "I was to leave it in the cloaks," he said quietly, looking around. "Ah, up there." He boosted the bag up onto the shelf above the coat rack, gave it a shove to ensure that it was stable, then walked back into the hallway and pulled the door shut behind him. His heart hammered as he saw the woman watching him. She hadn't moved, and her eyes narrowed as she watched him lock the door.

"This is irregular," she said. "Spare bags should have been delivered to the porter's lodge." She looked up at his face. "I think you'd better come with—" A bell rang, and she twitched away, looking toward the staircase. "Oh dear," she said quietly, "I'm late." She was clearly torn between a duty to be elsewhere and her suspicion at finding a strange man loose in the women's quarters.

"Ma'am." Hulius bowed again. "By your leave, I need to return these keys to Captain Bertrand *in person*." It was a total bluff, but taking the name of the Princess's chief bodyguard in vain was all he could come up with. The alternative was to kill or disable this woman, whose only crime had been to be in the wrong place at the wrong time—a course of action that would be both reprehensible and counter-productive, for her disappearance would undoubtedly set up a hue and cry.

"Captain Bertrand." Her expression was calculating. "Very well, then. What did you say your name was?"

"I didn't." Hulius drew himself up to attention. "Sergeant Brosz, my lady. At your service. May I have the pleasure of knowing my captor's name so that I can include it in my report?"

"Certainly! I am Madame Vishnevski, and I am running late for the geography tutorial that I am supposed to teach in the next period." She bobbled him a shallow curtsey, with an impish smile, then brought her hands together appreciatively. "Very well, Sergeant, by all means go and report to the Captain. I assure you that the next time you come this way you will not go unnoticed, either. You are quite *out*-standing!" She winked at him, clearly quite taken by her own cleverness in deducing that he was here to probe the school's security.

"I will tell the Captain, I assure you," Hulius said gravely. He turned and headed back toward the storeroom, feeling all the while as if gun sights were aimed at his back. *Not* seizing her in a headlock and rushing her ahead of him was one of the hardest things he'd ever done—that, or bolting and declaring the mission blown. But if the geography teacher went missing, continuing his mission would become impossible. By the time he reached the storeroom—less than a minute later—his back was beslimed with a cold sweat and his knees were weak with the aftermath of the adrenaline crash. He stepped inside, shoved the wedges back into position, and collapsed with his back against the door, breathing fast. For a moment his vision darkened. Pins and needles and a burning pain behind his eyes bespoke the unwisdom of mixing high-dose antihypertensives with the fight-or-flight reflex.

That was entirely too close for comfort, he told himself, wiping the perspiration from his face. But he'd delivered the package: a disguise for Elizabeth during her brief exposure to time line two's Berlin, and a final set of instructions. She was to breakfast as usual on the morrow, but should complain of stomach cramps and return to her rooms. At ten o'clock Hulius would return and, if the potted plant was present, he would knock on her door and politely invite her to follow him back to the storeroom. It combined the virtues of simplicity, and of not requiring him to penetrate Captain Bertrand's security cordon outside the building. If anything went wrong, he could world-walk to safety at any point, the only risk being a sprained ankle in the pine forests of time line one if he had to jaunt from the second floor. At least, that had been the theory—right up until his encounter with Mme. Vishnevski.

She was late for class, he reminded himself. *And she bought my story.* With luck, she'd forget about the incident. If not, she'd most likely tell Mme. Houelebecq, who might smell a rat—in which case she would write to the Captain, who would *definitely* smell a rat. But there'd be a jurisdictional argument. Madame was not happy about stationing soldiers among her girls (a position that Hulius, as a father himself, could appreciate). Probably nothing would be arranged before this time tomorrow. And if it was, the Princess would remove the plant pot, sending the signal to postpone.

I'm going to have to go with it, Hulius decided. It would be better if he could bring everything forward, but he'd already delivered her instructions. From this point on, nothing could be permitted to go wrong.

NEW LONDON, TIME LINE THREE, AUGUST 2020

Another morning dawned. Rita had survived the recording session and a strained private dinner with Brilliana, unpacked a baffling array of costumes that had been delivered while she ate (*No, they're not cos-tumes*, she told herself, *they're just ordinary clothes in this time line.*), then she'd spent a night tossing and turning sleeplessly. Now she was neatly turned out in an unfamiliar outfit that felt as formal as an interview suit, standing in the huge corner office of the man whom her birth mother had married—*no, in this world he's my* stepfather—and she had run out of silence.

"What do you *want* from me?" Rita demanded. "I mean, what are you planning with that interview? Do I get a say?"

Erasmus shrugged. "Of course you do! And I don't know every detail of what's going to happen, or I'd tell you. Like everyone else, I'm playing this by ear. If you don't want to participate, I understand, but—"

"No, it's not that." Rita walked across to the bay window. The side window of the Minister of Propaganda's office had a spectacular view of a formal garden. She'd seen pictures of the royal palace at Versailles: the garden here reminded her of it. According to a staffer, it had been commissioned by the Royal Pretender's grandfather. (Apparently superpower politics during the fifties in this time line had focused obsessively on closing the Imperial Topiary Gap.) "You're using me as a chess piece in two games simultaneously, aren't you? The message I was sent to bring you, and the head game my employers want to run on your wife."

"Who happens to be your mother." Erasmus turned deceptively mild brown eyes on her. "All right, your *other* mother, the one who didn't raise you. But you're right: there are two matters between us. One is the message. It's going to take us some time to prepare a response. Quite frankly, it's above my pay grade. It would normally be a matter for the Central Committee as a whole, with the First Man overseeing it. Unfortunately the First Man is . . . indisposed."

"What's that supposed to mean?"

Burgeson glanced away. "Your mother was like that when she was younger," he murmured. "Direct. There are some things we don't like to talk about." He turned back to her, worry lines forming on his forehead as he took a deep breath. "Adam Burroughs is the First Man of the Commonwealth, the ideological lodestone of the Party. He's our head of state—President for Life, if you want. Supreme Adjudicator. He isn't a president, as such—he's a head of state, but rather than being a chief executive, he's a judge . . . but you don't need to know the constitutional minutiae. The point is, he's terminally ill. He has cancer, and he's unlikely to see out the month."

She stared at him, disbelieving. "But isn't there a vice president or someone he can delegate to?"

"Not really, no." Erasmus stretched his arms out behind his head, fingers interlaced. "Many powers are delegated, of course, and not necessarily in the way you'd imagine if you're familiar with the United States—strategic nuclear retaliation, for example. And then there are the everyday activities of the various ministries, the drafting of legislation. The First Man actually has less executive power than your president—he's not meant to be a *monarch*." He said the word with marked distaste. "But he's the supreme adjudicator. Policy changes can't be approved without someone in his role to arbitrate between contending factions and rule on their constitutional legality. We did not copy the constitution of the United States when we were drafting our post-revolutionary settlement." He smiled thinly: "It contains subtle flaws—Huw Hjorth calls them 'emergent bugs'—that only become manifest after centuries. We studied it deeply and decided it placed an excessive weight on, ah, *liberté*, without a sufficiently clear idea of exactly whose freedom was to be protected, or why. And it undervalues *égalité* and *fraternité*. Not that the French republican constitutions of your eighteenth and nineteenth century were much better, or Stalin's constitution of 1936, let alone Nazi Germany. But your mother gave us a unique, priceless opportunity to study your time line at a point when our own constitutional settlement was still tentative. She delivered a set of studies to us in our first year, a, what she called a CliffsNotes dossier, of revolutions of your time line and their failure modes. We ended up adopting most of our guiding principles from a successful revolution in your time line. One that built a strong deep state to defend it from a predatory superpower, while placing a heavy emphasis on democracy and a universal franchise. Admittedly *our* Deep State aims to entrench democracy and foster human rights and respect for diversity, rather different priorities from the Islamic Republic of Iran, but the constitutional framework—"

"Hang on." Rita shook her head, then shoved her hair back: "*Iran?*" Vague visions of black-clad women and fanatical clerics made her head spin. "You're pulling my leg—"

"No: we ran a best-practice analysis on revolutions in your time line— you've had so many more of them! So many more experiments in over-throwing hereditary dictatorships! So many hopeful monsters! So many interesting failures to study!—and all things considered, Iran turned out to have done very well indeed under severe external pressure. Did you know that the half-life of a revolution in your time line is just three years? Most revolutions very rapidly decay into dictatorship or are ended by a counter-coup. We didn't want to do that, and we were determined to learn from other people's examples. So after making some adjustments to reduce nepotism and feather-bedding, we built a similar framework. Ours promotes the radical humanist ideology of equality and fraternity between all humanity, rather than a religious faith, but the underlying framework is similar. We're trying to build something new, Rita, to pro-mote a new outlook in a world dominated by the imperial power of ab-solute monarchs. Equality before the law, a universal franchise for all adults, protection from discrimination on the basis of race, sex, gender, caste, nobility . . . it's our task to lead and to set the standards we aspire to, even when the populace are less enlightened. It worked quite well for a generation: but Adam, our first and so far only Supreme Leader, is dying. So we can't send your Secretary of State a binding commitment to enter into negotiations, until the Party committee has met to vote in a replacement for the First Man." He shrugged.

Rita tried not to flap her jaw. "How long will that take?"

"Oh, for that we copied the Catholic Church," he said with a blithe smile. "The Central Committee gets locked in a sealed room and the doors aren't opened until they signal that they are in accord on the identity of the new Pope. First Man. Or First Woman."

"That doesn't sound very democratic . . ."

"Isn't it? The Party is open to all, and the Committee delegates are elected, just like your electoral college. It's not the kind of political party you're used to. We've got those, too: we call them Factions and they operate at a different level, running for seats in the Magistracy and passing laws, the legality and implementation of which is supervised by the Party. But the Party exists to protect the constitutional system. It functions like your Supreme Court, if the justices were elected by other government employees, ran the police and military, and had nuclear weapons."

"But that's—" With an effort of will, Rita pulled herself back on track. "You're telling me you won't have a reply to take back to Dr. Scranton and Colonel Smith until after the First Man dies? Which could be up to a month away. Am I right?"

Erasmus's smile vanished. "Not that long, I fear. The Foreign Affairs Committee has been discussing the letter, and there's a draft communiqué. Signing it will be the first matter for our new supreme leader to consider, I assure you, even before the official mourning period is over. Which I, and my wife, will be expected to attend—if you are still here, perhaps you could accompany us?"

"I'm not a diplomat!"

"No, but you're the nearest thing we've got to a representative of the United States government, and it would look good." He paused. "Also, he was a friend. And an inspiration to me. Many years ago."

"Oh hell." *I could go back, if there isn't going to be a reply for weeks,* Rita realized. *But then I'd be out of the loop.* "You're asking me to stay here indefinitely, aren't you? I need to go back and report in, Mr. Burgeson: they were only expecting me to be away for a couple of days. I don't think they'll have a problem with me staying here, but I have to keep them informed."

"We can arrange that." Erasmus picked up his pen—a fountain pen, Rita noticed: she hadn't seen any sign of ballpoints—and began to write a letter. "I'm sure Inspector Morgan can take you to a secure rendezvous location and wait a few hours. In the meantime, I'll draft an acknowledgment of receipt, and request your urgent continued attendance, pending our response. And a formal invitation to the state funeral. I don't expect them to say no . . . Does that meet with your approval?"

Rita had the distinct feeling that she was being toyed with, but not in a manner or to any ends that she understood. "Yes, yes it does," she said, wishing she had the nerve to push for more time to herself, for precious hours with Angie, hours in which she didn't feel like a lab rat trying to run a maze designed for the children of politicians. She paused. "Who do you think will succeed Mr. Burroughs?" she asked.

His smile evaporated. "That's the wrong question, Rita. You should be asking *what* will come after Adam dies."

"Why? What do you mean?"

He sighed. "This has never happened before in the Commonwealth's history. We all hope that our constitutional mechanisms weather the storm, and in a few weeks' time we are conducting business as usual under the aegis of a younger and healthier supreme adjudicator. We know that our framework *should* survive: it worked elsewhere, after all. But if ever there is a window of opportunity for a coup d'état, or an attempt to restore the monarchy, this is it. It is *very* important to us that your superiors fully understand the scale of the coming succession. Which is why I am doing my best to get you a ring-side seat, and to introduce you to as many of the key players as possible.

"You're in a unique position, Rita. If we publicly acknowledge you as the daughter of a Party Commissioner in an important Ministry, that has one set of consequences. Or we can introduce you as an overt agent engaged in a diplomatic exchange on behalf of the nation you are a citizen of, which will have a different set of outcomes. But either way, you will be able to give your Dr. Scranton a level of observer access that she probably didn't dream of—and which it is strongly in our interests to give her. We don't want the US government to meddle in our internal affairs during a succession crisis. And the best way to deter them is by giving them a clear understanding of the stakes. This is the first-time-ever transition to a new First Citizen within the Commonwealth—a superpower that has nuclear weapons and para-time-capable strategic bombers, just like the United States. The potential for meddling to end in disaster is very high. So I want you to do your best to ensure that your bosses understand that."

PANKOW, BERLIN, TIME LINE TWO, AUGUST 2020

Hulius returned to time line two's janitorial closet, trudged down the corridor to the exit, and slunk back to his rented apartment. He drove manually, despite the killer headache and bone-deep sense of fatigue that came from world-walking six times in five hours. Once back in the apartment bedroom, he didn't bother crossing over again to the furrier's warehouse. He was, he hoped, done with the stakeout staging area. Instead, he collapsed on the bed and set his phone's alarm to wake him after a couple of hours. Tomorrow he'd have to make a high-tempo return trip, rest up for a few hours before escorting the kid to the aerodrome, then make a final hazardous double world-walk. But afterward he'd be able to chill for as long as he wanted—even take a vacation with Ellie and the kids. *At last.*

At five that evening the doorbell rang. Refreshed and alert, Hulius checked the entryphone camera. It was Fox. "Come in," he said tersely, stepping back to make room.

"It's all set up." Fox sounded smug "I brought the goods." He kicked the duffel bag he'd dropped just inside the doorway. Hulius suppressed an involuntary twitch: some of the goods in question were explosive. "The contractors are scheduled to do a deep clean here the day after tomorrow. In seventy-two hours there'll be no sign you were ever in this apartment."

"Good," Hulius grunted.

"And here are the keys you wanted." Fox handed over a small key pouch. "Alarm code's on a piece of paper inside."

"Also good." Hulius glanced at them, then slid them into a pocket. "I've got one last job for you."

"Oh yes?"

"I want you to buy me two fully flexible tickets on Air France, flying CDG to MAR, business class if you can get them, premium economy if not. One-way, one checked bag per passenger." He pulled a folded sheet of paper from his pocket. "Full details here, with flight numbers, passport numbers, and full advance passenger information. You can do it online, or via an agency, I just don't want to do it myself. Flights to de-part in two days' time. When you've got them, print out the confirma-tion numbers and drop a note through the mailbox here."

"That's going to cost you. You want it on paper?" Fox looked dubious.

"Yes, fucking paper. I know it's old-fashioned and I know it's going to be expensive at this short notice, but I don't want to do it over the Inter-net. It's like hanging out a sign saying 'hack me here.'"

"Oh, you tinfoil hat guys crack me up." Fox relaxed visibly as he got a handle on where he thought Hulius was coming from. Paranoid clients were clearly something he understood all too well. "I didn't figure you were afraid of the CIA setting you up for a drone strike."

"Don't joke about that sort of thing," Hulius said flatly. He decided to shut this down fast by feeding Fox some of the second-level cover story. "They don't only target terrorists these days, and they're more subtle than you think. They use all the forces of the state to back up their multina-tionals, just like the Russians and Chinese. They pay lip service to the free market, but if you try and outmaneuver them they'll find a way to stash a kilo of heroin in your luggage while you're changing flights in Singapore"—while most countries had decriminalized over the past few years, Singapore was still gleefully hanging drug couriers—"or even poi-son your toothpaste." The best bit about the second-level cover story was that it was all true. The expansion of the Deep State and the outsourc-ing of security operations to corporate contractors had been accompa-nied by a huge wave of back-scratching and the subsequent diffusion of black ops techniques into the private sector. Outright bribery (officially illegal and fraught with difficulty in this brave new world of surveillance of banking arrangements) had been replaced by bullying and sabotage. It wasn't an improvement.

"Man, you're really tense. Is it that bad?"

"You have *no* idea." Hulius paused for effect. "The sector of the GM rubber market my people are in is worth about five hundred million a year right now, but it's poised to grow by a factor of ten in the next six years, and the bastards know it." He grimaced fiercely. Fox looked duly impressed. "We're determined to be the first to market, but there are people who don't want to see that and they will happily put a spike in our wheels—or a bullet in my head, if it comes to it. All over the fucking share price. Hence the cloak and dagger."

"Well, now I understand," said Fox. "Your secret is safe with me, my friend."

"It had better be, if you want the follow-on business. Will you stay for coffee?"

"No, I must be going." Fox sounded nervous, which was good. (The real purpose of the second-level cover story was to motivate Fox to keep his yap shut and his head down.) "Thank you for your confidence, Herr van Rijnt. And I hope the rest of your trip is uneventful."

"So do I," Hulius said fervently. "So do I."

After Fox left, he dragged the heavy duffel bag through into the spare bedroom and unpacked the suit of body armor. Piece by piece he checked the fit of each segment, loosening and tightening straps as necessary. Laid it out, it covered the bed like the shed carapace of a cyborg Gregor Samsa. Next he unlocked the flat Peli gun case. The FN P90 personal defense weapon and accompanying Five-seveN pistol were unloaded, their magazines and spares empty. He spent the next hour carefully loading and checking them. (Both firearms used the same small-caliber ammunition.) He disassembled the guns again, inspected them and applied lubricant, then put them back together, installing their suppressors but leaving their magazines out for the time being.

Finally he ate a microwave meal from the apartment's refrigerator, set his phone's alarm for six the following morning, showered, and bedded down in the other room.

PHILADELPHIA, TIME LINE TWO, AUGUST 2020

Gomez was taken by surprise when Rita strode into the control office wearing an oddly tailored tunic-and-trouser suit. "Where's the Colonel?" she demanded.

"Unavailable." Gomez stared, too taken aback by her sudden arrival to upbraid her. "Where have you been? You haven't reported in for three days."

"I've got two hours." The girl sounded tense and uncharacteristically assured. "I really need to talk to the boss right now." She held up a sealed envelope. "And get this to him."

"I said he's unavailable." Gomez pulled out her phone. "Undisclosed location, no specified ETA. What's got your ass? Report."

"Not to you." Rita shot right back. "Is there a secure phone in here? If the Colonel's offline, I need to talk to Dr. Scranton instead."

"Not until you explain where—"

"You're not in my reporting chain, Sonia. I need to brief Colonel Smith or Dr. Scranton *immediately* and you're obstructing me. I've got just under two hours here before I go back, unless I want to cause a diplomatic incident. Are you going to give me a secure voice terminal so I can report in, or are you looking forward to explaining yourself to the Colonel?"

"Fuck you." Gomez raised a finger, turned it into a gesture in the direction of a desk at the side of the office. "There's the terminal. You get one call, then—"

"Call Dr. Scranton then put me on the line if it makes you feel better." Rita crossed her arms aggressively. Her sudden self-confidence made Gomez bristle.

"I will do that, girl. You'd better be on the level."

A minute later Rita was holding the old-fashioned wired handset to her ear. "Rita, I'm in a meeting so let's keep this brief. What do you have to report?"

"I made contact and passed on the message, as ordered. I was then invited to stay and socialize." Rita glanced across the room at Gomez, who wasn't even bothering to pretend not to be listening. "Agent Gomez is present. Do you want me to continue?"

"Go ahead." Scranton's tone was dry as dust. "Hand me over to her afterwards."

"Okay. Mrs. Burgeson and her husband are a major political power couple. They're in the middle of a succession crisis right now, because

their pres—sorry, their *equivalent* of a president, he has different powers—is dying of cancer. There's no well-defined chain of succession
because he's been in charge since the revolution seventeen years ago.
Everyone is walking on eggshells. Mr. Burgeson says that a reply will be
forthcoming, but they're delaying until the new head of state can sign
off. In the meantime, he wants me to stick around as an observer—in
public—on the understanding that I'll tell you everything I'm allowed to
see. My identity as his wife's, uh, only surviving child, also has implications. If she publicly acknowledges me it can be used to open doors. Is
this what you were hoping for?"

"More or less. Very good, Rita. How long can you stay here for?"

Rita glanced at the time display on the phone: "I'm expected back in
an hour and a half. And I have a sealed letter for you or the Colonel. I
was told it's a written request for my attendance. And an invitation to a
state funeral."

"You said their head of state is dying." Scranton sounded thoughtful.
"How is this expected?"

"I was told if he lasts out the week they'll be very surprised. He has
terminal cancer and is being given palliative care. For the time being
their executive arm is running on autopilot. Uh, I was also told this
explicitly includes their nuclear weapons release authority. And I was
told to tell you that they've got para-time strike and retaliation capability. They're totes squirrelly about the possibility of some faction or other
attempting a coup—the royalists, or possibly hard-liners within the
regime."

"I see. Please hold on." Dr. Scranton was silent for almost thirty seconds.
"Very well. You'd better write up whatever you've got to report, then get
back over there. Try to report in every two to three days in future. You
can leave the letter with Gomez when you go. Now pass me over to her,
I have some instructions for her."

"Okay." Rita extended the handset to the other woman, who stared at
it as if it was an angry hornet: "It's for you." She placed the sealed envelope on the desk as Gomez took the phone. "I need a clean tablet: I've got
a report to write before I go back."

Rita was still peeling the plastic wrapper off the disposable tablet, preparing to type up a quick summary, when Gomez handed the phone back to her. "Hey. You. The doctor wants to talk," Gomez said, refusing to look her in the eye.

Rita took the phone. "Yes?"

"I have some instructions for you from SecState." Rita tensed. *What kind of meeting is she in?* "Current thinking is that we would rather deal with a governing faction who understand us than with radical or disruptive elements who don't. So we want you to cooperate with the Burgesons' requests, within reason. If they want to publicize your existence as either Miriam Beckstein's daughter or a direct special envoy from the United States, you should play along. However, remember that you aren't a diplomat and do not represent the government—you're just a courier and possibly an informal agent of influence—so you should not under *any* circumstances agree to any demands or requests on behalf of the government. If anyone makes such demands, tell them to write us a letter. Stay within their laws and keep your nose clean: you *might* be able to claim diplomatic immunity if you get into a sticky situation where someone is messing with you for political reasons, but we can't back it up from here and you shouldn't expect a get out of jail card. In event of civil unrest or serious threats, you have JAUNT BLUE capability. To make reporting easier you should take a clean tablet from the office supplies. They've got enough industrial espionage going that it's not going to give them anything they don't already know. Use it to write up notes and we'll drain it whenever you bring it back over. Have you got all that?"

"I think so. You're setting me up as an agent of influence with the former Clan world-walkers, who are the faction within the Commonwealth government most associated with para-time activity?" Rita's brow wrinkled. Across the room, Gomez frowned furiously.

"Yes, that's pretty much it. Goodbye and good luck."

The phone went dead, leaving Rita to stare at it: a dead lump of plastic in her hand. "I don't understand this," she subvocalized. Louder: "Okay, I'd better take this tablet, Sonia. Did she tell you that?"

"Yes." Gomez picked up the envelope. "I'll see the Colonel gets this. Or Dr. Scranton, depending."

"Thank you." Rita tried to smile, to walk the tension between them back down to something reasonable, but the other woman's expression was stony. "I'd better be going. There's a reception at seven and I'm expected to attend."

"Listen to you," Gomez said coldly. "Forgotten your girlfriend already. Just *go*, Douglas, you've got a job to do."

BERLIN, TIME LINE TWO/THREE, AUGUST 2020

Hulius rose before dawn and showered while the coffee machine burbled in the kitchen. It took an effort to stay centered. Today was going to be very busy, and he wouldn't be human if he felt no anxiety or unease about everything that could go wrong. So he tried to focus on the liberating awareness that it was nearly over. Weeks of patient planning and positioning were coming to a head. If all went well, by this time tomorrow he'd be on board a ship in the Atlantic, heading back home to Elena and the girls with his defector safely delivered into the custody of the DPR's debriefing officers.

He dressed carefully in long underwear before he strapped on the body armor. Then he donned a loose shirt and combat pants to conceal the protective gear. The Five-seveN pistol went in a concealed holster in a modified hip pocket. The short-barreled P90 he carefully loaded and installed in a bulky messenger bag, the main compartment of which held a compact first aid kit and a sheaf of documents. The butterflies in his stomach were a new and unwelcome side effect. After a bit he realized something strange: *I'm afraid. I must be getting too old for this shit.*

A pang of worry intruded: Elena would be getting restive and anxious at the long silence, angry with Brill for taking her husband away for nearly a month with no communication. He'd seldom been away for this long before, and they'd argued afterward. Last time she'd been afraid that he'd been captured and was undergoing enhanced interrogation in some hideous dungeon. This time she'd be livid, although if the scheme worked she'd understand why it was necessary once the Princess went public. But she might not wait. And if Ellie got really mad, the consequences could be very bad indeed. She *seemed* content to be a wife and mother, happier with the role than his sister-in-law, anyway, but if they'd followed a slightly different path it could easily have been Ellie checking that the guns were properly loaded. *And there I go again, wool-gathering.* Hulius worked his arms into the sleeves of a fleece jacket, leaving it unzipped. *Let's get this over with.*

He picked up the messenger bag and slung it over his shoulder, drained his coffee, left the apartment, and walked to the BMW.

The car started perfectly. Traffic was morning-heavy. He drove carefully, using the ritual as another distraction focus. It was too early for the schloss to be open to the public, but the car park was unlocked and he parked as close to the entrance as he could. A path around the side of the building led to a discreet servants' entrance. He pulled out the 3-D printed key duplicates Fox had obtained. They turned in the lock: *Now let's hope he got the alarm code right, too.*

An urgent beeping started as soon as Hulius pushed the door open. He glanced around then spotted the alarm cabinet. Taking a deep breath, he punched in the five digit code: the beeping slowed, then the ARMED message on the small display panel flipped to CLEAR. He turned round and locked the door, then moved on into the museum. The disarmed burglar alarm would probably worry whoever opened up an hour hence, but his wasn't the only vehicle left in the car park overnight. They'd probably assume the caretaker forgot to set the alarm when they closed up the evening before.

Hulius headed for the janitor's closet, messenger bag still slung over his shoulder. He world-walked to the forest, where it was raining lightly, so he cut short his rest period and jaunted immediately to the storeroom in Mme. Houelebecq's finishing school. The familiar headache bit hard at his temples. He winced, wedged the door shut, took his prescribed dose, and sat down on a dust-sheeted chair to wait it out.

An hour and a half passed. Outside his hiding place the young women awakened and conducted their morning ablutions, dressed for breakfast in the Hunter's hall downstairs, then returned to their rooms. Most of them would then take themselves to their morning classes. But Elizabeth Hanover had other plans, plans that involved declaring herself to be sick and retiring to her rooms. *Please be ready,* he prayed. *No surprises, let this be a routine extraction.* Long habit pulled his hands through a genuflection to Lightning Child, a god from a now-dead land who he had barely believed in even as a child. *Time to go.*

Hulius Hjorth stepped into the cold morning light, climbed the servants' staircase, and marched briskly along the corridor to the Princess's rooms. Seconds passed: he was alone between worlds, senses keyed up to a crystalline clarity. The flower arrangement on the side table was present. *Good.* He approached the door and quietly turned the key in the lock.

"Oh! You made me jump."

The target was waiting in her day room, wearing the headscarf, long skirt, and buttoned-up coat of a Turkish woman. Hulius inclined his head. She looked at him in surprise, eyes wide at the sight of his strange attire. "Elizabeth Hanover? If you wish to leave, follow me. We need to be swift."

"Where are we going?" she asked, not moving.

"You asked for extraction to New London," Hulius said, as patiently as he could manage. "I am a courier from the Department of Parahistorical Research." A little white lie. "We are going to walk up the corridor to a staircase, then into a storeroom, and I will carry you across to a version of Berlin that your security guards have no access to. An aircraft is waiting for us there. Is that acceptable?"

"I suppose"—her eyes glistened—"yes, yes it is." Her chin rose. "Are you armed?"

The tearing-cloth sound of the Velcro flap of his bag opening coincided with the slam of the door to the girl's study room. *"Halt!"*

Hulius turned, simultaneously reaching into the bag as he stepped between the girl and the doorway. Booted figures clattered out of the study, swearing as they collided in their enthusiasm to lay hands on him.

Three men in guards' uniforms, an officer raising a pistol and drawing breath to scream *halt* again—

There was a loud triple-bang as he squeezed the trigger of the P90: and a deafening report as the officer discharged his revolver, recklessly shooting even though the woman he was sworn to protect was standing right behind Hulius—who staggered, gut-punched by the bullet. The guards went down in a flailing mass. "Come *on*." He reached back and grabbed the target by the arm, took a lurching step forward, stepping over the dead or dying men. "*Fast.*"

"You—you shot—" He could barely hear her over the ringing in his ears.

"Do you still want to come?" He demanded. Her eyes were wide open, her expression shocked.

"Yes!"

"Then come *quickly.*" A bell began to clang. His ribs felt as if he'd been kicked by a horse. Something was broken: if not for the body armor he'd certainly be dead or dying. He dragged the target into the corridor. She wasn't hurrying fast enough for his liking. "Through here." The stairwell door gaped before him. He tugged her after him, trying not to gasp at the repeated jolts of fire as the devil played his ribcage like a xylophone with every step. There would be other guards, a detachment rushing in from the gate house. He turned and hurried the target down the short hall to the storeroom then through the door, grabbed her around her waist, noticing absently that her eyes were very dark, pupils wide. "Hold on," he said, lifting and tensing past the breath-stopping pain in his ribs. He shoved his left wrist up past the back of her neck so that he could see the knotwork on the wristband. "Now—"

Elizabeth squeaked. "You're hurting me!"

Hulius relaxed his grip, allowing her to slide down to the ground. His ribs were on fire and his head throbbed. It was raining gently, and the air smelled of resin and rotting humus. In the distance, a cuckoo called.

"What—where—" She looked around, stunned.

"We have one more jump—wait, don't move." He tried to catch his breath.

"Are we in another world?"

"Yes." His head hurt almost as badly as his ribs. "I need to pick you up so that we can complete the next jump," he said as gently as he could. "I'm not going to hurt you. But we can't afford to stay here. This is a wilderness world. Do you understand?"

"I—" She nodded, face pale and eyes wide. "Yes."

This time she helped, wrapping her arms around his shoulders as he lifted her. Dark spots swam in his vision as ribs grated. He jaunted, and everything went black as he dropped her.

A clatter of plastic told him she'd stumbled into the cleaning cart. "Don't move," he said quietly. "I'll get the light."

His flashlight lit up the cluttered closet. Elizabeth's eyes were wide, either appalled or excited—it was hard to tell which. Hulius breathed hard, trying to ignore the ache in his chest. "Where are we?"

"In a janitor's closet in the schloss—it's a museum in this version of history."

"A museum?" She shook her head and half-smiled ruefully, as if amused by the absurdity of the proposition. "So you're one of them? It's true, then." Her smile faded. "You, you shot those men. I think you killed them."

"I hope not." Another deep breath. "They fired, too. They forgot you were there."

"But Lieutenant Gorki shot—" Elizabeth stared at him. "*He* shot *you!*"

"I'm wearing armor." Perhaps it was better not to tell her that it had barely done its job. The lieutenant's revolver was a cavalry pistol, firing a big ball round. They were designed to blast a rider out of the saddle or kill his horse. Even if it hadn't penetrated, it had definitely cracked one or more of his ribs. "Now, I want you to sit down and try to compose yourself for a minute. We need to walk through a public space to get to my automobile, and it will not do to look agitated. Do you understand?"

"I understand that we're in a museum in another world," she said slowly. "Is this how they dress there? Is there still a finishing school—"

"The schloss is a museum," he said, trying to contain his pain-driven impatience. At this stage it was critically important not to frighten the target, to keep her in a pliable frame of mind, willingly cooperative rather than struggling to escape. "There will be some visitors, but it's early. Pretend you, too, are visiting a museum. Follow my lead and talk to no one: there will be no more shooting." He paused. "You will find many things in this world extremely confusing, but try not to react. Do not talk to anyone, just pretend you do not understand. If they see you they will think from your dress that you are poor and Turkish, maybe Romany. We will walk to the entrance, then out to an automobile parking lot. I have a vehicle waiting. I will drive you to the airfield." Just talking was taking all his energy. And there was something he'd almost forgotten to do. "Just one minute."

He reached into the ripped messenger bag—firing the PDW through its end had sprayed lining fabric everywhere, and it stank of gun smoke and hot brass—and fumbled in one of the interior pockets until he felt a cheap candy-bar phone. His hands were trembling as he pulled it out and switched it on. He sat and waited for the phone to connect, trying to control his shakes and beat the after-fight terror back into whatever dark cupboard of the soul it had emerged from. *That was far too close!* After thirty seconds the phone beeped. There was only one number in its memory: he dialed it.

"Hello?" said an unfamiliar woman's voice.

"Is that John?" he asked in English.

"I'll just get him."

A moment later, a man's voice came on the line: "This is John. What news?"

"I have the package. Experienced some damage during pick-up. Delivery scheduled for the usual place, usual time." Hulius ended the call, then switched the phone off and dropped it into a bucket. There was a sluice in one corner of the janitor's closet. He stood painfully, slopped bleach from a bottle into the bottom of the bucket, then topped it up from the tap until the phone was fully submerged.

Elizabeth was watching him curiously. "What did you do that for?" she asked.

"Communication security." Shorted-out burner phones told no tales, .

and strong bleach was as good an anti-DNA agent as any. "Come on, it's time to go."

Hulius stood up painfully, trying not to shake his head or breathe too deeply. He felt ill. It wasn't just the physical after-effects of combat. Few men of his age had come through the Clan's disastrous final civil war without experiencing violence, and he had shot at men before—possibly killed men—but this had been more than an unwanted complication. He was gripped by a sense of something having gone irrevocably wrong, even though he knew his actions had been justified, at least in terms of the mission. "The guards in your room. They shouldn't have been there. What happened?"

Words tumbled out: "Yesterday, when someone, when you, delivered the bundle of clothes and the note, you were seen. One of the teachers. Captain Bertrand was notified and he obtained Madame Houelebecq's permission to station guards. They searched my room and ordered me to follow your script, they wanted to catch—"

"I see, yes." Hulius nodded. Dark spots danced in front of his eyes. If they'd caught him alive, a world-walker attempting to abduct Princess Elizabeth, the repercussions would have been seismic. They might still be. With a pile of bleeding bodies and a missing heir, nothing could silence accusations of assassination short of the sight of the Princess, smiling and shaking hands with the First Man in front of the TV cameras. *We're committed now.* "Well, we're safe from Captain Bertrand, but this is not your world. There are other hazards. I must get you to a place of safety as fast as possible." He reached for the door handle, suppressing a whimper of pain. "Follow me."

AN UNDISCLOSED LOCATION, UNDISCLOSED TIME LINE/AN AIRLINER, TIME LINE TWO, AUGUST 2020

Freedom, Paulette reflected, was multivalent; an idea so flexible that if you applied yourself diligently you could invoke it to justify almost any atrocity. As she watched the prison clerks process her release documents, she didn't feel very free at all. Or perhaps it was just the realization that she was swapping a cell in a supermax prison for a jail the size of a continent that stifled her sense of relief.

The thing strapped to her right ankle itched.

They'd shoved a change of clothing through the slot in her cell door that morning, underwear and a dress and jacket taken from her own bedroom wardrobe. They'd even provided shoes and some toiletries. But before they let her out of the cell they'd manacled her again, and then fastened a plastic cuff below her shin. It made an odd bulge under her leggings, as if her ankle was deformed. "Don't tamper with it," the technician who fastened it told her. "Don't immerse it in water, don't try to cut the band, don't try to open it up. You don't want it to activate."

"What if I need a shower?" she asked. "Is it a tag? Or something else?"

But he didn't reply. Instead the guards marched her through a series of claustrophobic, windowless corridors punctuated by doors like coffin lids that buzzed as they closed automatically behind her. The white noise of air conditioning was everywhere, deadening and enervating. Finally they came to an office with desks and a control station and a warden with paperwork. "Do you know who's meeting you?" the warden asked, incuriously.

"I was told I'm being released into the custody of another agency."

"Sit down." He pointed at a chair.

She sat. Things were looking up: they didn't chain her to a ring in the floor, or hit her.

After a while, another door opened. It was Colonel Smith, with a couple of people she didn't recognize but whose posture toward him was deferential. "Ah, Ms. Milan." He nodded at her, then held up an ID card for the warden to scan. "I'm her pick-up."

They unlocked her cuffs and removed the manacles. Then there were more tunnels, a couple of checkpoints guarded by headless robots shaped like German shepherd dogs with gun muzzles for heads. Finally they came to a yard flanked by flagpoles flying the Stars and Stripes, and a tall motorized gate surmounted by razor wire and laser beams. "Welcome to freedom," said the Colonel. *Freedom* apparently meant the backseat of a gray government car that smelled faintly of stale sweat. "It must be kind of disorienting. Would you like a coffee?"

To her surprise, Paulette burst into tears. They were tears of anger directed at this tissue-thin simulation of compassion, but the Colonel seemed oblivious, or mistook them for something else. He even offered her a Kleenex.

The car drove itself, but the two minders up front—a black guy called Pat and a Hispanic woman called Sonia—kept an eye on it. Pat, at least, was packing a concealed carry, if Paulette was any judge of such things. The jail was set in its own patch of land, surrounded by high fences and camera masts, then a bare killing field before they reached the tree line. At the end of a short driveway they entered a windowless garage and parked up briefly, while a screen on the wall opposite counted down to zero and her ears popped. Then the next door opened, onto a feeder road leading to a four lane highway surrounded by strip malls. "Where are we going?" she finally asked.

"Starbucks first." Smith raised his voice so that the two riding up front could hear: "Then the airport." He continued in a lower tone, pitched for her ears: "It's going to be a long drive, so we're going to make a couple of rest stops. Don't bother trying to get away. The cuff you're wearing has got a Taser component and a sedative injector as well as a tracker."

"How nice." Paulette looked out of the back window. They were some-how in the middle of suburbia: there was no sign of the trees or the jail beyond the windowless garage as they pulled away. The supermax prison was stashed in another, uninhabited time line. The DHS had entire con-tinents to use for their GULAG, not so much an archipelago as a galaxy: even if she'd managed to escape, there would have been nowhere for her to go.

"We got them from China by way of Saudi Arabia. The Saudis use them to control servants and women. We use them to control valuable assets who might go walkabout if given the opportunity. Keep your nose clean and cooperate, and we might take it off . . ."

Paulette grimaced. "There's no point running," she said, then bit her tongue before she could add, *you've turned the entire world into a prison.* It was amazing what you could do in the name of liberty if you felt the need to defend it strongly enough.

They left the highway, paused at the window of a drive-through Starbucks, and were on their way again before Paulette could get the smell of stale automobile aircon out of her lungs. Three hours, two hundred miles, and one toilet stop later they left the interstate, this time taking a feeder road that led toward—

"An Air Force base?" Paulette asked against her better judgment.

"No, we get to fly Air DHS." They were waved through a checkpoint with speed and efficiency that suggested they were expected, then drove toward a hangar well away from the row of menacing gray drones parked alongside the runway. Inside, an unmarked C-37A was waiting for them. Polite but professionally incurious ground crew ushered them up the steps to a cabin kitted out in austere Federal grays and blues, rather than the walnut and leather luxury of a commercial Gulfstream. The door had barely closed behind them when the engines began to spool up. "Next stop, Tempelhof Air Force Base. We should arrive there around nine p.m. local time, five in the morning here."

Paulette took a deep breath. She hadn't really believed the Colonel's glib patter until the moment the pitch of the engines rose to a full-throated howl and shoved her back into her seat. "Why are you taking me to Berlin, Colonel? What do you want me to do?" *And what will you do to me if I try to say no?* Since he'd shown her the photograph of Hulius Hjorth, she'd had a horrible suspicion that she knew exactly what he was going to ask of her. And she wasn't sure she could live with herself if she did it.

Smith looked at her mildly. "In about eighteen hours' time you're going to talk an armed fugitive down from a hostage situation. In doing so, you're going to save a number of lives. Do you have a problem with that?"

She licked her too-dry lips. "How many lives?"

The Colonel glanced away. "At least *eighteen million*," he said with heavy emphasis, "more likely over a hundred million. That's our best estimate of the minimum death toll from a limited nuclear exchange between the United States and the North American Commonwealth." He settled back in his recliner. "Try to get some sleep. You're going to need it."

Exception Amber

Julie had handed Jose, Max, and Dr. Scranton their coffee cups when things began to go wrong.

"That's funny." It was Jose.

"Could you be more specific?" Scranton asked.

"There's something up with the feed from the wide-angle array . . ." The wide-angle cameras on ERGO-1 that were to give them their first close-up view of the inner debris belts and the inner accretion disk of blazing-hot gas that circled the black hole like a hellish parody of Saturn's rings.

"Where's ERGO-1?"

Julie looked at the big status board. According to the mission schedule, ERGO-1 was now less than a thousand nautical miles above the black hole, diving ever-faster toward it—traveling at nearly two-thirds of Earth escape velocity, in fact, faster than a satellite in low-Earth orbit. Off to one side, a display showed the distribution of known debris in the inner field, five hundred nautical miles below the plunging probe—

"Fuck me." Max winced apologetically. "Flare in progress, Doctor. There are lots of raw gamma emissions coming from the accretion disk"—the whirling disk of white-hot gas and debris swept up around the equator of the black hole—"it's heating up like crazy—"

"Forget the accretion disk." Jose pointed to the density map of the inner debris field, a couple of hundred miles further out than the central disk (a mere half mile in diameter). "Shit's *moving* down there."

"Define 'shit' and 'moving,'" Scranton demanded. She didn't seem offended by the language: merely impatient.

"Objects Alpha-104 through Alpha-118 are moving, Doctor. They're not where they ought to be anymore."

"How long have they been in stable orbits for?"

"Since observations began—"

"How fast are they accelerating?"

"If I had active primary radar—"

"You don't, so just give me a best guess."

"Alpha-104 is now . . . oh shit, oh shit." Jose hammered on his keyboard, old-school, pulling up simultaneous equations from an orbital mechanics worksheet. "I make that about thirty meters per second squared. Uh, no. Make that forty-four, forty-six. Uh, the acceleration is increasing."

"Five gees?" Scranton asked. Her face was colorless.

"The accretion disk is *flaring*, Doctor." Max's tone bespoke urgency. "Two degrees off-equator, six orders of magnitude brightness increase across the spectrum in the past minute." A millionfold increase of brightness in under a hundred seconds. "Still growing. Black body temperature just doubled to eighty-five million degrees."

Julie glanced over her shoulder, toward the door.

"Where's ERGO-1 now?" asked Scranton.

"Perigee in just under two and a half minutes. Main engine ignition and high bandwidth recording are go in one-twenty-two seconds. Five hundred and sixty miles to go—"

"Where are the moving bogies? What are they doing?"

Jose mumbled to himself. Louder: "They're killing their angular velocity relative to the hole. Means they're going to drop in closer, as if they're getting ready to execute a slingshot intercept on ERGO-1—"

Never awaken anything you can't put down again, Julie jittered in the privacy of her own head, suddenly aghast. They'd rattled Xenu's cage:

was it any surprise that the old enemy's sleeping war machines might lumber back into life in orbit around the black hole? She half-raised a hand to clutch for the Scientology bangle she used to wear around her neck. *Silly.*

"Ms. Straker." It was Dr. Scranton. "Please activate the bridge evacuation plan. Then phone Camp Singularity and notify Colonel Sanderson that I'm declaring an amber alert. That's amber alert."

Julie reached for the hard-wired guardhouse phone, trying to keep her hand from shaking. Scranton had been in the army: she'd been a junior officer during the Kuwait war, hadn't she? The GI bill sent her to Stanford, then ascending into the stratosphere of the national security complex during the current administration. Right now her voice had a flat lack of affect that hinted at the overcontrol of an officer trying not to spook her troops with bad news.

Julie worked her way through the phone tree until she reached the officer commanding Camp Singularity, vaguely aware that in the background Max and Jose were frantically tracking ERGO-1 and the ominous unidentified objects maneuvering deep in the black hole's gravity well. Scranton watched transfixed. In the distance, partly blocked by the sound-deadening foam of the trailer walls, a klaxon began blatting, the racket reverberating across the interior of the dome.

"Accretion disk flare rising to X-1, about forty-five percent coverage and rising. We're getting 4×10^{-3} watts per square meter in soft X-rays. Good thing the crew are all clear . . ." Max sounded shaky, for good reason. Julie's skin crawled. The hole was pumping out a stupendous amount of hard radiation now. If the flare intensified much further they'd need to evacuate the control room and the trailer on this side of the gate: the aluminum airlock doors wouldn't keep the sleet of X-rays out. "Alpha-104 now accelerating at one two one meters per second squared, a little under thirteen gees. If ERGO-1 fails to ignite Alpha-104 will make intercept in three minutes."

"It's definitely an interceptor?" Scranton asked.

"I see no other—" Jose interrupted himself. "ERGO-1 main engine ignition in twenty seconds—no other reasonable alternative." At thirteen gees, a human pilot would be mashed flat and unconscious in the cockpit. And the radiation level down there right now would cook them from the inside out in minutes, like a reactor core after a nuclear meltdown.

"Fascinating," Scranton murmured. And it was, in a way, Julie saw: the "debris" they'd been watching for the past sixteen years, orbiting far below the Bridge to Nowhere, was now fully alive, accelerating to intercept the probe package. And it had somehow woken up at the same time as the huge flare of fusion activity that had pulsed through the roiling donut-cloud of gas and plasma around the black hole. Almost as if the black hole was somehow powering the alien interceptors—

"Ignition." The ERGO-1 status display shifted, numbers spinning up in real time as it came under acceleration. "Looking good so far. High bandwidth link streaming. Perigeon in eighty-nine seconds, camera rolling. We should have video—"

A new window opened on the screen. It showed a backdrop of stars centered around an angry flare of light. The center of the disk was black, the sensors overloaded, like a battlefield laser burning through a wounded soldier's retina.

"Bogies are maintaining acceleration and changing vector." Max sounded shaky. "Intercept in three minutes and fifty seconds if they don't increase acceleration further."

"Not good," Scranton said mildly. "How much delta vee do they have?"

"So far? Three point seven kilometers per second and rising." Max and the Doctor shared a loaded glance. Julie racked her brain: whatever this meant to them, their reaction was significant. Like anesthetists in an operating theater watching the patient's vital signs deteriorate.

"Two hundred nautical miles to perigeon," Jose announced. "ERGO-1 is starting its Oberth maneuver. The differential gravimeter is picking up tidal forces on the order of one centimeter per second squared per meter at this point, and climbing."

"Flare is up to X-5," said Max. "We ought to think about moving. Or at least closing the storm door. If it goes much higher ERGO-1 is going to drop into safe mode. We'll lose most of the observations."

"Close the storm door now, unless it's going to sever the telemetry feed," Scranton directed. "We want to see this but we don't need to die for a few seconds of extra footage."

"Bogies Alpha-106 and Alph-109 accelerating much faster!" Jose bounced upright in his seat, his back tense. "Thirty gees and rising."

Max swore. "It's not going to—"

The violet pinprick glare in the high-definition video window from ERGO-1 suddenly flared green. The window froze.

"I've lost the ERGO-1 carrier signal," said Jose. He poked at his console then slumped. His forehead was shiny with perspiration: "Was that what I think it was?"

"Flare strength X-10 and rising." Max stood up. "That looked like a directed energy strike to me. Are the bogies—"

"Alpha-106 through 112 are still accelerating," said Jose. He sat up again, rattled his keyboard. "They're doing a close flyby, almost as if—"

Dr. Scranton stood up. "I've seen enough. Slam the storm door and let's go, we're evacuating *right now*, people." She calmly picked up her handbag and phone, then lifted the flap covering a big red button on the wall beneath a dog-eared sign saying NEVER PRESS THIS. "This is *not* a drill," she added in Julie's direction as she pushed the button firmly. She strode toward the door, coffee abandoned. "Hurry up!" She shouted over the chorus of sirens: "Unless you want to still be here when they find the bridge! Whoever and whatever they are."

PANKOW, BERLIN, TIME LINE TWO, AUGUST 2020

Hulius led Elizabeth through the back-office corridor and out into the public spaces of the schloss. A handful of visitors—clumps of tourists and graying local pensioners—were exploring the building. They ignored the big man with the baggy jacket and the ripped messenger bag clutched to his chest. The Turkish woman was even more invisible, easily mistaken for an off-duty cleaner. Together they made down the main staircase and out through the vestibule. Hulius waited a few seconds for Elizabeth to catch up. She looked haunted. "It's *different*," she whispered.

"The most familiar places are the most alien when you travel to other time lines," he told her, then drew a shallow breath and winced. "Come on."

Despite his earlier admonition, Elizabeth's head swiveled like a cat's at a rat fanciers' convention. Everything caught her eye, from the recessed external floodlights to the cars in the parking lot—cars which admittedly looked like weird, half-melted blobs of glass and metal compared to the chugging boxes-on-wheels of the Empire. He headed for the BMW, barely noticing the girl's quiet gasp as its lights flashed and the doors whined open at his approach. "Get into the right-hand seat," he told her.

"The right—" Elizabeth circled around the car warily. "There's no engineer. Who pilots it?"

"That would be me." Hulius dumped his bag in the leg well behind the driver's seat and slid behind the wheel, suppressing a gasp of pain. "Shut the door. Just a gentle tug. Now fasten your seat belt—it's that thing behind your right shoulder, pull it, it plugs in down there."

Elizabeth fumbled hesitantly. He reached past her, gritting his teeth, and tugged the seat belt. "It's the law here. We can be stopped by the police if you are not visibly wearing it."

"Why?"

"Because." He resisted the urge to rest his forehead on the steering wheel rim. "It's part of a safety system. To save your life in event of a crash."

"Does it work?" Elizabeth gave the seat belt an experimental tug as he pushed the start button and selected forward drive. "Hey, how are we moving? Did the brakes fail? Oh, it's so quiet!"

Hulius concentrated on controlling the vehicle. He didn't have the mental bandwidth to explain plug-in hybrids to a curious teenager. He felt hot and cold chills, a strange lassitude creeping over him. *I should not be flying today*, he thought grimly. Either the bullet had done more damage than he realized, or he was close to overdosing on the antihypertensive cocktail that allowed him to world-walk rapidly: maybe both. He coughed up something and swallowed instinctively, a hot metallic taste that was both familiar and worrying. The car park exit lay ahead. He squeezed the throttle, barely registered a quiet *eep* from the passenger seat as Elizabeth's fingers whitened on the grab bar, then spotted a gap in the traffic and squeezed into it.

He tapped on the dash and she gasped again as the satnav display switched on. She didn't gasp at the head-up projection, but her eyes grew wide when the car began to give Hulius spoken directions in English. And the speed of traffic on the autobahn, even in the suburbs, clearly scared her. "I see why you need safety systems," she said shakily.

He concentrated on staying alert and not drifting into the wrong lane. His ribs still ached brutally and he couldn't seem to get enough air in his lungs. "Car, enable lane following, constant distance, and preferred speed," he said to the dash, then took his hands off the steering wheel and fumbled with his fleece. There was a hole to the right of his heart, just above the red-hot wire in his chest. He stuck a finger through, felt the rough edges of a hole in the ballistic vest. *Shit.* The horse-killing slug had punched deep into it. At point-blank range it probably packed as much force as a .45 Magnum round. He shoved harder, and nearly blacked out with a sudden rush of hollow, nauseating pain. His chest throbbed and he swallowed again, recognizing the taste this time: it was definitely blood. It didn't matter if the jacket had stopped the slug—the slug had punched a couple of centimeters of Kevlar right into his ribs, probably puncturing a lung.

Hulius moved his hands back to the steering wheel. There was no blood on his fingertips but he felt dizzy and weak. *Shock,* he realized, *I'm going into shock.* "Change of plan," he said tightly. There was a junction coming up. He slid the car over to the right and turned off the highway, into a local main road connecting residential streets. Another turn, drifting slower, and he brought the car to a halt. Now he knew what was wrong, the pain was worse, sickening. He poked a wobbly fingertip at the satnav touchscreen, pulling up the address of the apartment he'd never intended to return to.

"What are you doing?"

"Getting us to a safe house," he said shakily. "Can't fly like this. Maybe tomorrow." He knew it was a fatuous idea even as it passed his lips.

"What's wrong?"

"Bulletproof vest stopped the slug. Think it cracked a couple of ribs. So I'm setting up"—a last stab at the screen and the satnav display changed, plotting a route across town—"a route to take us to an apartment. I'll get a doctor in." He grimaced, glanced in the rearview screen, and eased the BMW back out into the street. "Don't worry, we planned for hitches. It's just a delay." *More than that*, his conscience murmured in the privacy of his head.

He winced as he reached the end of the street and followed the instructions, turning back toward the autobahn, this time heading into the city. He wanted to cough something up, but his chest felt full of razor wire. There was something in his lungs. He was tired. Driving took all his attention and more, even with the calmly measured voice of the satnav directing him. Hostile horns blatted when he changed lanes erratically.

He must have zoned out, because he only realized where he was as he turned into a familiar street. The car had automatic parallel parking, for which he was grateful. Liz's eyes were as big as saucers as the car backed and crept into the space, steering wheel spinning without his input. "C'mon," he grunted as the engine finally cut out and the parking brake engaged. "Out."

Liz fumbled with the seat belt release button until he pushed it for her. Then he was leaning against the front door of the apartment, forehead against the cold painted wooden surface and feet braced apart as he pawed ineffectually in his pockets for the door keys. He felt cold and hot and sick, and he couldn't get enough air. A latch clicked and he stumbled forward into the flat. He heard footsteps behind him as the door closed.

Hulius stomped unsteadily toward the abandoned bedroom and dumped the messenger bag with a clatter. Lights came on. He slid out of the fleece and tried to unbutton his shirt with fingers that felt like swollen sausages. He heard the Princess say, "Let me do that." Cool fingers undid the fasteners and the shirt fell open. A small gasp. "Oh dear God."

He was sitting on the edge of the bed, bowed over, almost falling on his face. The rigid edge of the bulletproof vest shored him up like scaffolding around a building on the edge of collapse. He tried to remember something important about the messenger bag. "Bag," he mumbled.

The bag was in front of him. He reached inside. *Side pocket. Phone.* He tried to focus, but it was hard to think. Like being drunk or stoned, only with pain instead of euphoria. The screen swam before him as he swiped his PIN then speed-dialed a number in memory.

"John here. Hey bro, I thought you'd cleared this gate?"

"Doctor," he gasped: "Get me a doctor."

Then the phone was speaking in a tinny, angry crackle, but he didn't hear whatever it was because the carpet came up and hit him in the side of the head with a thud like the descending lid of a coffin.

TEMPELHOF, BERLIN, TIME LINE TWO, AUGUST 2020

The Gulfstream drilled on through the stratosphere, the afternoon sunlight dimming toward nightfall as it raced north and then east across the Atlantic. The cabin lights dimmed and the seats reclined: it was Paulette's first experience of darkness in weeks, and she luxuriated in the drowsy twilight until falling asleep, somewhere over Greenland.

Some time during the night she awakened to the sound of one-sided conversation. Colonel Smith was on the phone, talking quietly to a beige handset that looked as if it dated from the previous century. *Satellite phone,* she thought sleepily. He sat across the aisle from her. Eavesdropping was difficult. ". . . Trace on the subject," he was saying, ". . . went wrong? What? Called private paramedics? Excellent . . ."

She drifted off again, dreaming incoherently of a white-room interrogation by a faceless man who kept asking if she spoke German. The next time she awakened it was still nighttime outside the cabin windows, but there was a smell of coffee in the air, and the Colonel was sitting up in his chair, reading something on a tablet. "Ah, I see you're with us once more, Ms. Milan." His smile was feral in the undershot twilight cast by his illuminated screen.

"Bathroom," she husked, standing up unsteadily and making her way aft to the toilet. When she finished and returned to her seat she found someone had set it upright and swung it sideways to face the Colonel across the aisle. "What?"

"Sit down," he told her. She sat. There was a small side table propped up beside his chair, with lidded cardboard cups of coffee waiting. He passed one to her without asking. "Milk, no sugar, according to your file."

"Thank you." He wanted her to know how thoroughly they knew her. "What do you want?"

"We will be landing in a couple of hours," he told her. "I have a job for you. If you do it to the best of your ability, and successfully, I will release you into the custody of Major Hulius Hjorth, who will extract you to the Commonwealth. Where you are *Colonel* Milan."

What? It sounded too good to be true: much too easy, even leaving aside the question of involuntary exile versus life in prison. "Why? Why are you doing this?"

"To send them a message." He grinned like a skull: "Pawn takes queen: check, Ms. Milan. Can you remember to say that, verbatim, those precise words? It's a message for Miriam Beckstein—or Mrs. Burgeson, as she styles herself these days. *Pawn takes queen. Check.*"

"What does that even mean?"

Smith took a sip of his coffee and grimaced. "It's a fucking *chess move*," he said. "She'll understand. We've been playing this game for sixteen years. Don't tell me you never learned chess?"

Paulette shook her head.

"Well, that's your loss."

They sat in silence for a couple of minutes, sipping their gradually cooling coffee. "You said I had a job. What do you want me to do?" Paulette finally asked, hating herself for this display of weakness.

"I thought you'd never ask. We're going to land at a major NATO base. From there we will drive to . . . well, there are a couple of possible target locations. One is a hangar at a regional airport. Another is an apartment in the suburbs of Berlin. Either way, the local police will provide security. You will simply walk inside the building, locate Major Hjorth, and give him a different message."

"What message?" She rubbed her lips with the back of her right wrist.

The Colonel shrugged. "I'll tell you when we arrive. What you do afterwards is immaterial, but you should be aware that by order of the Secretary of State you've been stripped of your US citizenship. My advice would be to go with Major Hjorth, *Colonel*, because you won't be welcome in the United States—or Germany—afterwards. Just remember this—when you see her, tell Miriam, *pawn takes queen: check.*"

Behind them, the distant roar of the engines abated. Beyond the cockpit door, the pilots were starting their descent.

PANKOW, BERLIN, TIME LINE TWO, AUGUST 2020

The Major fell forward in a dead faint.

Elizabeth froze for a few seconds, appalled and fascinated. From the moment he'd picked her up—shocked into paralysis by the violence erupting around her—she'd felt a terrible freedom: a precipitous sense that, for the first time in her life, she was truly the agent of her own destiny. But with the Major's loss of consciousness it threatened to slip away.

The glowing glass gadget he'd been talking to slid from his nerveless fingers. It was buzzing, in a tinny emulation of telephonic conversation. *How strange*, she thought. She'd heard the sensational reports of course, the deranged-sounding claims that the Commonwealth was benefiting from super-advanced technology from another world. But until she'd sat in the passenger seat of the Major's automobile she hadn't quite credited it. Now, though, the presence of a telephone disguised as a self-illuminating pocket mirror seemed quite mundane compared to the things she'd glimpsed from the speeding motor's window. She picked it up, worked out which end was the earpiece, and held it to the side of her head, using her fingertips. "Hello?" she said.

"Fox speaking. Who is this?" asked a man's voice.

"I'm Elizabeth. The Major just fainted. I think he needs a doctor. He's been shot."

The man swore, most indelicately. "I'll be right round. I have the backup tickets. You are at the apartment, yes?"

"I think so." She looked round. "White painted walls, a front door with the number sixty-eight on it—"

"Ten minutes. Do you have any first aid training?"

"Some," she said doubtfully.

There was a musical chime and the sound of silence disappeared: the phone-thing darkened, and when she looked at it, it displayed a tiny printed message: CALL ENDED. The letters writhed and moved across the screen as if alive. Disturbed, she stowed it in a pocket of the long coat-jacket the Major had given her, then dropped to her knees beside him. He was breathing, but there was a trickle of blood from his mouth and a wet sucking sound from his ribs. The stranger was coming, but could she trust him? On impulse, she went through the Major's pockets. There was a wallet, made of some unfamiliar harsh fabric. Opening it she found a number of cards made out of stiff, glossy plastic, two bearing photographs of the Major's face, and a handful of small, colorful banknotes. *I'll take it for safekeeping,* she told herself, and tucked the wallet away in her coat pocket. His other hip pocket held a holster and a vicious-looking black pistol. She set it to one side to think about, then dropped the jacket over it.

Stricken by uncertainty, Liz tried to remember what she'd learned about treating gunshot wounds—a not-uncommon hazard for hunters— then bent to work at the unfamiliar straps and fasteners that held the Major's odd breastplate together. With the shirt out of the way she could see the deep crater where Lieutenant Gorki had shot him. There was blood: the slug had penetrated the full thickness of the armor, losing energy and distorting on the way through. Otherwise it would have killed him instantly. Now the blood bubbled every time the Major took a breath. *Pneumothorax,* she remembered from the field aid course. What to do about it? The most important thing was to stop more air getting into the wound, until help arrived . . . assuming, of course, that help was on its way. She was past having second thoughts about this whole enterprise, and was well into third and fourth ones. Seeing this brave new world put everything in a new and unnerving context. The Commonwealth really *did* have access to something like the future, which meant . . . *am I fooling myself about my own importance to them?* It was too much to think about right now, so Liz dealt with her confusion by compressing the Major's chest.

Twelve minutes later the front door opened. She looked up at the man who entered and stood over them, looking down dumbly. "Well!" she said, crossly—for this was absolutely *not* the defection she had signed up for, "you took your time! Are you the doctor?"

"I called the paramedics. They'll be here shortly—" The newcomer's hair was as long as a woman's, but he sported a full beard: his clothes were no more outlandish than those of the other people she'd seen around, but something about him made her acutely uneasy. "What happened? Was it the Americans?" He stared at her. "Are *you* American?" he asked slowly.

It seemed there were layers within layers here. This man clearly didn't know who she was, or who the Major was working for. Elizabeth frowned. "Make yourself useful, hold this in place." *This* was a blood-soaked towel from the kitchen. "It's vital not to let any more air get into his chest. Otherwise the lungs collapse. I need to go and find another one."

The stranger paled. Then he knelt down and took hold of the damp cloth. While he was distracted, Liz casually picked up the shoulder bag the Major had carried and moved it close to her side, allowing the flap to fall open. The bizarre carbine he'd shot the guards with was still inside: she wasn't sure she could bring herself to use it—wasn't even sure the Major hadn't expended its entire magazine—but if strangers were going to barge in and out of this odd little tenement she wanted to keep it close. *Especially* strangers who didn't trust Americans, and who thought she might be one. She scooped up the Major's jacket and the concealed pistol. "I'll just move these," she said quietly, sidling toward the hallway.

A bell chimed: a doorbell, Liz realized. She shouldered the bag and walked to the door, then recognized a spy-hole. A man in a lime-green coverall, carrying a bulky bag with a strange flag on the side—a plain red cross in a white circle—gesticulated from the doorstep. She let them in. "Are you a doctor?" she asked.

"*Nein*, no—paramedic." His voice was oddly high: in a dizzying perspective flip Liz realized she was talking to a woman. "Where is the patient?"

"Come with me . . ."

The shock-haired green-overalled medic took control in the bedroom. Liz went to the bathroom to wash her hands, then succumbed to a moment of acute disorientation. The fixtures were aggressively plain, starkly unadorned, but made to the highest standard, as if for an operating theater. It was as if these people took joy from the purely functional. *So strange.* She had imagined big differences, but it was the small things that shook her to the core.

She collected bag and jacket and pistol and retreated into what she guessed was a parlor, judging by the plain leather sofa facing what had to be a film projector screen (for no television could possibly be that big or flat). The Major's glassy pocket phone was incomprehensible, and in any case nothing she did made it work—it kept showing messages asking her to *look* at it as if it really *was* a magic mirror, then showed her a warning about "face unlock"—so she took the time to inspect her other spoils. The gun in the bag was a stubby black plastic thing, with a half-melted-looking handle near the front of the barrel. She gave up on it almost immediately and set it aside. The pistol was another matter. It looked not unlike the military automatics some of the royal bodyguards had carried, but felt ridiculously light in her hands, although the grip was oddly fat. She located the safety catch and magazine release then put it in the bag. There were papers, but they made little sense: diagrammatic maps of what appeared to be an airfield, technical listings of some sort. It was all very confusing.

As she pondered the papers, the doorbell chimed again.

I spoke to Fox. Fox called the doctor-nurse-whatever. So who is this, and who called them? The new visitor *might* be harmless, but she didn't intend to take any chances. Elizabeth glanced at the corridor through the apartment. There was a front door, of course, but there was also a side door at the opposite end of the passageway. She stood up and slung the Major's bag over her shoulder, then marched to the back door. She turned the small twist-handle and the door unlatched. It opened onto a cobbled courtyard with some small flower beds planted in wooden boxes and a shut gate. There were other doors to either side, clearly rear entrances to neighboring apartments.

Squinting against the daylight, Liz closed the back door behind her and walked to the other side of the courtyard. She rapped on a random door paneled with frosted glass.

There was no reply. Liz rapped again. There were no lights showing, so she unslung the bag and punched it hard against the glass in the bottom panel. The glass starred but did not shatter under the impact of the gun. She reversed the bag and hammered it against the panel again, heart pounding in her throat. She had a sense of imminent doom, like the unnatural calm before a lightning storm. The glass finally shattered all at once, turning into a spray of strangely smooth pebbles without jagged edges. She squatted, reached through the hole carefully, and fumbled around for the handle. There was a protrusion, a key negligently left in a lock. She turned it, and the door opened.

She found herself in another apartment, colder and more cluttered than the one the Major had taken her to. "Hello?" she called, palms sticky and hot. She relaxed infinitesimally as the seconds inched past without an angry reply. As her eyes adjusted she saw a door leading into an interior corridor. There was a front door at the far end, on the other side of the block from the Major's entranceway. The apartments were mirrors of each other. *Yes, I can do this,* she thought.

She unlocked the front door and stepped out. There was a tram stop not far away. Tugging her headscarf tight around her hair, she scuttled along the sidewalk.

If the Major was right, nobody here would pay any attention to one more dark-skinned Turkish woman shuffling along with bowed head.

If her fears were baseless, she could return in an hour or so: Hjorth or van Rijnt or whatever he was called wasn't going anywhere soon.

And if not . . . well, this was just another Berlin. Fast, half-melted automobiles and glowing glass magic mirrors. How different could it be?

NEW LONDON, TIME LINE THREE, AUGUST 2020

Everyone in the Brunswick Palace seemed to be holding their breath in the calm before the storm.

Erasmus Burgeson was chairing a meeting of the broadcasting budget committee when the news everyone had been dreading arrived. The red telephone on the table at one side of the boardroom buzzed for attention just as the Assistant Commissioner for Cable Communications was glibly replaying his pitch for an increase in the backhaul budget: "Demand for long range computer internetworking between metropolitan nodes is bound to double every fifteen months for the next two decades, and our current coaxial infrastructure is already overloaded—"

"Thank you, Joe." Erasmus nodded. "Excuse me." He took the receiver from the receptionist: "Commissioner Burgeson." He listened for a few seconds in total concentration. "Yes, I see. Thank you."

He put the phone down. "Ladies and gentlemen." (There were indeed three women on this committee: the Party's commitment to emancipation was slowly gaining ground.) "That was the First Man's residence. They're calling the primary list now."

"Oh." Maria Smith (Board of Governors, Committee of Radio Broadcasters) looked stricken. "Adam's condition is . . . ?"

Erasmus shook his head. "This meeting is adjourned," he said tiredly. "Minutes will show that a two-minute silence was observed out of respect for the First Man's passing. People, your departments all have death plans and you should activate them after you leave this meeting. You can go now—or stay with me for those two minutes." He folded his hands, bowing his head.

I regret to inform you the First Man has been pronounced dead, the switchboard operator had told him. *He passed away peacefully, in his sleep.* The Party Central Committee had decreed that two weeks of state mourning would follow this event. Then there would be an election by the Commissioners, and a new First Man would be sworn in.

What are we going to do now? Erasmus wondered uneasily. An unwelcome sense of dread leached the warmth from his soul. Until this moment, he'd always known that the state was in safe hands. The first large-scale experiment with democracy in this time line had been secured by Adam Burroughs, whose commitment to the principles of the revolution was above question. Erasmus had known the First Man since he was plain Sir Adam, a firebrand agitator in exile: and he'd trusted him, hero-worshipped him as an object of emulation. But the ship of state was sailing into uncharted waters, making first official contact with a nuclear-armed and presumptively hostile alien superpower, and the captain had just left the bridge for the last time. Nor had he heard whether Miss Thorold's high-risk/high-payoff scheme to protect the revolution from the machinations of the royalist threat had succeeded. *I need to talk to Miriam,* he resolved. *She'll know what to do next . . .*

PANKOW, BERLIN, TIME LINE TWO, AUGUST 2020

The doorbell rang for a second time.

"Make yourself useful and answer that," the paramedic suggested to Fox. "It's probably the ambulance." She was busy with a bag and a sterile plastic tube, trying to stabilize the shooting victim. Not enough hands, not enough backup. Her rapid response bike was parked outside but it wasn't going to get this patient to an emergency room, which was what he clearly needed.

Fox stood up. He hadn't been under any illusions about Herr van Rijnt's shady activities—industrial espionage and smuggled GM organisms were a fine story, but why the light plane with the interesting vertical landing parachute system?—however, between the clearly not-Turkish girl with the odd English accent and the gunshot wound, he'd made up his mind to leave. *Walk fast and don't look back.* The medic was here, van Rijnt would survive, and van Rijnt could help the Bundespolizei with their inquiries when they got their claws into him. If it wasn't the Bundespolizei it would be the BND for sure. This affair had the fishy stench of terrorism hanging over it: concealed guns, women in Islamic dress. Fox had no intention of sitting here and waiting to be arrested.

He walked to the front door and checked the CCTV screen. A woman stood on the doorstep. Long dark hair, office clothes. Not a paramedic, but she didn't look dangerous. However, he'd have to get rid of her before he could leave. Fox opened the door, keeping his right hand in his pocket. "Who are you?" he demanded in German.

The woman, who on closer inspection was middle-aged and thin-faced, gave him a weary look. "Do you speak English?" she asked.

"Who wants to know?" Fox replied in the same language. *Get out of my way.* He bounced on his toes, eager to escape.

The woman pushed her hair back distractedly. "I'm so sorry," she said apologetically, "but is Major Hjorth here? It's important."

"Major who?" Fox didn't have to feign bafflement.

"If he's inside, tell him Paulette Milan is here, and I'm really sorry about this."

Fox took a step back and aimed his pistol at the American woman through the lining of his pocket. Her eyes widened slightly. "You'd better come in," Fox told her. He took another step backward. "Slowly. Follow me slowly. Don't move suddenly."

"What happened here?" Paulette stared at him. Suddenly she looked terrified. "Is the Major okay?"

"I don't know who you're talking about." Fox gestured with his left elbow. "The doctor's trying to keep van Rijnt alive. He was shot. It wasn't me."

"Van Rijnt—who—have you seen Elizabeth Hanover? Is she with him?"

"A Turkish girl?" Fox shifted his grip and began withdrawing the gun from his pocket: *Maybe she's worth something.*

"You'd better put that down. They're going to storm the building and if you're holding a gun they'll shoot you for sure." The woman's vehemence took him by surprise: "They want the Major and the woman alive," she continued urgently. "Listen, whatever you do, *don't trust the Colonel.* They've got the apartment doppelgängered by world-walking special forces—"

She was cut off in mid-sentence by the loudest noise in the world.

NEW LONDON, TIME LINE THREE, AUGUST 2020

"They *what?*" Olga exploded with disbelief.

Brilliana glared at the staffer who stood before Miss Thorold's desk. "You'd better repeat that from the beginning."

"Uh, yes, ma'am." He looked almost too young to shave, and absolutely terrified of the two women focusing on him like a pair of cats confronting a cowering rodent. "Ma'am, the communiqué is from desk four, Operation CROWN. A transmission was received at nine twenty-eight local from Major Hjorth, indicating that all preconditions were nominal and he was going in. A second transmission at eleven zero six from Major Hjorth indicated that he had made the pick-up and was continuing to the next phase of the operation. But at eleven nineteen we received a copy call intended for Asset FOX, from Major Hjorth, requesting medical backup. Hjorth was then replaced on the call by a woman calling herself Elizabeth, who said, quote, the Major just fainted. I think he needs a doctor. He's been shot, unquote."

"*Lightning Child,*" Olga muttered in Hochsprache. The staffer looked confused. In English: "What happened next?"

"At eleven thirty-one, Asset FOX called a private medical service and requested that a paramedic attend an unspecified emergency at the safe house."

"And then?"

"We don't know," said the staffer. His body language screamed *don't hit me.* Possibly because Brilliana appeared to be taking the news personally— too personally. "Attempts to call Asset FOX were unsuccessful. Desk four logged some sort of major police incident in the next fifteen minutes, probably in the vicinity of the safe house, but we don't know exactly what happened between then and—"

"Play it again," Brilliana said wearily. "Play it, Sam."

The reel-to-reel tape deck held the transcript of a conversation that had required an out-of-schedule courier delivery. Luckily the station chief in time line two was bright enough to recognize an emergency when it took a dump in his lap. The technical trooper, who trailed the staffer around like a sad-eyed spaniel, pushed the button.

"Good morning, people." The voice was male, with an East Coast American accent. "This is Colonel Smith. I assume I'm addressing Miriam Beckstein, Olga Thorold, or Brilliana Hjorth." A pause. "In the course of his operation in your Berlin, Major Hjorth managed to get himself shot. This was not, I assure you, anything to do with me. Luckily my people managed to secure his safe house before the BND could move in and muddy the waters. He is currently stable but poorly in the base medical establishment at Tempelhof AFB, being treated for a collapsed lung and two fractured ribs. His future disposition is in your hands. Obviously, a positive outcome to the forthcoming negotiations will make it much easier to negotiate his repatriation."

A pause. Then the voice continued: "We are also holding Paulette Milan, or should I say *Colonel* Milan of your Department of Parahistorical Research."

"Stop. Stop!" Olga gestured at the techie, who mashed his finger on another button on the tape deck. "Oh dear Sky Father, tell me this doesn't mean what I think it does."

Brill stared at her. "Not going to say that."

"If they've got Paulie and Hulius, then they've got the, the target."

"Restart the tape," said Brilliana.

"—We trust future negotiations will be fruitful and I look forward to your concrete proposals as soon as you have resolved your current leadership crisis. Goodbye." The call trailed off into smug silence.

Brilliana looked at the staff officer and the technician, her gaze harsh: "You two, wait outside."

"Yes ma'am . . ." They beat a hasty retreat to the outer office, leaving Olga and Brill alone.

"They got Elizabeth," Olga said flatly.

"What about Paulie?"

"We ran out of time with the rendezvous protocol. They probably tracked Hulius on his last trip over, picked her up and drained her. I'm guessing they planned to use her as a stalking-horse to get close to him, only he somehow managed to get himself shot. Gods. Huw is going to be pissed."

"Huw"—Brill took a deep breath—"is not the only one. Someone's going to have to tell Elena. Don't get me started on what the HUMINT Oversight Group is going to make of it, either. But it's the blowback that I'm really worried about."

"Think we've been penetrated?"

"I'm not willing to go that far just yet. But something tipped them off and they got inside our decision loop. Instead of neutralizing the Pretender's claim, we're now wide open to accusations of abduction by the French, accusations of monarchist revanchism by the Radicals—and at the Department of Homeland Security's mercy whichever way we play it. The question is, what do they *want*?"

"We've got to get her back. By any means necessary."

"Yes, but getting her out of an Undisclosed Location that's armored against world-walkers is going to be just a little bit harder than lifting her from a Ruritanian clown school in imperial Berlin, isn't it?"

"Wait one." Olga waved a hand tensely. "Wait. I just had a thought."

"Just the one?"

"Smith didn't say anything about the Princess. He didn't mention her."

"So? Either he doesn't know what she is, or—"

"Or he doesn't have her."

"But Hulius sent the extraction code!"

"What if"—Olga looked thoughtful—"what if Hulius succeeded in extracting Elizabeth, but between him getting himself shot, and that last phone call, and Smith arriving, Liz took a hike?"

"That's what our friends call a Hail Mary pass."

"Yes, but think about it: Smith *doesn't know*. If he had her and knew what she was he'd have us over a barrel, wouldn't he? However, our English Rose isn't a shy and reticent wallflower. She's bright and determined enough to defect. If the extraction went wrong—"

"But that would mean she's in Berlin in time line two, on her own and on the run! Is that what you're thinking?"

"Yes. Of course, as soon as Colonel Smith gets a chance to question Hulius he's going to figure out what slipped through his fingers, but that could take a while. It all depends how badly Yul's been hurt. Shot, fainted."

"Could be blood loss, could be anything, really."

Olga made a pistol of the first two fingers on her right hand, aimed them at Brilliana. "You've been shot. Bang. Stayed functional long enough to get your charge to a place of safety—twenty, thirty minutes. Then collapsed. Shock, exhaustion. Hulius's going to be out for a couple of days, minimum. We can factor in Colonel Smith being reluctant to apply enhanced interrogation to a high-value captive who's recovering from a gunshot wound and who may have value as a hostage. Hulius's a stubborn son of a bitch, isn't he?"

Brill nodded. Her eyes glistened. "He won't give them anything easily."

"So if the Colonel doesn't have Elizabeth Hanover already, he isn't going to find out about her for a good one to three days."

Brill nodded again. Her expression hardened. "You know what? I have a feeling it's time we spoke to Rita's grandfather . . ."

PHILADELPHIA, TIME LINE TWO, AUGUST 2020

"Hi Kurt! It's Angie!"

"Hello, Angie. Have you heard from my granddaughter?"

"No, I think she's still working on that job they sent her on? I was just wondering if you wanted to do dinner tonight."

Kurt thought for a moment. Only a moment: his memory wasn't as sharp as it had once been. It was on the tip of his tongue. "Dinner, you say?"

"Yes, dinner."

She was insistent. *Dinner.* Well, then. An interesting choice of words. "Dinner," as opposed to "supper" or "Chinese" or "drinks." His pulse raced for a moment as he replied. "Very well. Do you want to pick me up?"

"Sure—are you still in that motel?"

In only thirty seconds the conversation was at an end. They had a date. Kurt slid his phone back into its padded case with a rueful snort. Fifty years ago—even thirty or forty, if he hadn't been married—he'd have been overjoyed by the thought of a date with a green-haired muscle goddess like Angie, even if she wasn't interested in him in the same way. Now it was just ironic, and a bit worrying. *Dinner* meant that Rita had been in touch. (Best not to know how.) *Dinner* meant news. But any unscheduled contact held an element of risk, so Angie wouldn't have requested a face-to-face meeting without a good reason. *I hope trouble has not found Rita*, he thought. But of course, if Rita was in trouble how would she have signaled Angela?

An hour later Kurt was downstairs in the lobby when Angie pushed through the doors. "Kurt!" They embraced loosely: Angie was willing to air-kiss, but a bit standoffish. He tried hard not to give offense, but the mores of the younger generations frequently left him confused and uncertain. *Such an old and ugly man I am*, he thought ruefully. "Come on, I was thinking we could pick up burritos together, there's this great little carry-out—"

He was half-expecting the usual tradecraft runaround, with a chatterbox bag for the phones and a last minute diversion to a random destination, but true to her word Angie drove him straight to a taqueria with a sit-down area that did indeed serve burritos as promised. They queued for a few minutes, then Angie led him to a table near the front window where they ate and chatted of inconsequentialities. Partway through their meal she backhanded her 7UP, tipping it onto the table: "Oh, I'm sorry!" she chirped as she grabbed at it. "Excuse me." She followed through with a handful of the serviettes she'd heaped on his tray, then dumped them back in a soggy mass, with something else folded among them. It was a note, scrawled on paper. Kurt smiled and nodded, and resisted the temptation to read it under the watching eyes of the diner's CCTV. The restaurant only had a low-grade commercial system, but if the DHS felt the need to tap its stream they could do so without a warrant. And even cheap CCTV cameras recorded in cinematic high definition these days.

"Have you heard from Rita's employers?" Kurt asked Angie, smiling for the cameras.

"Not a tweet." She looked worried. "You'd think they'd at least be able to confirm or deny to an employee's publicly-acknowledged partner, but no . . ."

"I imagine if they expected her to be away for any length of time they'd say something."

"Weather looks good. Why don't we walk our supper off?" she suggested.

"Ah, yes. Let us do that." Kurt kept a straight face. He'd been doing a lot of walking lately. It was good exercise as long as his knees and hips held out, and he'd been careful during his middle years not to put on more weight than his joints could carry. But his old shanks were tired today, and although Angie's suggestion made good tradecraft sense he'd regret it afterward.

Before they left, Kurt went to the restroom and used the stall. There were no cameras present when he unrolled Angie's smudged pencil-scrawl letter and read it. MESSAGE FROM RITA'S CONTACTS. HER MOTHER'S PEOPLE WANT YOU TO VISIT THEM. SAY IT'S URGENT. IF YOU AGREE, RDV DETAILS ARE . . .

Kurt read the rendezvous instructions three times, then continued to repeat them silently as he pulled wads of toilet paper from the holder and dropped them in the pan. He quietly tore the note up and scattered it on top before flushing. He continued to repeat the directions to himself as he walked out of the diner and found Angie. "Yes," he said, "let's walk. I think . . . yes, it's past time I went on a journey."

She glanced at him, questioning. He nodded infinitesimally. Then they walked around the block—a couple of blocks, in fact—before returning to her pickup for the drive home.

When he got back to his lonely hotel room, Kurt set his phone's alarm for seven o'clock the next morning. Then, before he went to bed, he laid out clothes and a day pack in readiness for the ride of his life. He lay awake in the dark for nearly an hour, repeating the instructions and working out for himself the steps necessary to minimize his risk of being observed. And then he drifted off to sleep for the very last time in this America.

NEW LONDON, TIME LINE THREE, AUGUST 2020

Even though she was still half-asleep, Rita realized something was wrong the instant she stepped through the parlor doorway in search of breakfast. It was something about the angle of Huw's shoulders, or the way Brilliana, at the other end of the table was furiously poring over a pile of documents. They were taut yet subtly broken, like overwound clock springs. They were also both dressed from head to toe in black, which after a few seconds she pegged as anomalous.

Brilliana looked up. "Ah, it's you." She paused with her pen in a death grip, poised in mid-air to stab a defenseless form. Her eyes were saggy, as if she'd been up half the night. "Take a seat. We need to talk."

"Go easy on her." Huw sounded equally tired. "Coffee, Rita?"

"Um, yes." Rita looked between them apprehensively. "What is it?"

Brill broke into speech with the suddenness of a mudslide: "It's not about you," she hastened to reassure. "But we've—well, there's a minor crisis. And a major one." She ground to a halt.

Huw looked at her questioningly, then leaned back in his chair and faced Rita. "Adam died yesterday afternoon, while you were away," he said quietly.

"Oh, I'm—" Rita hesitated. "I'm sorry for your loss," she said woodenly. Retreat into formula seemed somehow less false than gushing regrets for a man she'd never met, who had meant nothing to her personally. He wasn't her president, after all.

"Well, we knew it was coming." He sounded phlegmatic. "It *does* shove us into two weeks of official mourning, a state funeral, a possible constitutional crisis, and a power struggle—but that's not your problem."

His forehead wrinkled. "Although, come to think of it, your managers will need to be informed."

"There's a mourning dress in the wardrobe Cook and White's supplied for you," Brill reminded her sensibly. "In case you need to make any public appearances in relation to the funeral." She seemed preoccupied. "That's not going to be a big problem. I mean, the protocol has been planned in minute detail already. Which ambassadors are seated next to which Commissioners, who rides in front of or behind the gun carriage, the speeches, obituaries, and documentaries for public consumption. The real problems are all behind closed doors."

"Problems," Rita echoed, curiosity getting the better of her. "If it's all planned, if you knew he was ill—" She paused. "Is there something else going on that you want to tell me about?"

"Quite possibly, though I think we need to wait a little while." Brilliana gave her a guarded look. "Rita, I have a favor to ask of you."

"A—" Rita put her coffee down. "Is this work, or personal?"

"To the extent that politics is sometimes frighteningly personal, it could be either or both."

"What's that supposed to mean?"

Brill looked at Huw, whose blank look was disturbingly artless: "Dear, would you mind leaving us for a minute?"

"Wait what"—Rita paused until Huw closed the parlor door on them—"is *that* about?"

"Ears-only. Rita, I'm about to ask you to do something that falls outside anything your bosses expect of you, and which they might consider to be treasonable. You can say no and I won't hold it against you. If you're completely, robotically loyal you can even report it to them and—well, if you do so it means I've misjudged you. But I want you to be aware, up front, that the consequences of you saying yes are open-ended and drastic. You might not be able to return to the United States afterwards. If that happens, we have the resources to look after you and yours—but it's up to you."

It's the pitch, Rita thought faintly. The one she'd been expecting them to throw at her sooner or later. Only it was premature, far sooner than she—or the Colonel—had expected. They hadn't even tried to soften her up: they must *know* she couldn't say yes without— *What's she playing at?* "I'm listening," she said.

"It's not about you." If Brilliana had been waiting for Rita's double take, she was not disappointed. "We—Miss Thorold and I, after obtaining the consent of Mrs. Burgeson—reached out to your adoptive grandfather. Kurt Douglas. We need his help on a matter of some delicacy. Of course he isn't a world-walker, so we have set up a rendezvous, and we would like you to go and fetch him for us. Alice Morgan will organize ground transport and security. The thing is, we need a world-walker who is not on the DPR's books, or on our watch list, and who has a plausible reason for visiting time line two."

Rita opened her mouth, then closed it again. Picked up her coffee cup to take a mouthful, covering her confusion. "You want Gramps? What for?" *You want a world-walker who* isn't *one of your own to do this? Why?*

Brill's lips thinned. "I mentioned a major crisis and a minor one. The death of the First Man was the minor one. The *major* one—we've lost track of an asset, and we want to retrieve it. Kurt Douglas has skills that are uniquely applicable to the job in question. Skills you may be aware of, I think."

Rita suppressed a horrified shudder. *What does she know?* If Olga's people knew about the Wolf Orchestra they had her over a barrel. It wasn't just a minor indiscretion: it was blackmail material. The proverbial handle you wanted to have on a covert asset. They could mail an anonymous tip-off and she'd be in the shit so deep she'd be lucky to ever see daylight again. The Colonel and Dr. Scranton would bury her alive.

"His background is not a problem *for us*—quite the contrary. We're prepared to offer him asylum, a state pension, and just about anything else he can reasonably ask for, if he helps us out in this matter."

"What?" Her eyes blurred with cognitive whiplash. *If she knows about Kurt how can she* not *know about me?* "What matter?"

"That's his business, not yours. All I'm asking of you right now is that you let Inspector Morgan take you to a surveyed rendezvous point, cross over, pick up your grandfather—literally, pick him up—and come back.

Oh, and if he turns the job down, you're his ride home. He has no reason to trust me, but he certainly trusts *you*."

Rita crossed her arms, a sick sensation settling in her gut. *So this is what a conflict of interest feels like.* She decided to bluff, weakly: "I can't agree to you recruiting my grandfather for some kind of illegal operation on US soil—"

"It's not going to be on US soil. And it's almost certainly not illegal, either. Well, it might involve violating another nation's immigration regulations, but that's about it."

"What?"

Brill paused, clearly choosing her words very carefully. "The asset we've lost track of is in Germany. Germany in your world. And by the way, if you report this to your superiors before the meeting with Kurt, the deal's off the table."

"Germany." *You're kidding me.* Rita shook her head. *Carrot and stick.* "What?"

"Your grandpa's old home. That's where the job is."

"Oh." Rita thought about it for a few seconds. "It's not directed against the United States, is that what you're telling me?"

"Exactly. I swear it, on my honor." She made an odd gesture, fist over heart: something about her phrasing sounded formulaic rather than quaint. "If anything, if your grandfather agrees to do this for us, it will make our ability to negotiate with your government more secure."

"You just want to talk to him?"

"Yes, we just want to talk to him. Although I was hoping you might be willing to help us with another job in the meantime, if he agrees to help us out." She cocked her head to one side and stared at Rita thoughtfully. "You hoped to pursue a career on the stage, or in the cinema, at one time. Is that right?"

Rita, head spinning, could only nod dumbly.

"Well, we may be able to help you fulfill that ambition," Brilliana continued. "We want you to attend the First Man's funeral and related events, of course. We need to introduce you in public and ensure that you are recognized as the daughter of Miriam Burgeson and acknowledged as a diplomatic messenger from the United States, to maintain appearances—the only perfect alibi is the truth. But while you are doing that, how would you like to try out an acting role on the side?"

"Acting? *What?*"

"We think you can probably successfully impersonate a not-terribly-well-known figure in front of the media. Just for a few days—while we locate the original, who has managed to lose herself at the worst time imaginable. You bear a strong resemblance to her, and—" Brilliana shrugged.

"This figure. Their disappearance wouldn't by any chance be connected to your sudden need to talk to Kurt, would they?" A thought struck Rita. "You want this to be totally deniable, don't you? It's off the books and you're trying to run an ad hoc recovery operation involving as few people as possible. Something's gone wrong and you're in trouble—"

"Please stop speculating." Brilliana frowned. "All I am asking you for *now* is to bring your grandfather to a confidential meeting. You can sit in on it and discuss it with him—if *he* wants you to—and with Miss Thorold, to decide whether you are willing to help us out. All the cards will be laid out on the table, I promise. It's up to you."

"You *are* in trouble!" Rita drained her coffee. "This acting role. I want to know who it is. Tell me and I'll go fetch Kurt and we can talk. But"—she pointed a finger at the other woman—"I want *that* card on the table first. Or no deal."

"All right." Brilliana nodded slowly. "You know about the succession issue. For some time now, we've been negotiating with the—with the only child of John Frederick IV, the pretender to the throne. Offering an amnesty and a pot of gold if she'll come home, take up an oath of citizenship in the Commonwealth, and renounce the throne. It would . . . well, a royal defection would badly damage the Monarchist faction and spike the wheels of the French claim to some of our peripheral territories. It would reduce the risk of a superpower conflagration. And from your employers' point of view, it would stabilize the current configuration of the Central Committee, enabling us to push for direct negotiations with your government. And *that* is vital.

"Everything was running smoothly until the wheels came off her extraction in the early hours of yesterday morning. We're going to get her back, but it's important that she's seen making the right speeches on the timetable dictated by Sir Adam's funeral. So once we've established your public alibi, it would really help us if you would agree to spend a few days—at most, a week—standing in front of the cameras, playing the role of Princess Elizabeth of Hanover, fiancée of the French Dauphin and heir to the Crown."

CAMP SINGULARITY, TIME LINE FOUR, AUGUST 2020

When Dr. Scranton risked *severe* professional embarrassment by pushing the panic button, she did so in the full knowledge that she was kissing goodbye any remaining hope of recovering the ERGO-1 probe, thereby writing off nearly two hundred million dollars and two years of R&D. Even at her level, this was a potentially career-ending move. But she didn't do it on impulse. She'd entered the Bridge Control Room having memorized a set of planned responses for various outcomes. As she walked carefully down the steps and out onto the apron inside the dome (carefully, for she dared not risk breaking an ankle at this point), she was already speed-dialing the base commander's phone.

"Sanderson here. Who is this?" He sounded distracted.

"Scranton speaking. Colonel—"

"We're in the middle of an evacuation drill, some idiot pushed—"

"It was me, and it isn't a drill, Colonel. I want you to evacuate Camp Singularity all the way back home, immediate effect. I say again, this is not a drill, this is an Exception Amber emergency. Abandon in place and pull everyone back to time line two *immediately*."

"I'll do that." A pause. "I'd like it in writing." (Not that he needed the paper trail. All calls via the Camp Singularity picocell network were recorded. But it was a line in the sand.) "Can I ask why?"

Dr. Scranton picked her way around a fenced-off dig site and sped up, power walking toward the cinderblock wall bisecting the interior of the dome (and the airlock leading through it to the waiting trucks outside). "We just lost ERGO-1. Hostile action. We tickled the dragon's tail and the dragon woke up. We now have unidentified objects maneuvering in the gravity well. They're accelerating, they're unmanned, and they're heading for the bridge. We've got five minutes, tops. Best case, it's a false alarm. Worst case, we've got incoming hostiles."

"Understood, get yourself to a place of safety and clear the line."

"Good luck. Scranton out." The inner door gaped open: beyond it Dr. Scranton saw the boot barrier, the decontamination room—and the outer door also agape. The launch crew had legged it, which was exactly what they were supposed to do. She glanced round. Julie Straker was following her, looking slightly lost. "Keep moving, woman." Dr. Scranton walked into the tunnel. "Have you seen Jose or Max?"

"I thought they were right behind us. Jose said something about shutting down the bridge power supply to reduce its emission signature . . ."

Eileen swore. "Too late for that: there's no horizon in space. Come on." She high-stepped over the boot barrier and kept walking. "When you drove down today, did you take a pool car or reserve your wheels?"

"Reserved."

"Then you're driving. Take me to the transporter. We'll pick up anyone we've got room for on the way, but we're going straight back to time line two."

"But the contamination—"

"Forget it, this is an emergency."

The dome was almost half a kilometer in diameter. As Dr. Scranton left the airlock she dialed a number that rang straight through to voicemail. "This is the proxy voicemail dropbox for Dr. Eileen Scranton. Dr. Scranton is unavailable at this time. Your message will be transferred to her main voicemail in not more than one hour. Please leave a message after the—"

"Roy." Her secretary. "This is Eileen. I'm at Camp Singularity and I've just ordered a full evacuation. Exception Amber applies. We've lost ERGO-1 and there are presumed live Forerunner hostiles inbound. If I don't make it out, you need to call Larry Stern at NSC and tell him to brief the president on BLACK MONOLITH and BLACK RAIN. You then need to call Eric Smith—yes, I know he's out of the country—and tell him he's running the shop and reporting direct to Larry until otherwise ordered." She pulled up the keypad and punched a numeric shortcode in. The voicemail would be flagged as urgent and dumped into the next automated store-and-forward transfer to time line two: with luck her message would make it out even if she didn't.

Eileen tucked her phone back in her bag and concentrated on walking. She and the youngster were no longer on their own. All around them archaeologists in bunny suits, guards in fatigues, and ordinary base personnel in civvies were leaving their trailers and hurrying toward the huge crack in the edge of the dome. Diffuse daylight streamed in, illuminating the fine dust kicked up by dozens of pairs of boots. *Decontamination later*, Eileen thought absently. "Where did you park?" she asked, breathing harder.

"This way." Straker reached for her hand. Together they broke into a jog, heading for the path up the hill. The vehicle park was beyond the generator truck and tank farm, half a kilometer farther away from the dome. It had seemed close enough back when she'd helped lay out the plans for Camp Singularity. Now, to her sixty-year-old legs and lungs, it seemed much farther. "What *happened* back there?"

"You know as much as I do. Less talking, more running." Eileen worked out daily, Pilates and swimming. Jogging uphill on a dirt path did things to her joints that she didn't want to think about. But the thought of the unidentified "debris" circling in the gravity well around the black hole on the other side of the bridge kept her moving, despite the shooting pains. The president would have to be briefed, of course. But, more than that, the evidence of Forerunner weapons systems that were still active after all these centuries put many things in an unwelcome new light. The Clan's world-walking ability, for example. The implications of the current lethal diplomatic tango with the Commonwealth. That the program for which ERGO-1 had been a proof of concept and a busted flush at birth was the least of her worries. There were other ways of getting up to escape velocity without burning kerosene and LOX, beside relying on the dangerously active corpse of a murdered planet, if you had para-time technology . . .

"Nearly there." Julie wasn't wheezing, but she sounded more breathy than usual as she gestured toward the row of dusty SUVs and trucks parked in the clearing. People were climbing into every available vehicle and peeling out as fast as they could.

As they approached Julie's SUV the doors popped automatically. Dr. Scranton was about to climb in when a couple of archaeology staff staggered up. "Room for passengers?"

"Get in back." Julie climbed in the driver's door. Eileen glanced at her watch. Five and a half minutes had elapsed since she hit the big red button. Maybe it was already all over. She clambered into the front passenger seat and nearly collapsed. Her thigh muscles were suddenly rubbery and her knees had been replaced with hot spheres of pain.

"Drive," she gasped.

"On it." Julie hit the throttle as the archaeologists pulled the rear doors closed. The single-track road leading to the transit gate past the main encampment was full but the queue of vehicles was moving at nearly twenty miles per hour. Excellent traffic management under the circumstances. Nothing was coming the other way.

It took them three minutes to drive the mile uphill to the fence around the permanent camp. The gates were open and guards with rifles were waving the traffic through. More soldiers marshaled a queue of traffic— now backed up all the way to the perimeter fence—as it jerked forward to the doors of the para-time transporter. It was like some kind of stage magic trick. The door opened: cars and trucks drove in. Then the door closed and reopened a few seconds later, revealing an empty garage. Eileen closed her eyes and breathed slowly. The archaeologists in the back were asking each other what was going on. "Are we going to make it?" Julie asked in a voice pitched for her ears only.

"Yes." There was no other answer she could give. If they made it, it was the honest truth. And if they didn't, if the bogies somehow broke through the bridge and the gate, then it didn't really matter. Better that the kid should spend her last minutes calm and hopeful than panicking on the steps of the scaffold.

Bump.

It wasn't a hard impact. At first Dr. Scranton thought someone had gotten impatient and nudged the SUV. But then she realized they were five yards from the car in front and ten clear of the next astern. Her eyes turned to the rearview screen. She turned her head and squinted. Then she sat up, very straight. "Julie. New orders."

"Uh, yes?"

"Drive over there." She pointed at a spot fifty yards past the transporter building. "Park. Abandon wheels, we're going across on foot."

"On it." Julie put the car in gear and began to inch aside, out of the queue. One of the soldiers marshaling the vehicles jogged over, waving, and she wound her window down.

"Hey, you can't—"

"She can, on my authority." Dr. Scranton held up her ID badge. "There's no time for this. We're going over on foot, immediately: I want you to get everyone out of their vehicles and into the transporter. Pack 'em in like sardines if you have to."

"Ma'am, I don't know—"

Eileen glared at him. "Do not make me get Colonel Sanderson on the line. Did you feel that earth tremor just now?"

Nobody could accuse the Army of assigning idiots to their para-time installations. He turned pale, snapped a shot of her badge with his glasses, then tapped his headset and began talking urgently. Julie continued to creep out of line, then stopped. "Will this do?" she asked.

"Yes." Eileen unsnapped her seat belt. "Everybody out. Follow me."

She marched toward the transporter building as the big vehicle door began to open again, and saw a sergeant raise his hand to block the truck that was about to roll through. Up and down the line soldiers were approaching drivers, giving them new instructions. The ground chose that moment to tremble again. It wasn't much, magnitude three at the worst, but that it was happening *at all*—

"Come on!" She waved the archaeologists over and pointed at the door at the far end of the transporter. "Everyone in! Close up tight! Let's get as many people out as we can, folks!"

Evacuees began to crowd in, blocking out the light. A babble of conversation, questions, and consternation. "What's happening?" "Why are we evacuating?" "Why not stay with the trucks—"

By the time there were nearly fifty people in the transporter it was becoming claustrophobic. The space would normally have held a couple of trucks or four SUVs. Dr. Scranton kept calling people to close up, move to the back. Julie cowered against the rear door and tried to keep calm as the gate at the entrance rose from the floor and then the door swung shut. The light overhead was dim. Her ears popped: a moment later a bell began to ring and the door she had her nose up against rose toward the ceiling, admitting a different shade of daylight.

Julie stumbled forward. Dr. Scranton caught her elbow and led her out of the transporter. "Are they all going to make it?" she demanded.

"I don't know." Scranton's tone was abruptly grim. "But *we* made it and we were in the Bridge Control Room."

"What does that mean . . . ?"

"It means you're coming with me, Ms. Straker." Scranton's usual calm reasserted itself. "We're not in immediate danger, but I've got a job to do." People around them were spilling out into the parking lot; HMMWVs and civilian minivans were drawing up at the opposite end, doors opening as some nameless saint on the base logistics team organized an ad hoc shuttle service to get the evacuees to a processing point. Scranton waved, marching toward an HMMWV and waving her badge. "We're going to the forward control office to get an update on whatever's happening back at the dome. Then Baltimore."

"Baltimore?"

"Yes, Ms. Straker. Where we will be debriefed separately—you as a witness, myself as, as the officer responsible."

"Responsible for what?"

"I don't know, yet." Dr. Scranton's eyes glittered. "Disturbing, isn't it?"

APPENDIX

A short, opinionated political overview of events leading up to the foundation of the New American Commonwealth

The history of our time line, and that of time line three—the home of the Commonwealth—appear to have been uniquely similar prior to 1745. However, to understand why they rapidly diverged from that date onward, it is necessary to review some earlier history. The Commonwealth, like the United States, has its roots in British imperial colonization efforts in the New World. However, as a result of a motion carried by a single vote at a council meeting held on Wednesday October the 30th, 1745, these two continental superpowers were destined to develop along unimaginably different lines.

The New England colonies settled in the seventeenth century—and the middle and southern colonies—were political ventures. Religion and politics were almost impossible to disentangle in seventeenth-century Europe, and in England in particular Catholicism was seen as a subversive, hostile doctrine. In the wake of King Henry VIII's expropriation of the monasteries that controlled 20 percent of the nation's wealth, Catholicism was synonymous with subversion and treason, much like the perception of Communism in the United States in the 1950s.

Grants of land were made by King James the First of England and Scotland (two nations with a shared crown, which later merged to become the United Kingdom) against the background of a global struggle for supremacy with other imperial powers. Spain and Portugal (both

Catholic powers) had gained an earlier lead in the central and southern Americas; France (a Catholic power), the Netherlands, and England were locked in a centuries-long struggle for domination over the northern coast of Europe and now focused on the northern continental mass. Thus, the colonization of North America can be seen as part of an ideologically motivated struggle between great powers seeking to encircle and strangle one another.

Different groups, at different times, sought wealth in the colonies. In 1620, the Puritan colonists who set sail in the *Mayflower* from England and the Netherlands to found Plymouth Colony could be described as religious fanatics: their motivation was separatism and doctrinal purification, and a deep distrust of the suspiciously Catholic-leaning King Charles Stuart (Charles the First). Religious turmoil and a fiscal crisis combined boiled over when the King attempted to override the rule of Parliament in the late 1630s, resulting in the Wars of the Three Kingdoms (England, Scotland, and Ireland), of which the English Civil Wars were the most notable. The King was executed, and a revolutionary Commonwealth declared: all sorts of radical politico-religious doctrines flourished under the rule of the Puritan Protestant Cromwells. But the Commonwealth did not long survive the death of its first Lord Protector, and the Stuart monarchy was restored under King Charles the Second. Charles II ruled cannily, giving the Protestants in Parliament sufficient sense of security, but his son, James the Second, proved both autocratic and suspiciously Catholic: the result was another parliamentary revolution in 1688 which invited in an invading Protestant Dutch monarch and his English Protestant queen—and the exile of the Stuart dynasty in France.

Importantly, this period saw the creation of a Bill of Rights, resolving the tension over constitutional power between the Crown and Parliament and confirming that England would not be subjected to a Catholic monarch. Finally in 1714, after the death of Mary II, the crown was offered to a relative, George the First of Hanover, who was both in direct line of descent from the Stuarts and satisfactorily Protestant.

If the period between 1620 and 1714 sounds chaotic and turbulent, it was: and it generated radically different groups of colonists at different times. During the Puritan-ruled period of the Commonwealth, many former aristocrats and supporters of the Stuart dynasty left to found plantations in the West Indies and the southern colonies. Irish Catholics exiled by Cromwell's invasion, and later captured Scottish Covenanters, found their way to the New World as indentured laborers.

These groups frequently retained their religious and national loyalties, and in some cases were ill-disposed toward each other. Even today the Deep South and its foundational mythology of aristocracy bears cultural echoes of the Stuart loyalist Cavalier exiles who founded many of the plantations, as New England bears the stamp of Puritanism. While the significance of the Reformation split has faded from contemporary American political memory, in the eighteenth century it was still raw.

We cannot be sure precisely when the histories of time lines two and three began to diverge, but we first become clearly aware of the growing rift on Wednesday, October the 30th of 1745.

King James the Second of England did not take well to being chased into exile on the continent by his own Parliament, for the crime of being Catholic. And his son, James Francis Edward Stuart, maintained his claim to the throne in the face of the Hanoverian Protestant interlopers, despite being denounced as a pretender to the throne. With the transfer of the throne to a new monarch and a rocky transition of power—in 1715 the new Whig government proposed to prosecute the previous Tory ministry for financial irregularities—James, the pretender to the throne, fomented a rebellion by Jacobite loyalists (those loyal to his dynasty). It was badly mistimed, and James ended his life in exile.

However, his son Charles ("the Young Pretender" as the Hanoverian dynasty and their loyalists dubbed him) also held to the goal of retaking his throne. And in 1745, during the War of the Austrian Succession, he saw an opportunity to mount an invasion and coup while the British army was largely operating overseas.

In our own history books, those of time line two, "Bonnie Prince Charlie" landed in Scotland, raised the Stuart standard at Glenfinnan, rallied the highland clans to his banner, and marched on the Scottish capital, Edinburgh. After a brief battle at Prestonpans he captured Scotland: and then, on October 30, in a fateful council meeting, he announced his decision to go for broke and march on London. Militarily, it was a terrible decision. The Jacobites overran their supply lines and were fighting through increasingly hostile territory as their advance neared Derby. Meanwhile, Parliament had time to recall divisions from the continent and pursued the retreating Jacobite army to the site of their decisive defeat, at the Battle of Culloden.

But in time line three, sober heads prevailed. We do not have the minutes of the meeting, but his advisors prevailed on Charles Stuart to hold Scotland, and await reinforcements from the French Crown before he attempted to take England. In the absence of railways and roads, the rugged countryside of the Borders formed a substantial barrier to any army advancing from the south. Traditionally, English monarchs had attacked Scotland from the sea: the Royal Navy attempted to establish a blockade of the Firth of Forth, but with questionable success in the face of a strong French naval presence in the suddenly friendly waters of the North Sea.

In late 1746 a Jacobite army did indeed march south and attempt to take Berwick-upon-Tweed (which it held successfully until 1748). But there was no go-for-broke dash on London, and consequently no pivotal defeat for the Stuart Crown. Despite Hanoverian and Whig anguish, the Union between Scotland and England was severed, and Scotland became a hostile power once more, its lowland Presbyterian elite and highland clans warily united in loyalty to its new Catholic monarch largely out of fear of the old enemy to the south.

The British army—for the Hanoverian Crown in London did not relinquish its claim to Scotland—was faced with a difficult mission: to secure a northern border as well as maintaining its grip on overseas colonies and a presence in continental Europe. It was a mission made considerably harder by Louis XV of France, who knew a wedge when he saw one and who generously offered the Stuart kingdom the use of an army (freed up by the Treaty of Aix-la-Chapelle in 1748, as the War of the Austrian Succession wound down). Louis XV was aware of the unpopularity of his territorial concessions in that treaty, but preferred to be seen as a peacemaker rather than a conqueror. Accordingly, he allowed an increasingly paranoid and beleaguered British Crown to back itself into a corner.

War between England and France in the mid-eighteenth century was inevitable: the two powers were locked in a centuries-long conflict for control over the northern European coastline—sea travel being the most effective transport method in the pre-industrial age—and were rivals for imperial expansion in the New World and elsewhere. France, although larger and richer, was constrained by the difficulty of movement overland across its interior. Both powers had extensive maritime empires and sought to expand in North America.

In time line two, the Seven Years' War broke out in the mid-1750s as two alliances formed: Britain allied with Prussia, while France allied with Habsburg Austria (overturning two centuries of hostilities). In the colonies, the French and Indian War escalated, until in mid-1756 Britain declared war on France.

But in time line three, England was isolated. With French warships operating out of the Clyde and the Firth of Forth, and Franco-Scottish armies garrisoned in Carlisle and Berwick-upon-Tweed, much of the English army was pinned down at home. The French victories of the War of the Austrian Succession were repeated in a series of crushing defeats, as Ferdinand of Brunswick's attempt to defend the Protectorate of Hanover ended with the defeat of the Anglo-German army—and a string of victories at sea left the door open for the French invasion of England in 1759 which, in conjunction with the Stuart Crown's victorious march south, ended in defeat for the armies of King George II.

But this was not the end of the line for the Hanoverian monarchy.

Frederick, Prince of Wales, born in 1707, was first in line to the throne—but thoroughly estranged from his father the King. In our own history, Prince Frederick died suddenly of a ruptured abscess in 1751. But in the wake of the Stuart seizure of Scotland George II sent his eldest on a tour of the colonies, possibly to get him out of the way of political maneuverings in London, but also as an insurance policy.

When word reached New England in early 1760 that London had fallen to a Franco-Scottish invasion, and that the King had died of an aneurysm in the Tower of London, Frederick, Prince of Wales wasted no time. He sailed to Boston and, landing, rode to the Massachusetts Town House in that city where he declared himself King of Great Britain and King-Emperor of the British Empire in North America.

News of the English defeat and occupation by France sent shockwaves through the North American colonies—themselves intermittently under threat of French military expansion on the continent. News that the Hanoverian heir to the Crown had established himself in exile in Boston caused considerably more contention. Today in time line two we remember the War of Independence as being about taxation without representation, and about onerous terms imposed by a remote overseas empire. Having the King-Emperor appear on one's doorstep, announce that the capital was moving (first to Boston, then a decade later to Manhattan Island, which was to be renamed New London), and announce a Continental Congress, the establishment of a House of Commons with tax-raising power, and start raising an army to fight the French, must have been shocking.

One particular group felt the shock most acutely: the southern aristocracy descended from those loyalists to Charles Stuart who had chosen exile in the New World over bending their neck beneath the Puritan yoke of the Commonwealth. Although Protestants, this group despised and disliked the Hanoverian dynasty as a matter of principle. Faced with the prospect of a King-in-Exile levying taxes on their tobacco, sugar, and cotton plantations, a group of the wealthiest nobility in the West Indies and the Southern Colonies met in the council of the Lords Proprietors of Charleston, South Carolina, in 1762 and agreed to raise an army. They wrote to the French King, issuing a petition and calling for aid; and then they repudiated their membership in the British Empire. When the governor of Georgia refused to join them and denounced their rebellion as treason, he was hanged before the statehouse in Atlanta: and this began the incident known as the Slaveowners' Treasonous Rebellion.

The Rebellion lasted from 1762 to 1770, and was utterly devastating. In time line two, the American Civil War lasted four years and killed an estimated 3 percent of the US population; as many as 18 percent of all white males of military age in the South were killed. But the Slaveowners' Treasonous Rebellion was far worse, with consequences that can only be compared to time line two's Thirty Years War, or the War of the Triple Alliance, in which Paraguay attempted to conquer South America, attacked Brazil, Argentina, and Uruguay simultaneously, and suffered nearly 80 percent fatalities (90 percent of the male population and 50 percent of the women and children dying during the conflict).

From the King's perspective, there was no alternative to total war: allowing secession to go unpunished would result in the remains of the British Empire being gobbled up by the rival French, Dutch, and Spanish empires. England was already under enemy occupation: his back was to the wall. His prosecution of the war was therefore brutal to a degree that students of the American Civil War find shocking. The arrival of French and Spanish armies in Florida in 1764 escalated the conflict even before the inflammatory addition of a delegation from the *Tribunal del Santo Oficio de la Inquisición*. (This appears to have been the result of an initiative on the part of the Grand Inquisitor to shore up his office, already declining in influence at home. It was indulged by King Frederick VI, possibly in hope of allowing the Inquisition to undermine its own position—and was to have far-reaching consequences.) In particular, the mass executions and gibbetings of rebel prisoners along the Great Wagon Road between North Carolina and Augusta has few parallels in modern history other than the Siege of Vienna until we get to more recent post-nineteenth-century systematic genocide.

In the wake of the advancing Royalist armies, the widows and orphans of the executed rebels were enslaved regardless of race, as a punishment for treason, much as slavery had been used as a sentence in the wake of the '15 rebellion and against the Covenanters. Holdings were expropriated and titles granted to exiled British nobles, while former slaves were armed and used to police the conquered territory. In some cases, former slaves were placed over their ex-masters as overseers: by 1770 the geography of the planter states was unrecognizable.

This was not, incidentally, a war fought over emancipation, or over the issue of the expansion of slavery. A common misconception among people from our time line is that a civil war between the states in time line three must have similar causes to those of time line two. Rather, the cause of the war was the royal imposition of direct rule from the throne-in-exile. But it was not an unmitigated despotism. As the war progressed, the Crown traded privilege and power for support, allowing the establishment of a formal parliament with houses for the Commons and Lords, and a new Bill of Rights.

Emancipation and the end of chattel slavery followed the war (as early as 1811 throughout the continental dominions of the New British Empire). Popular sentiment for emancipation grew after the subjugation of the white southern population after the rebellion; the French blockade of the Atlantic coast following the occupation of the British Isles acted to sever the three-cornered trade cycle that brought slaves from Africa to the New World, throttling the supply of new slaves, while indentured laborers emigrating from the Scottish lowlands, England, and Wales boosted the population of the northern colonies. Finally, because of the role of the slave-owning estates in fomenting the rebellion, the practice of slave-holding was seen as questionable and unpatriotic.

Although the term "World War" is historically associated in our time line with the great conflict between the Central Powers and the Triple Alliance, and the later emergence of the same geopolitical stresses in the shape of Hitler's war, it is worth remembering that these were not the first global conflicts. The rise of the Spanish Hapsburg Empire in the Netherlands and Central and South America during the sixteenth century was inter-continental in scope; and the two-hundred-year-long struggle between the British and French empires in the late seventeenth to early eighteenth centuries could certainly be described as a global war, although not as all-embracing as the wars of the twentieth century.

In time line three, the French occupation of England in 1760 had several consequences of global geopolitical significance that gave rise to a series of world wars.

For the first time since the fall of the western Roman Empire, the northern coastline of Europe was dominated by a single power. Furthermore, the French treasury was far stronger at this time than in our own history. On occupying England, the Emperor granted the Farmers Generale a license to farm taxes in the newly conquered territory: customs tariff barriers were installed along the English canal system, breaking up what had hitherto been the largest free trade zone in Europe—and coincidentally making it difficult for organized resistance to emerge. Where in our time line the 1770s were a decade of repeated failures to reform the French taxation system, culminating in the fiscal crisis and subsequent revolution of 1789–91, in time line three Louis XV was able to pay off many of his creditors—and bought sufficient breathing space to make some moderate reforms of the tariff system, notably through selling titles of nobility to the new territories across the English Channel (and, highly optimistically, in the Americas). Consequently, the pressures that gave rise to the French Revolution were diffused, if not avoided entirely. The inevitable day of reckoning for the French Crown's finances arrived in 1812, but by then events had taken a radically different turn and rather than outright revolt the issue was settled by relatively peaceful means.

Free from the ruinous costs of continuous war with England, French trade around the Mediterranean flourished. An alliance with the Austrian Crown took place, between Louis XVI and Marie Antoinette: in the absence of the French fiscal crisis that led to revolution she was considerably less unpopular and when, in 1791, Russia attempted to annex East Prussia, the Franco-Austrian alliance not only repelled the invasion but reasserted the protectorate over the former Holy Roman Empire and Poland. French hegemony over Europe grew until in 1809 Tsar Alexander I attempted to regain his western possessions, triggering a genuine first world war.

Friction between the European imperial powers and the American Empire had been growing in the Caribbean colonies: the New British navy, still weak (for the Crown was focused on suppression of internal dissent in the South), was ill-equipped to play a part in a trans-Atlantic war. Nevertheless, an Anglo-Russian entente in 1810 saw the Crown send warships as far as the Baltic to help the highly inadequate Russian navy interdict ships supporting the French invasion. It was to no avail. A well-supplied French grand army *not* commanded by Napoleon Bonaparte (who, living in obscurity in Lyons, ended his military career as a colonel in the 1820s) laid siege to St. Petersburg in 1811 and, with supplies delivered by sea, carved the Grand Duchy of Finland and much of Western Russia away from the Tsar's Empire.

The French fiscal crisis finally arrived in time line three much later than in our own history. It also arrived at the gates of a Versailles that ruled unchallenged over Northern Europe, with the wealth of England, Poland, the Holy Roman Empire, and much of Russia added to its assets—and a strong army organized along modern lines with which to enforce the King's decrees. Of which there were many, as it turned out. A headlong reform of the system of aristocratic privilege, by which titles conferred exemption from taxes and the right of corvée (forced labor) over peasants associated with that title, caused considerable unrest among the nobility (who by this time numbered nearly 8 percent of the French population). But with decades more experience and an empire's assets to draw on, Louis XVI was able to buy off much of the unrest with grants of land and titles at the expense of the peripheral new territories. Worker and peasant revolts in England were suppressed viciously, and the special taxation suppressed much of the development that in our time line gave birth to the industrial revolution: it simultaneously secured the future of the French Crown, as long as it could continue to expand, buying off its creditors with future income derived from new territories expropriated from their previous owners.

Expansion to the east thus became the pattern of the French empire during the nineteenth century, while the British Crown in the Americas expanded to the west and south, digging aggressively into the vulnerable underbelly of the Portuguese and Spanish Empires—the creators of which were too busy fending off the French at home to focus on their possessions overseas.

The French invasion and occupation of England came about at a time when the building blocks of the British Industrial Revolution were coming together. The construction of canals coincided with the development of low-pressure steam engines for pumping water out of coal and iron mines: the lack of internal trade barriers and growing external, international trade made England a growing hub of industry in our own history. But with an uncanny effectiveness the French occupation shut down these harbingers of the modern. Canal transport was taxed. Mines were taxed. Engines for raising water by means of steam were taxed. The construction of ships and the harvesting of the oak from which their timbers were made were taxed. Road travel was taxed. Indeed, the whole of British industry was taxed, ruinously hard—as a deliberate policy to immiserate the capital-forming classes among whose ranks opposition to French rule might accrete over time. The industrial revolution was stillborn in time line three: the same ingredients came together a century later in the foothills of the Appalachians, but it is worth remembering that time line three's first steam-powered commercial railroad was laid between Irontown (in a location roughly congruent with our world's Philadelphia) and New London (the fortified imperial capital city on lower Manhattan Island) in the 1890s. And the first steam-powered ship, a tug boat, came into service on the Manhattan docksides in 1898.

The role of the monarchy in North America can't be said to be entirely negative in this respect. Nobody in time line three knew that industrial development was even possible. The Crown's overriding obsession lay in securing itself against the threat of aggression arising from secessionist movements at home and foreign imperialists overseas—and the French Empire was a global threat to the North American colonies from the 1760s on. There were no Federalist Papers and no constitutional convention in time line three, but a Bill of Rights was nevertheless negotiated in the 1810–1818 period, in part as a measure by a newly crowned monarch to burnish his popularity by contrast with the absolutist Continental System. It seems outlandish to American ears, but the subjects of the New British Empire prided themselves on their freedom and liberty compared to the subjects of rival empires overseas, even though in the post-Rebellion period from 1761 to approximately 1810 the British monarchy reigned as an absolute despotism of a kind that had not been seen in the British Isles since the days of Charles I.

Globally, the political pattern that emerges in the nineteenth century is not one of absolute monarchies set against post-revolutionary republics such as France and the United States, or constitutional monarchies like Great Britain: it is a pattern of absolute despotic monarchies set against somewhat more moderate absolute monarchies that permit representative assemblies of citizens and allow a free, albeit licensed, press to exist.

The ideological climate of totalitarian monarchies was very different to the turbulent growth of free speech in the English-speaking world of our own history. It is important to understand this in order to comprehend the impact of these changes on philosophy, science, economics, and literature. A monarchical system is as much a hereditary dictatorship as North Korea: criticism of the monarch's good taste, ideas, or philosophy is dangerous in the extreme. Adam Smith, who in our own history was the father of modern economics, engaged in his research and writing in the Stuart-ruled Kingdom of Scotland rather than the more economically liberal and outspoken Great Britain of our own time line. *The Wealth of Nations* appears to have been written, but was never published— suppressed by the censors of the Court of Chancery. Some highly circumspect papers discussing the theory of the division of labor and Smith's criticism of tariff barriers were published during his lifetime, but no general theory of trade emerged to challenge the eighteenth-century consensus of the physiocrats. In the nineteenth century, the unrest during the decades following the French fiscal crisis claimed the life of the young Karl Marx: the only trace of Friedrich Engels to be found in the historical records identifies him as a Hessian mercenary who died in obscurity in Panama. Prince Peter Kropotkin was apparently never born, in a Russian territorial appendix to the French Empire. And so this was a time line bereft of the ideologies of industrial civilization—both capitalism and communism were stillborn.

By the mid–nineteenth century, the growing distance between the macro-level history of time line three and our own history is such that most historical figures are absent or unrecognizable. There is no record of an Adolf Hitler, a Vladimir Ulyanov (Lenin), or a Benito Mussolini. These people simply never existed. On the other hand, many of those killed during the Terror of the French Revolution survived. The noble and chemist Antoine Lavoisier did not die on the guillotine, and went on to triumphantly pioneer stoichiometry and, subsequently, to make the first partial draft of a periodic table of the elements, a full fifty-five years before Dmitri Mendeleev did so in our own time line. Similarly, the germ theory of disease spread rapidly after Agostino Bassi's research in the early 1810s came to the attention of the French army's surgeon-general. While industrialization was retarded for up to a century by the invasion of England, scientific progress was not automatically impaired and in some aspects advanced *faster* than in our own history—until it ran up against the barriers imposed by the lack of an industrial establishment able to provide funding, personnel, and equipment for research institutes.

Another important point to bear in mind is that knowing something is possible means that you are halfway to achieving it. In the absence of a model for an industrial revolution, nobody in time line three went looking for one. This was not because they were stupid or thoughtless: the industrial revolution constituted the most drastic upset in human economic history since the bronze age/iron age discontinuity circa 500 BC. One does not go looking for sources of disruption on such a scale unless one has been trained by experience to seek them out.

In our own history, the American Frontier was closed by the end of the 1880s. With worse transportation technology and no telegraphs, the frontier in North America was nevertheless fully settled by the same time in time line three: a more structured state with a policy of imperial expansion saw to it. It also saw to the First Nation's "problem" with singular brutality—either conscripting the more warlike tribes and sending them south as soldiers to support their settlers in South America, or killing them if they could not be put to use. Similarly, the growing New British Navy first enforced a blockade of the Spanish and Portuguese colonies during the middle of the nineteenth century, then provided transport for a wholesale invasion of Central and South America during the latter half of the century.

This was not the ad hoc economic imperialism of our own history, but a deliberate program of conquest by an empire with a large, well-equipped conscript army that was determined to leave no territorial toeholds for the continental enemy. The Crown, as a matter of policy, used the descendants of freed slaves as the cutting-edge of their troops: they were believed to be hardier and less vulnerable to tropical diseases, and more ruthless in their treatment of the subjugated population. A century later, much of the aristocracy of South America was black—and notoriously loyal to the house of Hanover.

By the 1920s, the industrial revolution was gathering steam both in the New British Empire and on the continent. The construction of the Two Continents railroad, stretching down the spine of the Americas from the Bering Straits to Tierra del Fuego, mirrored that of the Trans-Siberian railway. The British navy adopted steam and oil almost simultaneously: the French had access to the oil fields of the Persian Gulf and did likewise. Both the major hegemons were beginning to modernize and had closed their internal frontiers.

The proximate trigger for the Third World War was the same as that of the Great Game fought between Britain and Russia in our own history: access to the riches of India through the passes of the Himalayas. The British Empire's toehold on India was far weaker in time line three than in our own history—the British East India Company controlled trade within much of the territory around the Bay of Bengal, but could not by any stretch of the imagination claim the entire subcontinent as a dominion. The threat of French expansion kept the rulers of Baluchistan, the Kashmir, and Afghanistan anxious, but these nations remained independent, as did the Persian Empire.

The stage for the global conflict was set by a conclusive struggle for domination of the Mediterranean Sea between the French Navy and the Ottoman Empire in 1918–20. As the Ottoman Empire ceded territory to France—including the right to build a canal at Suez—the French Crown became convinced that with control of the oil fields of Persia they would be able to control the Indian Ocean. Louis XX was a canny strategic thinker, obsessed with consolidating power over an entire hemisphere: his ministers were able to make the Persian emperor an offer he couldn't refuse, and when the first French ironclads arrived to take up their basing rights in Tehran in 1926 it became clear to all that a war with the British was inevitable. Both sides were already fighting a battleship construction race, with oil-fired reciprocating steam engines, iron-clad hulls, and, by the early 1940s, breech-loading rifled artillery in turrets.

The details of the conflict for the Indian Ocean are not germane to this briefing. The outcome is another matter. The French Empire won the war of attrition once their canal at Suez became fully available, culminating in a major naval victory—the Battle of the Andaman Islands—that traumatized the New British Navy for a generation. At the same time, the breakdown of the Qing dynasty's authority in China (which in our time line took place in the latter half of the nineteenth century, running to completion with the declaration of the Republic of China in 1912) came to a head with the declaration of the French Protectorate and the expulsion of non-allied powers from the trading cities of Hong Kong and Shanghai.

By 1950, the French Empire—the capital of which was now St. Petersburg—had established a hegemony across Eurasia, with a trade empire in India and China as a protectorate. Africa was largely under French and Dutch rule, and the much-diminished Ottoman Empire was reduced to a rump around the eastern Mediterranean. Persia, officially neutral, was encircled by and dependent on the French. The British Empire in the Americas had been effectively excluded from the eastern hemisphere, with the exception of certain territorial dominions—the Australian colonies (including the islands known as New Zealand in our time line), and the Japanese Empire (for the Shogunate saw in the British a valuable ally in maintaining their independence from the expansionist French).

The stage was thus set for something never seen in our world—the complete partition of the eastern and western hemispheres into two opposing totalitarian power blocs, neither possessing sufficient leverage to attack the other within its own territory.

It is important to note that, although it industrialized substantially between 1880 and 2002, the New British Empire lacked many of the values and political structures of the United States of America.

The US Constitution enumerated the balance of powers and rights of the arms of government in terms that would have been familiar to a British monarch in the 1770s—in our time line. The Hanoverian monarchy in North America was considerably more draconian in nature, having escaped from the crisis of the invasion of England only to be confronted by the emergency of a slaveowners' rebellion. Many of the absolute powers of the Crown, carved away by Parliament after the Wars of the Three Kingdoms, were reassumed, including the power to raise taxes directly and to dissolve Parliament and rule by decree. These powers were used during the conquest of South America, and again during the prosecution of the Third World War and the (failed) defense of the empire in India. By the 1980s, while Parliament still existed, it was little more than a rubber stamp on the monarch's legislative program: the judiciary was similarly an appointed bench, and the House of Lords packed with place-men who would vote for the crown that granted them their privileges.

The structures of a parliamentary democracy were not easily transplanted to an expansionist marcher kingdom spanning two continents, and were alien to the background of many of the colonists. While some of the New England colonies retained representative assemblies, large tracts of the southern continent were ruled directly by members of the House of Lords.

The separation of Church and State was non-existent in a realm governed by a monarch who was styled "the Protector of the Faith." Only considerable political caution—a huge majority of the population of the southern continent were Catholic, along with a substantial minority in the North—prevented the emergence of a Protestant theocracy: as it was, laws discriminating against the participation of Catholics, Jews, and anyone not of the Church of New England in public life were on the books right up until the revolution.

The broadly reactionary flavor of political life in the New British Empire, and the lack of recognizable free market capitalist or communist doctrines, should not mislead you into believing that there was no dissent. A strong tradition of radicalism with its roots in the dissenters of the British Isles during and immediately after the civil war flourished during the eighteenth and nineteenth century. The dissidence of Quakers and Ranters and Levelers, whose arguments found expression through religious metaphor and holy scripture, were both more dangerous and harder to deal with for a Crown with a role in the nominal state religion. In our own history, prior to the Arab Spring the suppression of political opposition by the dictatorships of the Middle East left religious radicalism as the only form of dissent available in the public sphere. Similarly, in East Germany during the cold war, the Lutheran Church experienced a degree of immunity to Communist oppression that provided a sanctuary for moral dissenters. Atheism and free-thinking were sheltered in the British Empire by reference to the Inquisition and the threat of a religious backlash against oppression: egalitarian religious communes that denied (at their own hazard) the primacy of the aristocratic landowner were not uncommon across the mid-west.

Growing industrialization and the spread of the mass media (newspapers and radio: television from the 1990s onwards) contributed to a rise in the political awareness of the general population of the Empire. Universal literacy emerged on the back of national educational standards intended to build a basis for indoctrination of the masses: just as Lenin's Bolsheviks wanted the Soviet workers to be able to read their propaganda, the New British monarchy wanted its citizens to be able to understand their policies. But universal literacy is a two-edged sword: once your citizens begin to read, it's very hard to make them stop.

It is against this background that we come to the character of Adam Burroughs. Raised as the son of a moderately wealthy baronet (whose fortune was built on his ownership of a steam locomotive works) it is speculated that the young Adam's interest in economics was raised first by his observation of factory production techniques—and his studies in turn led to his exposure and radicalization during a strike against his father's foremen. Many children of privilege, exposed to radical and threatening views, will cleave to their background; but a few, including Adam Burroughs, start to question everything. In the case of Burroughs, the result was a pioneering study of political economy that paralleled the philosophy of Voltaire and some of the class-based analysis of Marx, but which was infused by a fierce awareness of and aversion to social injustice—and a determination that something must be done.

The Ethical Foundations of Equality anatomized the power structure of the empire in terms of its regression from the early expression of the rights of man during the Long Parliament and the English Commonwealth, and highlighted numerous injustices: it then made the revolutionary postulate that a republic based on the mutualism implicit in Leveler ideology was a desirable objective, that the disestablishment of the state Church was a necessity, and that at the very least the royal court (which for most of a century had operated as an engine of favoritism and nepotism) needed to be reined in.

The book was of course banned, which made it an immediate underground best seller.

During the 1980s, King George VIII showed promising signs of reform-mindedness. Parliament in New London was given increased rights to introduce primary legislation, and the franchise extended to all adult males (the previous land-ownership requirement being abolished). The new monarch (crowned in 1977) keenly felt the chill of his nation's exclusion from the other hemisphere, and was attentive to the new schools of economic thought springing up in the wake of his country's accelerating industrialization. Under George VII it is likely that Adam Burroughs would have been imprisoned or even exiled for sedition, but under George VIII he was tacitly permitted to run for a parliamentary seat in hope of providing a safety valve for the radical sentiments finding expression among working men's self-improvement clubs throughout the realm. During this period, the League of Labor expanded and made some political gains in the northern continent, campaigning for reforms such as a right to free assembly, a free press, a fifty hour working week, and an old age or infirmity pension. With the labor force growing rapidly due to improvements in public transport infrastructure and agricultural productivity (internal combustion engines and artificial fertilizers were finally finding their way into farming) the League had considerable leverage: a reaction was perhaps inevitable.

On November 14, 1986, the reaction arrived from the other extreme. A group of extreme radicals—the Black Fist Freedom Guard—assassinated George VIII, the Queen, and one of his daughters; his son, John Frederick, witnessed the bombing. The new King ordered an immediate clampdown (just as in our own history Tsar Alexander III reacted to the assassination of his father), forcing Burroughs to flee to France, and having numerous members of the League arrested and tried for sedition. Over the next decade Parliament was reduced to a one month rubber-stamp session, the police (an internal security gendarmerie) were significantly expanded, and democratic and workers' rights activists were mercilessly hounded.

The technological developments in the Empire during this period cannot be ignored. As a novelist observed, "the future is already here: it is just unevenly distributed." The Empire began to undergo its industrial revolution late, in the 1880s, and the first heavier-than-air aircraft only took to the skies in 1969. However, between 1977 and 2002 the Empire acquired a telephone network, a continental electricity grid, the beginnings of an interstate road network (although the majority of freight and passenger transportation went by rail—the imperial railroad network was in many ways superior to that of the contemporary United States in our own time line), and many of the other seeds of modernity. The Imperial Air Army was experimenting with low-wing monoplanes and the first prototype jet engines: the Navy was bankrolling research into nuclear fission in the hope of finding a better power source for their battleships. For their part, by 2002 the French Imperium was on the threshold of detonating their first experimental atomic weapon. In 1890, the New British Empire had been more than a century behind the United States of 1890; by 1990 the gap had narrowed to perhaps 70 years.

The French hegemony in the eastern hemisphere was not absolute. In particular, a number of satellite powers retained considerable autonomy: the Persian Empire, the Netherlands, Spain, the Italies, and so on. The Bourbon Empire dominated continental trade and the northern interior, but did not dictate the course of all events.

In 1999–2002 it became clear that a war was brewing between two of the second-rank powers: the Persian Empire had designs on the territories of the Mughal Crown. Mughal appeals to the British Empire for assistance were met with incautious enthusiasm in New London, and the Americas were drawn into what should by rights have been a regional conflict. The presence of British warships in the Persian Gulf drew the ire of the French Crown, and soon a full-scale naval war was developing in both the Atlantic and Pacific theaters.

This was not a good time for the British Empire to enter a war. Anthropogenic climate change is as much a problem in time line three as in our own; the intersection of a large population with more primitive technologies aggravated many of the problems. Harvest failures in 1997 and 2000 led to famine in South America. Meanwhile, a rapid arms build-up—necessitated by preparation for war—coincided with a recession (partially induced by French trade sanctions) and raised the cost of government borrowing. Poor management of the economy was aggravated by the practice of granting tax exemptions with titles of nobility; much the same disease that had affected the French aristocracy in the late eighteenth century haunted the New British Empire in the wake of the closing of the frontier. For a while industrial output growth had masked the inefficiencies in the system, but from the mid-1980s onwards the Empire slipped into a period of low-grade debt-deflation, with interest rates pegged at zero (worsened by the King's obstinate insistence on sticking to a gold-backed currency standard—his reactionary rejection of modernity extended to the field of economics).

Rearmament provided a brief Keynesian stimulus to the New British Empire's economy, but now the secondary threat of inflation loomed. With further government borrowing blocked, the Treasury had no choice but to petition the King for permission to decouple the currency from the gold standard, to which he assented. If such a transition is conducted with due care it can be successful: but in time line three there was no cautionary historical tale of any equivalent to Weimar Germany. The Treasury printed money as the War Ministry demanded, and for a while there was a boom in employment in shipbuilding, munitions, and recruitment—but then the 2002 harvest also failed. The price of bread soared by 300 percent in two months in early 2003, and hyperinflation set in.

Great powers seldom win or lose wars due to their performance on an individual battlefield; rather, their ability to field and support armies and navies (which in turn depends on the soundness of their economic management) determines the ultimate outcome of the conflict. The British Empire was doing poorly in the Indian Ocean conflict even before the inflationary cycle commenced. The confluence of hyperinflation at home with a crop failure and overseas military setbacks was lethally toxic for confidence in the Crown's ability to honor its debts. In the summer of 2003 it became clear that the government would have to default. This precipitated a bank run and a liquidity crisis at the same time that bread riots broke out, all the way from Santiago to Boston. At the same time, naval squadrons on coastal defense patrols off the western seaboard mutinied after six months' non-payment of wages was followed by cuts to the sailors' rations. And in the Winter Palace a decision was taken that was as momentous as the German General Staff's decision to allow Lenin safe passage in a sealed carriage through the Central Powers to the Finland Station: Sir Adam Burroughs was given an exit visa and transport on neutral shipping to Mission City (on the San Francisco Bay).

Faced with a widespread uprising by the Radical Party—the consistently named and much more militant successor to previous decades' League of Labor—combined with a fiscal crisis and mutinies in the military, King John Frederick demonstrated far less resilience than his ancestors. He fled the capital, but was captured by mutineers at an army garrison in the vicinity of Lake Michigan. (Extensive conurbations exist in New Britain in the vicinity of major US cities including Chicago and Detroit, but due to the vagaries of naming and urban growth none of their names will be familiar.) Well-organized cadres from the Leveler underground movements seized control over the ministries and parliament buildings in New London. These forces were mysteriously well-funded under the circumstances. It is speculated that Clan world-walkers were even then liquidating their assets in the United States and using them to bankroll the quartermasters of the New England cells of Burroughs's faction. When the pound (currency) floated and began to hyperinflate, their stockpile of gold bullion became extremely valuable. This in turn served to cement the world-walkers' insidious leverage within the Radical party.

All revolutions take place against the backdrop of a power vacuum. The revolution in the New British Empire shocked everyone—this is a time line in which there was no French revolution, no American War of Independence, no Russian Revolution. The Year Zero for constitutional democratic government in time line three was 2002, and it remains a deeply shocking, ideologically radical proposition to the other natives of that time line. It is easy to forget just how revolutionary the United States of America seemed when seen through the eyes of outsiders in the nineteenth century; to the Bourbon Imperium and the other powers of time line three, the New American Commonwealth (as the post-imperial government renamed itself) is as utopian and as existentially terrifying as the Bolshevik Soviet Union must have seemed in the 1920s.

Internal factional fighting in the first six months of the new republic threatened to develop into a full-scale internal civil war, with death squads and blood baths on all sides. Somehow (world-walker intervention is suspected but cannot be proven) the Moderate Faction within the Leveler Party executed an end game that resulted in the death of the Security Commissioner, Stephen Reynolds, leader of the Peace and Justice faction, on the eve of a purge he was planning (which may be compared in scope to the Third Reich's Night of the Long Knives). This was rapidly followed by the consolidation of power under a Radical Party government led by Adam Burroughs himself, with Erasmus Burgeson as Minister of Propaganda (communications).

The Party government sued for peace immediately, settling with the French Crown on terms that initially seemed invidious—handing over a considerable number of warships, accepting liability for reparations, and losing Cuba.

And then the influence of the Clan world-walkers becomes clear.

A secret document circulating among the Party leadership in 2003 bears description. Titled "Revolutions and Their Deaths," and written in contemporary American English (hastily, by a variety of hands), it consists of a study guide to the revolutions in our own time line alluded to earlier in this briefing. It also describes a number of less well-understood revolutions and coups (Haiti 1791, Gran Columbia 1819, Germany 1933, China 1949, Egypt 1952, Iran 1953, Greece 1974, Iran 1979) in terms of the objectives of their leaders, and the administrative and ideological shortcomings that led to their failures to meet their goals (and on occasion, contributed to their successes). The framing rhetorical devices in this document are suspiciously familiar ("fail early, fail smarter, learn from your failures," "creative disruption," "the innovator's dilemma") and the perspective is somewhat Whiggish in tone: nevertheless, as a document that sets out to explain to a newly empaneled revolutionary government how not to shoot itself in the foot with the same caliber of ammunition used by its predecessors, it succeeds reasonably well.

A particularly frightening aspect of "Revolutions and Their Deaths" is the appendix containing a cynical, if not outright Machiavellian, analysis of two successful revolutions—the Iranian revolution of 1979, and the development of Communist China after the death of Mao Zedong. The Islamic Republic of Iran today is a (to Western eyes, bizarre) fusion of republican democratic values with religious fundamentalism. Meanwhile, the People's Republic of China is nominally a communist state (ruled by the dictatorship of the proletariat), but in practice is governed by an authoritarian capitalist oligarchy. The appendix proposes that as the revolution in the British Empire is the first of its kind, and the people are not accustomed to democratic forms, it will be necessary for the Party to operate and maintain a Deep State for at least a generation—a disciplined ideological cadre (like the Communist Party, or the Iranian Shiite religious academy) to stabilize and hold in place the structures of democracy within tightly delineated boundaries until such time as the embryonic forms of representative government take root and can survive autonomously.

As of 2005, the Radical Party appeared to be following this prescription. Adam Burroughs was enshrined in office as "the First Man," a President for Life with constitutional powers approximating those of a cut-down monarchy. The Radical Party itself occupied key ministries in his cabinet by way of the People's Commissioners. Parliament is open and a universal franchise (including women and anyone aged sixteen or over) elects representatives from any political party that does not espouse a return to monarchism or the abolition of democratic norms—but the Party also maintains control over the Treasury, and has its own armed formation in the shape of the Commonwealth Guard, which occupies a role approximately equivalent to the Iranian Revolutionary Guard or (within the Soviet Union) the KGB's troops. The Radical Party is built around an ideology of revolutionary republican democracy and resistance to aristocracy and the principle of monarchism. As the first flowering of modernist post-royal politics in time line three, the Party is a deadly existential threat to every other government on the planet: they are unflinching and fanatical proponents of a form of politics that we are taught to take for granted, and this often causes confusion on the part of Americans when they are first introduced to Commonwealth politics.

We come from a time line where democracy unquestionably won. This is by no means the case in time line three. They speak our political idiom—but in their own world's context they are extremists and zealots. They will use the tools of fanatics, if necessary, to achieve their goals, because they are deeply unreasonable about democracy. Their ideology is not congruent with our time line's views on economic liberalism, capitalism, free trade, or socialism. It is vitally important that the reader not project their own preconceptions of the meaning of democracy onto the statements of the Radical Party's ideologues, lest in doing so they blind themselves to subtle warning signs of difference.

After all, if there is one person a fanatic is predisposed to hate, it's a moderate who is almost but not completely aligned with their program.

And the Commonwealth has nuclear weapons.

(TO BE CONTINUED in Invisible Sun, *coming January 2019)*

GLOSSARY OF TERMS

Accretion disk
A "whirlpool-like" disk of extremely hot gas that gathers around a black hole. As matter is sucked into a black hole it heats up until the radiation pressure from the inside of the accretion disk balances out the attractive force of the hole. It thus limits the rate at which a black hole can absorb matter. As most black holes rotate, the accretion disk is dragged round at very high speed: temperatures range from several millions of degrees up.

ARMBAND
Device used by US military and DHS to transport aircraft between parallel universes. Mechanism is secret; believed to include neural tissue harvested from world-walker "donors."

BLACK RAIN
Code name assigned to time line three (home of the New American Commonwealth) by the US government.

Bogies
The chassis or framework carrying wheels, upon which a railway carriage rests.
Alternatively: hostile airborne/spaceborne missile or object.

Clan

An umbrella organization consisting of five (previously six) families of world-walkers, formerly resident in the Gruinmarkt in time line one. Co-ordinated the world-walkers' inter-temporal trade and smuggling activities, provided security, and a framework for the arranged marriages required to keep the world-walking bloodlines alive. The Clan was effectively disbanded in 2003, and the survivors sought asylum in time line three (with the New American Commonwealth).

Corvée for the Clan postal service

An obligation on world-walkers from time line one (who were members of the Clan). They had to make themselves available to transport goods between time lines a certain number of times every month. The organization is now defunct.

CVS

A big, well-known American pharmacy chain.

DHS

US Department of Homeland Security: in time line two, the agency responsible for transportation security, counter-terrorism, and para-time security (interception of world-walkers). Also responsible for organizing security of government and corporate sites in other time lines, and countering threats from all other time lines.

DPR

Department of Para-historical Research: a para-time industrial espionage agency established within MITI in the New American Commonwealth.

Engram

Among world-walkers, a knotwork design that can trigger the world-walking ability to transport them to another parallel universe.

Family Trade Organization
Precursor to the Office of Special Projects. It was a cross-agency organization established within the US government in 2002 in response to the discovery of world-walkers and the Clan.

FISA Court
United States Foreign Intelligence Surveillance Court: a US federal court established to oversee requests for surveillance warrants and other espionage-related secret legislation.

Gruinmarkt
A small kingdom on the eastern seaboard of North America in time line one, founded by Viking colonists in the twelfth to fourteenth centuries. Home of the Clan. It had reached a late medieval level of political and economic development before it was destroyed in a nuclear holocaust instigated by the United States.

Hochsprache
A Germanic family language spoken in the Gruinmarkt; now effectively extinct, remembered only by former members of the Clan.

HUMINT
Human Intelligence: intelligence gathered by means of human agents and informers (see also SIGINT, ELINT).

ICBM
Inter-Continental Ballistic Missile.

MITI
Ministry of Intertemporal Technological Intelligence: a government agency within the New American Commonwealth. This body is tasked with accelerating technological development by disseminating new developments discovered in other time lines.

New American Commonwealth

Successor nation to the New British Empire, which ruled North and South America and Australasia in time line three from 1761 to 2003. The New American Commonwealth is a revolutionary republic created by the former Radical Party to pursue the goal of spreading democracy throughout time line three.

Niejwein

Capital of the Gruinmarkt. Destroyed in 2003.

NRO

National Reconnaissance Office: US government secret agency in time line two responsible for launching spy satellites and developing photographic/radar intelligence from satellites.

NSA

National Security Agency: the US government agency in time line two tasked with SIGINT and ELINT, the interception and decryption of enemy communications. Noted for monitoring all phone, Internet, and data communications worldwide.

Outer family

Among the Clan world-walkers, the world-walking trait is recessive: only the children of two active world-walkers inherit the ability. However, the children of a world-walker and a non-world-walker may be carriers. The offspring of two such carriers may have the world-walking ability. Such carriers were monitored by the Clan and known as "outer family" members (the Clan had a strong interest in maximizing the pool of possible world-walkers available to them).

Para-time

Umbrella term for parallel universes diverging from a point in time. The cause of divergence may be some quantum event which may have multiple outcomes with macroscopic (observable) effects.

POTUS
President of the United States.

RFID
Radio Frequency ID: "smart" inventory control tags found on many items of packaging or clothing. RFID tags can be interrogated remotely and used to identify the item they are attached to, unlike bar codes (which need to be scanned at close range). Same underlying technology as contactless payment cards.

SCEP
Special Counter-Espionage Police: a government agency within the New American Commonwealth of time line three. The organization is tasked with tracking down subversives, spies, and agents of both the British Crown-in-Exile and the French Empire.

SIGINT
Signals intelligence: intelligence obtained by analyzing metadata derived from enemy radio, telegraph, Internet, and other signals.

TL:DR
"Too Long; Didn't Read" (sarcastic dismissal of a long explanation or glossary).

USAF
United States Air Force.

World-walker
A person equipped with the ability to controllably teleport between parallel universes. It's an inherited ability, the hereditable mechanism presumed to have been invented by a high-technology civilization elsewhere in para-time.